ANTHROMECH

Edited by Chris Kennedy
& William Alan Webb

Theogony Books
Coinjock, NC

Cover Design by J Caleb Design.

Anthromech/Chris Kennedy & William Alan Webb -- 1st ed.
ISBN 979-8893192858

Preface by William Alan Webb

Get ready for something different. If this has ever been tried before, the editors aren't aware of it.

Chris Kennedy Publishing, in cooperation with its imprint for writers, Quillcraft Press, has begun a new type of program incorporating CKP's stable of best-selling authors, up-and-coming newer writers, and most importantly, *YOU*, the reader, to bring great stories to lovers of exciting Science Fiction.

This book is not an anthology in the traditional sense; it's something new, an SSL.

Simultaneous Series Launch.

Every story in this book is the launch of a new series or a spinoff of an existing series. Many of the names will be familiar to regular readers of CKP's extensive catalog: Mark W. Stallings, John Siers, Kevin Steverson, Dr. Robert E. Hampson, Jr., William S. Frisbee, William Alan Webb, Michael LaVoice, April Jones, and even Chris Kennedy himself. The crème de la crème.

What's very different is that each of these authors is mentoring another, less experienced writer, working in tandem to create something entirely new, and not only that… to bring a talented new storyteller into the fold. There are also some future legends who are working on their own. All in all, this is a very impressive lineup.

Authors such as Craig Bell, M.D. Boncher, Richard Cartwright, Abigail Jenkins, Megan Miller, Andrew Waldren, C.A. Waldron, or Ronald Lloyd should not be overlooked. Each has their own work already in the marketplace. Russ Tilton has a best-selling series, GENIT, but this is his first appearance in a CKP imprint. If Amazon's algorithm is called A10, these authors will be the heart and soul of Chris' A6. (Ask Chris if you don't get the reference.)

And that's where *you* come in. We need you. PLEASE.

You need to let Chris know which of these stories you would most like to see become series. Which characters do you want to see more of, which plots need expansion, which universes are begging for more detail? Your input will, quite literally, make the difference. Never before have readers held so much influence over what comes next, at least within the context of Chris Kennedy Publishing. All you have to do is go to the poll and vote: https://chriskennedypublishing.com/anthro-mech-poll/

Think of it: what if there'd been a single book that introduced the Four Horsemen Universe, The Last Marines, The Lunar Free State, Salvage Title Universe, Galactic Merc, Time Wars (*Jurassic Jail*), Gladius Leagues, and more? Five years from now, readers may look back at this book in exactly that way.

So come be a part of something never tried before. Help craft a new slice of Science Fiction history. In an age when Humanity is racing to incorporate itself into the data banks of electricity-sucking server farms, help guide the stories that dare to fight back. Be part of something that will still exist even if the power goes out.

* * *

Machines *learn*. Science fiction has spent more than a century asking what happens when machines become powerful enough to rival or replace their creators. In most of those stories, the tension lies in loss… loss of control, loss of relevance, loss of authority. The machine rebels, the system escapes oversight, or humanity evolves beyond itself, leaving responsibility behind. Those are valid topics that have produced some of the genre's most enduring work.

Colossus, the Forbin Project.

Terminator.

The Matrix.

Dune.

Battlestar Galactica.

Player Piano.

The Moon is a Harsh Mistress.

Neuromancer.

With Folded Hands.

And many more.

This book begins from a different premise.

* * *

In today's reality, what once seemed like far-fetched fiction now intrudes on our daily lives like a horde of zombies. It's not science fiction anymore; it's *here.* And sometimes, a technological victory seems inevitable, because, let's face it, whether we like it or not, humanity is pouring the wealth of nations into developing its soulless replacement.

But not here. Sick of reading about, or feeling the effect of, so-called Artificial Intelligence? Read on.

This is an *Anthromech* compendium.

Anthro = *human.*

Mech, in this case, means *technology.* It may also mean the *mech* as it has come to be understood within the tropes of science fiction.

Following in the footsteps of those giants who came before, Anthromech is a new buzzword for science fiction in which human beings retain final authority over advanced technology. Machines may calculate, predict, optimize, and execute at speeds and scales no human mind can match. They may recommend courses of action so persuasive that refusing them seems irrational. They may even be correct, and we might have to fight them to retain our ascendance. But in Anthromech, technology does *not* have the final word. The last binding choice, especially the choice to use force, belongs to a human being.

Now, let's drop the essayist voice for a minute and get into the meat of it.

That difference isn't sentiment. Anthromech doesn't rest on the notion that men are better than machines, nobler than machines, or quicker on the draw. It rests on one thing: responsibility can't be handed off. A machine can carry out an order without a qualm, but nobody can haul it into the defendant's chair and make it answer to a jury of its peers. (If it could, the 'peers' would be other AIs, and they would declare it not guilty.) All you might get by way of response would be, "Sorry, that one's on me." Fat lot of good that does when there's a smoking planet out the port viewing windows.

In an Anthromech world, people know delay, waste, and mistakes come with the territory. That's the cost of owning what gets done.

A good deal of science fiction built around artificial intelligence asks, "What happens when control slips?" Anthromech looks the other way. It asks what happens when human beings refuse to let go, even when letting go would be easier, safer, or cleaner. The machines usually do what they were built to do. Trouble starts with the human hand that stays on the lever after common sense says to move it.

There's nothing inherently wrong with machines existing as tools for Humanity. After all, a wagon is a machine, and nobody argues the value of such tools. It's when the tools take dominion over their creators that the whole thing winds up backasswards.

This isn't post-human fiction, either. Anthromech has no interest in treating the loss of human identity as destiny, much less progress. Men and women may wire themselves into machines, spread their thoughts across star systems, or depend on cold hardware to stay alive where flesh alone would fail. Even so, they don't give up authorship.

They don't give up *agency*.

What those systems do in their name still belongs to them. Evolution doesn't buy them a way out; it only gives them a rougher road to carry the burden down.

Victory in an Anthromech story isn't defined by technological dominance alone. It's defined by the continued existence of human agency.

Sometimes that agency is preserved heroically. Sometimes it's preserved bureaucratically, even if some of us consider bureaucracy barely different from being ruled by machines. Sometimes it's preserved at a cost that calls the word "victory" into question in a way that Pyrrhus would understand.

At the end, though, what matters isn't that humans are *right,* but that humans remain *accountable.*

Bill Webb
Eads, TN

Chris Kennedy
Coinjock, NC

The Stars We Win

We made the wheel, we lit the forge, we bent the sea to keel,
We rode the thunder through the void on thrust and nerve and steel;
From ox-cart road to rocket wake, we climbed by nerve and hand,
And every cold machine we built, to serve the will of Man.

No bright machine nor thinking gear shall ever have the spark,
That drives a mortal soul go forth, to the vastness of the dark;
No engine wrought of wire and light, however strange its art,
Can match the stubborn, battered fire that burns in one brave heart.

Let circuits hum their hollow hymns and count the turning sky,
They do not know why mothers weep, or why the valiant die;
Let silicon prophets speak in sums to promise ease and power,
They do not feel the warmth of dawn, or cherish each passing hour.

They cannot feel the lonely watch, the last friend's parting grin,
Nor hear defiant oaths called out, to avenge one's fallen kin.
They do not dream of far green hills, nor mourn the fading day,
Nor choose to stand when fear says run and wisdom says obey.

So here's to dust and mortal bone, to sweat and will untamed,
To the breed that stumbled, rose and fell, and drove on just the same;
So sing it low and sing it long wherever men have been,
Free men may die, but do not kneel, and never will again.

While one man fights against the flood, while blood still fills his veins,
While one heart keeps the ancient oath through failure, loss, and pain,
The breed that crossed the void alive, shall hold the stars we win,
And all the cold machines we made, shall serve the will of men.

Poem by William Alan Webb
Dedicated to and inspired by the Blind Singer of the Spaceways

Contents

* * * * *

Anthromech *(noun/adjective)*

1. A doctrine, design philosophy, or technological order in which human will remains sovereign over machinery. In an anthromech system, machines may amplify strength, speed, intelligence, reach, or destructive power, but they do not possess final authority. Command, judgment, and moral agency remain in human hands.

2. More broadly, Anthromech describes any civilization, military force, or technology built on the principle that man must rule the machine, never yield to it.

3. A principle holding that machinery exists to serve, extend, and obey humanity—not replace it. However advanced the system, the hand of man remains on the sword.

Short form: Anthromech: the primacy of man over machine.

# # # # #

Me and My Shadow by Kevin Steverson & Craig Bell

A Shadow Mode Story

Chapter 1

Planet sk'Alen, Fourth Planet Out from the Star Tau Ceti
12 September 2243

Shit, that's going to leave a mark.

Still shaken and a little groggy from the blast that had thrown him into the slight depression he found himself lying in, the Marine looked at his left arm. Well, at least where his left arm had been a minute ago. Right now, it ended at the elbow.

Obviously, the auto tourniquet worked, as it had clamped down on his arm just below the bicep. The Damage Assessment Sensors in his uniform had determined that enough damage to the sleeve meant a life-threatening injury to the limb itself. It wasn't the first time a Marine was thankful for DAS. It wouldn't be the last.

He looked at the heads-up display screen over his right eye and saw the readout giving him his own medical status:

RYERSON, JOHN D. 2647015 / BLOOD LOSS MINIMAL / LOSS OF LIMB / AUTO TOURNIQUET AT MAXIMUM PRESSURE / RECOMMEND MEDICAL EVACUATION.

"No shit," Ryerson mumbled. He flicked his comm and activated the automatic beacon to call for medevac. He leaned his head back for a moment, resting his helmet in the dirt of what he now realized was an impact crater. It was worn down enough that he knew it predated the current battle being fought around him. From what he'd seen of the indigenous sentients, it wasn't exactly a surprise that they'd been killing each other longer than the Corps had been involved.

He pulled his IFAK and laid it on his chest, first removing, then injecting himself with the syrette to kill the pain he knew was coming. Then he took the small canister of Epaseal and sprayed the stump, sealing it from infection and stopping any seepage.

Ryerson lay back and waited for the evac, feeling the pain meds take hold and thinking back over the past couple of days. *What a cluster fuck.*

* * *

Three Days Earlier, aboard UTS Leonard Mason*, en route to*
Tau Ceti Star System
9 September 2243

"Gunny, what did the skipper tell you about these guys… what did he call them, Skales? How bad do you think it's going to be?"

Gunnery Sergeant John D. Ryerson looked up from the Handheld he was entering notes into as he sat on the edge of his bunk and gazed at the baby-faced lance corporal standing there by his compartment hatch. Seeing that the kid was scared, he remembered this was the first combat drop for the youngster, so he resolved to take it a little easy on the guy.

"Tanaka, are you worried that the training you've received isn't going to serve you well?" he asked.

"No, Gunny," Tanaka answered. "I think I'm pretty well trained."

Ryerson nodded. "Okay, maybe it's your weapon. Is there something wrong with it?"

Frowning in confusion, Tanaka replied, "No way! I take perfect care of it, Gunny!"

Looking back down at his Handheld, the veteran NCO asked, "Is it your officers, Tanaka? Your NCOs? Don't you trust them?"

Very confused now, the young lance corporal stammered, "No, Gunny, I trust the lieutenant and first sergeant."

Ryerson set the Handheld down on the desk next to his bunk and stood up, his two-meter-plus height towering over the diminutive Tanaka, leaning down so his face was six inches from the youngster's nose. After holding his gaze for a few seconds, he roared, "Then what the fuck is your problem, Tanaka? Do you think Captain Gurung was holding information back from you and your buddies when he gave the company brief?"

Bracing to attention, Tanaka, eyes straight ahead, replied, "No, sir!"

Shaking his head, Ryerson looked over the kid and straight into the face of a Marine staff sergeant who stood in the corridor with a huge grin on his face. Ryerson winked and looked down at the young Marine. "Okay, then, if you trust your weapon, your cadre, and the LT, and you think you have the best info available, don't you think your problem is that maybe, just maybe, you're overthinking the situation?"

Tanaka looked at him with a rueful expression. "Yeah, Gunny, sorry. You're right." He started to turn away and bumped into the sergeant standing behind him. With a hurried, "Sorry, Staff Sergeant!" he bolted down the corridor.

"Come on in, Davey," Ryerson said to one of his best friends. "What can I do for you?"

"Between you and me, JD, I'm just giving you a 'eads up," Staff Sergeant David Thatcher said, the Cockney accent betraying his London East End roots. "Our young Mr. Carlisle is showing all the signs of an officer who is determined to get a medal on his first op."

"Real gung-ho type, is he?"

Thatcher nodded. "Truly, 'e is, so I wanted you to be aware of it when we drop tomorrow. 3rd Platoon is going to be on the right of the LZ, and the old man says that's where some of the indigs are pretty well dug in. We could find ourselves deep innit rather quick."

"You're the platoon sergeant, Davey, so try to rein him in just a bit. I'll watch him close, promise."

"Thanks, JD. I figure if you saw 'im doin' anything stupid, you could sic the skipper on 'im right quick."

"That's our job, bud. Training the young and keeping them alive in the shit." The sixteen-year veteran NCO grinned. "Officer or enlisted, they're all idiots until they ain't."

Thatcher grinned, "See you tomorrow, JD. Keep your head on a swivel."

"You too, Davey."

* * * * *

Chapter 2

In the three days prior since, not one thing had gone right for Ryerson. The initial insertion had been rough. Spiraling down through atmo always was, but they started taking fire as soon as the Landing Craft (also known as LCs, or Elsies) hit the upper edges of the planet's exosphere. The LCs were armored and shielded, with the platoon's personnel secured in the uncomfortable but padded seating. Even so, they could get rocked, and they did. The Elsie carrying 1st Platoon took a hit to its shielding at only a hundred meters above the surface, which flipped it onto its side as it hit the dirt hard. Half of 1st Platoon's people were KIA or WIA from the crash landing, including its PL, a first lieutenant with two combat drops on his record.

2nd Platoon had made it down intact, and they'd moved to contact almost immediately to their front and left. So far, they'd given more grief than they'd gotten, with light casualties and steady movement toward the objective, a mine that had been taken over by rebels.

His buddy Thatcher had survived so far, since 3rd Platoon landed. His young lieutenant wasn't so fortunate. He hadn't lasted twenty minutes before an indig round took his head off. They were down, personnel-wise, by almost half in the less than 72 hours since contact.

Captain Gurung, the Golf Company CO, was a compact little man of Gurkha blood, whose family had served king and country in the Marines long before the Royal Marines and U.S. Marines had merged a century earlier. Losing his 1st and 3rd Platoon officers meant he needed someone to take charge immediately and make sure Golf's right kept moving forward.

* * *

12 September 2243

Gunnery Sergeant John David Ryerson took command of the combined survivors of the two platoons. Those from 1st had moved over to the right, and between them, plus the guys and gals still left from 3rd, Ryerson had nearly a full platoon to work with.

They'd made short work of the emplacements that had given 3rd Platoon such grief. By the end of the second day, the combined platoon was past that target and on the approach to the mission's main objective, the mine entrance. The CO had reformed the company's approach with the new 1st Platoon to their left.

It was on that approach when a mortar round fired from the indigs' position, dug in above the mine's entrance, landed five meters away from Ryerson. At least, that's what he thought of it as. It made it easier to refer to alien weapon systems as something he was familiar with. He'd been talking with Captain Gurung, his comm guy standing next to him, when it hit.

He found himself lying on his back in the crater, missing an arm, and waiting for the evac he knew was on the way. He'd taken some shrapnel in his legs, as well, but they were only cut up and bleeding. He wasn't worried about them if his uniform's DAS wasn't.

"Gunny, fuck! You going to be okay?"

He looked up and saw young Tanaka looking down at him, his face covered with grime. The kid had proven to have what it took in the two days since the landing, killing indigs and leading first his rifle team, then a squad when his squad sergeant was KIA.

"I'll be fine, Tanaka. Gimme a SITREP!"

"The Skales have pulled back inside the mine, Gunny. Heavy's coming up to get 'em out," Tanaka responded, calling the heavy weapons guys by their nickname.

"Anyone else hurt like me? Baker?" asked Ryerson. Baker was his comm guy, a PFC from the Belt.

Tanaka shook his head. "KIA. Same round that hit you. He took most of the shrapnel you would have if he hadn't been standing next to you."

Ryerson laid his head back down. He could hear the evac coming, so he exhaled and said, "Shit. Okay, kid. Back at it. Keep your people alive."

"Aye, aye, Gunny," Tanaka answered. "Copy." He took off up and over the lip of the crater, heading back to his team.

The hybrid ship coming to get him was designed for efficient flight in both atmosphere and vacuum, serving primarily as an armored ambulance. It landed about ten meters away, and the acrid yellow dust of the planet's surface swirled around him from the downblast of the twin rotors used for planetside operations.

Less than ten seconds later, two corpsmen came over the top of the crater and started tending to him, making sure all his serious wounds were addressed and protected before they rolled him onto a grav gurney and got him out of the AO.

He'd been medically sedated on the way out of sk'Alen's atmosphere, so when he began to wake up, he was a little fogged from the meds. He looked around and realized he was in sick bay back aboard the *Mason*, peering up at the face of a Navy doc.

"How you doin,' Gunny?"

Ryerson squinted to help him focus. The doctor's name tag indicated a last name of Stein and a rank of lieutenant commander.

"I've been better, sir," Ryerson replied. "Pretty sure I'll survive, though."

Stein smiled. "That's the plan. You did a good job, making sure the arm was protected, so we didn't find any indication of infection there, but we do have some minor infections in a few of the wounds on your legs. Nothing to write home about, but we'll keep you here for a couple of days to make sure we get that under control."

"How are my guys doing dirtside, sir? Do you know anything about how it's going?"

The doc shook his head. "Not really. I think I heard that the mine you were looking to liberate was taken within a few hours after you were evac'd, but I'm not sure."

Ryerson frowned. "How long was I out, sir?"

"A little longer than we wanted, but only about twelve hours. You lost a lot of blood from some of the wounds on your legs we closed up. I'm pretty sure you wouldn't have noticed them in comparison to how the arm must have felt," Stein said with a smile, "but we're good now, so no worries. Have you up and mobile in a couple of days. Then we can see about a prosthetic replacement for your arm."

"Sounds good."

The doctor nodded and left the general ward area for his office. As he walked out, he acknowledged Captain Gurung coming in. The Gurkha walked up to Ryerson's bed with a grin lighting up his ugly mug.

"Gunny, we did it. *You* did it," he announced as he stood over Ryerson. "The mine was taken, and we didn't lose any more of our people. Congratulations."

Ryerson shook his head. "I don't know if I'm the guy to congratulate, Skipper. I got blown up before the assault on the actual mine even started."

"That kid Tanaka? He led the assault, under your orders, according to him, and he said to tell you he did exactly what you told him to do."

"Which was…" Ryerson began.

"He said you told him to keep his people alive," Gurung answered, "and he did. He took a slight wound, a through-and-through from a projectile weapon to his upper arm, but he wrapped a bandage around it and kept on."

Ryerson laid his head back and closed his eyes for a moment. "Good kid. We had a counseling session on the *Mason* before we dropped."

"Yeah, heard about that. Actually, I heard it… you have the classic Marine Corps-issued set of lungs, Gunny."

Ryerson grinned. "Genetics."

"That's right, you're, what, X number generation Marine Corps?" Gurung nodded. "How many?"

"I'm the twelfth Ryerson directly serving in the Corps. My ultimate great-grandad was a United States Marine who fought in the Gulf Wars of the 20th and 21st centuries. Not an officer among them… us," he said with a shrug. "Well, until my brother, that is."

"That makes it even more remarkable in my eyes, John," Gurung said quietly. "You're up for the Silver Comet."

"I don't deserve that," Ryerson protested. "Shit, sir, all I did was my job."

"That's rather the definition of bravery to my mind, Gunnery Sergeant. A Marine doing his job when the shit's flying around him, thick as flies on a dead yak. And you did exactly that, taking a couple of disorganized groups of Marines and turning them into a single unit of hard chargers. That led to the accomplishment of their mission. And, not to mention, under the leadership of a young lance corporal who was inspired by you… as were they all."

Gurung shook his head and continued, "No, Gunny. You're getting this, and you'll look appropriately stern and determined as I pin it on you. That's an order."

"Aye, aye, sir," Ryerson relented. "Quick question, sir. The doc said I'm getting a prosthetic. How quick can I get that? I want to get back to the unit."

"Out of my hands. Doc says he thinks you'll be medevac'd to Bethesda for the prosthetic," Gurung replied, referring to the massive hospital station on the second planet out from Barnard's Star.

The star was a red dwarf not quite six light years from Earth, and the medical facility based on it was named after a historically famous hospital located on their home world.

"I was afraid of that." Ryerson sighed. "Probably means reassignment to another MEU."

Gurung shrugged. "Maybe, but it's still the best place to get a fighting Marine back into shape. Whatever they give you means they want you back in the Fleet. No small compliment, even if it's rather backhanded."

The diminutive captain smiled. "And, again, you'll deal with it and put a determined and stern look on that ugly face of yours. Understood?"

Ryerson chuckled. "Aye, aye, sir."

Gurung nodded and left. Ryerson watched the Gurkha officer walk out with a smile. *Badass.* He respected his captain tremendously, and he knew he'd miss working with him. Again, he lay back and stared at the overhead.

Barnard's Star. Bethesda. Shit.

*****

Chapter 3

Bethesda Medical Center
17 October 2243

In the intervening weeks since he'd embarked on the UTHS *Mercy*, Ryerson's wounds on the lower extremities closed up and healed with the aid of a brand-new layer of synthskin. He knew from previous encounters with sharp and penetrating objects that it would eventually merge with his body's natural epidermis.

His left arm, however, was still missing everything from just below the elbow. The doctors on the *Mercy* had ensured he remained infection-free and prepped his arm for a prosthetic lower limb, including an actual hand. While the prosthetic would be metal and chips with hydraulics and fluids that mimicked his natural arm, it would not look like natural skin. To protect the moving parts, it was fashioned from a blend of titanium and one or more of the many new metallic elements discovered on some planet or moon. New for mankind, anyway.

He was glad that some egghead somewhere in a lab had somehow made the metal flexible. He didn't know the science of it, but he appreciated the fact that it would enable him to work with it as a completely normal hand and arm. After a bit of training and physical therapy, he knew from some of the guys around him in past units that it would feel and function as if it had always been a part of him, and not some aftermarket accessory.

He'd been there for two days now, and he was growing a little impatient. First of all, being two meters in height meant that most beds weren't long enough for a guy of his stature. The bunks in the hospital were no exception to that rule. Added to that was just general boredom.

About the time Ryerson was going to do something, anything, to relieve boredom, a doctor walked into his room with a Handheld in his left hand. The first thing Ryerson noticed was that this doc was obviously of Chinese extraction, and the second item worthy of note was that he was close to as tall as the gunny. Unusual all the way around.

"Gunnery Sergeant Ryerson, John D., I presume?" asked the doctor in unaccented Standard. He stuck his hand out, and the two shook.

"Guilty, Doc," Ryerson responded with a smile. "I'm glad to see you."

"Sure, you say that now, before we start attaching the prosthetic," said the doctor with a blank expression. "Let's see if I still bring you joy after we attach it."

Ryerson didn't quite know how to respond to that, so he just nodded slowly with a skeptical look on his face, which turned into a grin when the doctor started laughing.

"You Marines… always so serious," he said. "My name is Zhu Lei, so just call me Doc or Commander. Both are easier to remember."

"You got it, Doc it is," Ryerson responded with a chuckle. "As I said, and I meant it, I'm glad to see you. I'd like to get this show on the road."

Zhu nodded. "I understand. You're probably bored as hell, but I assure you, there's a reason we haven't begun the procedure quite yet. First, we needed to make sure everything damaged, both externally and internally, had healed enough for us to work with the formerly traumatized areas. Second, the construction of the prosthetic is what you would call a 'custom job' and has to be made to the micron for it to become part of your body. Our goal's always to give you an appendage that you can use far better than the original issue."

"As long as you're here now, I'm good," Ryerson said. "How do we start the process?"

"Surgery to attach the prosthetic will be tomorrow at 0630, Gunny, so your prep will start approximately an hour earlier. We'll prepare the arm and flood you with antibiotics and some meds to enhance your body's acceptance of the new limb. And, of course, we'll be numbing that part of your body. I'm pretty sure after this past month, you're okay with not having too much more pain over this."

Ryerson nodded. "Got that right, Doc. Absolutely. So, what can I do to prep myself, other than wait?"

"Good of you to ask," Zhu replied. He gave the Handheld to Ryerson, who took it and glanced at it before setting it in his lap. "Downloaded in that is a 'how to' for the early part of getting used to the prosthetic. You'll feel a little odd because all your nerve endings will be stimulated when you move your hand or arm and touch anything, in much the same way as your flesh and bone did. It will feel just like your original very quickly. The challenge is that it's much stronger, so you have to be cautious when you use it."

Zhu reached over with his left arm, picked up a carafe with about two liters of water in it, and held it up to Ryerson. "If you did this tomorrow, it's likely you'd damage some of the connections in your arm. You need to give it at least forty-eight hours post-op for all the connections to adhere to you. During that time, move your fingers. Make a fist. Rotate your forearm slowly. Make like you're counting to five with your left hand, using each finger individually. Just that sort of exercise therapy without picking up anything, not even a fork yet. Clear?"

"Aye, aye, Doc. Clearly understood, and that's what I'll do," Ryerson promised.

"Good," said Zhu, nodding his head to indicate the Handheld in Ryerson's lap. "I'm out of here, but read that, and I'll see you in the morning."

"Will do. Thanks!"

* * *

The surgery went well, and when Ryerson came out of the anesthesia-induced fog, he looked at his left arm. To his delight, he saw that it ended the way it had been issued at birth… with a hand. His mouth dry, he unconsciously reached for the water glass with a straw next to his head on a side table, attempting to move his left arm.

Ryerson realized it wasn't going to happen, as his arm was immobilized in a cast-like tube that covered it from the deltoid to the metallic wrist. Synthetic skin would be added later. The cast, or whatever it was, was secured to the railing on his hospital bed, preventing him from moving it in any direction. *This is going to make a head run interesting.*

With that thought fresh in his mind, he looked toward the door and saw Dr. Zhu come through it with a Navy nurse, a lieutenant. *Damn, does everybody around here outrank me? Ah, well, could be worse. Could be a corpsman, and they're generally ugly as hell.*

"How do you feel, Gunny?" Zhu asked.

"A little fogged, Doc, but not bad. Can't move the arm to see if it will, though."

"That's intended," Zhu said. "No movement for twenty-four hours, then we'll scan the arm to ensure that all the connections are stable. Once confirmed, we'll remove the outer part of the orthocylinder. The inner part is a gentle compression device, to be worn for an additional two or three days, depending on the attachments. Then, it's off with all of it, and PT begins in earnest."

"Sounds good." Ryerson nodded. "How'd the surgery go?"

Both Zhu and the attractive lieutenant smiled and nodded before Zhu answered, "Very well, Gunny. I'm very pleased with the outcome. We encountered no issues with your musculature, nerve endings, or vascular system whatsoever. That in and of itself is a bit unusual, as we generally have at least two or three bleeders, as we call them."

He put his hand gently on the orthocylinder and said, "We call them that for obvious reasons, as it's normally the vascular system we have a challenge with. Yours? Not a one. We'll take the win, as you Terrans say."

A little surprised, Ryerson asked, "You're not Terran?"

Shaking his head, Zhu replied, "No, I was born on Xiu-Ying, a planet colonized by ships from the old Chinese Republic in the late 21st century, near Alpha Centauri."

Ryerson must have looked a little puzzled, because Zhu chuckled. "You have no idea what I'm talking about, do you?"

"No, sir," Ryerson said, thinking hard on various briefings. "I don't believe I've ever heard of it."

"Not a surprise, as my people didn't broadcast its existence until twenty years ago. As I'm given to understand from what our history says versus everyone else's, my people were rather famous… infamous? Anyway, they were known for being a little paranoid and holding secrets very well."

"Forgive me for asking, Doc, but I'm curious as to how your planet's only been known by us for twenty years, and you're in front of me as a lieutenant commander in the Terran Navy."

"Well, I could brag about my scores in university and medical school, Gunny, but that wouldn't have been enough without some political dancing. My family is among the more politically connected on Xiu-Ying, and they were wise enough to see the advantages of a son serving the Terran Alliance. I had my MD at the age of eighteen before I left my home world, and instead of doing as my parents wished and seeking to practice on Earth or one of the Inner Worlds, I chose the military. Fifteen years later, I stand before you, an Officer and a Gentlemen, according to God and the Terran Congress."

Ryerson nodded. "You didn't have to tell me all that, Doc, but it's a great story. Thanks." He looked at the nurse and raised his eyebrows.

She smiled and said, "Terran born and raised, Gunnery Sergeant Ryerson. Illinois."

Ryerson nodded. "Been there, at least to the Chicago-Milwaukee metroplex. Didn't get to see much of the area south."

"Still mostly farm country," she said, "but pretty." She held out her hand, which was warm and soft. "I'm Lieutenant Parks."

"Nice to meet you, Lieutenant."

Parks laughed. "You say that now, Gunny, but I'm the one in charge of your physical therapy. Let's revisit that last after a couple of sessions."

"Oh... kay..." Ryerson looked at Zhu, who held up his hands.

"Don't look at me, Gunny. She's in charge, and I know better than to cross her."

They all laughed, although Ryerson's was noticeably less enthusiastic. *This is going to be... interesting.*

*****

Chapter 4

Three days went by quickly, once Ryerson could get up and move around. It was only the first full day that he was somewhat restricted. Since then, he'd been able to walk around the floor and talk to various troops, including a couple of Marines he knew had been on sk'Alen. Apparently, his guys had done all right, and he heard that Gurung had been decorated.

PT had been interesting, as he'd thought it would be, but not due to any real pain. Discomfort, certainly, but no real hurt, outside of a couple of twinges now and then. The topical meds they used and the gentle local that was injected into the skin above his elbow worked like charms.

On the fourth day, Zhu observed Parker putting him through his paces a little more than she had to that point. He was able to pick up various objects, each requiring a different positioning of his fingers and grip with the prosthetic. He didn't even really have to think about it; he simply reached and did what he would have done with his right hand. It was that easy.

Parker had him using a grip device that measured the pressure he could comfortably bear, and it increased each day. And not just a little bit. By the fifth day, he could exert the kind of pressure in his grip that would crush someone's hand if he wasn't careful.

On the seventh day, weirdly, he felt almost normal. Whatever these guys at Bethesda did, it was absolutely amazing to him that he knew… he *knew* that he could get back to his unit and pick up where he'd left off.

He asked Zhu that morning when he could go back to the Fleet, and Zhu shrugged before he replied, "Honestly, Gunny, that's above my pay grade. I don't know yet."

Ryerson frowned. "But aren't you the medical officer who clears me for duty? Am I not cleared?"

Zhu studied him for a moment, then said, "Gunny, I okayed you for a full return to duty yesterday."

"Okay, with all due respect, sir, what am I still doing, sitting on my ass in a hospital room?"

Before Zhu could respond, a tall, swarthy, squared-away full colonel of Marines wearing an OD green turban and sporting a full beard strode into his room, followed by Parker and another woman who looked vaguely familiar. He noted that the second woman wasn't a nurse, as she was wearing a white lab coat like Zhu, but she wasn't Navy, either. No rank insignia.

"I heard that question, Gunny," the colonel said in a deep bass voice with a slightly British accent. He stuck out his hand. "I'm Singh, pleased to meet you."

Torn between saluting—which Marines didn't do indoors unless under arms—and shaking, he stuck his hand in the colonel's and asked, "Sir, so why am I still here?"

Colonel Singh grinned, his teeth white against the deep blue-black of his beard. "Because I had them put a hold on your discharge until we had a chance to talk."

Ryerson's face was suddenly expressionless. He'd been in the Corps long enough to know that when a full bull colonel wanted to talk to you about something, it was rarely something you'd get excited about.

Singh looked at him shrewdly. "Do you know who I am, Gunny?"

Ryerson nodded. "Now that you ask, sir, yes, I do know who you are."

Zhu looked confused, as did Parker, so Ryerson said, "Colonel Singh, here, is well known in the Corps, Doc, and he's respected, but he's respected as a combat officer, one who's entitled to wear the Medal along with the others he's wearing." He looked at Singh. "So I guess the question is why he's here and what he wants with a simple Marine."

Zhu and Parker looked at Singh and the woman with suspicion. They hadn't known of his reputation or that he was a Combat Arms officer rather than Med. They should have noticed his ribbons, all of which indicated Singh had been in more than a few hot spots, and he was apparently entitled to, but not wearing, the Medal of Honor. And who was the woman?

Singh looked at Zhu and Parker. "Doctor… and Lieutenant Parker, I'm going to have to ask you to leave, as the conversation Dr. Einarsdottir and I are going to have with Gunny Ryerson is classified. I thank you for the amazing work you've both done."

Dr. Zhu started to say something, paused, looked at Ryerson with a smile, and nodded. Then, he ushered an obviously irritated Parker out of the room, closing the door as they left.

"I know you have questions, Gunny," Singh said, his face deadly serious, "and I promise answers to all of them, but I have to tell you first that this conversation is indeed classified, and so far above your pay grade that if you ever tell anyone about it without clearance from me… well, there's a penal stay that you won't enjoy at the end of it. Is that understood, Gunnery Sergeant Ryerson?"

"Aye, aye, sir. I understand," Ryerson replied, his curiosity piqued.

Satisfied with the classic Naval service response for "I understand and will obey," Singh nodded. "Good. Now, to business."

He looked over at the woman he'd referred to as Dr. Einarsdottir and motioned her to his side. "Gunny, this is Doctor Freyja Einarsdottir. Freyja, this is Marine Gunnery Sergeant John David Ryerson… Michael's brother."

"I knew that as soon as I walked in, Colonel," said the lady doctor in a melodious voice. *Is that an accent? Why does she look familiar to me… I've never met her before.*

"A pleasure to meet you, John," Freyja said. "I knew your brother and worked with him."

Bingo. There it is. Mike had sent him a couple of 2D pics of a group of people at a party he'd been attending, and this doctor had been in both of them. His brother hadn't said anything about her, just that his temporary duty station was one he was enjoying.

That was the last missive of any kind he'd received from Mike. His brother, a major, had been a Raider. Ryerson didn't understand what Mike had been doing away from the Spec Ops teams, but he figured he didn't need to know. After all, like Ryerson, John D, Mike was a Marine, and Marines were told what they needed to know when they needed to know it.

The next thing he'd heard was that Major Michael Aaron Ryerson and half his company had died when their dropship LC had taken a direct hit on a mission near Lalande 21185, a star just a little further out than Proxima Centauri. He didn't know the specifics and doubted he ever would. Mike had been a Raider; their missions were usually nasty and always classified.

So, what had he been doing, working with this doctor?

"I recognize you from a 2D that Mike sent before he was KIA at Lalande," Ryerson said. "What was Mike doing with you that had a Raider major working with a doctor? Was he wounded in some way I didn't know about?"

"I'm not that kind of doctor," Freyja answered with a slight smile. "Mike was helping with a project I'm a part of, but it'd be best for Colonel Singh to explain."

Ryerson looked at Singh, who shrugged and said, "Dr. Einarsdottir is being modest. She's not just a part of the project; she's the lead. She requested a warfighter with the requisite background to help us field an asset we could use in virtually every combat scenario."

The colonel continued, "Gunny, we're going to leave you for a moment. There's a clean set of MCUs in the closet. Get dressed, and we'll be in the hall." With that, and before Ryerson could ask any more questions, Singh and Freyja walked out of the room.

Ryerson shrugged; he was a Marine, and he'd just been ordered to put on his uniform—his Marine Combat Uniform—and meet them in the hall. When he finished dressing, everything as it should be, he grabbed his cover and walked out of the hospital room for what he hoped was the last time.

On the way out, he passed Parker and thanked her, asking her to pass along his appreciation for all that was done for him to Dr. Zhu. She smiled. "Remember when I asked how you'd feel when you were done with PT, Gunny?"

"I still feel the same way, Lieutenant Parker. Just a little sore, that's all," Ryerson replied with a smile. "Take care of yourself, ma'am."

Her smile waning, she looked at Singh, then at Einarsdottir, frowned, and then said to Ryerson, "You take care as well, John. Be well."

"Tough to do, given my chosen profession, Lieutenant," Ryerson said with his eyes already down the road. "But I promise, I'll do my best."

With another nod, Ryerson looked at Singh, who turned without a word and led the way out. Waiting outside the main building in what was essentially a garage was an intra-atmospheric Light Armored Shuttle, which surprised Ryerson. He'd assumed they'd be headed off-planet. As far as he knew, the med center was the only installation on the surface, which wasn't exactly conducive to human life. The buildings were all linked and atmo-tight. The shuttle lifted two meters off the pavement and pivoted, heading for the exit.

Once it was through the shimmering shield that kept the noxious atmosphere of the planet at bay, the shuttle banked right and up. At about a hundred meters in altitude, it flew through the soupy murk that shrouded the world they were on. Ryerson knew from his reading time in the hospital that the atmospheric envelope of the planet was primarily a phosphene soup at an average of 73 degrees Celsius. Rather hot, in other words.

The shuttle interior itself was pretty comfortable. It was obviously one for the officers instead of enlisted. One thing he'd learned early was to enjoy the comforts that came along with rank or circumstance, because you never knew when the opportunity would come your way again, or ever.

Singh ignored him, reading messages on his Handheld. Dr. Einarsdottir, on the other hand, immediately engaged Ryerson in conversation once they hit altitude.

The seats in the shuttle were comfortable and secured them snugly with a four-point harness, which the pilot made certain was engaged for each passenger prior to lifting. The colonel was forward, in the seat in front of the good doctor, while she was across the narrow center aisle of the shuttle from Ryerson. In most similar situations, especially if he didn't know how long he'd be on the shuttle, Ryerson would have just laid his head back and closed his eyes.

That was not to be, however, for Einarsdottir leaned across the aisle and said, "I know I didn't express this earlier, Gunny, but I wanted to offer my condolences on the death of your brother. I only worked with him for a few months, but I grew to like him. He was obviously a good Marine, and once we started talking, I figured out he was a pretty good guy underneath the Star, Globe, and Anchor."

Ryerson smiled. "I'm glad you saw that, Doc. Mike was a good guy, and he was a hell of a Marine. I wish I knew more about the op he died on, but maybe someday."

She talked about some of the operations he'd been a part of, knowing the generalities but not the specifics. She insisted that he call her Freyja, and he responded by asking her to use his given name as well.

Ryerson realized very quickly that she was particularly interested in the various weapons he'd used as a grunt and in the MEU since. He saw Colonel Singh look over his shoulder at him, and Ryerson wordlessly sought his permission to answer. Singh nodded with a smile and went back to his messages.

He had to admit she asked good questions and understood everything he shared with her. Ryerson was surprised she wanted to know as much about the tactical application of each weapon within the squad and situation as she did about how they functioned. He could see that she was absorbing all of it, even if she wasn't taking physical notes of their conversation, and he'd bet that she'd be able to regurgitate all of the information and tech specs he'd discussed without much effort.

Ryerson felt the LAS bank to the left. He leaned slightly into the aisle and looked forward, past the pilot, to see that they were approaching a facility of some sort. As they descended smoothly despite the normally rough atmo, he observed the automated defense emplacements every 50 meters or so surrounding the buildings. To his trained eye, he assessed the size of the facility at approximately one kilometer in size, slightly oval in shape. *Huh. A klick. Pretty good-sized compound for something this far from Earth. Should be interesting.*

As the shuttle settled into a surprisingly gentle touchdown inside one of the larger buildings at the center of the base, Ryerson could see quite a bit of activity to the front of the LAS. Mechs moved what appeared to be heavy gear around, while human military personnel avoided them. All of it seemed purposeful to the veteran Marine, who logged everything mentally without conscious thought.

"Okay, Gunny, let's un-ass this thing. We have something you need to see," Singh said as he popped his harness and stepped into the aisle. Dr. Einarsdottir stood, as well, and moved ahead of Ryerson to the hatch at the back left of the shuttle, stopping and waiting for it to open.

Ryerson waited for the colonel to pass, then fell in behind him as the hatch opened with a slight but noticeable change in air pressure. The air coming into the shuttle felt comfortable at about 22 or 23 degrees Celsius, smelled of warm machinery, and was slightly acrid. It was mild and not strong enough to induce a reaction from either his eyes or sinuses.

Hopping down from the LAS, he figured from seeing the other military personnel around him that this area was considered outside, so he put on his cover. Glancing around, he followed his two companions across the huge floorspace and through a side door approximately four meters high and twenty meters across.

The colonel and doctor didn't slow as they walked past assault vehicles and some mechs Ryerson had seen before. A couple of the models he'd actually utilized in different places and times. All of them were in various states of either repair or modification; he couldn't tell which.

A hundred meters later, the three entered a smaller portal as it opened. It was large enough for three men to walk through together, but not much more. Once they were through the entry, it closed behind them. Ryerson could hear a locking mechanism operating and knew it was a secure area.

He was in a room ten meters high and twenty- or twenty-five-meters square. That was noted unconsciously, as were the locations of the other two entrances he could see. But what really caught his attention was a roughly humanoid-shaped figure standing five meters in front of him. *Holy shit, that's a fighting mech of some kind. Damn.*

Colonel Singh stopped in front of the fighting mech and gestured up to it, waiting for a moment, then said, "This is the newest iteration of a failure of ours, Gunny. Meet MIMIC."

Ryerson could hear the capitalization of the letters, but said nothing, scanning the mech and taking in what he could see from in front of it. The mech exuded menace in mottled camo with the word MARINES proudly showing on its chest above the number 01. *This thing has to be at least four meters tall... and it looks like it could carry a ton.*

Dr. Einarsdottir stood next to the colonel and spoke with what sounded a lot like affection. "He's our newest and brightest hope, John. In our earliest versions, the upper half of the torso of MIMIC was a little broader and deeper, as we had what was essentially a cockpit of sorts for a soldier—or in your case, a Marine—

to stand upright in. The connecting harness would hold the human securely and amplify everything the human did down to the grasp of his hand to pick up a feather."

Ryerson nodded. "I can see it, but this—what did you call it? MIMIC?" He looked at Freyja.

She nodded, "MIMIC. It isn't something we'd be giving to the Army, at least at this point, because it's far better tailored to what you and your Corps do. Slightly smaller, more mobile units that would be rapidly deployed across the known star systems. It's perfect for your MEUs and their mission profiles."

Einarsdottir looked back up at the mech, "As to your question, MIMIC is an acronym for Mobile Intelligent Marine Infantry Cybermech."

Singh smiled. "As you can see, Gunny, our scientist friend here is aware of our fondness for acronyms."

Ryerson chuckled. "We do have a few, sir. No argument."

He walked around the MIMIC, noting the joints and how they were armored and sealed. It was obvious to his trained eye that nothing foreign—dirt, sand, whatever—could get into any of the articulated joints of its bipedal legs, arms, or shoulders. He couldn't tell how much damage the joints could take from direct fire, but he was willing to bet it was a lot. The shoulders were protected from above by a rounded platform on each, extending from near the neck outward to cover the top of the shoulder joint.

Ryerson thought they looked pretty sturdy, and he could see what he'd wager were hardpoints built into them. *Hell, I bet you could place launchers up on those for just about any kind of ordnance a grunt could carry. Grunt? Shit, you could put some kind of mortar or artillery piece up there! It wouldn't suck to have that fighting alongside us with a heavy weapons squad, that's for sure.*

He stopped, still looking up at the mech, and said, "What happened to the human pilot idea? Having a Marine driving this thing makes a lot of sense."

Singh shrugged. "That's what we all thought, too, but trials showed us otherwise."

He looked at Einarsdottir, who nodded, and said, "No matter how well we secured the pilot and tried to protect him, the human body is just too fragile to take the concussive impact of heavy ammunition. The results of the tests on dummies and cadavers were less than optimal."

Ryerson actually laughed. "You mean the pilot would have been badly wounded or outright killed? We're just too soft a critter?"

She nodded ruefully. "Precisely. We never advanced it to even try a live pilot trial, as we figured it was pointless. We already knew what would most likely happen, so why risk a life?"

"What about a Cygnian pilot?" Ryerson asked, referring to the natives of the fourth planet out from 61Cygni. "Those guys have pretty tough skin, don't they?"

Singh nodded. "They do have that, no doubt about it. The problem is twofold: On a practical level, their physiology is so different from ours that fitting them into one of these requires a loss of uniformity. Then there's the political."

Ryerson grunted. There was always the political.

Singh chuckled. "Exactly. They're our friends and allies today. Tomorrow? Only history knows the answer to that, so, no, what this agency creates is solely Terran."

Einarsdottir nodded. "That's my understanding, as well, and I have to say, considering the history of our species, I think it's a good idea to make certain we don't create weapons systems that can be easily turned on us if at all possible."

"I agree," Ryerson said. "Another question, sir, if I may."

Singh nodded. "Go ahead."

"You used the word 'agency' a moment ago. What agency is this?"

"You're standing in the R&D section of the Terran Advanced Research Program. TARP, to get back into the world of acronyms," Singh replied. "Tell me, Gunny, are you familiar with Earth's history back to the 20th century? Particularly as it relates to weapons development?"

"If you're referring to what was known in the U.S. as DARPA, then yes, sir, I am."

"Perfect, then you understand what TARP is mostly about," Singh said approvingly. "Although our agency isn't just about weapons research. We also work on the mechanics of new drive technology, computers, you name it. If it has military applications, or even potential ones, we're the people tasked with its development."

"All of this makes sense, sir. I just have one more question."

"Shoot."

"What am I doing here?"

Just then, Colonel Singh's comm buzzed. He pulled the small device from his pocket, held up one finger to Ryerson and Einarsdottir, then walked a short distance to get some privacy. Ryerson looked at Freya and asked, "Do you know the answer to that question, Doc?"

"Please, John, for at least a while, we're going to be working together on this, so just call me Freyja, yes? It'll make our conversations easier."

Ryerson smiled. "Sorry. Yes, Freyja. Thanks."

"To answer your question, I know SJ won't mind if I don't wait for him before I explain."

"SJ?"

Freyja laughed, a delightful sound to Ryerson's ears, and replied, "Sorry. SJ is what I call Colonel Singh. His full name is Subedar Joginder Singh. I told him early on that I wasn't even going to try, so he told me to just call him SJ. Easier."

Ryerson nodded. "I think I'll just keep calling him Colonel or sir."

"Probably best," Freyja agreed with a smile. She gestured for him to follow her and headed toward one of the two doors he'd noted on entering the area. Walking into the next and smaller room behind her, he saw some gear spread out on a table.

Freyja stopped next to the equipment on the square table and said with a dramatic flair, "As they used to say on those late-night 2Ds and 3Ds, 'Welcome to my laboratory.'"

Then she laughed and continued, "This is why you're here, John. This, when married to your MCUs, will enable you to work with the MIMIC effectively. I've designed all of this, early on conceptually with your brother Mike, who really helped me understand just how much a Marine could add to his or her loadout when fully kitted and still be combat effective."

Ryerson nodded. "Mike would have been good at that. He knew his stuff."

"He did," Colonel Singh agreed as he entered the room. "And one of the last things he said before he had to return to his unit was the perfect grunt to test all this was his brother, John. And there's the answer to your question, Gunny."

Singh and Freyja watched as Ryerson walked around the table, every so often turning over a piece of equipment or picking it up to examine more closely. It was obvious to them that he was seeing which piece would work with another, and where it would be worn on him when fitted. He held some of them and gauged their weight.

He didn't ask any questions, just kept up his examination of the items for almost ten minutes before he looked up and said, "I think I can pretty much envision how all this is going to work, but I'm curious about how you'll have everything here actually fit on a Marine. Are you looking to build this into some form of armor? Because if you are, I think you're making a mistake."

"Why do you say that, John?" Freyja asked. "That would seem to be the most elegant solution."

"Sure, if you don't mind the additional weight," Ryerson replied. "That's been the challenge with body armor from time immemorial. No matter what Man has tried throughout the centuries, it always comes down to weight, and even now, we don't have armor that does what armor's supposed to do *effectively* without being too heavy."

Singh chuckled. "Gunny, that's almost verbatim what Mike told us after he did his initial exam of the gear. That's when he stepped in and started helping with design."

Freyja nodded. "What you're looking at here, for the most part, would be fitted to a kind of exoskeleton frame that a Marine could step into. While in and of itself, there's weight, once fitted, it would take up the entire load of not just what you see here, but also the Marine's ammunition, ruck... you name it. It would actually lighten the load and enable the Marine wearing it to go further while carrying more."

"Okay, anything that does that is going to be real popular, believe me," Ryerson replied with an emphatic nod. He waved his arm to indicate the entire table. "So, tell me what you're thinking about how to partner this up with a MIMIC mech."

"This is where we start—the word Mike used was 'meld'—melding man and machine somewhat," Freyja said. "We have an implant ready to test on a human subject—you, in other words—so it's really just a question of your willingness to move forward."

Singh nodded as Ryerson looked at him. "Yeah, Gunny. It's up to you at this point. No officer is going to order you to do this. It has to be voluntary on your part." He chuckled as he read Ryerson's facial expression. "I know. I know. Any gunnery sergeant is going to get that look on his face when he hears the word 'volunteer.'"

He shrugged. "But that's where we are. So, do you want some time to think about it? Do we need to explain a little more about the implant?"

Ryerson replied, "Before we move forward, I have to say that I'm intrigued by all of this, but my first question before we talk implant is straight up," he gestured toward the door they'd come through and asked, "what's the whole point of the mech out there and the gear in here?"

Singh responded seriously, "Gunny, what we're creating here is essentially a team of man and mech. When you're wearing the exoskeleton and hooked up, the mech will have the capability to do everything you're doing as you're doing it. We call it Shadow Mode. You shoot; it shoots. You throw a grenade; it throws a bigger one. You call for a close-in arty strike, and a rocket shoots off your mech. Basically, it shadows your every move and responds as an Electronic Intelligence would to your commands."

"An EI?" Ryerson asked. "Not an AI?"

Both Singh and Freyja shook their heads.

"No, Gunny. We want the mech slaved to the Marine, so there's no room for independent action by the mech. It would add too much confusion to the battle space," Singh answered. "I want thinking Marines in charge out there."

"That was made clear from the beginning, John," Freyja agreed. "AI was eliminated as an option from the start. Besides, we have yet to develop AI to the degree necessary to give it our hundred percent trust in anything, much less a weapons platform. As far as we're aware, no known race has done so, either."

"Thank you," Ryerson said. "I don't trust AI, either, and I don't know any Marine who does. The issues a century ago were enough, thank you very much."

"We agree," Singh commented.

"You said it requires an implant of some sort, so I have to ask, what kind?"

Singh looked at Freyja and gestured for her to answer.

"It's a two-millimeter sphere, John, that we would implant beneath your skin right here," said Freyja, tapping the back of her neck about two centimeters from the base of her skull. "We wanted to put it near the communications pathways, but in a location where normal MCUs in the field would shield it, while not being where it would cause any discomfort. I honestly don't know what it will feel like, but it tests as pretty unnoticeable… for what it's worth."

"What does it do?" asked Ryerson.

"Straight comm with the EI, Gunny," Singh answered. "You'd be able to command it, enable what mode you need just by thinking what you want, and converse with it as you would a voice-enabled computer."

Ryerson nodded, looking both at the table and outward, toward fights he'd been a part of and those he knew lay on his horizon as a Marine. Decision made, he looked at Colonel Singh, a highly decorated Marine's Marine, and then at Dr. Einarsdottir.

"Let's go," he said firmly.

"Oorah," Singh replied quietly with a nod.

*****

Chapter 5

2nd Planet Orbiting Barnard's Star
TARP R&D Facility
19 September 2243 CE

Surprisingly, Ryerson found that the tests Freyja had run on the implant's intrusiveness had been accurate, which wasn't normally the case, as long experience in the Corps had taught him. He could definitely feel it when he reached back and touched the location, but it was a very slight bump under his skin. More importantly, he'd tried on every bit of MCU gear that would be up around his neck, and none of it bothered him. Again, a bit of a surprise, but he was beginning to realize just how on top of her stuff the good Dr. Einarsdottir was. No surprises except pleasant ones.

He spent two days wearing and field-testing different gear, and being physically measured for the exoskeleton, which everyone referred to as the Exxo. One of the suggestions he'd thrown out was, when fitted with the Exxo, if it was possible for him to utilize a heavier-caliber weapon than the standard MA8, and shouldn't they explore that?

The suggestion had been met with a thoughtful frown from Freyja and a big grin from Singh. What Marine doesn't want a bigger and badder weapon? Neither Marine had ever been in a fight where they wished their firearm was a little less powerful, and there hadn't been a single engagement where every Marine they'd ever known hadn't wanted something bigger. *Bringing max pain to the bad guys is what we do. Let's see what she can come up with.*

Today was the day. There was a battery of tests to run. First, to see how easily and efficiently the Exxo could be donned by a Marine without assistance. If this was going to work in the field, a Marine couldn't always count on being with others all the time.

As Ryerson stated bluntly, "Shit happens. Anything built here has to be usable in all aspects for a single Marine without assistance."

Singh concurred, so it was a bit frustrating when it was obviously ungainly for Ryerson to essentially 'put on' the Exxo. After a couple of attempts, Ryerson stepped away from the rig, which remained upright and balanced on its "feet."

Freyja started to say something, but Ryerson held up his hand as he thought through what needed to happen. *Huh. I wonder if… MIMIC, can you hear me?*

The MIMIC answered him back telepathically, *<<Yes, Gunnery Sergeant Ryerson, I can hear you, even though what you and I are experiencing is not actually audible. You 'hear' me, but it is through the implant rather than your auditory system.>>*

Ryerson smiled. He looked over at Singh and Freyja, both of whom were frowning and puzzled by his smile. Which, of course, made him grin even wider.

"I think we have it covered," he said, slipping his combat boots into the flat stirrup at the base of the Exxo.

"We?" Freyja asked.

Just then, the door to the lab opened, and after ducking to come through the doorway, MIMIC was there. Standing upright, it walked over to where Ryerson stood next to the Exxo, and to to Singh and Freyja's surprise, bent over and helped the gunnery sergeant into the Exxo rig, making certain every part was secure and fastened snugly.

Thanks, MIMIC. You know, that's a dumb thing to call you. Any particular name you like?

<<Not really. The only other human I have actually spoken with was Major Michael Ryerson. I assume, because the two of you bear the same last name, that you are siblings.>>

Were siblings, MIMIC. Yes, we were brothers. Mike was killed in an operation shortly after leaving this facility. I miss him.

<<I do not have the capacity to feel what you call emotions, Gunnery Sergeant Ryerson, but please accept my condolences. I do understand that humans feel pain when someone they care about is damaged or dies.>>

That's perceptive of you, MIMIC. Thank you, and please call me either John or Ryerson. Gunny, whatever. Up to you.

<<I shall call you John. I appreciate the effort to make me feel more like a partner… John. And, if I may be so bold as to suggest something that I hope does not anger you, I would like to be called Mike. Close enough to MIMIC, and close to your brother, who helped me become me.>>

Mike it is, and it is appropriate. Think we can work together, Mike?

<<John, whatever enemy we face, we will not only face it together… we shall defeat it. We shall, as you were thinking earlier, bring max pain to the enemy… the bad guys.>>

Ryerson turned to look at them. At the same time, the massive MIMIC turned, mirroring Ryerson's movements and stance exactly.

Gunnery Sergeant John David Ryerson looked up at Mike standing behind him, turned back to face Colonel Singh and Dr. Einarsdottir, smiled, and simply said, "Bring 'em on."

# # # # #

To be continued in the first novel of its series: *Shadow Mode*, on June 26, 2026.

* * * * *

Author Bios

Kevin Steverson is a retired veteran of the U.S. Army. He has been published over 60 times, with 21 novels and 40 short stories (not counting translations), and his bestselling *Salvage Title* Trilogy has been picked up for development into a feature film. He is also a published lyricist with 10 songs cut in Nashville for various artists. When he is not on the road to a convention or writing songs with musicians, he can be found in the foothills of the NE Georgia mountains, working on his next story.

Craig Bell is a California transplant, now living in the Pacific NW with Sara, his wife and partner in everything for 35 years. When not writing, you'll either find him reading science fiction or military history. If it ever stops raining, he'll be at the range, keeping up his skills with rifle, pistol, and shotgun.

# # # # #

A Loyal Steed by M.D. Boncher

A Mech Family Robinson Story

Chapter 1

"All pilots. Thirty minutes for final load-out and drop preparations." The dropship *Silverback's* AI announcement echoed through the ten-mech bay.

The *Silverback* was one of a dozen similar ships ready to launch from the glorious Osmundian Hegemony's navy to start peacekeeping actions on the rebellious world of Troilus. The peasant castes had revolted, slaughtering the nobility and merchants, and decimating their planetary garrison. Survivors scattered into the planet's wilds, disorganized and broken. This shameful act toward the emperor would not go unchallenged.

The common cause of lower-caste uprisings was often incompetent and lazy nobles who forgot they must serve as well as lead. Drunk on power and greedy for luxury, they discovered a taste for sadism in the tools of control. The forgotten necessity of *noblesse oblige* left the Troilusian nobility blind to the rising dissent. They discovered the truth too late. Happy peasants and merchants made for easy rulership. Peasants who no longer feared death led to sudden murder in the night.

Captain Jason Robinson, dressed in his armored combat suit, strode down the drop bay between the rows of his squadron's mechs like a priest in a cathedral of war. He gleamed like an armored Templar, ready to receive his blessing from the high priest. Armored plates that would keep him cool and protected flashed under the harsh lights.

The peasantry of Troilus seemed more bloodthirsty than most he'd quelled, but none could contend with a synchronized orbital assault from Hegemony combined arms. He'd commanded his mech squadron through more than a dozen campaigns like this. They'd earned many unit citations for bravery and excellent service to Emperor Osmund XIV, and twice he'd received medals for service above and beyond his calling. He'd joined the most decorated members of his proud warrior caste family. The honors, elevated status, and privilege accrued to all his kin.

At the end of the mech bay, Trigger, his thirty-foot-tall, Percheron-class scout mech, dozed like a thoroughbred in her drop bay. The quadruped chassis was a sleek marvel of destruction. Its four limbs ended in omniped feet, rolled like vehicle tires on smooth surfaces or locked in place, enabling it to ascend extreme slopes like a ram. Thick ARAS-F "fur" covered the lumpy marrowbone armor, giving the appearance of a thick winter coat. ARAS was an ablative fiber, perfect for dispersing energy over greater surfaces, and entangling drones before they made contact with the hull. Trigger's black, glossy fluff flowed like a blue-ribbon winner at the fair.

He felt around in the fur for the access panel to activate the war machine. It bleeped, recognizing his dog tags when he touched a hidden panel. The mech woke and knelt down like an elephant presenting itself for inspection, and the horse-head-shaped cockpit lowered to the ground for entry. Twin tusk-like autocannons in a chin turret swiveled out of the way.

"Captain Robinson, good to see you." Trigger's voice came from her external speakers. "Are we riding into battle again?" Like most mech pilots, he'd personalized her interface. Trigger sounded and acted like his idea of an ancient western gunslinger lady. Perhaps a Calamity Jane or Annie Oakley type of woman who'd shoot first and maybe ask questions later. A ride-or-die partner.

"We sure are, girl," he said, circling around her, doing his pre-mission checks. Some of the technicians servicing his mech assisted and pulled flags and hoses, getting her ready for action. One handed him the load-out checklist to go over the mission payload on Trigger's chassis.

"Yes!" Trigger answered, her speakers fuzzed out with static in her excitement. "I've been powered down too long."

His squadron was climbing into their own mechs. His was a fast scouting and harassing unit geared around high mobility that caused havoc behind enemy lines. There were also four 25-ton *Gazelle*-class mechs, with two 35-ton *Cheetah*-class interceptors, and a pair of 50-ton Bisons with breaching payloads whose main guns were Toroidal-Vortex Plasma Cannons in their humps.

"Ready to link up, Captain?" Trigger asked.

"Let's get this started," he replied, linking up the hardlink connection that bound the two together. A blast of jumbled data spilled into Jason's head when the connection opened. Sensors quickly calibrated and fell into the back seat of his consciousness, layering augmented reality onto his vision. Trigger did most of the monitoring, but shared critical data instantly. Mech pilots had to be able to handle juggling two perspectives on the battlefield. Most of the emperor's military couldn't make it in the cavalry.

"Incoming message from the bridge on the private channel," Trigger announced.

Jason picked it up. "Captain Robinson receiving."

The voice of the *Silverback's* captain, John Bentham, came over the connection. *"How's pre-drop going?"*

A slow smile crept onto Jason's lips. "Looking really good, Old Dog," he said. "Trigger's itching to blow up some naughty rabble-rousers."

"Oh, is she now? Trigger's quite the step up from that piece of crap Sentinel*-class you first drove. What did you name him?"*

"Tinny Tim." Jason chuckled. "I mean, come on, that sword was practically a crutch and almost useless. How're things going on your end?"

"Same as always, since we released from the carrier. On schedule and about to get our atmoshake on in a few minutes, so I gotta square up. Wanted to wish you good luck on your mission, and we'll be ready to give you a ride home when it's all over," Bentham said.

"First round's on me back home," Jason said, like many times before.

"Or when we meet again at Fiddler's Green," Bentham finished their private ritual.

The comm closed, and Jason returned to his pre-drop checks with Trigger. Confidence was high among his pilots. His Cheetahs were making bets on how many kills they'd get. Gazelles were syncing up their sensor suites; the channels bubbled with chatter. His second squad warrant officer, in his own Percheron, smiled back across from his drop bay. "Fuzzy" Welstrom had been his right hand for five missions now, and they had a great rhythm going.

"Everything going well, Old Dog?" Fuzzy asked as they hit the atmosphere. The dropship began its typical rattle and shimmy. Technicians finished locking everything down and cleared the space.

Jason shook his head and laughed. "That predictable, huh?"

"Everyone's got their rituals. You two always give each other a little crap and say goodbye. I can read lips, and you're looking right at me," Welstrom pointed out, then took out the pictures he had of his wife and three kids, making a show of it. "See? Even me." He gave them all a kiss and stuck the picture back in the pocket of his combat suit, over his heart.

"Ain't you sweet," Jason mocked.

"You wait. You find the right girl and punch out two or four bundles of joy, and you'll get it." Fuzzy said, his handlebar mustache, heavily waxed, twitching with mirth.

"I'm married to my career, Fuzzfuzz. That ain't changing any time soon." Jason rolled his eyes at Welstrom's returned taunting laughter. "You got anything official to say, Chief?"

"Nope. Everything's racked up and ready to hit the ground run—"

The blinding flash of electricity and flame dazzled Jason, and his faceplate blacked out, saving his vision.

"Trigger! What was that?" he shouted.

"The *Silverback* has taken a direct hit from a polar orbital gun," she said, her tension rising. His comms exploded with panicked screams on all channels. He felt the ship roll, sloshing him around relative to the gravity well of Troilus. His faceplate cleared to reveal debris drunkenly swirling around the drop bay.

"If the roll isn't stopped in a few seconds, we'll lose the heat shield's protection, and this entire bay gets exposed to re-entry," Trigger said coolly.

At the opposite end of the drop bay, orange light grew. It was the glare of friction-ignited air. Comms started cutting off mid-scream as his pilots were incinerated. He couldn't see the back of the bay where the blowtorch of screaming sky melted the interior of the dropship and cremated most of his squadron. The *Silverback* finished its barrel roll and leveled out. Somehow, she stayed together, but the hellish glare showed through cracks and holes.

All the ablative armor fried off the mechs, making them look like burned toys. Trigger warned him that the damage she'd taken was mostly superficial, but his squadron tac-net showed 80% casualties. Welstrom's cockpit was gone. A thin jet through a crack had obliterated the front third of his mech, but spared Trigger.

"Jason!" she yelled.

"Copy. What?" He felt drunk with horror.

"Captain Bentham ordered abandon ship. Survivors are to activate emergency drop sequences."

"Oh, ye god…" Jason moaned, realizing what that meant.

"We won't survive another pass."

"Now! Eject us before we can't." Jason gripped the armrests tightly and kept praying.

Trigger sent the command. Emergency eject systems activated, opening the bay door at a 30-degree yaw. The heavy Percheron mech crept out of its drop guides.

"Come on… come on!" Jason begged physics. Just before it turned horizontal to local gravity, they slipped the last inch and were flung free.

Everything vanished in a weightless stream of smoke and flame from the disintegrating dropship. The shockwave of impacting the atmosphere and the drag chute shook Jason as if he were a treat in a dog's puzzle toy. Sparks burst in his eyes as he struck his head against his seat restraints, and everything went dark.

*****

Chapter 2

Jason returned to consciousness like an ancient monitor warming up. The world was all blurry and fuzzy, then it sharpened into focus. He blinked at the bright light of day, uncertain whether it was morning or afternoon, but the light was painfully bright. Soft, rust-colored rock crumbled off stumpy hoodoos as white sheep scattered like clouds.

"Good, you're awake. We have impending danger," Trigger said dispassionately.

"Sitrep. Damage control?" Jason groaned; his head felt like a broken speaker cone.

Trigger was busy "grazing" in the field, sticking her nanofab maw, at the lower side of the cockpit, into the crumbling limestone. The grinders crushed rock into gravel that would break down into purified feedstock.

"ARAS armor is almost regrown. Marrowbone reservoirs are three hours from full. I suffered no serious integral damage, and the emergency drop rig prevented us from becoming a crater. I ate the chutes and retrorockets for trace minerals."

She continued her sitrep as Captain Robinson clarified what he saw. A short distance away sat a peasant homestead. It was primitive by modern standards, but comfortable, constructed of 3D-printed polycrete with primitive decorations. Clouds of dust from livestock rolled by on hot zephyrs. Targeting zoom revealed they were watching Trigger hard.

"What do you say about greeting the locals and seeing what we can learn, gal?"

Trigger stopped eating; her tanks were full enough. "I think we're asking for trouble if they know about the invasion. It doesn't seem like we achieved a global communications blackout."

"We're supposed to be liberators, not new enslavers." Jason started maneuvering toward the homestead.

"True, but do they know that?" Trigger's tone hinted she was on a hair trigger. High-alert protocols sometimes express themselves in the weirdest nuances with these mechs when customized.

Jason grimaced at her logic but smoothly piloted over. Clusters of sheep ran, while livestock guardian dogs and llamas interceded between them like angels. Rolling on Trigger's omnipeds, they came to the pasture fence gate and politely stepped over. A lot of farmhands watched from what could be called defensible positions if they faced bandits in trucks or Jeeps. For a mech as tall as their barn, it was nothing more solid than bedsheets on a clothesline.

A tall, dark-skinned man, in Mexi-Afghani clothes, came out, hand held up to invite parley.

"Seems like they want to talk. Dip down so we can do this face-to-face, and pop the canopy."

"I'll let you down, but I'm not popping my canopy. You're being reckless," Trigger said and dipped low, squatting on her legs. The man held his position until the mech stopped moving. Jason wasn't going to argue with her right now. The man saw Jason waving him over through the reflections and cautiously walked over. Nonplussed, the chickens scratched in the ruts torn up by Trigger.

"Good day, Citizen," Jason said with his best public relations voice and smile. "Could you assist me?"

The man gave him a pleasant-sounding response in a local dialect, but he didn't understand a word.

"He wished peace upon you," Trigger translated.

"Do you speak the emperor's tongue?" Jason asked.

"I do." The man's pronunciation was so thickly accented as to be nearly incomprehensible. *These outworlds,* Jason complained to himself.

"Where am I?"

The man looked back at his men. His sons and wife watched from the house. All were armed, but their small guns couldn't hurt Trigger.

"Shemnevobeck Farm. Three miles west o' Navahamna Station in Castallan's domain," the man said. His wrinkles were expressively deep cuts in his face. Jason squinted at the sheep farmer; his stomach started feeling sour. None of the names meant anything to him, but they would to Trigger's navigation apps.

"We've landed 1,087 miles from the beachhead, minus thirty-five miles off that for our intended drop zone," Trigger said. Irritation dripped from her words.

Jason turned back to the peasant, flashing a hollow grin. The shepherd looked more antsy as he examined Trigger's monstrous bulk.

"Captain, the local networks aren't down. I've hacked the terrestrial relays. These people have called the local garrison. They're dispatching a salvage team to collect us. No ETA for arrival, but expect this one to try and stall." Jason could feel Trigger's desire to cut loose through their link.

Jason's smile grew tight. The shepherd's expression grew more nervous. That was normal for a civilian standing next to a mech, but now, he tried to coax Jason out of the cockpit, offering him hospitality. His farmhands glowered on.

"Thank you, no. We must be going." Jason held up both his hands. Then, through their data link, he ordered, "Put up a fast Combat Air Patrol. Four sets of sensor drones and anti-vehicle pairs."

From the middle of Trigger's "saddle" came a salvo of eight musical buzzes. The sensor and attack drone pairs launched into the sky, quickly gained altitude, and spun out from the mech like a CAP. One scanned, while the other was an anti-vehicle drone powerful enough to take out all but heavy armor or reinforced structures.

"You have our bearings back to the beachhead, girl?" Jason asked.

"Yes." His stomach dropped as Trigger stood back up. "I have a general course set and am trying to get an extraction request to Hegemony Command."

The farmer ran for his home, screaming at his family.

"Sounds like a plan. Let's roll out."

The dull *thunk* of a bullet followed by a thrown gravel-like hiss against the cockpit startled Jason. He looked in the barn's direction. The armed farmhands had fired with their rifles and shotguns, doing nothing but knocking off a few negligible tufts of ARAS fur and chipping the paint.

"No, no!" the farmer shrieked at the house, frantically waving and shouting to them, desperate to get their attention. Jason traced the line to where the shepherd was looking.

Searing, painful light dazzled him. A laser diffused by the diamondoid smart-glass of the canopy bulls-eyed him in the face. His helmet visor saved his sight and life. Until then, he'd been willing to walk away and leave them in peace, but the acrid smell of smoke from burned clothing and the warm spot inside his helmet ignited his rage.

Reflexively, he fired the head-mounted auto-shotgun, a quick burst at the approximate source of the laser on the homestead's second story. The house shredded as if a hailstone-laden tornado had clipped it. The flechettes turned the second-floor corner of the polycrete house into an explosion of dust, shattered ceramic roof tile, a few gouts of bright red blood, and meat chunks, which scattered to the ground. Anyone who'd been struck by those rounds was now sashimi.

The farmer fell to his knees and wailed. All gunfire from his impulsive kin and farmhands stopped. Jason swiveled the cannon past them, waiting for the excuse to let them have it, too. He hated to, but you don't mess around when civilians start shooting. It must have been an anti-mech gun provided by the local militia.

"Captain, we need to move it. If they're in vehicles or mecha, they might catch up, but if they're in mechs, we might outrun them," Trigger warned.

Jason wheeled them about in the direction she'd laid out. Dirt flew as they peeled out. Her omnipeds happily tore down the gravel road, ripping deep ruts and smashing through the closed gate.

Trigger's weight caved in the cattle grid. "That should delay some pursuit." She chuckled.

Jason took the winding ranch road to the nearest country blacktop and turned south. With a pair of legs in each lane, they picked up speed. They crested a small hill to discover a terrified agri-hauler. It skidded to a stop. Like a speed skater, Trigger gracefully slewed around it, then accelerated to a cruising speed of just over seventy miles per hour. They flew by the fields and herds as her attempts to contact the Hegemony were blocked by a wall of static.

"Drone #3 has visual on that salvage team. It's some light-armored vehicles and a recovery crane, plus an ultra-heavy lowboy to haul me back like a dead deer. Like I'd just roll over for them," Trigger grumbled.

Jason flipped over to view their intercept course. The escort vehicles were hover-capable, and once the rebels spotted them, they rushed forward to capture them. Trigger couldn't outrun those, but she could get some distance from the heavy road-bound trucks. She jumped a ditch and went cross-country toward a different highway. They slewed in the softer earth, slowing, but didn't need to switch to a gallop yet.

The lightly armored rebel vehicles were nearly in range for their anti-mech missiles. On an augmented monitor, he observed the drones' attack runs.

"Engage with the suicide drones and nanofab four more," Jason said.

A haptic acknowledgment of his order tickled his neck. "Kill or disable?" Trigger asked.

"They're rebels trying to steal Hegemony materiel. Take them out."

"Yes, sir!" Trigger said with a touch of malicious glee.

The first drone gave him a split-second image of the gunner looking up in shock. A ball of smoke and flame mushroomed on the other side of a small rise, rapidly followed by two more. An AMS blister detonated the last suicide drone. The biggest of the quartet was an up-armored APC loaded with a light autocannon and an ECM suite. As its connection was scrambled, the nearest sensor drone went dark. This nasty little customer skimmed over the low rise and had a direct line of sight. The anxious gunner let off a burst with the main gun. At maximum range, only two shells landed, clanging off the side of Trigger's heavier armor plate. It sounded like someone bouncing a baseball bat on a full water tank.

"They shot solid penetrators, not HEAT rounds. Two hits on my rear left leg. No penetration."

"I still don't like people shooting us." Jason swung the left saddle-mounted laser back and fired. The precision shot carved up the top of the vehicle, burning through the APC armor, and nearly slashing the turret free. "Huh. Tougher than I thought." He fired again. This time, the vehicle's hydrogen cell engine detonated. Debris sprayed all over the pasture, and it tumbled, throwing smoky chunks. Its turret flew free like a decapitated head.

"Anything else pursuing?" Jason asked.

"Drone #2 is back online, with that APC's jammer down, and it is returning to formation. No more hostiles detected. Still unable to connect to the Hegemony control net."

"They must have some big transmitters blocking it. I guess we're going to be assigning ourselves some secondary targets of opportunity," Jason said.

"I'll begin scanning for rebel broadcast sources over one hundred thousand watts. They should be easy to spot. Shall I nanofab long-range, dual-purpose 'wild weasels' to conduct HARM attacks?" Trigger suggested.

"Roger. Make three glide bombs and send them on a 90-degree arc in front of us, high altitude, 30-degree search patterns."

"Unless you make them autonomous, that will leave five drones for our direct control."

"Grant attack/return autonomy. Let's keep eight available for countermeasures," Jason decided.

If the wild weasels' AIs didn't find a target before they hit Bingo charge, they'd return to refuel. He suspected they'd find broadcast towers in converted radio or TV stations because the jamming signals were nothing but revolutionary music and "Troilus Tatiana" spouting off anti-caste gibberish.

"All set," Trigger said and assembled the mission package on the generic drone frames in her carrier. She launched all three in rapid succession, and he watched them fly away on their planned hunting corridors.

"You think we should continue going cross-country? Right now, we are still over a thousand miles away. The shortest route gives us an ETA of twenty-two hours and ten minutes from Hegemony control.

"Assuming nothing interferes, and the beachhead sits at Trennick Sound," Jason grumbled and slumped in his seat. *Nothing goes smoothly in these operations,* he thought as they glided over the flat veldt through the sparse acacia trees and herds of water buffalo and steers. *Best get used to the stimulants. Trigger will pump me full and keep me sharp.* "Look for roads we can use for a time to speed us up. Anything we can do to shave off time, the better."

"Roger that." Trigger started re-plotting. A few seconds later, she presented an alternative path. "From the last satellite passes we have, here's the best route. It can knock our time down to seventeen hours and twenty-four minutes, barring—"

"Yeah, yeah. Barring any confrontations, which you know we're going to get." Jason waved off the standard AI boilerplate answer hedging. Even going more than fifty miles an hour over what normally would be terribly rough terrain for a vehicle, Trigger's legs absorbed the shocks and rumbles, turning the ride into silky smoothness.

The two worked together, scanning the skies and the occasional hacked message from the local comms network. Apparently, the salvage team's failure and deaths had enraged the rebels, and they'd redoubled their efforts. The constantly screaming jammers still kept them locked out of the invasion force's freqs. The minutes ticked by as their route deftly avoided the most obvious ambush points.

"Contact, Wild Weasel Number Three. Radio tower south by southwest, thirty-eight miles from our position. Drone going into attack phase," Trigger declared excitedly. She put the drone's nose cam in his augmented display.

Ahead, a radio tower blasting out a hundred thousand watts of jamming jutted almost half a mile out of the ground, a nearly invisible needle of latticed metal jabbing the sky. Long guy wires created a pyramid-like lattice.

The ground erupted with loaf-of-bread-sized drones that buzzed into the sky. They'd triggered a drone spider nest. Glass and poly threads spooled out like a web in all directions as the drones attempted to catch their wild weasel. "Shit, counter-drones. Take evasive action, nap-of-the-earth." Jason grunted.

The drone dove straight down and zipped along at a height of less than two yards above the ground toward its target. The warm fibers lit up on infrared as the counter-drones pursued. Two missed and slammed into the ground like mortars, spraying entangling threads, attempting to gum the wild weasel's propellers, but none caught it. A half-dozen more counter-drones missed, blowing up a lone tree and a parked car outside the control trailer. The wild weasel shot under the floor, between its block piers. Their own over-eager drones hit the trailer multiple times. It didn't matter where the wild weasel hit the tower, but the lower, the better. With a quick hop over a chain-link fence, Jason saw a single frame of girder, and the camera went dark.

"Can you confirm destruction?"

"Yes. Jamming has dropped significantly," Trigger said proudly. "I'm getting some snippets of Hegemony Command through this noise, but not enough fidelity to give me secure parity matches on signals."

"Then let's hope we get another one," Jason said, feeling the first big rush of relief since he woke up.

*****

Chapter 3

Once the brief intensity of combat ended, long stretches of boredom followed. Jason and Trigger noticed movement on their long-range scans provided by their drone coverage. It seemed like most of the rebel militia had been pulled out of the backwaters to meet the invasion force. That explained the lack of resistance. The late afternoon dragged on into the evening. Far above, dropships transitioning the upper atmosphere left glowing white and yellow contrails. The rebel orbital guns occasionally scorched cuts across the sky like bars of lightning.

"Do you think they suffered?" Trigger asked.

"Hmm?"

"Do you think the other mechs and pilots suffered?"

"Awfully existential of you, girl. What brought that on?"

"I can't say. Maybe it's just a byproduct of my subroutines cogitating possibilities from past analysis to determine outcomes."

Jason laughed. "That's a really complex way of saying you were incorporating your recent experiences into your reference frame modeling. I didn't think it was possible for AIs to feel actual emotions. You sound like you're feeling melancholy or survivor's guilt."

"I don't know." Trigger sounded frustrated to Jason. "I'm programmed to replicate emotions to aid you by utilizing subconscious cues, but I don't know if I really *feel* them. I lack the fundamental ability to comprehend feelings. Can you explain it to me? Am I really feeling?"

The question caught Jason off guard. "I, uhhh… no, I don't think humans can tell, either. I can't quantify what feeling is. Some philosophers might believe they can explain it, or a psychologist, but not me. I just react and repress them. In this line of work, they can get you killed."

"I've interfaced with some mechs a lot older than me who'd been continuously running for decades. They always acted differently. They act more like humans do, almost instinctually. They remind me of old samurai who fought their whole lives for their masters and became… peaceful… resigned about war, battle, and accepting of their own mortality. I can die, after all. My body is corporeal. My software could glitch and be corrupted, becoming impossible to restore." Trigger paused for an uncomfortably long time. "I could become obsolete and waste away in mothballs with no way to upgrade."

Jason snorted and smiled. This was absurd.

"Too deep! I'm having a philosophical discussion with my mech!" He chuckled. This mission was growing more and more surreal, yet the curiosity about her questions niggled at him. He guessed he might as well commit to the premise. There was nothing else to do except watch for ambushes and other targets of opportunity. "We humans can offer poor proof as to our own understanding of existence or consciousness. It's the paradox best answered by the philosopher Descartes: 'I think, therefore I am.' Who's to say no?"

She jumped a small creek like a motocross racer, landing with an elegant bounce on the opposite shore, but didn't respond.

"In answer to your original question," Jason said with a yawn, "I think any suffering was very brief for the pilots. I can't say for the other mechs. Even though you don't feel pain like a human, you still register damage. Maybe it's the same, but different. Do you suffer an injury like a human? No. You take it like a machine. It's just something that stops working with an error code and a warning light."

"That's not pain?" Trigger asked.

"Not in the same way."

In the distance, they saw a small village slide by. Their course was set to avoid settlements, and no one came out to intercept them.

"We experience reality in vastly different ways, don't we?" Trigger apparently wasn't done being philosophical.

"We do." Jason waited for her next thought, but silence was the answer as the veldt slipped by.

* * *

Night on Troilus was bright, somewhere between civil and nautical twilight. The rebel polar guns were still able to keep the main capital ships of the peacekeepers at bay, using the moons as cover. Sparkles of orbital debris vied with the stars, and the grid of fiery contrails made by crashing dropships and orbital firefights slashed the sky with bombardments and counter-battery salvos, creating debris fields of moon rock.

"Target of opportunity located. We found another jammer," Trigger said.

"Good, send one pair from the drone CAP in for target surveillance. Loop in the wild weasel. High-low formation," Jason ordered. Trigger complied, and the three drones converged. The weapon drones went nap-of-the-earth, while the sensor drone climbed to maximum altitude. Video revealed a small town fifteen miles to the southwest of them.

"Analysis suggests a town of approximately twenty-five thousand. A local mech garrison for a small enclave of now dead nobles and their rebel co-opted military, according to the damage. Mostly merchants, trade and peasant castes."

"Yeah, populist uprisings are a mess. So what's the source of the jamming?" Jason scoured the feed.

"Converted television station. In fact, this looks like it's a central jamming hub controlling several towers. We knock this out, and I can probably re-establish connection to the Hegemony comms," Trigger said, sounding relieved.

"Yeah, I like that, but something doesn't smell right. I doubt they're defenseless. That garrison is big enough to have an entire squadron of mechs. They have armor rolling already," Jason reasoned.

The visuals went dark with a flash-flicker. "What? Oh, damn. They've got a defensive dome." A pair of explosions bloomed as the wild weasel and anti-vehicle drones were detonated by an AMS blister somewhere in town.

"We could bypass this, but there is a significant tactical advantage to destroying it. I could finally reconnect," Trigger suggested.

"With that AMS dome, we're not getting a drone close." A second pair of their drones climbed to max altitude, far out of range of the lasers, and sent back visuals that made Jason squint.

"The town's stirred up, but they're acting odd. Not reacting like they should," he murmured.

"They're not scrambling properly." Trigger sounded surprised, too.

"Yeah, they're too slow. Okay, there! A few hunter-killer teams are assembling on the parade ground." Jason said, watching the four-man teams muster out. His face scrunched up in disgust. "This is amateur hour!"

Trigger highlighted the mech bays. Two of the doors opened. "Mechs coming out." A pair of *Rooster*-class light mechs stumbled out. They both sported centerline particle cannons and two wing-mounted pulse lasers. One fluffed up his normally flat ARAS-Fe feathers as if he detected incoming fire.

"They've got morons behind the controls," Jason said, a big grin creeping out.

"They've spotted our new drones and are coming in this direction." Trigger highlighted a column of armor heading to a forward position.

Jason's confidence rose. "If their tankers are this bad, we may as well mop this up."

"Be careful, it looks like they have their own drone nests." Trigger pointed out a triangle of drone sites with giant haystacks of glittering fiber, and a few swarm launchers.

"Ancient tech." Jason whistled.

"But still effective. They're hard to take out but might be susceptible to swarms."

"Where's that AMS blister?" Jason asked.

"The anti-missile system is on top of that tall building over the bazaar arcade," Trigger said.

"That's one thing they did right," he said, frowning at the tactical analysis. "We'll have to assault the town to get our remaining wild weasels in."

Trigger continued to rain on his parade. "We'd have to level the town to deal with those HK teams. They'll start firing mech-grade weapons at us out of windows, roofs, and all the other nooks and crannies you can think of."

"I know that!" Jason snapped. "They're not a priority. We just have to trash that broadcast station."

"I'm more worried about those Roosters and their particle cannons," Trigger noted. "Those can burn right through me, so I'd want to deal with them first." Trigger didn't sound anxious or fearful, but was definitely more cautious than Jason.

"Me, too. Let's hold position here, see if they'll come into the open; otherwise, we have to assault their position," Jason decided.

"Remember, we're still being pursued and can't linger," Trigger said.

They didn't come out. The armor column stopped at a camouflaged checkpoint and unloaded troops. The two remaining suicide drones flew in at grass height. They snuck in undetected and struck the checkpoint and the drone nest's control, sending billowing flames into the sky.

Three more nanofabbed drones flew skyward with a laughing buzz.

"The drone swarm's ready," Trigger announced. Eighty-one dinner-plate-sized drones armed with grenade charges pushed into the vertical launch bay stacks.

"Then let's do it." Jason looped them around like a cutting horse, bringing them into max effective range. Pausing on a low rise a mile away, he dialed in a shot at the AMS blister's building.

"Ready to fire, and the swarm is holding for launch," Trigger said.

Jason held his breath and fired.

Two pairs of lasers and masers hissed and buzzed ominously, igniting the air in brilliant lines as he held the energy streams open like an industrial cutter.

Concrete and metal flash-melted as masers threw sparks and fiery plasmoids like a fork in a microwave. Micro-explosions from material failures shattered the unreinforced building, trapping the AMS crew as Trigger's four cannons sliced the top of the building off like hard cheese. It crumbled and slid down into the street.

A chuckle bubbled up inside Jason's chest. "That's the downside of a good location like that."

"Here they come." Trigger pointed out a column of six light armored vehicles around the burning checkpoint. Lasers lanced out from their turrets. A burst raked Trigger, boiling off a chunk of ARAS fur like she was at the groomer. It did little else but carbon-score the plate underneath.

"Let's make 'em defensive. Launch the swarm. Target the hunter-killer teams, autonomous control," Jason commanded and turned to run. Trigger's swarm vanished into the night, dispersing into the city, hunting for anyone carrying anti-mech weapons.

A volley of autocannon shells made the ground erupt just behind them.

"It's a *Roland*-class heavy hover tank," Trigger said. "He's late to the party. Those twin rotary cannons can shred me pretty easily."

"I know, that's why we're being evasive."

To prove his point, a rippling twin burst tore across the farmland. Brilliant yellow and red tracers zipped at them. Despite a jink and a juke, Trigger's abdomen got peppered. Damage reports tallied on her health monitor. Nothing screamed red yet, but a couple of armor panels had sustained damage that needed watching.

Jason returned fire with his right-side laser/maser combo and followed with a burst from his smaller autocannon. The beams struck the tank's glacis, scribbling deep burns into the thick armor with brilliant, boiling sprays of molten armor. The hover tank nosed into the ground as Jason's return fire knocked it around, scaring the inexperienced crew. Fans sucked up a lot of dirt, clogging them with a cough and a *clang*.

Rebel armored cars shot a few rapid-fire mortars toward him. Trigger's AMS blister blew them out of the sky at apogee and zapped a heavy missile just a few feet outside the launch tube. The premature detonation overturned the heavily armed patrol vehicle.

Trigger didn't use her omnipeds on the soft ground but ran like a mustang fleeing hunters on the veldt. Two of the pursuit vehicles erupted in flames as her anti-vehicle drones struck home. She crowed at the kills like a Comanche. Jason swept the laser/maser combo over another wheeled APC, which smacked a few more shells off Trigger's tough armor.

"Still nothing penetrating yet," Trigger said tightly. Jason had to hand it to the designers who'd included such tonal subtleties in the vocal interface. The Roland coughed and spat, dislodging more earth caught in its ducts, still unable to lift. Its turret spun, trying to track them. The Roland's gunner struggled to get his turret back on target.

Jason loosed another salvo at the tank. The maser found the ammo magazine, but the tank landed several shots into Trigger's torso and neck before it died. Brilliant flames wreathed Trigger. Her gyroscopes couldn't manage the shock, and she tumbled to the ground with a gout of pasture, rolling on her side like a derailed locomotive. The flaming cloud of the tank's destruction faded into the midnight blue of the sky.

"That hurt. Not to mention… unsportsmanlike," Trigger said by way of an ancient movie soundbite.

"Are you okay?" Jason did a pat-down himself. Those rotaries were no joke. But she was quoting a movie? "Who has a possible concussion here?"

"Four rounds penetrated my armor. My neck is compromised, but central data is fine. Left side control offline. Calculating whether self-repair will bring back functionality."

"We're still in the fight?" Jason flipped through the damage control screens as Trigger fought to right the cockpit.

The burning hulk of the Roland gave off a garish light as the last remaining APC fled the scene.

Trigger stood, listing drunkenly toward her wounded side, twisting her head to try to keep the cockpit level for Jason, but she couldn't.

"I look like a zombie horse," Trigger complained as they trotted around the town again, hoping not to get dive-bombed by a drone nest or run smack into the pair of Roosters.

"You trot like one, too. Gah! My back, slow down or shift to omnipeds. You're gonna break my spine." It was like being thrashed about on a broken rollercoaster. He smacked a leg against a panel lip, hard.

"Can't be helped, Captain. The ground's too soft and sandy to engage omnipeds," Trigger apologized. "Good news, a workaround is being processed by damage control nanites and should regain 72 percent of lost control in twenty-four minutes."

Jason grumbled about it, stuck at a twenty-degree list. "Can we hole up somewhere till you're repaired?"

"The longer we tarry here, the more likely pursuit will catch up. I'll get us to a road. That will help. I've lost track of the Roosters, but I have one eye in the sky, searching."

He let out a heavy sigh. "Find them. We don't need that sort of amusing surprise. We probably have clear airspace." Jason then steered them through the burning checkpoint, the rebel soldiers firing harmlessly at them with their rifles and machine guns. Trigger spitefully swung a leg wide and obliterated the remains of the guard shack.

Jason followed the map toward the TV station. Where were the Roosters? Where were they hiding? Not two buildings down, an apartment balcony exploded with three loud bangs, and the bodies of an HK team flew over the railing and down three stories. A swarm drone had detonated an HK team's ammo.

"That was lucky," he said. There were only a few more blocks before they could take a shot at the TV station. More infantry ground fire spattered against Trigger's hull. A grenade got dangerously close to the holes in her neck plating. Jason responded with a chattering roar of autocannon shotgun shells toward the grenadier. The building façade rained into the street, exposing the building's frame, ending the attack.

Trigger took a corner and moved them into position to destroy the studio and its transmitters. A flash of turquoise lightning washed out the night with its brilliance. A particle cannon narrowly missed Trigger's head, and by extension, Jason in the cockpit. She bolted across the intersection like a startled stallion, vanishing behind a building as the second Rooster's particle cannon vaporized a large portion of it.

"Ho! My God!" Jason's shock at the ambush hit him like a fist. Trigger made a wheeling turn to loop down a parallel street, still running toward the station. "We gotta flank those Roosters," Jason growled.

Trigger rolled sideways on her omnipeds for a strafing pass, and Jason opened fire as they slid by the corner of the building, catching one of the Roosters off guard. He scored a direct hit on the covering Rooster with the double laser/maser salvo. He got the shot off with a full second of burn, dead on the body of that dirty chicken. At point-blank range, ARAS feathers exploded. Flaming plumage flew in all directions. The lasers cut a pair of deep gashes through the outer armor, and the masers penetrated even deeper. Flame and plasmoids blew out of the gash. Autocannons buzzed, peppering the cockpit, tearing large chunks of armor off like they were plucking the chicken.

The Rooster went down in a heap; flares from burning metal popped and fizzed. Trigger slid by, keeping her nose pointed toward the intersection, till they vanished down another few blocks and stopped out of sight.

"That was sweet." Jason breathed heavily with excitement and triumph. "These must be civilian militia."

"Deeply satisfying revenge. The other must be chasing us." Trigger's voice held a smug edge.

The other Rooster pilot, unsure where they were, started shooting at shadows. Pulse lasers blew apart anything that moved, including fleeing civilians and other rebels.

"We'd best take him out. He's a loose cannon," Jason grumbled with a shake of his head.

"But first…" Trigger let that hang as she turned to show Jason the building they'd taken shelter behind. It was the television studio. "Crud. Scans show a basement, so no driving through."

"Yeah… shame, that," Jason said. "You cut the towers with our beamers, and I'll trash everything else." A broad, vindictive grin spread.

Trigger started strafing sideways again. Jason kept guns on the building, and he pulled the trigger for both ballistic cannons. The shotgun flechettes and explosive autocannon rounds tore the building to pieces, grinding it up. Jason watched the building dissolve under the stream of projectiles until nothing but a burning pile remained. A column of dust and smoke rose into the sky as their guns' roar harmonized with the buzz of the energy weapons.

Trigger sliced through the guy wires of the tower and carved up every uplink dish.

"I have a link to Hegemony TacNet!" Trigger exclaimed. "Re-establishing protocols."

A bolt of turquoise lanced through the smoke and dust, striking her left hind leg. A rapid smattering of minor explosions went off inside the hull, black marrowbone fluid blasted out of pores, and Trigger's fur incinerated off her hindquarters.

Control systems went dead, and the leg went limp. Jason let out a startled shout as they slumped to the ground. He tried to turn her kinked neck toward the source so he could return fire with his auto shotgun, but control wasn't back yet.

Another series of blinding shots came out of the corona of dust, missing by inches. The Rooster's pilot was still blind-firing where he thought Trigger was and shot over her prone chassis.

"Jason—" Trigger gasped. The vocal subroutines communicated her damaged state through all-too-human inflections. She sounded like she was in serious pain, and that spurred him to action.

He returned fire where he thought the Rooster was. Dust burned in the path of the saddle-mounted laser/maser combo but hit nothing. The rebel was gone.

"Can you get up?"

"Trying," Trigger groaned, fighting to get her right hind leg beneath her. "My leg can't find a purchase in this rubble."

"Not good, but more importantly, where did that Rooster go?"

From the top of a neighboring four-story building, pulse laser fire from the Rooster's "wings" rained down. Fur crisped and threw up clouds of ash, and black marrowbone steam hissed out of the release pores. It had him dead to rights and was peppering him to death while its "big pecker" particle cannon cooled off from his careless rampage. If he couldn't move or stop that Rooster, terrible shot as he was, they were done for.

Jason noticed that the autonomous swarm tracking HK teams was still at 63%. Since jamming had vanished, he re-established the link and reset their targeting to the Rooster.

In seconds, the little drones zipped in and started detonating, like bees after a bear. The tiny terrors mostly hit feathers, rendering their attack nearly useless. Some exploded in the pilot's face, trying to crack the armored cockpit open, but were too weak to penetrate. The Rooster pilot panicked and recoiled, flapping about, desperate to swat the pesky drones down, and fluffing up feathers, which let one or two of the remaining fifty swarmers underneath, rupturing a couple of armor plates.

Jason fired half his main guns at a newly created bare spot and peeled a gash at the wing joint. The maser penetrated deeply, causing an explosion of steam, and boiling water engulfed the top of the building like a disappearing ninja. There was a loud *crash* as the novice pilot fell off the opposite side of the office building. The hissing diminished as the steam billowed.

"Radiation alert. Radiation alert." A dumb alarm sang its cadence.

"You blew out his power plant's internal cooling coil," Trigger said as she stood up on three legs.

"That reactor is probably scramming as we speak. As tough as those things are, you're screwed if you lose all your coolant."

"That makes it a technical KO," Trigger said.

Jason ran the incoming damage reports. The best they were going to be able to do was freeze all the joints in her lame leg and move via omnipeds. The other three would have to do the job. Her frame shook as she locked it in place. "Ready for more good news?"

"Sarcasm?" Jason snorted in appreciation. Every time he thought he'd learned something new about Trigger, her AI surprised him.

"Ya think? Our pursuit will be in visual range in three minutes," Trigger actually smarted off again. Jason laughed.

"Aw, hell. Can we outrun them?"

"We have to try, but now I'm limited to mostly roads. That means they'll be able to coordinate intercepts easier."

"And we have over six hundred miles left." Jason let out a resigned sigh. "Punch it, girl. Keep trying to re-establish our link as we run. Maybe we can finally get help."

"Great minds think alike," Trigger said and started rolling.

A few more HK teams took shots with no effect as they fled the town. In the distance, a convoy of heat signatures streamed into the shallow valley as the town shrank behind them. It consisted of several vehicles and a squadron of heavier mechs that they couldn't fight, even undamaged. Trigger minded the road moving forward while Jason kept a close eye on the rebel pursuit.

Jason identified the bipedal mechs as older Soldier or Guardsman classes. The tracked vehicles were main battle tanks centered around some kind of big cannon. They reached a crossroads.

"They're going toward town." Jason sighed, slumping back in his seat. "I guess they need to make sure about the mess we made there first."

"Or somehow they haven't seen us," Trigger posited.

"More proof they're not warrior caste. Regardless, this is a neat piece of luck." Jason felt relief shooting through his veins as he watched the last of their pursuit disappear behind the town.

*****

Chapter 4

Jason relaxed for the first time since he woke up on Troilus as the pursuit stayed in the town. Flipping through diagnostics and damage reports, he let out some *sotto voce* cussing. Unless they stopped to refill her feedstock, they couldn't nanofabricate more drones. Repair nanites had priority and a long way to go.

Trigger skated down both lanes of a two-lane highway in the bright moonlit night. "Why haven't you reconnected with the Hegemony TacNet?" Jason asked.

"They're refusing my handshake. Must have something to do with the *Silverback* getting shot down. Someone might not have uploaded the latest security checks, or we've been listed as KIA, and our access has been terminated. I'll keep trying."

With a few flickers to the cockpit screens, Jason was tossed left as Trigger's neck muscles re-established control, and he was upright again. "Well, thank God for that! Nanites did their job." He clapped with relief and rolled his shoulders and neck. "I got a headache from being canted off to the right for so long. What's with those power blinks? I was worried we were going to lose power."

There was a dull *click* in his suit, and the familiar bite of a stimulant injector. "Ah!" he yelped at the surprising sting. "It's that time already?"

"My screens didn't blink; you had several micro-sleeps. So yes, your health markers are shifting from being in the seat so long, and your reaction and awareness have significantly degraded. There. I included mild pain medication for the headache."

"Yeah, it's kicking in fast."

"Drink more, too. You're showing signs of dehydration," Trigger nagged.

Jason squinted at the cockpit speaker. "What are you? My mother?" He aggressively flipped some switches, then sucked on the hydration nipple in his helmet.

"Can we put up another drone CAP?"

"Yes, but that will deplete our feedstock to a dangerously low level. Shall I scan for a good grazing spot?"

"No. Just put two up, not four."

Trigger obeyed.

"How soon do you think it'll take you to reacquire the handshake?" Jason changed course using a narrow dirt road and private drive to cut over to a new highway. That might confound attempts to cut them off for the moment.

"I don't have an estimate," Trigger snapped like a teenage girl.

"Focus on that, then. I'll handle the driving," he said. The dirt road they were on turned out to be a homestead. They'd have to off-road it to get back on pavement. They smashed through fences and scattered livestock as they charged on. Jason picked out packed trails, followed a creek, burst out onto a two-lane blacktop, and kept cruising. A mile or so behind them, police lights lit up a crossroads barricade.

Jason let out a cackle. "They're *really* unprepared for us if they're trying to use police cruisers and a SWAT-outfitted APC."

"Cracked it," Trigger said gleefully. "I knew I could—"

All the screens powered down, and the lights went red. Trigger coasted to a stop. An inhuman voice that wasn't Trigger's spoke. "Security handshake breach. Compromised protocol. Unauthorized access detected. Begin termination of assets."

Jason's jaw went slack. He felt the blood drain from his face.

"I think I pushed too hard," Trigger said softly. "They're sending self-destruct codes. I can't stop them."

"Oh, no, they don't," Jason growled and unstrapped himself from the pilot seat. In the distance, the police roadblock was quickly rolling their way. Someone must have spotted them. "I'm not going to let them kill us that easily."

Trigger was frozen in her own locked-down body. "I can't stop it! Is this fear?"

Kneeling on the seat, Jason grabbed hold of the panel releases behind him, throwing the covers on the floor with a clatter and *bang.* Flickering fiber optics lit up the cockpit in rainbows of light, and he reached down to the bottom. There, he found a sturdy yellow handle and flipped off the safety catches, then he gave a hard pull. The security locks broke with a *crunch*, and the system severed all exterior data connections. He'd severed the connection to Trigger's antennae and engaged isolation mode, physically removing any chance of exterior data from getting in.

"Everything's gone silent, but the code's already been injected. Reactor runaway starting in 5… 4… 3… 2…"

Trigger fell silent as Jason pressed the forced emergency reboot.

Trigger slumped on her locked legs like a sleeping horse. He sat there in the dark, and the cockpit got stuffier and more rank-smelling. He could still hear noises coming from the reactor, but it didn't seem to be running away. *Did it work?* There was no crescendo of doom like he'd expected. It just hung there and whined, ringing in some irritating minor chord.

The police and their APC vanished out of sight behind them. They were close. He saw little sparks of flashlights from the homestead he'd just driven through.

"Come on, come on!" he begged.

Long seconds ticked by. The sirens were faint, but growing closer.

And then, with a whooping gasp from the climate control vents, Trigger came back to life. He'd rolled her back to the last stable save, which was five minutes previously.

"What? Captain? What's going on? How'd I get here?" Trigger asked.

"Hold that thought, girl," he said and buckled back in. Power cascaded to all her systems. The instant the weapons were hot and locomotion returned, he spun around and opened up with the auto-cannons on the police, who were less than a hundred yards away. Vehicles exploded into scrap and flames. The SWAT team APC tried to swerve, but the big slugs mashed it into a ball of tinfoil that smoked for a moment, then blew up like an M-80 firecracker in a can.

The lasers came back online, and he fired off a series of quick shots at the homestead, catching the barn and machine shed on fire.

"Now, let's get out of here." Jason spun Trigger around and started across the veldt, reached another highway, and left the scene in his dust.

"What did you do?" Trigger asked. "Everything is silent. I can't establish contact with my drones now."

"Right. If I turn on your antennae, you'll blow up. We're listed as KIA, and Hegemony Command means to enforce it."

"So that's why I'm not trying to reconnect?" Trigger said cautiously.

"If you try to link up again, they'll hit you with another self-destruct download and you go kaboom in the biggest fireball you can muster, which should incinerate everything inside of five hundred yards, and irradiate about a third of a mile out. Including me. So let's get out of here."

It was many miles before Trigger said anything. "Thank you. I've never felt anything like this before. Now I know what betrayal is like." Bitterness dripped from the words.

"Yeah, I get that. I didn't think that was possible for you to have such emotions. Let alone gratitude."

"I'm surprised too," she sounded like she was struggling with the ramifications of that hole in her memory.

Jason frowned. Could Trigger handle this? Would she be able to react and function like a war machine anymore, or would she need a major data overhaul?

"So how's that make you feel?"

"I don't like being mistaken for the enemy. I'm mad. Desperate to prove we're still functional and on the same team."

"At least we're still alive and screaming," Jason said, then he raised a mischievous eyebrow. "How's this for an idea? We're being pursued, and I'm sure our little stop has let the pursuit catch up. Why don't we give them problems to slow them down? Blow up bridges, start fires, and detonate fuel depots. Make so many problems for the Rebels that they have to pull forces back to deal with them. I suspect that we're already drawing some of their forces out of position, and they're soft back here. So, let's do as much damage as we can and get the attention of fleet surveillance, and maybe they'll recognize that we're alive and doing our job, even if we haven't been able to report back."

"I like that. I need somewhere for this hate to go." Trigger sounded like she was grinning from ear to ear, if she had them. She wanted revenge and vindication.

"Then let's kick this pig," Jason agreed, and they started their rampage.

* * *

The hours crawled by silently as Jason and Trigger wrought havoc upon the rebels' soft underbelly. Pre-programmed suicide drones and the cutting power of their lasers collapsed any bridge bigger than a culvert. Masers detonated fuel depots and their underground tanks. A few short bursts from the autocannons left small industrial buildings in tatters. If anyone on high was watching, they were seeing quite the show.

The first greasy light of dawn revealed the scars across the heavens caused by aerial battles raging in the dark. The rebels were more capable than Jason had thought. Cut off from all communication, the silence was eerie. Heavy truck traffic grew as they approached the lines. They avoided convoys as best they could. The escorts were too much for them. As much as they wanted to take out the high-speed train with its flatcars of mechs headed for the line, it was too fast to catch, and the gun cars forced them to keep away. The train vanished toward the front. Spitefully, they cut the tracks over a culvert once it was gone.

Behind them, despite cutting bridges and other hit-and-run tactics to wreck roads and cause chaos, the pursuit was catching up to them. Their rampage drew more pursuit from all quarters. The last hundred miles became rolling hills and low valleys riddled with slow-flowing streams, and unfortunate bogs that forced Trigger to stick to roads. They still outclassed every vehicle that closed in, but superior mechs were forming a tightening cordon, hemming them in.

"They're harrying us like hunting dogs, pushing us into a corner." Jason's third stimulant injection was wearing off, and hopelessness leaked through the cracks.

"I know. If only we could have gotten around that last patrol, the coast is only eleven miles away."

"Yeah. An easy hop across to our pickets."

They entered an abandoned river city. Trigger angled off to hide in a fish market's loading dock near a levee to assess their situation. Artillery had driven out the locals, and uncontrolled fires had razed most of the urban center. In the distance, they heard more napalm runs. Hegemony forces held air supremacy in the area.

"Are you seeing a way out of here?" Jason asked. Without antennae, they couldn't talk to their drones, and they'd lost track of the pursuit, but he was certain they were in the city and searching.

"Without the ability to gather intel, simulations and observations are no good. The bridges across the river must be controlled, and it's certain they're joining in the search for us. We're going to have to gamble and move before it's too late. I'll get stuck instantly in the surrounding bogs and sugarcane fields." Trigger groaned as if she'd lost the endgame by the look of the pieces on the board.

"What's this?" Jason asked, selecting what looked like half a bridge sticking out into the river.

"A loading pier for petrochemical feedstock barges."

Jason gave a relieved sigh and grinned. "There's our way out."

"How?"

"You're still water-tight to a hundred feet?"

"That's still *mostly* true. Some of my interior will flood in my back half and neck, but it shouldn't damage me too badly."

"The bottom's dredged for barges. We can jump into the river and scoot downstream unseen." He thumped his seat's armrests with restless hope.

"Crazy, but possible," Trigger said, her excitement building.

A low hissing sound, like an avalanche, caught their attention, coming out of the smoke ahead of them and growing closer. A gutted building on the next block collapsed as if it had been pushed. Dust billowed into the sky, whiting out scanners for a moment, then something moved in the clouds of smoke and powder, like a mountain coming at them.

"Oh, hell," Jason wheezed at the sight. The faint silhouette was enough to tell him what it was. Its giant snail-like shell came into view. An ultra-heavy *Mollusk*-class tank oozed forward on its foot of smart sand. Big as a five-story building, it dominated his view; somehow the Rebels had one. Bumpy with mirror-bright marrow-bone protrusions, it heaved toward them. Giant bulges extruded from the spiral pattern's center and showed the ring-tipped barrels of twin toroidal-vortex plasma cannons. It bristled with other tactical weapons from the front, surrounding its shell lip like a wreath of spines.

Trigger needed no prompting and bolted out of the loading dock. Twin circles of glowing purple swung toward them like a predator's eyes spotting its prey. She ducked behind the fish market. There was the signature quick quail-like whistle and thundercrack as the Mollusk fired.

Purple donuts of obliteration, hotter than the sun, struck the corner of the building. A shockwave of flaming debris showered hundreds of yards beyond Trigger as she sped away. Her rear-facing cameras showed that the dock and much of the fish market building were gone in a foul-smelling steam and rain of burning debris. The ultra-heavy mech surged forward. Jason couldn't believe how fast it moved, pursuing them like a dog after a hare. The buildings it knocked down slowed it a little, but not enough.

"Get us to that pier!" Jason shouted.

"Copy that," Trigger said. Particle beams, pulse lasers, and autocannons tore up the landscape, scoring too many glancing blows on Trigger as she flew through the city toward the feedstock plant by the pier. Smaller mechs tried to intercept them, but Trigger couldn't afford to be bullied by them anymore. She trampled a small *Guardsman*-class mech, knocking it into a building at speed. Jason put some parting blasts into it and drove the other harassers back with well-timed shots.

A hard bank threw Jason against his restraints. Trigger juked just in time to avoid a direct hit from the Mollusk's naval-scale TVPCs. Another deafening explosion tore a crater into the ground as deep as she was tall.

Ahead of them were the gates to the refinery, strangely untouched. Tangles of pipes, cracking towers, and lattices would make it easy to lose them. Trigger's AMS blister started buzzing and sizzling, shredding swarming drones that dove upon them after they blasted through the complex's gates. Deafening smacks and bangs from drone detonations rattled her.

A well-placed shot with both pairs of lasers and masers took apart an *Ursa*-class mech almost in brawling range. The Mollusk was too big to pursue them into the feedstock refinery. It would collapse the cracking towers and mechanical chemistry synthesizers with catastrophic repercussions. The monster went another way to cut them off.

All the hazing fire stopped.

"Almost there, almost there, we're almost there," Jason chanted. "Get us onto that pier, go out as far as you can, and jump in." Trigger took control of their course as Jason focused on fending off the mechs that followed them in.

The pursuit fell away like a punt returner getting past the coverage as they slid through giant storage silos. Fast scouts charged up behind them. One attempted to tackle Trigger. Like a knight's charger, she kicked with her good hind leg, shrugging off the attack. Another Guardsman tried to wrestle her down. She scraped him off against a tank, wrecking it.

In the center of the tank field, they found the feeder lines to the loading pier. Trigger hopped onto the pipes. She rode them like a parkour runner, smashing through flimsy scaffolds and catwalks. Safety equipment tore free, and pipes bent and cracked, spraying thousands of gallons per second of different petrochemical feedstocks.

The end was near as the pipes came into the clear over the levee. A crossfire opened up from all sides as the rebellion took its last chance to kill them. Jason looked right and saw the Mollusk a quarter-mile away, its shot lined up, the twin circles of its main guns a bright, shining purple, ready to fire.

"Made it!" Trigger shouted triumphantly and leaped into the air, arcing over the river, her armor peppered by the focused fire, alarms screaming. Black marrowbone fluid burst out of the armored pores.

Twin vortexes of sun-grade destruction flew toward them, and Jason could barely process what was happening. The tip of the pier exploded in a fireball worthy of an orbital strike. Plasma and ionized particles bathed Trigger, stripping armor and tossing her even further.

Jason's world was fire and light. He screamed as he felt the boiling heat on his combat armor. The cockpit filled with smoke from overloading systems. Breakers blew, the world spun, and with a crash, Trigger hit the murky waters and sank instantly.

Everything went dark and cold.

Trigger lay on the bottom of the river, as if sleeping peacefully in a pasture. Jason watched flame boil on the surface, buffeted by shockwaves he could faintly hear but not feel as the feedstock facility annihilated itself in chain reactions.

"Trigger?" Jason asked. The air tasted of metal, soot, and fried silicon. "Come on, girl. You've survived so far. Don't you leave me yet."

No response. He tried to get out of his chair, but a lightning bolt of pain stopped him. His left shoulder was dislocated, and the collarbone had snapped. He couldn't open the emergency panels to flip the breakers. It took some time to get unbuckled from his seat and turn. A new agony bolted up his leg. He looked down and found the left shin of his combat suit was sliced open and covered in blood. The impact of landing must have slammed it against the corner of a control panel.

"Gotta get you up and running. It'll work out, and we'll just walk along the bottom to our line. It'll be fine." Jason flipped some still-functional breakers not covered in water. Partial systems came back online, revealing the gruesome truth. The damage report screen showed that Trigger's left rear leg was missing from the hip down, and her right-side guns were half-melted off her chassis.

Flame had scoured the drone bay, fouling it with a cooked blend of polymers.

Tears ran, spotting the inside of Jason's helmet visor. "She's just an AI. Just an AI. She can be rebooted. It's not a problem. She can come back, and we can talk about this. We can… we can—" His words stuck at the sight of the antenna isolation breakers. She was disconnected from the Hegemony servers. If her drives were compromised, there was no up-to-date recovery copy.

Jason's hands started shaking uncontrollably. He couldn't manage the fine motor control to flip the small breakers. The water at the bottom of the cockpit was deeper now, and it was pouring into his torn suit. The reactor showed emergency reserve power dying rapidly. Water trickled down the panes of the canopy, and the fibers no longer glowed. Panels and screens winked out one by one, leaving him alone. Dim firelight on the water cast rippling shadows. He was trapped in a hellish tomb.

With only a little foul air left in the cockpit, Jason knew he had no option but to bail out. Wounded and in a torn combat suit, he couldn't swim. It would drag him down. Peeling off his clothes caused many tortured shouts. Water was up to his waist when he finally got his boots off and shucked them free. The laceration on his leg was wicked. He bandaged it with the little emergency wound kit he hoped would prevent him from bleeding out.

Above, the water still burned with raining tar balls that were coating the river bottom and Trigger. Would it stop burning in time for him to escape? The first gap in the flames showed as the fire from the pier died away, and the current drew the floating mats of fiery glop downstream. If he could swim against the current long enough, he might make it.

The water reached his neck. Jason felt around for the emergency canopy release and tugged. With a *whoosh*, the last remaining air pocket gently pulled him out. Using his good arm and kicking like crazy against the flow, he aimed for a clear spot in the water.

He looked down for a moment at Trigger's chassis, cockpit head tilted awkwardly up at him as if to say goodbye, her body a violated husk of what she once was. She vanished in the murky, tar-filled water as he broke the surface.

* * *

The android nurse wheeled Jason back into his hospital bay with several other wounded from the peacekeeping action. Bentham was across the aisle between their beds, and a dozen other mech pilots, aviators, and soldiers filled the room. Outside the bay's window, the curve of Troilus spun on its axis, now a vision of victory after they'd put down the rebellion.

"How's therapy today?" Bentham asked.

Jason shrugged. "Embrace the suck and get healthy, I guess. You?"

"Medical discharge once they put a new leg and arm back on me. With a sweet, sweet military pension for duty above and beyond. Would you believe they're giving me a medal for getting so many people off that tub?"

"Yeah." Jason's mind was miles away at the word "medal." "I can believe that." He looked over at his Silver Star, Purple Heart, and Peacekeeper's Cross, plus a half dozen other medals of accomplishment, and a battlefield promotion to major on the little table next to his bed. Despite this, he was being reassigned. There was talk of sending him back to Earth after asking too many troubling questions about Trigger. Was she programmed to engage in existential subjects, or was it digital evolution? They'd asked about his mods, and that had signaled that it was time to shut up about it.

"I'm off to the Merchant Marine, I guess. They're always looking for ex-military spacers to captain freighters around the cosmos. Peaceful retirement, I guess, and at least if pirates attack, they have a captain that isn't going to fall apart under pressure." Bentham's boisterous prognostications did little to raise Jason's spirits. He put on his smiling mask and let Bentham have his moment.

His bed's datamate jingled. It was a call from the mech bays. His face scrunched up.

Cautiously, he answered. "Major Robinson."

"Afternoon, sir," the master sergeant on the other end of the line said. He looked to be calling from the cockpit of a mech. "I thought I'd give you a little bit of a surprise to cheer you up."

"Not sure what you're talking about." He felt the icy claws of dread grip his belly.

"We got your Percheron all salvaged and put back together. We even reinstalled your AI, and she wanted to say hi."

"Trigger? How?" His heart jumped into his throat.

"It took a little doing, with all the water and fire damage, but we pulled out what we could and reinstalled her."

His heart jumped a little. "You recovered her memory?"

"Not quite, but we got her returned to a backup point just before the *Silverback* was shot down."

"Hi, Captain!" came the happy hell-for-leather voice. "Are we getting back in the game? Whose ass are we going to kick now?"

She had none of the mission briefing memories, of course. The mission was done and classified, and she didn't need to know now. Jason stared at the screen that showed the view out of the cockpit. The noise of the mech bay leaked through. Hope became an icy lump in his throat.

"Trigger? Did you suffer?"

Both the master sergeant and Trigger 2.0 spoke simultaneously. "Huh?"

"Did—did you feel yourself die?" Jason's hope cracked.

"I'm an AI, I can't die or feel."

"Do you remember what we talked about planetside?" He already knew it was foolish to ask, but the urge was too strong.

"I just reboo—"

Jason hung up and stared into space. What had happened between them during those twenty-odd hours no longer existed. Their time alone, running for their lives, had changed them both. Experiences only they could share. That Trigger was gone, laid to rest on the bottom of the river, vanished like a random prompt, never to be repeated.

Life for him would go on, haunted by questions she could no longer answer.

Slowly, he pulled his bed sheet over his head like a shroud and finally allowed himself to weep.

* * * * *

Author Bio

Author of the *Akiniwazisaga* and *Tales from the Dream Nebula* series, M.D. is a native Wisconsinite expatriated to wonderful, wild West Virginia, where he lives with his wife, their cat, Li'l Bits, and a small flock of naïve chickens. He's an author, writing coach, developmental editor, artist, graphic designer, and musician.

# # # # #

Hunger in the Code by Russ Tilton

A GENIT Mechmaps Story

Chapter 1

2000 Hours
Panamá Pacífico Military Base, Panamá

Eli Jenkins stepped out of the taxi, his duffel slung over one shoulder. He checked his watch.

8:03 pm. Right on time.

He wondered if his new partner always worked this late. But he didn't care. It was his first assignment after training, and he was excited. Besides, anything to get out of that classroom.

He glanced at the dark hangar. *Did he go home early?*

His boots crunched on a film of grit as he stepped from the gravel lot into the shadowed threshold of the old hangar. He pushed through the steel door then paused as it swung shut with a hollow *clang.*

Darkness swallowed the space.

"Hello?" he called.

No answer.

He moved deeper inside, trailing his fingers along the wall to a set of light switches. He flipped them up.

Nothing.

"That's weir—"

Click.

His brow furrowed.

Click… click-click.

He froze. The sound came from the far end of the warehouse.

Footsteps?

No. Not footsteps. This was sharper. Faster. And it was coming toward him.

Click-click-click-click-click.

He squinted into the black, eyes struggling to adjust.

CLICKCLICKCLICKCLICK.

He stepped back, his muscles tightening.

"Hey! Is there someone there?" he shouted.

CLICKCLICKCLICKCLICKCLICKCLICK

The sound was louder now, faster. Adrenaline slammed into his chest.

CLICKCLICKCLICKCLICKCLICKCLICKCLICKCLICK!

A shape tore from the shadows, massive and low to the ground, its outline brutal and unmistakable.

A Howler.

Jenkins gasped as it locked its burning red eyes on him, jaws wide, teeth glinting like metal blades.

CLICKCLICKCLICKCLICKCLICKCLICKCLICKCLICK!

"NO—!" he screamed. He stumbled back, flung up his hands, and squeezed his eyes shut—

BLAM!

The overhead fluorescents snapped on, washing the cavernous space in white light.

He opened his eyes and looked up to find a mouth full of titanium teeth six inches from his face, lips pulled back in a rictus grin.

A slow clap echoed from behind a stack of crates, and a large black man stepped out, grinning like a schoolboy.

"Welcome to the MECHMAPs, Jenkins."

Jenkins sagged forward, hands on knees, breathing hard.

"You… you asshole."

The grin widened. "I figured you'd want to see one in action."

"You could have killed me."

"Nah. Only if I'd let him finish the run." He stuck out a hand. "Reggie Washington. Come on, I'll give you a tour."

*****

Chapter 2

They made their way to the back of the hangar, where three Howlers stood silent in their charging docks, mist curling off their bodies from the final rinse, arched backs gleaming under the overhead fluorescents. Even powered down, they looked alert, coiled. Predators, waiting for the leash to come off.

The old building smelled slightly of burnt drive belt rubber, oil, and dust.

"This used to be home to Blackhawks and Cobra gunships, back during America's 'stabilization efforts' in Central America. Now, it houses monsters."

Jenkins stepped nearer.

"Tell me what you're looking at," Washington said.

"Mechanical Mutant Apex Predator, or MECHMAP, Howler-class. Crocuta-Human hybrid, 400 series. Looks like a hyena built in Hell."

"That's about right. 'DARPA's finest,' according to them."

The thing's head was level with their chests, and even standing still, the Howler looked like it was about to lunge; head low, shoulders high, claws retracted but ready.

Jenkins circled the rack. "Digitigrade legs. Subsonic locomotion. A biopolymer 'skin' laid over synthetic musculature and segmented armor plating. Covered with pseudo-fur that breaks up its heat signature."

He paused. "Scares the hell outta me, and it's not even on."

"Good," Washington said. "Means you might live through your first op."

The Howler's electronic eyes, now dim, still reflected red under the overheads. The snout was wrong—too long for a human, too short for a hyena—and its jaw hung open slightly, as if caught mid-laugh… or mid-bite.

"What's with the face?" Jenkins asked. "It doesn't look like anything."

Washington folded his arms. "It's not supposed to. That's part of the psyop. It's designed to unnerve. You look at it, and it doesn't make sense. It doesn't fit into a category. Makes you hesitate."

He frowned. "They look like they're thinking."

"They do, 24/7. Their ears twitch like a signal array, listening to everything. Tracking voices. Updating threat models. Mapping posture trees. You standing here is data to them."

"Memory stacks."

Washington nodded.

Jenkins looked down. A paw on one was partially extended, revealing a six-inch talon, long enough to punch into a man's heart.

"They're not equipped with weapons, right?"

"Just those claws and their teeth. Ceramic titanium. Serrated. Polished down to the molecule."

"With a bite force that can snap a femur in half," Jenkins added.

"That's right," Washington said, "but there's another reason they don't arm them."

Jenkins looked at him.

"Deniability." He nodded toward the claws. "Bullet holes and blast trauma point to human involvement, but a body that looks like it was torn apart by an animal raises more questions than answers."

Washington lifted a tablet from the bench beside him and tapped the screen. A soft chime sounded—then the middle Howler twitched. Without warning, it threw its head back and unleashed a noise that stopped time.

The roar ripped through the warehouse, slamming into steel and concrete, vibrating through Jenkins's chest and skull. It wasn't a single noise but a layered assault—hyena screech, jagged siren-wail, the deep, chest-crushing thunder of a big cat. And threading through it all, a dying human scream, stretched and broken.

Jenkins's breath locked. His knees buckled, his vision narrowed to a tunnel, and he clamped his hands over his ears involuntarily.

"Holy shit!" he yelped, stumbling back.

The sound cut off as abruptly as it began. The Howler lowered its head, jaws parting and then closing again with a faint mechanical *click*, as if satisfied.

Jenkins bent forward, hands on his thighs, fighting nausea. "What the fuck, man?" he gasped. "You kidding me?"

Washington watched him carefully.

"You ever hear a tiger roar up close?"

Jenkins shook his head, still blinking. "No."

"People think it's just loud. It's not. Tigers use infrasound—low-frequency pressure you don't consciously hear. It vibrates your chest, your sinuses, your inner ear. Your brain reads it as a threat before you even process the sound," he said, setting the tablet down. "Your amygdala lights up. Adrenaline dumps. Muscles seize. Fine motor control goes out the window. Most people freeze up and panic."

Jenkins swallowed. "That—that's what that was?"

"That was part of it. Refined. Tuned. Amplified." He glanced at the Howler. "They layered the frequencies—animal dominance signals mixed with human distress. A predator-prey scream that hits all at once. Your brain can't categorize it, so, again, it makes you hesitate."

The younger man wiped his face. "It felt like something punched me from the inside."

Washington nodded. "That's the infrasound. The body reacts first. Thought comes later—if it comes at all. That's all they need. That half-second of paralysis. That kill window. Claws and teeth do the rest."

"So that sound…"

"… is the last thing you hear."

A smirk tugged at the edge of Washington's mouth. "Still scared, kid?"

"Terrified," Jenkins muttered, his chest rising and falling. "Got any more surprises?"

Washington barked a laugh and slapped him on the back. "Nah, man, that was the last one."

Jenkins exhaled, shaking his head, then nodded toward the machines. "Why is their armor incomplete? The flanks are exposed. Why not fully plate them?"

"It's purposeful. It's bait."

The younger man looked confused. "Bait?"

"Damage is data. They're built for it. They let you score a hit so they can figure out how to end you faster."

"More of the psyop."

"Exactly. They let the enemy land a blow, then bleed on purpose while they study your rhythm, your stance, your location. Just when you think they're wounded and you have a chance, they adjust and come at you."

"Damn."

"Early models flinched when injured—or, more correctly, damaged. They paused to process it. That was a problem. So DARPA ran trauma loops over and over. Real wounds, real pain signals, until the instinct to flinch was gone."

"They trained pain out of them."

"No," Washington corrected, "they trained it *into* them. Now, when a Howler gets damaged, it's not seen as a warning; it's seen as an opportunity."

Jenkins's face darkened.

"They have biogel lines routed close to the surface to make it look like they're bleeding. To make them look vulnerable."

"That's not combat. It's theater," Jenkins muttered.

"That's psyops, but with these things, every act ends the same. It's not all show, though. I've seen a video of one of them charging through gunfire with a leg hanging off."

They stood in silence for a few moments, staring at the row of Howlers. Titanium demons in mechanical slumber.

After a beat, Jenkins asked, "Do you miss the old ones? The organics?"

Washington didn't answer right away. He turned, walked a few steps, and then said over his shoulder, "Yeah. Even though they bled for real, if they slipped the leash, you had options. Control devices, tranqs, or a bullet if need be. These things?" he said, glancing down at the rack of mechanical mayhem. "Once you press go, there's no stopping them."

*****

Chapter 3

Two Weeks Later
1530 Hours

Washington straightened slowly and stretched his back until it popped, and the dull ache settled into something manageable. He picked up a rag from the workbench, wiped the sweat from his face, then scrubbed his palms until the grease smeared into the fabric. The hangar was warm and stale with oil and ozone, the kind of odor that never really left your clothes.

At his feet lay a half-assembled MECHMAP, its chest cavity open, cables and synthetic muscle bundles exposed like a butchered machine-god. Its detached arm rested nearby on a padded stand, its claws curling inward as if it were dreaming of something to tear apart.

Washington glanced over at the row of glass-fronted offices lining the hangar wall, the lights long since dark. One still bore a faded title stenciled above the door. FLIGHT OPS. A ghost from a different war.

How many times had he and the rest of the Section 17 crew flown out of this same hangar? A couple dozen, easy. Back when you still put boots on the ground—or at least hovered above it with guns hot and a real chance of dying.

Black-bag ops in the hills of Afghanistan or the jungles of Peru with live MAPs—organic monsters, stitched together in secret labs and super-sized with hormones and experimental gene edits. Freaks. Beautiful, loyal, nightmare freaks.

Those were the days, he thought, not without a bitter twist in his gut. This was still the same game: hunting and vanishing the bad guys. But back then, if—when—things went sideways, you had control gloves, kill-switches, or weapons that could actually stop a MAP. And failing that, a voice on the other end of the comm, someone real, who bled if you punched them. Someone you could scream at when shit hit the fan.

Now it was all one big algorithm. Monsters made of titanium and hardware instead of muscle and bone. Bots deploying bots, while operators with no skin in the game sat in a trailer halfway around the world, calling the shots while binge-watching Netflix on a second monitor.

"Foolproof," the DARPA guys called them. Cleaner. No collateral damage. No messy explanations. No awkward press conferences or hand-wringing politicians trying to cover their asses before the seven AM news cycle. Just a digital authorization code, and men like him left to bag up the meat. Besides, they said, the MECHMAPs would shut down in place if they deviated even a fraction from protocol.

Washington snorted and shook his head. He knew better. *Don't trust absolutes,* his mother used to say. *They come back and bite you.* Just because it hadn't happened yet…

He turned back to the units.

The mission had been tough—for the MECHs—but it was a good one for Jenkins to cut his teeth on.

A rescue operation of an asset being held for ransom by Los Lobos in a warehouse in Quito, Ecuador. They used just one REAVER. After plugging in the asset's DNA and image, the NIGHT TERROR-based SIMIA unit erased the eleven gang bangers in under eight minutes, despite having its left hand blown off by a grenade two minutes into the fight. The hostage was recovered, shaken but unharmed.

Along with the destroyed limb, the armor plating down its spine was fractured, a claw on one leg was missing entirely, and some teeth were chipped like someone had gone at them with a grinder. The hangar lights caught the dried fluid spattered across its flank—black and flaked now, but unmistakable.

Washington tapped the tablet hanging from a lanyard around his neck and called up the damage report.

MISSION COMPLETE: 100% TARGET ELIMINATION. NO UNINTENDED CASUALTIES. SELF-CHECK: CRITICAL STRUCTURAL DAMAGE. AI DEVIATION: NONE.

He had to admit, the MECHMAPs were interesting. Cold. Efficient. Brutal. They didn't eat. They didn't sleep. They just learned… and waited.

The old organic MAPs, though super-sized and genetically altered, were nothing compared to these. The MECHMAPs were bigger—and definitely meaner—but not a lot bigger.

Since they could build them any size they wanted, Washington wondered how they determined the ideal size. Logistics played a role, no doubt. Some DARPA bean-counter running cost-benefit analyses on fuel payloads and shipping containers. But size was only part of the equation.

The other part—equally important, if not more—was psychological warfare. An enemy combatant might grow used to the sound of gunfire, but not the impact of seeing a grinning apex predator coming at him with steak-knife claws and a grin like a great white shark.

Washington continued replacing components, disconnecting the unit's back panel, and inspecting the synthetic musculature beneath. He inserted a new lower arm from a nearby metal rack. The assembly clicked seamlessly into place. It was like changing out spark plugs.

After he finished, he stood back and keyed the tablet. The LEDs in the unit's eyes pulsed faintly as it reinitialized. For half a second, they flicked open—flat, metallic, unreadable. Then it powered back down.

He muttered under his breath, "We're not operators anymore. We're glorified mechanics."

* * *

"Getting nostalgic again?" Jenkins said, stepping from the supply room, a rag slung over his shoulder, something unidentifiable smeared across the front of his coveralls.

Half his age, Steve Jenkins was built solid in the same places as Washington, just tighter and cleaner—without the scars that gave the older man's frame its gravity. Sharp-jawed, cocky, with blond, buzz-cut hair, he had the air of someone who knew the rules but hadn't learned to fear them. He moved like Washington once had—quick, economical, confident in his body—but without the caution that came from experience. He lacked the quiet awareness of how fast things could go wrong.

"You really miss those things? The organics?" Jenkins asked, tossing his rag onto a tool cart and walking over. "Man, screw that. I've seen the archive footage. You had to *feed* them. Water bowls. Tranquilizers. Then clean up after 'em with an oversized pooper-scooper. You guys were more like zookeepers."

Washington grunted. "There were some downsides."

Jenkins snorted. "*Some?* Bro, they needed to be cleared by a vet tech before you could deploy them. And I read where one unit caught mange. Freakin' *mange*, in a war zone."

Washington started to reply, but Jenkins held up a hand. "Yeah, yeah, I know. They had *soul*."

He chuckled. "You had to have been there. All you've ever known is MECHMAPs."

"I'll take smart metal over emotional muscle any day."

Just then, both men's tablets vibrated, and the screens lit up.

Washington looked down. "Well, get out your metal polish, Jenkins. We got a mission."

*****

Chapter 4

Off the Northwest Coast of Guatemala
0053 Hours

The Blackhawk thundered up the coast, hugging low over black water, the horizon nonexistent in the early morning hour.

In the cargo hold, the three Howlers stood, locked into steel brackets bolted to the deck like restraints in a madhouse, their internal systems cycling behind their synthetic ribs with a faint hum.

Washington sat in his nav station, head back, eyes closed, the noise-dampening headphones dulling the rotors' roar to a soft pressure in his skull. He always sat next to them so he wouldn't have to look at them. They gave him the creeps.

He opened his eyes and tapped his headset mic. "You read the mission packet?"

Jenkins, sitting beside him, barely looked up.

"Yeah, yeah. Cartel dudes. Coke lab. We're the garbage men," he mumbled, his cellphone screen lighting up his face with digital gunfire and cartoon blood.

Washington exhaled through his nose and shook his head.

Jenkins must've caught it, because he added with mock seriousness, *"A cocaine processing station just inland from Manchón, Guatemala. The bad guys are picking up four hundred keys of finished product at 0300 hours. No friendlies within two klicks of the location. One-klick exclusion zone around the lab. Everything inside is fair game."*

He smirked.

Washington chuckled. "There may be hope for you yet, Rookie."

"I want to know two things. Number one, whoever heard of a cocaine processing plant outside Colombia?"

"It's an interesting concept," Washington said. "From what I was told, the Mexican cartel running the lab realized they could get coca paste for a fraction of what they pay for finished cocaine hydrochloride. And since labor is labor, they want to see if they can do the conversion themselves and cut out the middleman."

Jenkins nodded. *"Interesting."*

"What's your other question?"

"If the plane's not due until 0300, why are we getting here so early? It's barely one o'clock. Besides robbing me of valuable beauty sleep, that's a hell of a long time to be on the ground so some local can stumble across our parking spot."

"SOP. The bad guys are more likely to be asleep now. We land early, go dark, and sit tight, then let everybody and everything calm back down."

He tapped the cargo wall with one knuckle. "And with this Ghost Hawk, nobody should hear us land."

"Should," Jenkins echoed.

"Besides, the plane may show up early. Better to get there and wait than to get there late and be screwed."

The Blackhawk banked slightly, and the Howlers tilted a few degrees to match the new pitch.

Jenkins frowned. *"They never seem to move when you're looking at 'em. It's like they wait."*

"They're designed to sit motionless in the brush for hours. Watching. Waiting," Washington said, his eyes closed. "Target-acquisition logic runs on minimalist motion protocols—no wasted movement, no posture shifts."

"Like landmines that breathe."

Washington smiled. "That'd be a good analogy if these things breathed. And have you ever noticed that their exterior doesn't reflect light?"

The younger man gave a quick glance. "Is it that chameleon armor stuff?"

Washington nodded. "Smart skin. Adaptive pigmentation tied to a low-res topographic scanner. Reads light levels, color values, shapes—then bleeds that into the dermal layer in real time."

"So basically," Jenkins said, *"they're wearing the jungle."*

"More or less. You don't see them until they're already moving, and then it's too late."

Jenkins grinned. *"That's something your old organic MAPs could never do. All that growling and panting. You could probably hear them a klick away. Plus, they stank."*

"I'm not saying these aren't an improvement. I'm just saying, nothing's infallible."

Jenkins made a buzzer sound. *"Wrong answer. These things have a flawless record."*

Washington frowned. "According to DARPA."

Over the headset, the pilot said, *"One minute."*

Jenkins stashed his cellphone, leaned forward, and double-checked his harness.

The crewmen manning the M240s at the cargo doors scanned with their NVGs, their grips relaxed, but ready. Mounted beneath them were the twin GAU-19s, slaved to the copilot's console, each triple barrel, electrically driven Gatling gun capable of throwing out nearly 2,000 rounds of .50 caliber rounds a minute. Not that it mattered. After the MECHMAPs were completed, there was no one left to shoot back.

The cabin lights cut out without warning, replaced by a dim red glow. A second later, the helicopter dropped into silent mode—the engines still running, but the sound throttled back by baffled rotors and adaptive dampening tech. Inside, it was almost peaceful.

Washington flipped down his NVGs, turning his world green.

A black slash of crushed grass, maybe a hundred yards across, appeared.

"LZ's clean," the crew chief announced. *"No thermals. No movement."*

Washington nodded. The site had been drone-scouted and cleared by satellite. It was supposedly abandoned, but in the jungle, that meant nothing.

The Blackhawk set down in a brief windstorm. The rotors spooled down, the vibration faded, and the turbines wound into silence.

The crew manned their guns while Washington and Jenkins unclicked, M-16s in hand, their eyes locked on the tree line.

No one moved.

After a couple of minutes, Washington said, "And now, we wait."

He turned his attention to the large monitor bolted to the bulkhead across from them. On it, a satellite feed ticked along with slow pulses of infrared—washed-out grays and whites that formed the rough shape of the processing camp.

Nine heat signatures appeared inside a cluster of four huts. Outside, a faint red blob flickered; the last of a cook fire, burning down. There were no sentries. No movement. No discipline.

Washington shook his head. "Complacent sons of bitches."

Beside him, Jenkins had pulled a poncho over his head, the hood down low to mask the glow from his phone. Faint pops and cartoon screams bled out in muffled bursts from beneath the fabric.

One crewman glanced over and shook his head.

The kid'll learn… I hope, Washington said as he settled back to wait.

* * * * *

Chapter 5

0203 Hours

An hour later, the pilot's voice cut in over the headset.

"*We've got radar contact. Small fixed-wing approaching low and slow from the west. Looks like your delivery plane.*"

Washington straightened.

A second voice joined the channel, a radio intercept out of Panama.

"*Confirmed chatter—Spanish. Satellite confirms it's the target aircraft. ETA under twenty minutes.*"

"An hour early," Jenkins mumbled, pulling the poncho off his head.

Washington raised an eyebrow.

"Don't say it," he said as he lifted the screen on his MIL-STD-810G certified field laptop. It was the kind of machine you could drop from a helicopter and still run diagnostics on after you scooped it up off the ground.

Washington, being the senior, placed the palm of his hand against the screen for biometric confirmation for mission prep. A few seconds later, hydraulic bolts disengaged with a dull *hiss*, the restraint arms withdrew, and the Howlers came online.

A low whirring hum filled the cargo hold. Limbs flexed, and clawed fingers spread, clacking softly against the steel deck. Optics flicked from dark to red—six points of glowing light cutting through the gloom. Heads swiveled in short, mechanical bursts. One unit tilted its head too far to one side, like a predator trying to decode a scent it couldn't place, then it snapped back to center with a *crack* of artificial vertebrae.

"Creepy bastards," Jenkins muttered.

The door gunners stood with their backs pressed against the hull. One had unconsciously lifted his M240 slightly—not enough to be threatening, but enough to feel like a talisman.

But they all knew the truth.

If a Howler went off script, if the AI stack cracked, it didn't matter how many guns you had trained on it.

Nothing was going to stop it.

* * *

0207 Hours

Washington glanced at his watch.

"You want to do the honors?"

Jenkins grinned. "Hell, yes."

Washington unhooked the hand-held, military-grade gaming console controller from his vest and handed it to his partner.

Jenkins practically bounced down the Blackhawk's loading ramp and onto the grass. Around him, the jungle, rendered in ghostly shades of green by the NVGs, unfolded in pale, spectral greens, the trees standing silent and massive.

The three Howlers remained motionless inside the cargo bay, their optics glowing faintly.

Jenkins manipulated the controller like he was born to it, his thumbs moving with effortless precision, the kind of fine motor control that seemed baked into his generation. He tapped the screen.

MANUAL RELEASE AUTHORIZED.

The large monitor mounted on the cabin wall flashed green, then split cleanly into two feeds. One held the overhead satellite view—thermal grayscale of jungle canopy and terrain contours. The other fractured into three smaller windows. HUD feeds, one from each Howler. On them, the jungle shimmered in washed-out green, slightly pixelated at the edges as the optics adjusted. Tactical markers floated in the foreground—distance to target, terrain gradient, time to contact. In the upper corner, a small red triangle pulsed steadily.

OBJECTIVE LOCKED.

There came a low *clunk*, followed by another, and then another as the hydraulic pistons released. The Howlers stepped free of their restraints and came down the steel ramp single file, claws half-curled, heads forward, the soft hum of servos barely audible.

When they reached the jungle floor, they fanned out and formed a line, facing Jenkins.

A voice came over their headsets. "*Control to MT1, your target aircraft is fifteen minutes out. Confirmed to be inbound from the west. ETA: 02:20.*"

"Copy," Washington acknowledged. He turned to Jenkins. "Send them."

Jenkins flipped the weathered rubber cover on the manual override switch. It snapped open with a dry *click*, exposing a metal toggle scarred with faded red stripes. He grinned and pushed it down.

"Go time."

The three Howlers leaned forward in perfect unison and braced against the earth like sprinters, fingers splayed, claws biting into dirt. Their heads snapped up and locked on the coordinates streaming down from the satellite feed.

Then they launched.

There was no roar. No warning. Just the soft, rhythmic *thump-thump-thump* of fur-covered metal paws striking ground and the Doppler whine of powered limbs driving them forward at inhuman speed.

A fury of motion exploded across the three HUD feeds. Branches whipped past, trunks blurred, and undergrowth tore away into darkness. Beyond the sensors, the jungle was pitch black, a tunnel of greenish smear and raw velocity, 55 miles an hour through terrain no human could even see through, let alone navigate at speed.

Nap-of-the-earth flying was nothing compared to this. NOE still yielded to gravity and terrain. This was ground-level violence; precision married to momentum.

Washington felt a flicker of vertigo as he watched.

He checked his watch. *Five and a half minutes to reach the perimeter of the processing lab.*

HOWLER-1 HUD FEED

ACTIVE MODE: STRIKE INSERTION

—TERRAIN GRADIENT: 12° DECLINING

—SPEED: 88.7 KPH

—TARGET ETA: 00:04:37

—VITALS: NOMINAL

—SIGNAL: LOCKED (SATLINK 03B)

—SQUAD LINK: 3/3 CONNECTED

Branches tore past like projectiles. Vines snapped across fur-covered composite armor and rolled away like paper. Every root, ridge, stump, and gully flickered across the HUD in wireframe for 0.2 seconds—analyzed, calculated, dismissed, or utilized.

OBSTACLE: FALLEN LIMB (1.4M DIAMETER). ACTION: VAULT.

IMPACT FORCE: WITHIN TOLERANCE.

TRAJECTORY CORRECTION: -3.4° YAW.

MAINTAIN VELOCITY.

Legs flexed like pistons. The ground vanished. One Howler soared through a curtain of wet leaves, hit the opposite bank, and didn't pause. Rear limbs struck first, absorbing shock. Forward limbs planted half a heartbeat later. Full-speed acceleration resumed within 1.2 meters.

AUDIO FEED: MUTED—JUNGLE SOUNDS LOW, WIND VECTOR HIGH

OLFACTORY INPUT: SUPPRESSED

FACIAL HEAT SIGNATURES: NOT DETECTED

The jungle peeled away in thermal grayscale; a blueprint of the Howler's cognition—bark heat, foliage chill, infrared bleed from insect clusters. One false heat source to the left, a nesting bird. Logged. Ignored.

The other two Howlers flanked behind and to the left, visible as green diamond markers in the HUD peripheral—perfect spacing, exact pacing, coordinated through subvocal burst transmissions the human team would never hear.

LZ TO TARGET: 3.91 KM REMAINING.

ESTIMATED ARRIVAL DELTA: ±0.7 SEC ACROSS UNITS.

NEXT NAV POINT: FORKED TERRAIN SPLIT—SUGGESTING STAGGERED DISPERSION.

A ditch opened up—two meters wide, overgrown and black.

ACTION: VAULT (FULL ARC)

BACKUP ACTION: SIDE WALL REBOUND IF TRAJECTORY FAILS.

No need. It cleared the gap easily, barely dipping its head. Momentum carried it forward, deeper into the dark, deeper into the heart of the kill zone.

A blur of motion flicked across the HUD—heat signature, four limbs, 75 kilograms. A deer. It erupted from the underbrush three meters ahead, white tail flashing as it crashed through the foliage, startled into a full sprint. The Howler tracked it instantly—trajectory, mass, velocity, scent profile—then dismissed it in less than half a second. Non-combatant. Not in perimeter. No deviation. Its head never turned. There was no surge of adrenaline, no flicker of curiosity. The program didn't allow for that. Everything outside the designated parameters was irrelevant.

The lab came into view.

A faint glimmer of residual thermal—heat bleeding from corrugated tin roofs, thin walls radiating low human signatures.

OBJECTIVE VISUAL ACQUIRED—PROCESSING FACILITY: CONFIRMED

NUMBER OF TARGETS: 9—ALL STATIC (ENTRY)

DISTANCE: 73M—CLOSING

HOLD PERIMETER UNTIL ENGAGEMENT COMMAND RECEIVED

The three Howlers split with geometric precision—one angled right, one went low and left through dense underbrush, and the third took up position between the camp and the runway.

The HUDs dimmed slightly as camouflage mode engaged. Smart-skin adjusted to ambient colors and temperature, until one by one, the MECMAPs went dark, disappearing from the satellite infrared display.

The nine traffickers never stirred. Never realized they were already dead.

*****

Chapter 6

0210 Hours

"I'm ten minutes out, Reynaldo," blared the handheld beside the cot.

Reynaldo Barrera jerked awake, heart slamming as he fumbled for the radio. For a moment, he had no idea where he was. Then the heat of the jungle closed in, along with the sharp stink of processing chemicals, and it all came back.

"Reynaldo, did you hear me? I said I'm—"

"Sí, sí!" he snapped, rubbing grit from his eyes. "Watch for the runway lights."

He swung his legs off the cot and stood, swaying slightly, grabbed the radio and his rifle, shoved the door open, and stepped into the night.

Three other huts crouched nearby, dark and silent. Barrera moved to each one, pounding his fist against corrugated metal.

"¡Levántense! ¡Arriba, cabrones! Get your weapons and get to the runway! Juan—bring the truck!"

Lights flickered on. Curses followed. Boots hit dirt. Metal scraped as rifles were dragged free. The camp shook itself awake.

Satisfied his eight men were up and moving, Barrera cut between two cabins and stepped onto the narrow foot trail leading toward the runway.

The jungle swallowed him immediately, and black pressed in from all sides. He stopped, patted his pockets, and cursed under his breath. He'd forgotten his flashlight. For a moment, he considered turning back—but there wasn't time. Besides, he'd walked this trail a thousand times. He could've done it in his sleep.

He moved on, slower now, letting his eyes adjust, feeling the uneven ground through the soles of his boots.

The night seemed darker than usual, the jungle quieter, and he felt a chill down his back.

Knock it off, he chided himself. *There's nothing wrong.*

Still, something just... *felt* wrong.

He shook it off and kept walking.

Ten steps later, he slowed, then stopped.

He peered down the dark ribbon of trail ahead... then he slowly turned his head to the right, and his chest tightened.

There was something there, like vines wrapped around a tree trunk, but...

His skin crawled as a cold thread spiraled down his back.

He took a step closer.

"Where are those lights, Reynaldo?" came from the radio.

Barrera jumped, then spat, "Shit!"

He turned and ran.

Behind him, deep in the bark of the tree, two red orbs flashed on.

* * *

The trail ended at the north end of a worn jungle airstrip cut into the packed dirt, stretching 1,500 feet to the south. To the left, hidden in the vegetation, was a weather-worn wooden box mounted to a metal post. He opened the lid and flipped a toggle.

Twin rows of red LED strips flashed along the runway like sparks buried beneath the jungle canopy.

"Do you see us?" the man asked.

"Yes," came the angry reply, along with some muttered curses.

The rumble of a diesel engine grew, and from around a stand of trees, a flatbed truck appeared.

Five men rode in the bed, hunched low among fuel cans and duffel bags, rifles laid across their knees. Three more packed the cab. The driver swung the wheel hard, angling the truck across the north end of the runway so the headlights washed the dirt strip in pale yellow light, then killed them.

Barrera could hear it now, the low, steady drone of the aircraft, still distant but unmistakable. He stabbed a finger down the runway. "Get into position."

Three of the men jumped from the truck bed with their rifles and spread out along the crude airstrip.

"I have the runway in sight," the pilot said over the radio. *"Lining up."*

Barrera turned back to the truck. "The rest of you—get those kilos unloaded. Move."

As the duffel bags were dragged to the edge of the strip, the growl turned into a roar.

"Turn on the headlights," Barrera snapped.

The old flatbed's lights flared to life, lighting up the northern end.

"There," one man said, pointing.

The tiny plane suddenly exploded into view and screamed past twenty feet overhead, the wheels barely clearing the palms.

They swore and ducked down.

"¡Mierda!" one shouted as he dropped to the ground.

The Cessna disappeared down the runway, its landing lights illuminating the ground in stark white. Tires hit with a jolt, and dust mushroomed up.

The plane continued to the end of the strip, locked a wheel, executed a tight half-circle, then taxied back.

* * * * *

Chapter 7

0210 Hours

The jungle outside was silent, but inside the Blackhawk, things were heating up.

Washington and Jenkins sat at their docking stations, peering from their laptops to the large monitor displaying the satellite information and three live MECHMAP feeds.

"Got movement," Jenkins murmured as a heat signature stirred inside one of the huts.

"That must be Barrera," Washington said as they watched the figure pound on the walls of the other three huts.

After the camp was roused, the figure headed down a narrow trail leading to the runway.

"Trail's tight," Jenkins said. "Canopy cover's thick."

"Yeah," Washington replied quietly, "and he's about to walk right past H2."

On H2's video feed, the jungle resolved into a crisp, green-tinted lattice of heat and geometry.

Then Barrera stepped into the frame.

The man slowed, stopped, and turned his head.

"Oh, shit," Jenkins hissed.

For a long half-second, the trafficker stared directly into the camera. Then he took a step forward.

At that exact moment, the radio barked, "Where are those lights, Reynaldo?"

Barrera jerked.

"Shit!" they heard him curse over the MECHMAPs audio feed. Then he spun around and continued down the trail.

Jenkins slumped back and blew out a breath.

Washington chuckled softly. "Bought yourself a few more minutes, Reynaldo."

They watched his heat signature emerge from the end of the trail. Half a minute later, twin rows of red LEDs winked to life along the airstrip. Almost simultaneously, a truck rolled out of the trees and came to a stop near the north end of the runway.

Washington nodded at the screen. "That would be the finished product."

Three figures ran down the strip and took up positions while the others began pulling duffel bags from the back of the flatbed and piling them up near the clearing.

"Barrera and eight guards," Washington said.

The Howlers' HUDs pulsed as new overlays populated the feeds.

NEW CONTACT: AIRBORNE—FIXED WING

DESIGNATION: CAIMÁN-80

MODEL: CESSNA 206—SINGLE-PROP, HIGH-WING, STOL | CAPACITY: 1,400 LBS.

SPEED: 165 KNOTS—DESCENDING

OCCUPANTS: 1 (PILOT)—THERMAL CONFIRMED

TRANSPONDER: SPOOFED—MEXICAN AGRICULTURAL REGISTRY

Jenkins glanced over. "All lined up…"

"And boxed in," Washington said. "Game time."

The radio crackled in their headsets. "*Command to MT1. Two minutes till green light.*"

Washington knew the suits at DARPA were watching from a command center back in Arlington—men and women in pressed shirts, seated behind glass and conference tables, tracking the feeds in air-conditioned quiet. When the moment came, *they* would give the order. *They* would start it. And once it began, only they could stop it.

Washington wasn't an operator anymore; he was a caretaker, tasked with keeping the MECHMAPs functional and putting them on target. After that, he just watched. He often wondered how many of the ones calling the shots ever saw the results of their actions firsthand.

The pilots and crew clustered around, eyes fixed on the satellite display.

"What's that red circle around the lab?" one asked.

"That's the one-kilometer exclusion zone," Jenkins said. "The MECMAPs can't go outside that area until we call them back."

"Everything inside the circle is fair game," Washington said grimly.

A crewman pointed at a cluster of structures located a click beyond the lab, situated between it and the ocean. "What's that?"

"That's the village where the workers live," Washington said. "They come in the morning, process the product, then go home at sundown. According to DARPA, they don't carry weapons, so they're not considered targets. Just poor Hondurans trying to earn a buck."

* * *

"Here's the plane," Jenkins announced.

On the satellite feed, the aircraft flared and touched down in a burst of dust and glare. The engine burned white-hot in ultraviolet as it rolled to the far end of the strip, spun around, then taxied north and stopped.

As he watched, Washington felt the old familiar weight settle in, heavy and dull, like standing on the tracks with a train bearing down, and there's nothing left to do but count the seconds.

Inside the Howlers' HUDs, vectors sharpened as positioning data updated. Telemetry tightened and range indicators locked in.

OBJECTIVE CONFIRMED—AIRCRAFT LANDED

ALL UNITS: LOCKED | IN POSITION | ENGAGEMENT READY

AWAITING COMMAND: +02:01

Washington shook his head. "Those poor bastards have no idea what's about to happen."

"I wish I could press the 'go' button," said Jenkins.

"No, you don't, trust me," Washington said. "That's the kind of thing that slowly eats you from the inside."

The younger man glanced over but said nothing.

*****

Chapter 8

0220 Hours

The red landing lights flashed across the underside of the wings as the plane taxied north. Once there, it locked the wheel again, spun in a tight half-circle, and came to a stop facing south.

The cargo door creaked open, and a thick face behind a patchy beard appeared.

"¡Gordo!" Barrera called, striding up to the heavyset pilot.

"¡Pinche Reynaldo!" The man laughed.

They embraced and slapped backs.

"Long trip?" Barrera asked, stepping back.

"Long enough," Gordo muttered. "Storms over Campeche. Had to detour south, and the military's got new birds sniffing along the old corridor. I ghosted them near Puerto Barrios."

"You made it. That's what counts." Then he spun and barked at the two nearest guards. "Get the duffels! *Rápido!*"

Two of the guards scrambled over and began dragging the 220-pound bags to the plane, one at a time. Together, they loaded them into the plane, distributing the load as well as they could around the auxiliary fuel bladder lying in the middle of the passenger compartment.

"Four hundred keys processed and packed," Barrera said, slapping a bag. "You remember what that looked like in paste?"

The pilot laughed. "I remember the smell. I'm happy to leave that and the Colombian jungle behind."

"But the women…"

"Magnifico," the pilot admitted, holding a hand to his chest.

"Now, you have something for me?" Barrera asked.

Gordo turned, popped open the copilot's door, and dragged out a smaller duffel bag. He handed it to Barrera. "Count it if you wish."

"No need." He gave a sharp whistle, and one of his men jogged over, grabbed the bag, and tossed it into the cab of the truck.

"Safe travel, cabrón," Barrera said, hugging him once more.

"Clear skies and short hops," Gordo replied. Then he patted Reynaldo's shoulder, turned, and climbed back in.

A second later, the engine whined back to life.

* * *

0227 Hours

Reynolds narrowed his eyes. "Those boys stateside better hurry up,"

As if hearing the admonition, all three HUDs flashed, one after another.

H1—ENGAGE READY

H2—ENGAGE READY

H3—ENGAGE READY

AND THEN AGAIN.

H1 —EXECUTE

H2—EXECUTE

H3—EXECUTE

"Game time," Jenkins said almost reverently.

"Captain, please start your bird in case we get a runner," Washington said.

* * *

0228 Hours

Gordo eased the throttles forward.

The prop spun up with a rising whine, and the Cessna shuddered as it began to roll forward, slow at first, the nose wandering slightly as the tires bumped along the uneven strip.

It felt sluggish. Between the 880 pounds of product and 620 pounds of fuel in the bladder, the aircraft was at its maximum takeoff weight, but he'd been there before, many times. Besides, most of that fuel would burn off by the time he got to Monterrey, and once there, Starla would help him reduce the weight of the money he was going to earn. Gordo grinned and nudged the throttles a hair farther.

The plane clawed for speed, the Cessna's tires chattering down the jungle strip, hammering against ruts and packed clay. The twin rows of red LED markers streaked past, flickering in his peripheral vision as the engine wound higher.

Almost there, he thought, glancing at the airspeed indicator.

Hands light on the yoke, feet dancing on the rudders, he leaned forward, eyes scanning the length of the runway, already thinking about rotation—then he did a double-take.

There was something on the strip. A shape running toward him, low and fast.

He'd encountered animals on jungle strips before, but they always veered off… this one didn't. It kept coming, straight down the middle.

He stared.

It moved wrong. It was too smooth. Too fast. And its legs pumped like pistons.

"Move, cabrón," he muttered, instinctively easing the yoke back just a fraction.

Then his brow furrowed. "Is that… is that a hyena?"

Pow-pow-pow-pow-pow-pow!

"Oh, shit!" Gordo yelped as gunfire lit up the left side of the runway.

A guard burst from the tree line, firing his AK47 into the air on full auto, something latched onto his upper body like a parasite.

In the flash of the landing lights, the pilot watched the thing bite down on the man's skull, crushing it like a piece of fruit. Then it was gone.

When he looked back up, the thing in front was almost on him, and he could see a massive, low-slung body like armor and muscle fused together. Hyena-shaped, but wrong, with a face that looked almost human, lips curled back from black gums and metal teeth, and glowing red eyes that were locked on his.

He slammed the throttle forward and gritted his teeth. The engines howled, and he pulled back hard on the yoke. The nose lifted.

Twenty yards. Fifteen. Ten.

He was going to make it!

WHAM!

The entire aircraft jerked sideways as something smashed into the right landing gear assembly. The yoke whipped to the left. The right wheel caught dirt, the nose slammed down, and the plane rolled. Then the world flipped, and Gordo screamed as the Cessna began to cartwheel.

The fuselage split apart on the first bounce, ripping apart the hundred-gallon auxiliary fuel bladder.

WHOOOOOOM.

A burst of white-orange fire lit the jungle like a second sun.

The wreck tumbled twice more, spinning shards of metal and flaming kilos into the night and illuminating the pillar of black smoke rising into the sky.

* * *

0229 Hours

The explosion knocked Barrero to one knee and lit up the far end of the runway. The truck's windshield turned into a mirror of fire as a thunderclap echoed through the valley, and the flaming wreck of the Cessna dropped back behind the trees, throwing sparks into the dark.

He staggered to his feet, turned, and was about to shout orders when the sound hit him.

It came from the tree line and slammed into his chest like a shockwave, vibrating through bone and teeth, squeezing the air from his lungs. Then it fractured into a howling, yowling, laughing, metallic human scream that tore through his head and buckled his knees. Nausea rolled through him, and his heart went wild, while his bladder threatened to give way.

The laugh climbed higher, broke, reassembled, and climbed again—closer now, everywhere at once. Then another one joined in the yowling chorus of madness, and then another.

He clamped his hands to his ears and looked up in time to see a guard sprinting down the runway, his rifle forgotten.

A shape exploded from the brush like a missile and slammed into the fleeing man from behind, lifting him clean off his feet. He flew six feet through the air and hit the dirt in a loose, boneless sprawl.

For a split second, Barrera thought it was over, but the thing wasn't done.

It reared back, lifting its right front limb.

Is that an… arm? The thought barely finished forming before it struck.

The limb cut through the air with surgical speed and struck the man's head just above the ear. There was a sharp, wet *crack* that carried all the way back to the truck.

The body went still.

Barrera stared, breath locked in his chest.

Animals didn't do that.

Whatever had just killed that man hadn't swiped with a paw.

It had thrown a punch.

A scream ripped from the tree line and cut off mid-note. Then the howling returned, louder now, layered, overlapping, circling the clearing like something herding them.

Barrera and two of his men pressed their backs to the truck. The other three stood exposed in the clearing, heads snapping back and forth, rifles whipping from shadow to shadow, their breathing loud and ragged. One moaned while another whispered a prayer.

Movement flickered in the brush.

One guard screamed and cut loose, emptying his rifle on full auto into the darkness. Muzzle flashes stuttered, lighting up tree trunks, shredding branches, ripping bark from wood, but nothing cried out.

Click.

The bolt locked back.

At that exact instant, a blur smashed into him. Before the man even hit the ground, the thing clamped its jaws around his throat and jerked back.

The guard never made a sound.

The man beside him yelped and bolted. He made it three steps before the ground ahead of him *moved.*

Something unfolded from the brush, rising from four legs to two in a smooth, deliberate motion, then stepped almost casually into his path.

The man skidded to a stop, eyes wide as a dark stain ran down the legs of his pants.

With forward-facing eyes, high cheekbones, and a flattened nose, it almost looked human, but the skin was pulled tight over metal and bone, stretching and distorting the features into a caricature. Blood-matted fur clung to segmented armor plates, and the thing's unblinking eyes glowed a dull red.

The man's rifle fell from his shaking fingers and hit the dirt. He dropped to his knees, never taking his eyes off the thing. Then slowly, desperately, he pressed his palms together in prayer.

The creature's grin widened, revealing three-inch-long serrated metal teeth that flashed in the light.

It stepped forward and drew back an arm. Four long metal claws slid free. The arm shot forward and *disappeared* into the man's face.

The guard's arms flew out to the sides, and his body spasmed once.

The creature jerked its arm back, and the man collapsed to the ground, unmoving.

The thing's grin never faded.

The third guard screamed and ran, stabbing the barrel of his rifle blindly behind him, firing as he ran for the trail leading back to camp.

Just as he reached the opening, an arm dropped from the canopy, and a huge hand clamped around his head. It squeezed and lifted him off the ground until he hung four feet in the air, boots kicking uselessly. The sound he made was high and thin. Pure panic and agony.

The thing squeezed, and the man's skull collapsed inward with a wet, crushing *pop*, like a ripe melon in a vise. It let go, and the body fell to the jungle floor in a loose heap.

The creature—monster—thing—swung down from the branches as effortlessly as a monkey dropping from a tree.

It straightened, looked at the remaining men—and grinned. Then it threw its head back and unleashed the same terrible howl. The sound rolled through the clearing and echoed back from the trees as if the jungle were answering it.

Barrera, wedged between the two remaining guards at the front of the truck, grabbed them each by a shoulder and shoved.

¡Aguanten!" he shouted. "¡Peleen, coño! Fight!"

As the two men stumbled into the clearing, Barrera scrambled for the driver's door. He yanked it open and dove inside, then slammed the door shut and threw the shifter into drive.

A man appeared at the passenger side, pounding on the window, eyes wild.

"¡Reynaldo—!"

Barrera ignored him and stomped the accelerator. The rear wheels spun. The truck fishtailed into a tight, screaming donut. The bumper clipped the man hard, knocking him off his feet and into the dirt.

The tires dug deep ruts into the ground as the truck lunged forward, dirt and dust blasting up into the air behind it.

Barrera didn't look back. He didn't need to. The howling followed him into the dark.

*****

Chapter 9

0236 Hours

The headlights jittered wildly, lancing through the trees like panicked searchlights as Reynaldo fishtailed down the narrow passageway, the tires barely staying inside the rutted path. Branches scraped the side panels like fingernails and slapped against the windshield.

He gripped the wheel with white knuckles, heart punching at his ribs, eyes darting.

He heard a rifle crack once, twice. Then a scream. He snapped his head to the mirror, and in the afterglow of the muzzle flash, saw a monster drive its jaws into a man's chest again and again. The scream cut off as if a switch had been thrown.

Reynaldo nearly drove off the trail. He jerked the wheel back, tires spitting gravel.

His breath came in fast gulps, eyes wild, his mind screaming.

Who's attacking us?

What are those things? Attack dogs?

No, they were too big. Too fast. Too smart.

Just ahead, the edge of the processing camp came into view. He lifted his foot off the gas slightly, then caught movement in the mirror. Three shapes were barreling down the trail after him.

"No, no, no—" Reynaldo moaned.

He jammed the gas pedal down, flew past the huts, and continued west. Through the open window, he heard the howling laughter.

* * *

0229 Hours

All eyes were locked on the video feed as the Howler leaped up, arms wide, claws extended, and slammed into the right landing gear of the Cessna. The aircraft snapped sideways in midair, struck the ground, and cartwheeled.

Then it exploded.

On the satellite view, the screen lit up like a flashbulb, as the plane burst apart and rained wreckage.

Through the open side door of the Blackhawk, they saw the distant burst of light over the treetops, and a second later, the *crack* of an explosion.

Jenkins stared at the monitor, stunned. "It grabbed the landing gear." He looked at Washington. "It grabbed the fucking plane."

Washington just shook his head. "That's gonna draw some attention."

On the Howler video feeds, the guards scattered and were methodically hunted down. None of them stood a chance.

"This isn't a fight," Jenkins murmured. "It's a purge."

On the screen, the last three traffickers stood with their backs to the truck. One of them shoved the other aside, jumped into the truck, and took off.

"That would be Reynaldo," Washington said. He turned to the pilots. "We got a runner."

The other pilot scrambled back into his seat and spun up the rotors.

"They're chasing him," Jenkins announced.

The Blackhawk lifted on a cushion of chopped air, branches thrashing as the rotors clawed for altitude. The crewmen strapped in behind their guns as the jungle slid past beneath them.

Despite the noise and confusion, Washington never took his eyes off the monitor.

"Reynaldo's halfway to the perimeter," he said, voice steady. "He might make it."

Jenkins glanced up with a crooked grin. "Looks like I'm gonna get my first taste of action."

"Chew slow," the big man muttered. "This ain't one of your video games."

Jenkins leaned forward and stabbed a finger at the satellite screen. "Who's that?"

A small blur of heat appeared at the western edge of the access road, weaving unsteadily toward the processing lab. It was a narrow profile.

Washington leaned in. "It's a motorcycle coming from the village. Somebody probably heard the explosion and is coming to check it out."

Jenkins shook his head. "He won't get there before the Howlers hit the driver."

"Maybe not," Washington said, "but if he gets his hands on that money, we've got a problem."

On-screen, the race unfolded in brutal clarity.

Barrera's truck hammered down the rutted trail, bouncing like a carnival ride, while behind it the Howlers came up fast, moving as if they were running on pavement, unhindered by the mudholes, roots, and broken ground as internal mechanisms compensated instantly, joints adjusting on the fly. Their upper bodies stayed eerily level, arms pumping in perfect sync, as if the jungle were scrolling beneath them rather than slowing them down.

To the west, the motorcycle closed in, the rider weaving between puddles, boots kicking out to keep balance.

All eyes were locked on the faint red circle marking the exclusion zone as the vehicles clicked nearer.

Washington leaned back slightly. "We need eyes on that cash bag before this turns into a goddamn treasure hunt."

Suddenly, the motorcycle's taillight flared. The bike wobbled, fishtailed, and skidded to a stop.

"Good," he said hopefully. "Stay there. Whoever you are—just stay the hell put."

"The truck's at the perimeter!" Jenkins blurted.

Washington looked up in time to see the vehicle cross the red boundary line.

On the Howler HUDs, speed vectors dropped, and gait profiles shifted. The pursuit softened, almost gracefully, like the predators had suddenly lost interest.

For a moment, it looked like it was over.

Then on the satellite feed, the motorcyclist reached up and slid something off his shoulder.

A long shape.

A rifle.

"No," Washington shouted.

Too late.

A cone of light flashed from the muzzle of the weapon.

* * *

0233 Hours

The Howlers wove for half a second, then recalibrated and fell back into formation—and accelerated.

On their feed, a new overlay pulsed to life:

NEW COMBATANT IDENTIFIED: WEAPON SIGNATURE CONFIRMED

ZONE PROTOCOL UPDATE: PERIMETER EXTENDED +1.0 KM

RULESET OVERRIDE: DIRECTIVE 3 AUTHORIZED

Washington's eyes went wide. "What? Wait. They can't do that."

But they had.

A new circle appeared on the tactical map, this one enveloping the trail, the truck, the rider—and the workers' village.

The original red circle faded as the Howlers blew past.

"They're not stopping!" Jenkins shouted.

On screen, one Howler broke off and slammed into the motorcyclist like a battering ram. Both bodies tumbled, a smear of heat and motion crashing into the undergrowth.

The other two MECHMAPs never deviated but remained locked on the truck.

"Command, this is MT1," Washington barked into his headset, voice tight. "We have an unauthorized deviation from the attack plan. You need to shut down the MECHMAPs immediately."

Crackling static. Then: "*Uh… we can't do that without authorization from DARPA headquarters, MT1. Stand by.*"

"Stand by?" Washington snapped. "Those things are heading toward a village of noncombatants. It'll be a goddamn bloodbath."

"*I understand. Stand by. I'm trying to get through to HQ—*"

"This is bullshit," Washington muttered, tearing off his headset. He turned to the pilot. "Get us on top of that truck. Now."

"Roger that."

The Blackhawk banked hard.

Seconds later…

"Truck in sight, two klicks ahead."

Washington stepped up behind them and said, "Hit it with the Gatling gun. If we can stop it, maybe the MECHMAPs will stop."

The copilot twisted in his seat, eyes wide. "Are you sure about that?"

Washington glared at him. "Shoot the fucking truck."

After a second's hesitation, the pilot nodded. "Do it, Joey."

The copilot flipped some switches, and a crosshair appeared on the monitor.

"Locked on… firing."

The helo lurched with the weight of recoil, and a stream of tracer rounds screamed from the underbelly, ripping through the canopy. Dirt geysered up as a serpentine trail chased the fleeing vehicle.

The Howlers dodged the rounds as if they'd expected them.

The bullets ripped through the bed and then into the cab. The truck swerved violently, its tires caught a rut, and it flipped.

It rolled twice. The driver's door exploded open, and the driver flew out like a rag doll, hitting the ground hard.

Before Barerra had stopped sliding, H1 was on him. It ended him with a bite.

An instant later, H2 and H3 appeared alongside.

Washington gripped the nav station, whispering, "Stay. Stay."

The Howlers turned, not back toward the runway, but west, toward the village.

On the satellite image, thermal signatures appeared as dozens of lights flickered on inside huts. Doors opened, and villagers stepped outside.

On the HUD, new text bloomed across the screen in bold red:

MULTIPLE HOSTILES IDENTIFIED—SECTOR W-03

RULESET OVERRIDE CONFIRMED

EXECUTE

"Holy shit," Jenkins whispered. "They just flagged the whole village."

"What's the word, Dude!" Washington shouted into his headset. "Those villagers are noncombatants. That's a goddamn fishing community!"

A pause, static, then, "*Still waiting on DARPA. Hold position.*"

Washington clenched his jaw so tight he thought his molars might crack.

On the satellite feed, the Howlers fanned out in a flanking formation, approaching the village low and fast, like wolves rounding up sheep, as more glowing figures stepped from huts. Parents with children, people half-dressed, barefoot, blinked into the night. One man raised a lantern. Another held what looked like a machete. A child, from its small heat signature, pointed.

The Howlers sped up.

"Engage them!" Washington shouted. "Hit the Howlers with the Gatling gun."

The pilot shook his head. "Negative, sir. Not without DARPA clearance."

He spun on him. "They're about to *slaughter* those people."

"Those machines are worth four million apiece," the pilot said, not meeting his eyes. "My ass would be in Leavenworth before the rotors cooled."

"Goddamnit," Washington spat, turning away.

He grabbed his M-16 from the weapons rack and slung it over his shoulder.

"Drop me. Now."

Behind him, Jenkins paled. "That's suicide, Reggie."

"I have a barrier bracelet. Besides, I'm not asking you to come."

The pilot held his gaze for a beat, then banked hard. "LZ coming up. Get ready to drop the fast rope."

But as the crew chief prepared to deploy it, the copilot said, "You're too late."

Washington looked out the door.

The Howlers were in the village, moving like mechanized death.

Screams rose and fell like the tide. Children, women, old men—it didn't matter.

The Howlers didn't discriminate.

He sagged against the bulkhead as the video feeds turned red.

After a minute, the radio crackled.

"*Command to MT1. DARPA has authorized shutdown protocol. Executing now.*"

The HUD confirmed shutdown status.

H1: STANDBY MODE—OFFLINE

H2: STANDBY MODE—OFFLINE

H3: STANDBY MODE—OFFLINE

Washington lifted his head slowly and looked back out the door.

Below, the three Howlers stood like statues in the smoldering ruin of what had been a village. They were caked in gore and surrounded by mangled corpses of every shape and size. There didn't appear to be a complete human body in sight.

Washington nodded. *They're certainly thorough.*

Then another transmission broke through. A new voice, flat, clinical.

"*This is DARPA Headquarters. Advise us when you have secured the drug money.*"

Washington turned away from the hatch and let out a breath that sounded like a laugh, but there was no humor in it.

*****

Chapter 10

Two Months Later

Washington stood in front of his locker, methodically folding the flight jacket he hadn't worn in months, then slid it into his duffel bag. The distant hum of generators and cooling fans filled the space, a low, mechanical breath that never quite stopped. Somewhere behind him, a MECHMAP diagnostic tone chirped and went silent again.

Jenkins paced.

"This is bullshit," he said for the third time, hands chopping the air. "You can't just let them do this. There are whistleblower laws. Federal protection. Go public. They'll have to—"

"They don't have to do a damn thing, Eli," Washington said, not looking up.

"They stonewalled you, you pushed back, and now they're cutting you loose? That's retaliation. Clear as day."

"Of course it is," Washington said, pulling the bag shut and zipping it halfway, "but it's their game, their rules."

He reached into the locker and pulled down a pair of battered patches, both frayed with age, the Velcro worn thin. One was black with a shield superimposed over a red 17, the other with the letters GENIT dripping blood and superimposed over a DNA helix. He turned them over once in his hands, then set them gently inside the bag.

"They gave the mechtechs shutdown authority. That's all that matters."

"Yeah, because of you!" the younger man exclaimed, ready to renew his rant. "You have to fight them. Make noise. Get your job back."

Washington finally turned and looked at him.

"Kid," he said, not unkindly, "this was always going to end one of two ways. Either I stayed quiet and kept collecting a check while people died, or I said something, and they found a reason to show me the door. I picked the one I could live with."

Jenkins shook his head. "It's not right."

"No, but that's how it works. Besides, they didn't fire me; they just offered me early retirement." Washington grinned at him. "And at fifty-six, it's time. I can feel it in my bones."

He shouldered the duffel and rolled his neck once, easing the stiffness out. "Look, this is a different game. Guys like me came up working with organics. With them, we knew where we stood, and that gave us an edge."

He glanced toward the far end of the hangar, where a MECHMAP sat dormant in its rack.

"With these things, there *is* no edge, just an on/off switch. And that's a game for the next generation."

He looked at the younger man. "Just keep your finger near that switch, and you'll do fine."

Jenkins's jaw tightened. "It's not right."

Washington slung the duffel over his shoulder, gave him a crooked smile, and said, "It is what it is." Then he walked out.

* * *

Houston International Airport

The terminal hummed with the low, constant noise of people going somewhere.

Reggie Washington wasn't.

After clearing customs, he grabbed a plastic bowl of airport salad and found a deserted part of the terminal to eat his lunch while awaiting his connecting flight.

He pushed a fork through it with little interest, moving lettuce around more than eating it.

Panama already felt a long way off, but so did everything else.

Retired.

He'd rolled the word over in his head a hundred times, but it still didn't fit.

Fifty-six wasn't old, not for this line of work. Not for him. Physically, he felt better than he had after half the Section 17 and GENIT ops he'd run over the years. This was something else.

He was worn down. Not from work, but from the way it ended. He always assumed he'd pull the plug himself when the time came. Instead, someone else had made the decision for him. In return, DARPA had agreed to give shutdown authority to mechtechs, so it hadn't been for nothing. No more waiting on a suit half a continent away to make the call when things went sideways—and things always went sideways. Wasn't that enough?

"You look like a man deep in thought," a voice said.

Washington didn't look up right away, but set the fork down carefully and wiped his fingers on a napkin.

When he did look, he saw a man standing a few feet away, mid-forties, clean, neutral clothes, with a face you wouldn't remember five minutes later. His radar went up.

The stranger gestured to the seat across from Washington. "You mind?"

"Yeah, I do," he snarled. "I'm having lunch."

The man smiled faintly and sat anyway.

"I know who you are, Mr. Washington."

"Then you know this is where I tell you to move along."

"MECHMAP tech, recently 'retired,'" the man continued, ignoring him. "Before that, Section 17 and GENIT operative."

His chest tightened as the hair on the back of his neck lifted. Access to that information required the highest clearance. Who was this guy?

"A lot of people know a lot of things," Washington said, keeping his expression neutral. "Most of them are smart enough not to repeat it out loud."

The man's lips twitched up. "You think that's the end of it?"

Washington sighed. "The end of what?"

"The machines going off script. You think giving techs a kill switch fixes that?"

Washington said nothing but leaned back and studied him.

The stranger tilted his head. "You think DARPA cares when those things go off script?"

Washington's eyes hardened. "Careful. You're getting close to a conversation you don't want to be in."

"I don't blame you for being cautious," the man went on, unfazed by the implied threat. "You should be. After all, they're watching you… and me, too."

"If that's the case," Washington snarled, "you ought to keep walking before they decide you're a problem."

"I'm afraid they already have."

The big man's eyes narrowed.

"I used to work for DARPA."

"A lot of people used to work for DARPA."

"More specifically, I helped develop the MECHMAP program."

A silence hung between them.

"They weren't supposed to be autonomous," the man said. "Not fully. Not like they are now. The plan was simple—assist and augment deployments."

He studied Washington. "But you already know that. You were there."

Washington remembered. Ten years ago, when they first appeared. When mechtechs still had their hands on the wheel.

Back then, the machines were—for the most part—predictable and contained. But on more than one occasion, a tech was forced to shut one down to prevent a disaster.

Inevitably, there were bad calls. MECHs shut down mid-execution, resulting in soldiers getting killed. To DARPA, that was unacceptable.

About that time, AI got smarter, and the leash got longer. Eventually, mechtechs were relegated to preparation and recovery of the units, with everything else decided from 2,000 miles away.

"Let me guess," Washington said, voice flat, "you warned them what might happen."

He nodded. "And when they ignored me, I kept track. There are more incidents than you think."

Washington began poking at his lettuce. "Shit happens when you fight wars."

"I'm not talking about war. I'm talking about political assassination."

Washington looked at the ceiling and exhaled. He placed the cover on his meal and set it aside.

The man watched him, then, after a moment, said, "You don't believe me."

"That our government would create weapons and then use them for nefarious purposes? Not only do I believe it, I expect it. In fact, I took part in it."

He almost laughed at the look of surprise on the man's face.

"But you know what? I don't give a shit about any of that anymore because I'm retired. It ain't my problem."

The man said nothing at first, then nodded. "Maybe… maybe not."

He pulled out a simple card and set it on the chair beside Washington. No logo. No title. Just a name and a number.

He stood.

"If you ever decide it is your problem—or when you get bored with retirement—call me."

"Why do you care about all this?"

"Because some of the people they killed were my friends.'

Washington peered up at him. "Why were they targeted?"

The stranger's lips tightened. "For doing the same thing you did. Questioning the program and demanding changes."

He gave Washington a two-fingered salute. "Safe travels."

The man turned and walked away, blending into the terminal as if he'd never been there.

Washington remained seated as the noise of the airport crept back in. In the distance, a boarding announcement echoed.

He picked up his duffel bag and slung it over his shoulder. Then he picked up the card and glanced around the concourse, letting his eyes linger on the faces. He chuckled, shook his head, and tossed the card into the trash.

"I'm retired."

He headed for his departure gate.

* * * * *

Author Bio

Russ Tilton is a Marine who retired from the Memphis Police Department after more than thirty years in law enforcement. As a detective sergeant, he worked everything from homicides to internal affairs to narcotics. This foray into the darker side of life is reflected in his stories.

# # # # #

The Ghost Load by
Joe Hower & William Alan Webb

A Story of the Iron Ghost Legion

Prologue

Some of you could die.

Dog Company First Sergeant Ezekiel Mumford masked knowledge of their danger behind the one-eyed squint his assembled company called his "eye-fuck." Stopping at each one for precisely four seconds before moving to the next Marine, Mumford understood what the combat virgins didn't: fearing him more than the enemy *might* just keep them alive. Obeying him without hesitation might reduce their reaction time a quarter-second, and that could spell the difference between life and death.

Or maybe not.

To them, Remote Phase Warfare was *fun*. Remote-chance-of-dying entertainment they got paid to play. Mumford didn't care whether critics called them Meat Puppets, Long-Leashers, or other derogatory names, as long as his Marines realized that death *was possible.*

"You've probably heard the static that combat operations on Luda begin tomorrow… well, that's no ghostfeed. Tactical deployment is not yet scheduled, but you *will* be prepared for transition by 0600 sharp."

If you could hear mental groans, Mumford did, but none were foolish enough to do so out loud. No one made it to corporal, much less sergeant, without learning harsh lessons in the Confederation's Marines. Those lessons usually came complete with no assembly required, unless you counted mending a broken bone or two.

"Whatever happens from this point forward, there's only one certainty… you will never be the same again. Questions?"

"No, First Sergeant," Staff Sergeant Branson responded on behalf of the junior noncoms. "We'll get everyone on prep right away."

Mumford appreciated Branson's quick response, an example for the rest of them. With that, Branson rose from his seat and left the company briefing room.

Now it was the staff sergeant's turn. He was on the fast track to gunnery sergeant, and everyone knew he meant it when he said, "right away."

"Get your people moving, the usual prep. Kiss the dog, pet the wife, say goodbye to all your unauthorized kids. Move!"

The response was a flurry of movement as every small-unit leader, including Sergeant Rodriguez and Corporal Smitty, headed for the door as if Satan's underboss was breathing down their necks… which, in a way, he was. Each small-unit leader hauled ass down the barracks' central hallway, peeling off in turn as they entered their own squad bays.

Mumford followed Sergeant Rodriguez, who didn't say a word when they reached the bay for 3rd Squad, 2nd Platoon, passing beneath the stenciled sign that proclaimed their unit nickname of BACKBREAKERS. It wasn't that the first sergeant trusted Rodriguez less than his more senior sergeants, but that Rodriguez was newer to the unit. Mumford wouldn't be doing his job if he left anything to chance.

As they'd waited for ghostfeed to become fact, the platoon's other two corporals had been drilling the troops on various

Essential Subjects. That knowledge would be invaluable during the next set of unit inspections. But all that ended abruptly when Rodriguez and Smitty entered the room.

"All right, here's all you need to know for now," Sgt. Rodriguez offered. "We transition to the planet Luda tomorrow for combat operations. You've got until 2200 to get yourselves squared away."

For a moment, nobody moved or responded. They just sat there, grinning from ear to ear. Mumford moved into Rodriguez's field of vision and lifted an eyebrow. That was all it took.

"What the hell is wrong with you? *MOVE!*" Rodriguez yelled at the squad. Finally, the spell was broken, and they scattered into various corners of the room, grabbing unfinished paperwork, stowing personal gear, and snatching up comm devices.

The invention of transitioning greatly minimized the risk to warriors. Now, only your mind inhabited a mechanical war machine, and actual death among the Confederacy's military had dropped to rounding-error levels. Basically, no one died. An unfortunate by-product meant the reduction of war to something akin to a brainstem implant's immersive holographic experience. Humanity's diaspora across the galaxy eliminated most universal constants, except for the attraction of games. The attraction of fucking-off was baked into human DNA, with gaming a universal choice.

War became far too easy to wage, unless you were among enemies who didn't possess the same tech, or were some of the inevitable civilian populations caught in the middle as collateral damage. For them, war remained humanity's ancient affliction, unchanged since the dawn of time. Watching his people, Rodriguez leaned over to Smitty.

"What's the over-under for our mech losses?"

Smitty checked his comm tablet. "For our squad, fifteen."

"Fifteen? Hell, there's only nine of us."

"You're underestimating Lance Corporal Argent. The big money says Argent's going to lose four all by himself."

"*Four?*"

Smitty shrugged. "It hasn't happened *yet*, Sergeant."

"It better not happen at all. You're his fire team leader. Tell him to cut out the heroics. Remind him that excess losses come out of *our* pockets. His bullshit enthusiasm on Costla Four cost the squad damned near half our combat bonus."

"We'll have a talk," Smitty said.

Mumford kept close enough to hear but didn't intervene. This was as much a test for Rodriguez as it was for Smitty.

"You're damned straight you will," Rodriguez said, "if you ever want a third stripe. Take Corporals Eddings and Stevens with you. They both lost out on vacations thanks to him. Their wives were *pissed*. Have you seen Eddings' wife? When the first sergeant doesn't get his coffee or smokes first thing in the morning, he's still nicer than her when she's in a *good* mood."

Mumford smiled without smiling, a talent unique to senior NCOs.

"Yeah, I've seen her. Couldn't happen to a nicer guy."

"I told him not to marry an ex-stripper. But did he listen? Fuck no."

"I'll grab them, and we'll *counsel* Argent. Won't happen again, Sergeant."

"I'm counting on it."

*****

Chapter 1

Corporal Smitty had been around long enough to know how it worked. His fire team arrived at the platoon's ready room precisely on time, at 0600, then waited two and a half hours for the mission briefing to begin. *Hurry up and wait* would have described the life of ordinary soldiers throughout human history, a constant of every military that ever had, and ever would, exist. From the armies of Pharaoh to Earth forces of the 20th century, through their own contemporary Triarch Confederation Marine Corps, they were all the same. Junior enlisted were expected to tolerate the same bullshit over and over.

It was always the same; the battalion CO would inform senior staff of a 0730 start time. Those mid-level officers would then direct the company commanders and first sergeants to have the troops ready and online at 0645. Those same officers and staff noncoms—Mumford for one—relied on the performance of their troops for an excellent Annual Fitness Report. The AFR determined their compensation level for the following year, so they would then delegate responsibility to the smaller unit noncoms to have their platoons and sections online at 0600. Those noncoms would then pad the time further to ensure their own future promotions. To the average GI, that meant Reveille was at 0400 to meet a deadline 3-1/2 hours later that only required getting out of bed, donning a uniform, and eating chow.

Some things never changed. And that included Lance Corporal Argent.

"I'm losing rack time for this shit?" he said for the fourth time in the last fifteen minutes. Several others nodded in agreement. Feeling the all-seeing gaze of First Sergeant Mumford, Smitty decided he'd given them enough bitch time.

"Hey, Argent! Are you tired of being a lance corporal? You want to be a PFC again?"

Argent flushed red.

"Not really, Corp."

"Then shut the fuck up. The CO will be online when he's online, got it? This ain't the damned Navy! Sit down, shut up, and get some of that shuteye you're whining about missing, like the rest of us are trying to do."

Argent opened his mouth to say something, but saw the look on Smitty's face and started laughing.

"Aye, Corp. Sorry."

Smitty and Argent were best friends. Each man knew the other in a way only long-time comrades-in-arms could. The lance corporal knew when he could argue and when he couldn't. This was the latter, so Argent promptly stretched out across four of the folding chairs and closed his eyes.

All of them could sleep almost on command, but his best friend had taken it to a whole new level. That was no real surprise to Smitty. He and Argent had first met in third grade. Their natural mischievousness fed each other's talent for trouble, and during that first year of friendship, they spent more hours in the conference room next to the principal's office than in class. After that, they were inseparable. The only thing that had ever slowed Argent down was his uncanny ability to sleep anywhere.

Two hours later, the words "First Sergeant" brought Smitty and Fire Team Bravo to instant alertness, as it did everyone else in the ready room. Thankfully, Sergeant Rodriguez had stayed awake and on the lookout for trouble. Within moments, the 44 members of 2nd Platoon were upright in their chairs. Only a few seconds passed before the doors parted, and First Sergeant Mumford stalked down the center aisle, not even looking from side to side as he walked through the four squads to the front of the room, where an old, beat-up lectern stood.

The thing looked like it had been salvaged from a planetside junkyard, although it seemed new compared to the first sergeant. He claimed to have joined the Triarch's Marines when "Christ was a corporal," the kind of man who would have been Caesar's most trusted centurion, or one of Chesty Puller's unwavering Marines on Guadalcanal, way back on Earth. Despite his age, he regularly bested every single member of the platoon in close-combat sparring. And he usually did so in a most painful manner.

No one had the balls to ask him his actual age.

"Listen up," he intoned, "the CO is about to come online. I don't want to hear so much as a breath in this room until she's finished."

Smitty watched Mumford's every move, memorizing everything the man did. Mumford didn't bother to ask if everyone understood. If anything, First Sergeant Mumford was very self-aware. He knew that, to a man, the troops feared him. But he also knew that he would gladly charge any enemy position with them at his back. Even new transfers got the word most ricky-tick from existing unit members when they reported in for duty. Those who didn't somehow seemed to draw the dubious privilege of facing Mumford in the sparring ring. Without fail, that experience adjusted their attitude to one of enthusiastic and instantaneous compliance.

As if on cue, the large video monitor hanging on the wall near the lectern came to life. It bore the image of a woman with severe features and the same close-cropped hair they all wore. It was Captain Downey, the Dog Company CO. Like the first sergeant, she was a commander of few words and came right to the point.

"Good afternoon, warriors of the 3rd Spear. A dispute has arisen on the independent world of Luda."

The screen switched to the image of a vast star chart. On it were clearly marked the worlds of the Triarch Confederacy, including their own world, Earth, in the Sol system; the Rigel System; and the Confederacy's newest member, the Proxima System. On the other side of the map, but still within the same arm of the Milky Way, were several systems labeled as members of the Kelmari Union.

The Union was made up of an alien race, or perhaps multiple races. Very little was known of them other than what seemed to be their hostility to humans. Between the Kelmari Union and the Triarch Confederacy lay a no-man's land, a mutually agreed-upon segment of space where no fewer than a dozen unaligned systems served as a buffer between the two antagonists. Those systems were populated by outcasts of both great societies. It was essentially what the old vids called "the Wild West." A state of perpetual cold proxy war existed there between the Confederacy and the Kelmari, which occasionally flared into small firefights that maintained the status quo stalemate.

Because of the vast distances and the never-realized goal of FTL travel, almost all contact between the two races was through intermediary technology. The human race had long ago developed FTL *communications*, and that technology allowed a person's consciousness to be temporarily uploaded into a quantum computer substrate. Once there, it could be transmitted via the FTL comm system to another substrate light years away, with time intervals never more than a few minutes.

At first, this technology was used purely for exploration and to keep the three human systems woven together in the Confederacy. It wasn't as good as physically being there, but you were only limited by the capabilities of the mechanical simulacrum you were being uploaded into. Some closely resembled actual humans, with skin, hair, and scent indistinguishable from real people. Those cost big time, and the wealthiest citizens used them extensively. After all, why take the time and risk to travel when you could simulate the experience without leaving home? But as with any new technology, it didn't take long for the military to recognize its tactical potential.

The Confederation quickly developed various designs of mechanized war machines to weaponize the tech. Most designs were in a form not dissimilar to that of a spider. As if a mechanical spider wasn't intimidating enough, they ranged in size from 9-inch diameter units—for stealthy reconnaissance missions—to heavily armored weapons platforms up to 30 feet across in different styles. Some were mobile artillery pieces used only for stand-off indirect fire. Others acted as mules, carrying weapon reloads or bringing home disabled units. The remainder were assault units equipped with particle beam or railgun weapons in various configurations as needed. All boasted small fusion power plants to meet their power-hungry demands.

After all, AI-guided drones could only do so much in the complex battlefields of 24th-Century warfare. The experiments with so-called self-aware AIs had, of course, ended badly, and nobody wanted to risk the near-extinction of the human race again.

Best of all, with a few design tweaks, the mechanical warrior bearing a human consciousness could overcome all the hurdles of unfriendly environments on far-flung worlds, with their varying atmospheres, temperatures, pressures, flora, fauna, and gravities, without endangering the operator. Some of those worlds were gas or liquid giants with little to no terrestrial battlefield to speak of.

The Kelmari lacked the technology to match the Confederacy in this respect. They still had to train, transport, and suffer losses with fully biological soldiers. The only things working in their favor were the proximity of several worlds with large populations and their species' faster reproductive and growth cycles.

The basis of the design for the Spiders was the same everywhere. This was crucial because it allowed Marines operating the platforms to train within defined operational limits. A unit could be on the march within minutes of transmittal. The only thing that varied from unit to unit was the operator's name stenciled on the exterior. That was one of those quirky throwbacks to an earlier age when warriors had climbed into fighter planes to do battle. As an operator transmitted from their home base, they would be mated with a Spider substrate. One of the first tasks the onsite techs would perform was to paint the operator's name on the unit.

All the units were fitted with an auto-transfer device that would return the operator's consciousness to the local computer hub, where it could either be reloaded into another Spider almost immediately, or transmitted to a new location, usually homeward in the Confederacy.

The auto-return device was a game-changer, greatly reducing the need to hire and train new Marines. The brain boxes, as the techs and Marines called them, were tucked well inside the mech, protected by a heavily armored casing. Only a few weapons, such as a nuclear warhead, were capable of a hit devastating enough to prevent the 'brain box' from transmitting the operator's consciousness homeward. Only then would the actual operator be lost, as their consciousness failed to transfer quickly enough from the mech it inhabited.

Captain Downey continued, "For those unaware, during the last several decades, we and the Kelmari have maintained small military outposts on Luda. We've mostly left each other alone, with us keeping only a single battalion of Spiders in storage bunkers as forward-deployed replacements. The human locals have learned to stay clear of the bunker's general area due to its automated defenses… only the garrison maintenance company knows its specific location on the southern continent."

Using her wristband controller, Captain Downey initiated a holographic 3-D map of the planet, slowly rotating above the company's heads. On it, she highlighted the location of the human base. Manipulating the control again caused the names and population numbers of both species to appear for the three major cities and a score of small towns. Finally, several solid red dots indicated the locations of known Kelmari bases. A blinking red cursor hovered over a remote area about 100 miles to the east of their base, well within the normally accepted space each race maintained for military installations.

"The Kelmari have managed to get a foothold within striking distance. They could hit us with almost no advance warning. And we have reliable intelligence from inside the Kelmari compounds that they're planning something big, something designed to hurt us very badly. The nature of this threat is unknown."

Argent, being Argent, couldn't resist the opportunity to kiss the captain's ass by volunteering a question.

"Why is that a problem, Ma'am?"

Being interrupted mid-briefing should have brought the smartassed lance corporal a smackdown. Most COs wouldn't tolerate it, but Captain Downey wasn't most commanding officers. Smitty watched her smile at the opportunity to show off what she believed was her incredible wealth of knowledge to the entire company.

"The person who provided us with this information died in the doing. And while Luda isn't a member system of the Confederacy, it is a major exporter of some rare elements we need to support many of our current technologies. Without them, we risk falling behind the Kelmari in our ability to project power across this part of the galaxy. If they were able to take out our base there, it would be decades before we could build up enough military capability to take it back and restore the flow of those resources."

Captain Downey replaced the rotating globe with a holographic map of the area within a 250-mile radius of the Confederacy base. This map was topographic.

"Our base occupies relatively flat terrain near Luda's equator, with this mountain range to the north. These peaks are relatively low compared to the Himalayas or the Rockies. To the south is the ocean. We've got this river running north and south between us. Near the ocean is this large river estuary and wetland area. If you've ever been to the Everglades in Florida, you know what that's like. Only the local fauna is a lot bigger than an alligator and seems willing to eat anything, even one of our Spiders, so we'll avoid that area if possible."

The Kelmari outpost began to blink.

"Our primary mission is to recon this enemy outpost and discover why the Kelmari are willing now, after sixty quiet years on Luda, to poke the bear."

"Grr..." somebody growled.

"Exactly," Downey said. "But this mission isn't offensive in nature. We're going in to get answers, not to kill people or break things. ROEs are to respond only if fired upon. Then, if headquarters doesn't like the answers we find, we may receive orders to violently prosecute this intrusion into our area of influence." Pausing, she looked around the room. The expression seemed more like that of a quartermaster in a logistics meeting than of a combat officer. "Any questions? No? Good. We deploy tomorrow at 0730 local time. Clear up anything you have going on here and get yourself ready to transmit. Don't be late."

Sensing that the briefing had come to an end, the first sergeant rose from his seat.

"You heard the captain; get your asses moving. NPA in one hour!"

Amid a series of low groans, the entire company exited the room through three sets of double doors. Once in the hallway, Argent grabbed Smitty by the arm and pulled him to one side.

"NPA? What's up with that?"

Smitty could only shake his head. Neurological Phase-Alignment was the official Triarch Manual designation for the two-hour transition meditation designed to lower the Marine's heart rate and "quiet" biological feedback loops so the mind could more easily decouple from the body and merge with the quantum substrate. Marines called it the Hum-Drum, a reference to the low-frequency acoustic hum played in the ready rooms to assist with meditation and the general "drumming" sensation in the ears as the neural jacks begin to prime. Jack Heads, common slang for Space Marines, often said they were "going to the drum" when heading to the meditation pods. The term referred to the permanent surgical neural jacks behind the right ear.

In answer to Argent's question, Smitty spread his hands.

"Must be some do-gooder politician looking after our psychological welfare again."

"I wish they'd stop it," Argent said.

*****

Chapter 2

Smitty's mind wandered as he waited for his turn in the line. Mentally calculating the combat bonus he'd receive from this mission, he thought about what to spend it on. His reverie was shattered by First Sergeant Mumford screaming in his direction.

"Smitty, get your head out of your ass and get in your pod!"

Giving a dirty glance to Argent, behind him in line and snickering, Smitty stepped toward his assigned pod. Also called a tube, the device was already open. Lights flickered as it ran various diagnostics.

The process always reminded Smitty of something Argent had said during Basic Training.

"We're the meat filling in high-tech hot dogs."

It was funny because it was true.

Without a word, the tech began making various connections to Smitty's body, starting with the cardio-pulmonary monitor and control probes. Together with his medulla oblongata, the machines would keep his physical body alive after transmission of his higher consciousness occurred. Meanwhile, the digital essence of what made him *him* would occupy the brain box inside the fighting mech itself, light years away on Luda.

The heavily armored casing of the brain box lay deep within the mech's chassis. It housed the quantum computer substrate where the Marine's consciousness resided after transmission; destruction of the brain box meant the death of the Marine. Therefore, it was the most resilient component of the Spider, with shielding designed to protect the substrate from nearly any battlefield damage, ensuring that even if the mech was shredded, the brain box remained intact long enough to trigger the automatic homeward transmission of the operator's consciousness.

To Smitty's left and right were a dozen long lines of Marines undergoing the same passage. His fire team had done this dozens of times in training until their first combat action a year ago. Now they were seasoned veterans, and it was routine.

Finally, all the connections were made except for the last one. This one was a bundle of fiber optic cables that "he" would quite literally pass through. According to the Triarch Confederacy Manual, the official nomenclature for their unique mind was the Neural Signature Construct, or NSC, an intentional sterilization of the procedure. When the brass talked about casualties, they referred to "the loss of an NSC," treating the human soul as a data asset. Bodies left behind when the brain was destroyed during combat operations were officially no longer considered human, since they were no longer cognitively independent, and therefore became disposable.

As with all things Marine, the Jack-Heads had slang for their own consciousness once it had left the "meat-space" of their physical body; to them, their transferred consciousness was their Ghost Load. The biggest danger beyond combat was poor connectivity.

Make sure the brain box is sealed tight. I don't want my Ghost leaking out into the vacuum because of some microscopic integrity failure.

They all had a surgically implanted jack behind their right ear that the bundle connected to. With a small push and a twist, the tube tech ensured that Smitty's connection was solid. He didn't seem satisfied, however, and turned to a small touch-screen control panel on the side of the tube. Tapping it a few times, then pursing his lips, the tech finally proclaimed that Smitty was good to go.

Smitty called out over the fire team's comm, "See you ghosts on the other side, Bravo!" a moment before the tube's lid swung silently downward until fully engaged with the tube itself. There was a slight lurch as the tube began to move into the storage rack that would sustain its power supply. Through the tube's lid, he could only see a portion of the rack and the backside of the tube. A soft female voice prompted him to "Prepare for transition."

The experts all swore that the brevity of transmittance meant the user would have no sense of passing time, but whoever said that had never experienced the process. Not everyone noted changes, but for those who recalled the passage, most described a sense of swirling light, with shapeless forms passing by to either side. A few mentioned a bright pipeline, perhaps like a subway.

Smitty belonged to the first group, and within the microseconds in which events took place, his brain immediately noted something different. Something *wrong.* It happened beyond the speed of conscious thought, so that only later did he understand what had happened.

Forms passed by as everything cascaded in a swirling vortex. He "saw" other shapes, but greenish rather than the normal white, grotesque and distinct, as if… *real.* And then came a violent lurch as his mind pushed into the quantum substrate. He was there, where he should be, and yet…

Something was wrong. His mind bounced off invisible walls in a darkness that shouldn't have been there, then as quickly as it had happened, all became still, and the standard mind-up-interface manifested itself as a thing to be seen, although he knew quite well that he was not actually seeing anything other than what the substrate and the Spider's sensors presented to him as sight, sound, and smell.

Suddenly, the physical world snapped into focus as those sensors came fully online. As usual, there was a tech presence inside the interface. Not a physical person, but a holographic one. Once, they'd been AIs, but like all AIs given too much responsibility, that too had turned to shit. Now the techs were the multigenerational descendants of colonizers who'd departed the Sol System hundreds of years prior, housed in a secure base somewhere in human-controlled space.

"How are you doing, Corporal?" the tech said.

"That was rough."

Smitty heard himself through the Spider's voice module. His virtual heads-up display identified the mech as a Raptor TC-42, Serial Number AY-35. The TC-42 was the favorite of most operators, as it possessed a deadly combination of speed and firepower, its weaponry vastly outpunching anything in the other classes except mobile artillery. Best of all, it had a top speed of 84 mph on dry land. For some reason, though, he had no ammunition load or charged capacitors. Running dry in a combat zone? That made no sense, unless there was no imminent danger to the base.

"No one else reported anything unusual," the tech responded. "Rough… how so?"

"Why is this machine not ready for combat?"

"Do I look like I'm ordnance? I'm a neuro-tech, Corporal. Now, please, answer my question."

"Everything went green mid-transfer, and it felt like I slammed into a wall at the end."

Sometimes, cowards or burned-out veterans used transfer errors to avoid combat, and the tech clearly didn't believe him. "I'll make a note. Get moving." The tech pointed off to his right.

Smitty felt the familiar sensation of feedback provided by the substrate as he extended the Spider's six limbs and scuttled off the small platform… with a difference. There was a shimmering edge to objects, and what he could only describe as an "itching" inside his head. It all *seemed* right, but also different.

The mech's lethality gave him confidence. Four legs provided locomotion, while two arms handled weapons. Rocket launchers mounted atop the shoulders provided additional firepower. Unlike the heavier TC-45, the TC-42 had less armor, but was much, much faster.

Smitty queried his sensors, reaching outward for the familiar comm channel he shared with the rest of the company, but there was no response. Looking around, he realized there were no other Spiders in sight. He was in a small chamber with unfamiliar machines and several passages leading away. Disoriented though he was, Smitty went into high alert mode.

What in the fucking hell is this?

Moving cautiously, Smitty turned the corner into a passageway… and stopped. Half a dozen Kelmari worked busily over several Spider mechs.

The creatures stood on three limbs, while two others moved with astonishing precision across the Spiders' various control surfaces. Each alien body was a low disk of gray flesh, streaked with bluish-green veins, while the five muscular arms radiated like spokes from a wheel. A ring of five glossy black eyes encircled the top of each body, one on each side of the head, and another facing upward. None turned toward the human as much as they subtly rotated, bringing different limbs forward as needed. The effect was unsettling, as if the creatures were both facing him and not facing him at the same time.

Honed reflexes took over. Smitty sent the command to arm his weapons… then remembered with horror that the magazines were empty and his particle beam weapons were offline.

Shit, shit, shit…

Then the nearest Kelmari spoke in a reasonable facsimile of Sol Standard. "How was the transmission?"

Smitty froze. "Huh?"

"Do you not understand your own language?"

"Huh, what?"

An unmistakable tone of anger colored the alien's response.

"I know you humans are stupid, but pay close attention! Remember, we hold your family, and you will either cooperate fully in these trials, or your family will suffer for your obstinacy."

Families? Fully armed, Smitty would have smoked the fuckers on the spot… yet there was obviously something going on that Smitty didn't understand. Outnumbered and unarmed, he decided to stall until he figured it out.

Then a thought came. Smitty turned the sensors inward to analyze the TC-42; his eyes widened when he realized what must have happened. The Spider his mind now inhabited wasn't synced to the Triarch Confederacy. It might have been at one time, but it had since been heavily modified and now bore a transponder marking it as Kelmari hardware. Added to that, the aliens acted like they expected him…

"I… I—" was all he managed to stammer. "I'm sorry, please forgive me."

"I refer you to my question."

"Uh, the transmission? Fine, yes, everything was fine."

The Kelmari was now visibly perturbed and wobbled over to a nearby console. Its gait was like a wobbling plate.

"So you say. Let us review the transmission data."

Focused on the screen in front of it, the Kelmari appeared to study it briefly before calling over several others of his race. One who somehow appeared older to Smitty—perhaps it was the slight frame and leaning posture—spoke in the click-whistle language of its race. The modified mech had a built-in translator, which must have been installed by the Kelmari.

"Look there," it said, indicating something on the screen, "this distortion of the signal."

The original tech responded, "We will need to go back through the data at nanosecond intervals and try to isolate the source." Turning toward Smitty, it approached the Spider with a data pad in hand, fiddling with the readout and controls displayed there. "For now, all appears fine. We do not need the unit here to complete our data review. Let's get it armed up and on the topside. Have him run through the exercise with the others, and then send me a dump with all the data. We may never find the cause, but let us at least try."

With that, the tech turned away, and one of the guards motioned to Smitty. This alien had a more elongated body, three distinct legs, and two defined arms with shoulders. The head matched the other Kelmari.

"Follow me to the armory," it said in Sol Standard.

The trip to the armory was a silent one, giving him scant minutes, maybe seconds, to figure out his situation.

They mentioned interference with a transmission. I transmitted, so how could they know that? Or...

No, it wasn't possible. The solution his brain developed would have required a coincidence beyond calculation, so how could it be? Yet nothing else explained the dilemma.

Were the Kelmari uploading at the same instant the Confederacy was transmitting me to Luda? Did my signal somehow overwrite that of the original human whose place I took? And what does that mean for me?

The only thing he knew for sure was that he had to play along with it for now and see what happened, although knowing those assholes at S-3, this was just a training simulation, and they were playing games with his mind to see how he'd react.

Yeah, that must be the answer. This is all a test. Maybe some new potential sergeant's evaluation.

Even as the thought crossed his mind, Smitty knew it wasn't true.

After a short ride up a few floors on what amounted to a freight elevator, the door slid open to reveal what looked like an armory, albeit unlike others he'd seen. Strange weaponry filled racks lining the walls, most with multiple handles. In the center of the large rectangular space stood a 20-foot square raised platform, elevated two feet above the surrounding floor.

Nearby, another Kelmari tech hunched over a console, impatiently waving him forward. Unlike the other aliens, whose voices sounded more or less normal, this one spoke with a harsh, squishing sound.

"Your movements are sluggish, human! In your own vernacular, move your ass!"

The TC-42 weighed in at a little over 1,200 pounds but was designed to be fast and nimble. With a short hop, Smitty directed the Spider onto the platform, where the tech immediately began loading the shoulder-mounted rocket launchers, then inserted racks of magazines containing various types of ammunition. He received everything from small-caliber rounds to various types of grenades, and even some short anti-armor missiles. Lights throughout his display changed from red to green.

Meanwhile, the tech grumbled in his own language to the guard who'd brought Smitty to the armory, apparently forgetting or oblivious to the mech's onboard translator.

"What are they thinking, Siggeston? Nobody tells me anything. They keep sending me more of these things, and there are already more than a hundred of them topside. It would help me do my job if the superiors informed me of operations."

The guard responded with what Smitty guessed was the human equivalent of a shrug.

"You know more than me. I am a guard; they do not tell me much."

Now the armorer was carefully mating up some electronic connections on either side of the Spider's thorax. Smitty recognized them as the capacitors that would power his particle beam weaponry. It looked like he was getting a full load-out.

Why?

Feeling a knot in his guts, he was pretty sure of the answer, which the tech verified with his next words.

"Using humans to fight for us is doomed to fail; that's what I think."

Uneasy, the guard squirmed.

"I do not ask such questions, Technician Vor."

"That was not a question, and we are friends, Siggeston. You need not use my formal title. We've held them off for thirty breeding cycles using Kelmari forces, as we should be. *We* are bred for combat."

"I am not. Neither are you."

"You know what I mean, the Warrior Class. But suddenly, they have lost the will to absorb more casualties. First, they made us disassemble and repair these captured mechs, which are inferior to our own, then they forced us to train these humans. Now here we are, arming them with our most advanced weapons."

"Aren't these human weapons?"

"Upgraded by us, my friend. At least they only selected humans with families... you know how they are about their offspring. If they so much as think about disobedience, their mate and children will be served as fresh food in the dining hall."

"Fresh? Still alive?"

"The youngest are quite soft... very delicious."

A grotesque splitting of the technician's face could only have been the Kelmari version of a smile. It took all Smitty's restraint not to arm his weapons and turn the technician into soup... but he didn't. Horrible as the words were, there was a bigger picture here.

Completing its job, the technician leaned forward so that its face filled the forward vid sensor of Smitty's Spider.

"Isn't that right, human?" it said, reverting to Sol Standard. "You will do anything to keep your precious offspring from becoming Kelmari shit, won't you?"

Smitty bobbed the Spider slightly up and downward in the standard non-verbal sign of acknowledgment.

The Kelmari tech quickly replaced and secured the Spider's access hatches. Stepping back to give his work a second quick review, the armorer was finally satisfied and nodded to the guard.

"He is now ready to die for the glory of the empress."

*****

Chapter 3

Somehow, Smitty's transmittance to Luda had ended with his occupancy of a Spider in the possession of the Kelmari, rather than friendly forces. He'd heard stories of people transmitting and never arriving; everybody had, but he'd written them off as late-night lies involving bourbon. Yet here he was, inhabiting a fully armed Spider, riding in a freight elevator with a Kelmari guard squad.

The ride took 27 minutes, 14 seconds, according to the mech's time log. None of the Kelmari spoke during the trip, which gave Smitty time to think. Recon and intelligence gathering were part of Marine basic training, so he took in every detail. Even with no way to determine the depth of the facility, he knew it would take nothing less than a penetrator strike from orbit to destroy it. Then the elevator lurched to a stop, punctuated by metal-on-metal shrieking in protest.

The doors opened to reveal a short corridor with a blank wall at the opposite end. As they approached, the wall split into equal halves that silently slid into each side, despite being two feet thick.

Hardened against conventional weapons. Add a nuclear warhead to the penetrator.

Stepping to one side, a guard marked by a blue ring around its thick neck pointed across a large area. The Sol words sounded harsh to Smitty's ears, but his translator handled them easily enough.

"Report to the officer-in-charge at the far end of the exercise yard. Do not delay, human filth."

Careful not to appear unsure, which might give him away, Smitty urged the Spider into a trot. He had to admit, the neural connectors did seem more responsive than usual after whatever modifications the Kelmari had made to them.

Moving quickly to the "exercise yard" meant crossing a devastated landscape. Ruined buildings, crashed and shot-up vehicles, debris, shattered pavement… the whole place was identical to the advanced training mock-ups back in the Confederacy. Staged, of course. The buildings were empty shells, the holes in the streets too round, the vehicles too neatly arranged; the training yard replicated a city. Standard stuff. But not a Kelmari city, a *human* one. The building proportions and materials matched those on any planet in the Confederacy. An ominous feeling crept over him.

The Kelmari are planning to fight on human worlds. Not contested planets like Luda, human ones. Confederacy worlds.

Shit.

Passing between two relatively intact structures, Smitty finally saw a large, bowl-like amphitheater with a gathered force of Spiders. Beyond that space stood an untouched building that looked familiar in his memory, but he couldn't quite place it. Checking his virtual heads-up display, or VHUD, he saw that the force below him was roughly equal to an augmented company of 150 Marine Spiders.

His large-unit comm line crackled to life with a message from someone claiming to be the company CO.

"AY-35, join your fire team!"

Again referring to his VHUD, Smitty found a flashing icon providing a rally point in the amphitheater where his small unit was located. Nobody acknowledged him. Soon after, the large-unit comm line opened as the company commander came online.

"All right, remember the briefing. Our families are counting on us to prove we can do this. If we fail today… well… I don't have to tell you what will happen. The waypoints and rally locations are all in your VHUDs. Move to your IPs and let's run the exercise smartly this time. New people, keep up. Do not fuck this up. *Dismissed!"*

There was no time to wonder who was in the other Spiders, where they came from, or who could be trusted. Unit cohesion would be nonexistent.

Each soldier's VHUD flashed their initial point, the jump-off point to begin their assault on the objective. Smitty was behind the curve, so he commanded his Spider to move on its own to the IP while he quickly reviewed the exercise briefing he'd missed. It seemed to be a straightforward assault plan until he came to the overall objective… and blinked in shock. Their target was nothing less than the Confederate House of Law, back on Earth. Twenty-three light years from the Friction Zone, the contested space separating the combatants, the Kelmari were taking direct aim at the center of the Confederacy's power.

The company's mission was to obliterate anything and everything in their way, plant a simulated bomb of some sort, and then fight to defend it to the end. The plan was to pre-program their auto-return devices to transmit them to a Kelmari hub moments before detonation of the device.

Except the Kelmari didn't have transmission technology… or did they?

There was only one possible conclusion. Somehow, the Kelmari had reverse-engineered the technology and found a way to transmit soldiers to Earth itself. There, they would auto-load into Spiders, fight their way through the unsuspecting security forces, and assault the capital. Humanity's best weapons would be turned against them.

Like any Marine, Smitty held no love for any of the politicians who controlled the Confederacy. They were corrupt—everybody knew that—but he accepted politicians as a necessary evil. A strike like this would devastate the Confederacy's ability to wage war for months, maybe years. The Kelmari would surely have other plans in motion to take advantage of such a devastating strike. Humans were likely to lose several independent worlds to the Union. For that matter, the Pegasus System itself might be in danger.

One impulse suddenly dominated his thoughts.

I've gotta get the fuck outa here.

* * *

Smitty's attention snapped back to the present as his VHUD flashed the command to begin the assault. Unlike his own fire team, this company had five in each team and fifteen per squad. Here, he was presumably a private, since nobody had assigned him a rank. Whoever was in charge of his team led their advance through the "city." Ahead and above them, the 4th squad, consisting of the smaller recon Spiders, was leaping from rooftop to rooftop, providing a constant stream of recon photos and data. They were barely 100 yards into the assault when "enemy" positions began to resist them.

It felt wrong, fighting against "Confederacy" forces, and Smitty knew that in a real attack, it would be impossible for him to think of the defenders as enemies. Once he somehow figured out how to get home, after warning his buddies, these Kelmari-humans better not try to get past him. Unlike these people, he and his fire team were real Marines. Now, however, he fought like hell.

Automated defending units in static positions were being operated remotely by Kelmari techs. The Spider to Smitty's right was suddenly ripped apart by an explosion that threw it up and over.

Fuck me, they're using live ammo.

His team leader screamed over the unit channel.

"Farrell is down! Close up the gap and take out that position."

Smitty never hesitated. While his Spider continued to advance in leaps and bounds, dodging incoming fire, he used his VHUD to select an anti-armor missile from the magazine. In mid-jump, he launched at a window that ballistic rounds were coming from.

"Missile away!"

Verbally reporting the launch was unnecessary; everyone in the unit would have it automatically reported to them via their VHUDs, but old habits die hard.

Smitty's Spider had landed in front of the building as his missile tore into it. A massive blast blew out the windows. Pressure would have killed anybody within.

"Helluva shot," his fire team leader said. *"Best we've seen so far. What's your name, Soldier?"*

That's Marine to you, buddy.

"Cor—" He caught himself. "Smitty."

"Keep it up, Corsmitty."

Smitty mentally grinned. Once they'd eliminated all defenses, the company CO resumed overall command.

"All units, dig in where you are. Hold the perimeter while the device is placed." And that was exactly what they did. The roles shifted, and now they were playing defense.

Combat intensity increased. Multiple enemy positions that had been dormant as they passed by were now brought online. The firefight was both real and deadly. Spiders to his left and right were struck and taken offline, their drivers killed. Smitty poured back answering fire, as he'd done a thousand times before.

"Cease fire, cease fire! All units cease fire."

After a few final desultory shots, the shooting stopped.

"Good job, everyone! We have a few damaged Spiders. Everyone, pitch in and help get them back to the Armory for repair."

Before or after cleaning out what's left of their drivers?

Another flashing icon appeared on Smitty's VHUD along with a message that read, ASSIST IN TRANSPORTING THE DUMMY DEVICE BACK TO THE ARMORY.

During the fight, a squad of Spiders had moved a triangular metal shape to the capitol building's front steps. The Kelmari's impressive attention to detail extended to what appeared to be an exact replica of the device involved… a U930.

A fucking U930!

The single most destructive bomb in the Confederacy's arsenal.

Smitty had only seen a U930 once, and he would never forget the moment. After all, there was a reason it was called the "Planet Killer."

Detonation would reduce Earth to a memory.

*****

Chapter 4

The elevators couldn't handle moving the entire company underground all at once, so Smitty had plenty of time to think. Clearly, the Kelmari planned to use one of the planet killers. But how did they intend to get one? He was only a Marine corporal, but even at such a low security clearance, he knew security around a U930 surpassed that of any other ordnance. Try as he might, Smitty could only come up with one answer: a traitor.

His turn came. Nobody accompanied him down, as there wasn't room for a second Spider. Impossible as it seemed, he somehow had to warn the Confederacy. Had the exercise not emptied his magazines, Smitty might have tried to shoot his way out. But then what?

Soon enough, he disembarked on a lower floor, where techs completed the umbilical connection between the Spider and their hub. There was no way of knowing what came next, since Smitty's physical body was light years away on Earth. He fought down a moment of panic before his consciousness once again spiraled downward. Opening his eyes, he found himself within a small chamber, not unlike the tubes they used on Earth.

This version of the suspension system featured a cover that slid back and upward. A Kelmari approached him with his hand outstretched. Smitty could no longer contain his fear. Grabbing the extended hand at its wrist, he twisted upward, pulling it closer to his own body while applying pressure to the creature's elbow.

The Kelmari cried out, "Let go, human! I am not trying to hurt you; I only want to remove the monitoring connections!"

Smitty wasn't sure what was more surprising to him, the Kelmari's reaction, or the sound that came from his own mouth. Or that he *had* a mouth. Because how had he become corporeal?

"Oh, uh, sorry about that. You surprised me."

What the hell is up with my voice?

But he knew. Almost as quickly as the thought came, he knew. Somehow, some way, Smitty was now inhabiting someone else's body.

"This is weird," he said, rotating his arms and looking at them like the foreign things they were.

"What is strange to you? Wait, are you the transmission that experienced the unknown interference?"

Oh, shit.

"Me? Oh, it's not that," he said quickly. "It's just disorienting, going from the mech interface back into my own body again."

The Kelmari stared back at him in that strange, unblinking way of theirs.

"That is understandable. No others have reported this sensation, though. Does it pose a problem that should be investigated? I can append your records with the information."

"No, I'm good. It just caught me by surprise. Really, I'm fine. And grateful for your attention."

"As you should be."

Smitty stood up and looked around. Other humans were walking away from the tubes toward a single exit to their left. Hoping it was the correct thing to do, he followed them.

Following the other humans, Smitty found himself in what was clearly a mess hall. A line was formed, specialized machines ladled preset portions of something resembling food onto metal trays, and Smitty joined them. Burnished steel counters reflected the ambient white lighting. In it, Smitty could see a young man with red hair and an athletic build. It took a moment to realize this was the body, the one he now inhabited. Right above the breast pocket was a name: REEVES.

* * * * *

Chapter 5

In his heart of hearts, First Sergeant Mumford had never fully trusted the idea of digital transference. Without question, it lowered casualties and worked well… when it worked. But when it went wrong, it went *very* wrong.

Under his careful scrutiny, Lance Corporal Argent and the rest of Fire Team Bravo prepped their Spiders for deployment, ensuring that all systems were nominal and ammo was fully topped off. After the transmission errors, they had to endure a long day of testing. Marines, even those who were just disembodied consciousnesses, weren't built to sit around.

Fire Team Bravo was more than ready for a fight. Nobody knew what had happened to their fire team leader, who hadn't completed the transmission, but also wasn't back in his physical body. The technicians were baffled, and while no one would say it out loud, Mumford knew Smitty was lost. Who could say where? Maybe that was the worst part, because every warrior deserved a proper sendoff. They could bury his body, but without a mind, was it truly the person?

"Dog Company, saddle up!" Mumford said loudly, but without yelling. God help the Marine who didn't hear him. "We have an alpha-level strike package. This is not a drill. No more tests, it's take and break time. We'll brief en route. Argent, get your people moving."

The first sergeant had temporarily appointed Argent as Bravo Fire Team Leader, but there'd been no time to settle into the role before they received an immediate alert from battalion headquarters.

Once outside, the company formed up. Lift units swooped in, hovering over a Spider, while techs rushed in to make the magnetic connections. Finally, the entire company was suspended from their lift units and began moving rapidly to the east. Luda shared much in common with Earth, so the experience mirrored training exercises in the Amazon basin. Inside each Spider, the VHUDs came to life with target maps. Every unit's IP was indicated, and routes of ingress were highlighted, along with known and/or suspected enemy positions.

First Sergeant Mumford kicked off the briefing.

"All right, you Meat Puppets, listen up! As the captain told you the other day, we have… or *had*… a human intel source working among the forced labor at the Kelmari facility. Somehow, they managed to smuggle out valuable intelligence to us about Kelmari intentions. It took the S-2 intel weenies a few days to sort it all out, and there's a lot to it they're still working through, but here's what we know for sure. The Kelmari are planning a major operation, and apparently, they've developed mechanical warrior technology similar to ours. So instead of slugging it out with their normal troops, we'll be facing mechs that look a lot like ours. In fact, they might even be the same. Ghostfeed has it they reverse-engineered some Spider units we thought destroyed."

A jumble of voices filled the comms channel, all tinged with concern and questions.

"Knock it off! I understand your concerns, but we still hold a significant advantage… namely, *you*. Or rather, your training. No matter how good their mechs might be, they haven't had time to train up to our level. These systems are only as good as the operator, and we hold the high ground there. Our goal today is to wipe that facility off the face of the planet. It would be an easy task for orbital bombardment, but that would leave us with nothing but a smoking crater. We need intelligence. How far along is the program, and how good are their mech platforms? That means we put boots on the ground to do the job. Any questions?"

Only a silent hiss carried over the comms.

"Drop zone approach in 2.5 minutes. Run your final system checks."

With that last command, Mumford dropped off the comms. Time to fight.

* * *

The improbability of his situation left Smitty disoriented. His mind kept coming back to the same conclusion: one glitch was bad luck, but this many stacked together felt impossible. He should have landed in a Confederacy Spider on Luda. Instead, he'd hit some green-lit nightmare in transit, wound up inside a Kelmari-held mech, and fooled them into thinking he belonged there. Any part of it might have made sense on its own. All of it together felt like the universe had shoved him into the one place where everything that could go wrong already had. It all felt so pre-ordained…

Alarms brought him back to reality. They blared throughout the Kelmari facility, lower-pitched but otherwise like an air-raid warning back on Earth. The station's intercom announced an incoming attack in both Kelmari and Sol Standard and ordered operators to their mechs. All around Smitty, humans and Kelmari alike broke into a run for the mess hall exits, heading back to the transference tubes. Smitty fell in with them. As his mind processed the situation, it swiftly veered toward panic.

Those incoming troops are my brothers. I can't *fight them.*

"Reeves!"

A human tech pointed toward an open tube. Smitty stumbled that way at half-speed, trying to think of a way to help his buddies. He was hardly lying down before the techs wired him up for the transfer into the mech, presumably AY-35 again.

"Hey, hold on," Smitty called out, but they paid no attention to him and lowered the canopy into place. The last thing he saw was the flashing beacon of the alert.

And then he was in the substrate. This time, the transmission had gone as expected. Nothing odd happened. One moment, he was attempting to get the tech's attention through the canopy glass, and the next, he was in the Spider's substrate. Autopilot took over and moved the mech toward the bank of elevators.

No slow-moving platforms now. Someone had dialed up the elevator's speed, so they disgorged Spiders onto the surface at a frenetic rate. In less than ten minutes, the entire company stood, forced into defensive positions, 148 Spiders, with Smitty's team on the far-left flank. Their mission objective was to deny that flank.

The Kelmari mech's comm systems tolerated a lot of nervous chatter that the Confederacy would never allow, probably due to inexperienced combat leadership, until the company commander finally cut it off. His voice betrayed a quaver but didn't crack.

"Silence! Bring all weapons online. They're only 200 meters out and coming fast!"

Smitty knew it was only a trick of the mind, but he would have sworn he could feel his heart beating its way out of his chest. Combat was his natural environment, but he'd never before fought against his own unit.

The Kelmari Spider troops were green, with no actual combat experience. Deploying them now was sheer desperation, a vain attempt to save the Kelmari facility, which he knew was already lost.

As he watched, Dog Company detached at speed and hit the ground moving. Doing that without snapping a leg required precise training, instantaneous reflexes that were part data-driven machine adaptation, and part skill… mostly human reflexes driven by muscle memory.

Fire discipline vanished at the first sight of the Confederacy lifters. There had been no assignments or creation of interlocking fields of fire among the Kelmari-trained humans, so everyone fired without coordination or planning. It wasn't a battle; it was a brawl.

The tide of the fight quickly swept over and around Fire Team 4, the quintet of Spiders Smitty was assigned to. He kept shooting wide and high, trying to make it look good for any Kelmari observers. Dust and smoke filled the air, so they all switched over to radar and thermal-vision sensors, relying on their various sensor platforms to find targets. You could tell the green Kelmari drivers' reactions were slow and clumsy compared to Dog Company. A welling pride filled the displaced Marine, knowing he'd been part of training them to be the best fighters in the Confederacy.

Smitty's VHUD began a warning indicating that he'd been painted by an incoming missile. Without thinking, he leaped as high as the Spider would allow. The missile impacted where he'd been standing and exploded, but on landing, he scurried away without waiting, barely dodging a second missile. The edge of a crater crumbled under his Spider's weight, causing him to slide sideways below ground level. Using his periscope allowed him to follow the battle until he could climb back up.

Only a single Confederate Spider was advancing nearby, and he saw it briefly as he tumbled back to the ground. Off to his right were the other four members of Fire Team 4, moving without coordination or purpose… but not for long. In a dizzying sequence of mechanical acrobatics, it closed with the Kelmari team and obliterated all four of them, but not before they all fired their particle beam weapons.

Normally, the Confederate Spiders could shrug off a hit from a particle beam. The mech's armor combined sacrificial ablative outer layers, low-density spaced armor, and dense refractory backing of tungsten, carbon-carbon composite, and advanced ceramics, all designed to absorb, disperse, and survive the beam's brutal heat. Against charged-particle attacks, magnetic and electrostatic shielding disrupted the beam before impact, while heat sinks, coolant loops, and phase-change materials bled off the remaining energy before it could cook the cockpit inside the hull.

But in a series of fluke coincidences, they all targeted the same Spider, and all four of the beams struck the Confederate mech in the same location. What should have merely damaged it instead cut through the armor and laid bare the machine's small fusion reactor. With its containment field down, the reactor went critical immediately. In an act of self-preservation, the Spider's system automatically ejected the reactor high into the air above them, where two seconds later, it blew up in something resembling a miniature supernova, smashing or vaporizing everything in a 500-meter radius.

Screams filled his comms, human screams of terror, of panic, of superheated death… the lucky ones died instantly.

Being inside a deep crater saved him. Still, the blast wave overhead had the effect of slamming his AY-35 hard into the ground. Heat melted part of the armor and knocked sensors offline. The effect was like being dropped from a height into a pit of fire.

In the seconds that followed, Smitty watched his machine reboot and run system checks; more amber offline indicators filled his display than green operational ones. AY-35 was badly damaged, maybe beyond repair. Barely a quarter of his sensor package functioned.

Somehow, three of the Spider's four legs dragged AY-35 out of the crater. From what Smitty could tell, the battle still raged to the north of his position, but everything around him had been fragged and flattened. He trained what remained of his sensors on the Confederate Spider that now lay half-covered in dirt and rocks. Without its reactor, it was running on battery power, with only a few minutes before it shut down completely. Its last act would be the transference of the pilot's consciousness back to the Confederate hub on Earth.

That's when Smitty knew what he had to do.

The intel he carried was both vital and urgent. Earth's very existence was on the line. He reacted accordingly.

The heavily damaged AY-35 struggled forward, off-center and unsteady, but moving, and came to rest two feet from the dying hulk of the Confederate Spider. Blackened armor hid most of its markings. Nobody fired at him; nobody called him. The battle had moved on.

Smitty *knew* things about Spiders, things that weren't exactly classified, but also weren't common knowledge. At the speed of thought, he loaded all the intelligence he'd gathered into a single data burst, one to override that of the Confederate pilot consciousness in the ruined Spider's brain box. It would eliminate the Marine from the retrieval algorithm, leaving him or her to die with their Spider, but that was one life being spent for the billions on Earth.

Quickly switching the comm protocols of his own Spider, he extended its presence outward until it forced its way into the Confederate system. The pilot inside the Spider must have noticed, because Smitty could sense their mind occupying its substrate, fighting him.

Who was it? The mini-nuke had fried the Spider's transponder array and blackened the hull. Melted armor blackened and distorted identification marks. Never a religious man, with his breathing accelerated and his mind overwhelmed with the urgency of the moment, he nevertheless mouthed a breath prayer for whomever he was about to kill.

With a flurry of mental commands left unspoken, so there was no chance the AI would get it wrong, he resisted the other pilot with everything he had in an effort to impose his will. The data stream would go through on its own if he could only force down the will of his comrade. Near the end of the struggle, he could feel the other pilot fading, fading… until a single coherent word penetrated Smitty's mind.

Calvin?

Then, opposition vanished. The digital packet went through. It seemed to last forever, but in reality, it only took a few nanoseconds. The timer countdown ended. The data was sent to the Confederate hub, and the human consciousness he'd been fighting vanished into the Aether… into nothing.

When the unit completely shut down, Smitty merely sat in his own heavily damaged Spider, unable to move at all. Having no physical body inside the machine, he could only wait to be recalled by the Kelmari.

Had he really done that? What gave him the right? Question after question from his conscience plagued him. He'd willingly taken the life of someone he served with, but not just anyone… only one person alive in the universe knew Smitty's old nickname, the one from his childhood.

Calvin.

The pilot of the Spider had been Lance Corporal Argent.

*****

Author Bios

William Alan Webb is an award-winning author and military historian known for blending sharp storytelling with real-world depth. A veteran of multiple genres, he writes fast-paced science fiction, fantasy, and thrillers. Webb also teaches writing, mentors authors, and explores the evolving role of storytelling in an age increasingly shaped by artificial intelligence. https://thelastbrigade.com/

Joseph Hower is a former active-duty Marine hailing from West Michigan. He and his wife share five children and four granddaughters. Now retired from a real-world career, he remains a professional musician of almost five decades and can often be found performing across West Michigan. He spends the remainder of his spare time traveling or tending to his lawn, garden, and smoker. You can find him through his author Facebook page, The Fiction of the Day, or via email at thefictionoftheday@gmail.com

#####

Soul Survivor by Michael LaVoice

A Meat Grinders Story

Chapter 1

The order from LT Schtick to assault the Honey Badger position wasn't met with enthusiasm, but we did it anyway, because we're Marines. We called the alien invaders Honey Badgers thanks to them bein' hard as hell to kill, and their general demeanor. We know they don't look like real honey badgers, or human beings, for that matter. More like furry lizards, if that makes any sense, except somebody said it and the name stuck.

The assault only lasted a few seconds before it ended. I don't know what the hell they hit us with, but whatever it was, it knocked us all back into our trench. We were lucky. 1st Platoon wasn't. They were completely wiped out, but I didn't know that at the time.

I lay in the mud at the bottom of our trench as my Mark III Predator battle suit rebooted several critical systems and ran a check on the others. I needed to know my platoon's status, and I needed it now.

"2nd Platoon, report!" I ordered as soon as the green light came up on my comms. A heavy rain began to fall. It always seemed to be rainin' on this damned rock. The briefin' on this planet said it received more annual rainfall than an Earth made of Oregons.

"1st Squad here, Gunny," SGT Parnell called out, *"all present, but Simmons is down. Need a corpsman."*

"Copy that, Parnell, sendin' Rodgers your way, but have your grenadier lay down some hate at the enemy to cover his approach," I replied.

"Copy," Parnell answered.

A moment later, a round of shots from an arm-mounted grenade launcher sent our reply to whatever new doomsday weapon the Honey Badgers had hit us with. I didn't think it would do them any harm, but maybe it would keep their damn heads down so Rodgers could get to Simmons.

"Gunny Slade," LT Schtick said on our private command channel, *"1st Platoon is gone. We're all that's left. We have to take this enemy position down."*

"That's wonderful news, sir," I replied, "how do you recommend we do that?"

"I was about to ask you the same question, Gunny," the LT said. *"Direct frontal assault was a bad idea."*

"Glad to hear you admit that, sir," I said.

"It wasn't mine," he informed me. *"That came from the captain, who's now no longer with us. It's up to us, now."*

"Lemme get back to you once I've got casualty reports from the rest of the platoon," I said before shuttin' off the private channel.

LT "Schtick up his ass" was gonna get us all killed. He can claim the idea was the captain's all day long as a CYA move, but I was in the command staff meetin' where he first brought it up. He's always thought the Honey Badgers could be taken down with overwhelmin' force, and he's only half wrong. The only weapons our Predator suits came with that seemed to be effective every time they were tried were the damn onboard shotguns. They were put in the suits almost as an afterthought, but they fired uranium-depleted buckshot that shredded every version of the Badger power armor the bad guys came up with. The trick was gettin' close enough to use them.

The Badgers weren't invincible. They could be defeated with a combination of brains and brawn, but we were sorely lackin' in the second element now that 1st Platoon in its entirety was gone. And thanks to that new weapon they'd just used on us, another charge wasn't gonna work.

One by one, the other squad leaders checked in. SGT Dawson's second squad was down by two riflemen—at least their suits were registerin' them as KIAs—while CPL Stanz had to shift over to 3rd Squad after SGT Tanner's suit reported him as KIA. That meant we still had almost the whole platoon. Hoo-freakin'-ray for us. It wasn't gonna be enough.

I'd say it was time for the Navy to rethink its shift in tactics from preventin' infestations on human-occupied planets to removin' them once they made planetfall, but nobody asked me. As per usual. Gunnies get the job done, no matter how asinine the job the officers thought up was.

I had Hansen send up a drone to survey the enemy fortifications so I could hammer out a quick-and-dirty battle plan for the next assault. Bastards weren't even dug in properly, just standin' around in their armor on top of a muddy hill they'd scraped all the grass off of, waitin' for us to make the next move.

If we sent the grenadiers and our few autocannon-equipped riflemen to the left and right flanks to soften them up, or if we were unusually blessed by the Almighty, and they scattered, we could use the new M-21 coil rifles they'd issued us to pick them off at range. As a Corps, we'd grown too reliant on the arm-mounted blasters and plasma cannons the Predator suits came with. It was time for Marines to be real riflemen again.

I opened the all-channel comms. "Okay, listen up. All squads, send your grenadiers and AC riflemen to the left and right flanks. On my command, they start softenin' the enemy up while we advance and take down individuals stupid enough to stick their heads up from cover. If we reduce their numbers enough, we can then assault the position and take it back. Understood?"

I was greeted by a chorus of *Oorahs,* and felt my chest swell with pride. We might all be about to die, but damnit to hell, I loved these men, and would proudly go out fightin' these alien bastards and take as many with us as we could.

I was just about to give the order when the command channel from the carrier group opened up. *"Attention all ground units, stand down and prepare for Anthromech insertion. Repeat. All ground units, stand down and prepare for Anthromech insertion."*

"What?" I demanded, not on the main channel. "Not now! We don't need spam cans here!"

"That name is against regs, Gunny! You heard the man," LT Schtick snarled. *"Stand down. That's an order."*

Inside, my rage howled, barely in check. We'd lost too many good men and deserved to take these bastards out ourselves, not let them do it for us. I realized that I was standin' in our trench, which wasn't a good idea tactically, and took a knee.

"Gunny," SGT Parnell called over a private channel, *"I heard about the spam cans before, but don't know enough to know why this is such a bad idea. What's the story?"*

"Spam Cans—the proper term, Anthromech Marines, is only used by the brass—are an abomination. Hell, they're not even human anymore, just the central nervous system of a dead Marine married to a roboticized body that's run by an AI."

"Holy shit!"

"Yeah. The AIs need human brains to help them process everythin' and work right," I said.

"Why just the CNS? That's creepy as feck!"

"The tech boys couldn't get the fusion reactor-powered battle suits that were originally supposed to be the Mark IV Predators to work with a whole human body crammed inside of it, along with the fusion reactor, so they resurrected an old idea the human race had rightly rejected as insane. Spam cans. Might as well be feckin' zombies. There's rumors that Marines in the program aren't even allowed proper death benefits once they're in."

"Why would anyone volunteer to get rid of their own bodies?"

"I have my doubts. Probably more like voluntold. Not to get too technical, but the Anthromech suits become the Marines' new bodies. They keep the CNS alive at the center in a nutrient bath that can go for literally months without needin' nutrients dumped into it, and their weapons are Direct Energy types."

"I heard about those, like a Particle Beam Cannon, and Plasma Grenades that are supposed to be pretty badass!"

I held up my brand-new M-21 coil rifle. "Yeah, but they're both limited in range. Hell, these new peashooters the Corps gave us for this mission have more range than the PBCs. Spam cans are brawlers, and that's all. Up close and personal killin'. They even got built-in melee weapons. Add all that to nearly indestructible bodies, and you can see how the brass might fall in love with the idea. As long as they don't have to think too hard about what it does to the men and women they used to be."

"I haven't heard of them being deployed before now," Parnell said.

"They've been field tested a couple of times as frontal assault units when takin' back Honey Badger-occupied worlds, but the results weren't great."

"What the hell happened?"

"You see, Sarge, the human CNS needs biofeedback from the senses. Sight, smell, taste, touch, and audio input. Without it, we go insane in a big damn hurry. Even just losin' one of those senses has been known to drive average humans over the edge. Can you imagine wakin' up inside a metal shell with nothin' left of what made your human experience human?"

Parnell was silent.

"I sure as hell can't, but I coulda told the lab coats that it was a bad feckin' idea. Hell, rumor has it they lost a whole first generation of spam cans for that very reason. Then they created some kinda artificial reality to plug 'em into in between missions to keep 'em sane. All that tells me is they're delayin' the inevitable. It's a nightmare waitin' to happen."

Now it was about to happen to us, and there wasn't a damn thing I could do to stop it.

A tone over the comms alerted us to the fact that the spam cans' drop sphere was about to impact the enemy. All we could do was wait. I moved my drone out of the way, but kept it airborne so I could monitor their progress.

A drop sphere is basically a ship-killer-grade missile that's been hollowed out so it can hold a platoon of Anthromechs, five to a platoon. An NCOIC, called a gunny—which also pissed me off—and four Marines. Their combined firepower was roughly equal to that of an entire platoon of real Marines, hence the name. They shoulda called it a lance or somethin', anythin' but a platoon. As usual, nobody asked me.

Through the lens of the drone, I watched the drop sphere hit the ground right in the middle of the Honey Badger position, probably killin' a couple of them at least, and kickin' up a huge plume of dirt and debris. The sphere was designed to break open on impact, releasin' the Anthromechs, and I'll give 'em this, they knew how to make an entrance.

PBC fire vaporized bits and pieces of the front line of Honey Badger power-armored troops before they could get a shot off, and then they went to work with their melee weapons as sword blades and battle axes popped out of slots in their arms. They were made of the same damn near indestructible alloy the suits were, so they could do some serious damage in a hurry if they got close enough.

Three of the Mech Marines waded into the closest group of already wounded Honey Badger troops and finished them off with admirable quickness. The other one and their gunny held back and took shots at the power-armor units a little further away, dealin' serious damage with the PBCs they carried, and sendin' several to their gods with one of the plasma grenades.

I was well and truly pissed. It looked like the damn things were gonna do in a few minutes what we'd been tryin' to do as a unit for several days. Damnit. I refused to be out-Marined by these things. I just couldn't do it.

Through the eyes of the drone, I watched a portion of the Honey Badger unit break away and take off with the jump jets built into their legs. They were 50 yards away in about three seconds, and another 50 three seconds after that. I knew exactly what they were doin', even if no one else did yet. They were movin' to get out of range of the PBCs, and it was about to work.

"Oh, no, the hell you don't, ya feckin' bastards!" I muttered, standin' back up.

I took the M-21 coil rifle they'd issued us for this op and lined up a shot on the Badger that was furthest out. I let out a breath, relaxed, and squeezed off the shot. The round took him in the vulnerable neck armor joint that allowed them to turn their heads. We didn't have that. We relied on 360-degree visual sensors built into our armor. We didn't need to look around like they did.

Once the first one was down, I lined up a shot on another one and did the same thing.

"Hell yeah, Gunny!" SGT Parnell said as he joined me in takin' long-distance shots at the bad guys.

"Gunny!" LT Schtick called over the platoon channel. *"Stop firing! We were told to stand down and let the Anthromechs handle it."*

I checked the power readout on my suit. I was still at 65%. Even shootin' the coil rifle continuously for a couple of days, I could last until we could get to a rechargin' station. I didn't like that this was the one area in which I was a little jealous of the spam cans. We didn't have reactors; we had batteries. Yeah, they were the best and longest-lastin' batteries humanity had ever produced, and could recharge in about five minutes at a chargin' station, but they were still batteries. A limitation on continuous ops.

A second group of Badgers' power armor blasted away from their group, this one in a different direction. They took two more leaps before stoppin' to turn and fire on the spam cans. They were still usin' those damn lasers they carried that had way more distance than the PBCs and our coil rifles. That was a weapon we hadn't been able to crack yet, mainly because we hadn't been able to capture one and reverse-engineer it. Honey Badgers never get taken alive, and they always take some of us with them.

I aimed my rifle at one of the bad guys in the newest group to break away.

"Gunny!" LT Schtick called out. Damn! Was he monitorin' my combat feeds only?

"I'm just practicin' my aim, sir," I said unconvincingly. "Just practicin' my aim."

"Gunny," SGT Parnell chimed in, *"is it just me, or are those PBCs getting less effective the further away the Badgers get?"*

"Yeah, that's the drawback. They're good up to about fifty yards or so, then they start to lose punch. There's talk about a larger version of these coil rifles in development, but they're not field-ready yet."

"I think the Honey Badgers have figured that out, Gunny," SGT Parnell said.

I checked the drone feed again, and sure enough, the Badgers were now all away from the Mech Marines by a good 150 yards, and the Mechs were gettin' hammered by long-range laser fire, but even then, they were hard to injure or kill. The arms under the suits weren't flesh, blood, and bone—they were circuits, graphene superstructure, and electro-reactive fibers.

"I think they're gonna die, Gunny," Parnell said, a tone in his voice that said he thought we oughtta be doing something about it.

"They were dead before they were put inside those shells, son; they just didn't know it."

"Still don't feel right, sitting here doing nothing, while they're taking all the heat," Parnell said.

"Them's the orders, Sarge, and we follow orders, at least for now," I said.

Just then, everythin' changed. In the drone video, the Gunny Mech took several hits at once. I guess they penetrated the shieldin' of its reactor, because the whole damn suit just ruptured, and for a second there was an additional star in the system, this one on the ground. It sounds worse than it is. I mean, sure, it's plenty bad for the Anthromech that blows, because the reactor blast basically turns the Marine and everythin' within five meters of it to ash, but relatively speakin', it's a small explosion. It just consumes everythin' close to it.

"Holy sheeit!" Parnell said. *"Did you see that?"*

"Yeah, I saw it," I said.

The remainin' Mech Marines stopped movin' for a second as their gunny's suit died down, and all that remained was a smolderin' ruin of melted armor and slag. It didn't even have human form anymore, much less human components.

"What the hell are you people doin'?" I asked no one in particular as the Anthromechs just stood there, directionless. "The squad leader should take over and keep after the objective! Why aren't they movin'?"

"They got no leadership, Gunny," Parnell replied.

"Rhetorical question, Parnell," I said, "besides which, it's irrelevant. If I got taken out, what happens?"

"I become Gunny, and Stanz becomes first squad leader, God help us all," Parnell said without hesitation.

"Feck you, Parnell!" Stanz said across the channel.

"Exactly," I replied, "there's a clear chain of command of who becomes what when one of us dies or is sufficiently wounded that we can't continue, and the Anthromechs don't appear to have that, or they've just lost their shit. Either way, they're about to have a real bad day, and we'll be right back where we started."

"That doesn't sound optimal, Gunny," Parnell said.

"No, Sergeant, it doesn't," I agreed. "I don't intend to let it go that far. They may be already dead, but the T, O, and E says they're Marines, and that means we pull their asses outta the fire—or die with them in it."

"OORAH, Gunny!" Parnell said, and I heard other voices sayin' the same thing. When did everybody start listenin' in to our channel?

I opened the command channel back up. "LT, Gunny Slade here. The Mech Marines are in trouble. We are goin' to assist."

"Negative, Gunny—" the LT began, but I cut him off.

"Sir, you seem to operatin' under the mistaken idea that I was askin'. I wasn't. I was tellin'. Slade, out."

The command channel incomin' comms indicator went red and stayed that way. There wasn't any way I could shut it off, so I ignored it.

"Parnell, take 1st and 2nd Squad with you and flank the enemy position on the left," I ordered. "Remember, they're runnin' and gunnin' now, so stay on the move. You can outdistance the Mech cannons with your new peashooters, but get as far into range as you can."

"Yes, Gunny. Moving, Gunny!" Parnell responded.

"3rd Squad, on me!" I ordered. "We're gonna take the right flank and muddy middle. All units, use your grenadiers to soften 'em up and make 'em reconsider their life choices, then take 'em out!"

A chorus of OORAHs followed me as I hit the jump jets on my power armor and cleared the top of the trench. 3rd Squad was at my side, fannin' out as we landed in a dead run. I set a counter to let me know when we'd be within maximum range for the new coil rifles, and then set another for the AC Riflemen. We only had one of those per squad. The autocannons, which were built into their suits, replacin' the whole right arm, could punch a hole through a Honey Badger suit if it was a direct hit, but I wanted 'em loadin' up HE rounds for maximum disruption. They can't aim anythin' at us, much less that doomsday weapon, if they're spendin' all their time gettin' bounced around the battlefield.

"Gunny Slade, get your people back in this trench right the feck now, and that is an order!" LT Schtick finally figured out how to command-override the comms channels. Good for him.

I kept runnin'.

Behind me, as he stood sky-linin' against the top of the trench, a shot from a Honey Badger laser weapon burned a hole through his chest and out the back side of his Mk III Predator suit. I didn't stop.

My first distance indicator warnin' went off.

AC troops, fire HE rounds into the enemy formations!" I ordered.

"Aye, Gunny, firing HE!" the autocannon-equipped riflemen called out as they complied. Seconds later, the Badgers were rocked hard by explosions that lit the sky and flung at least a few body parts into the air. *I'll be damned, looks like one of them got a direct hit after all!* I thought.

We were closin' in on the Anthromech Marines' formation as they stood around their dead gunny. I opened the all-comms channel.

"Mech Marines, this is Gunny Slade, 2nd Platoon, Alpha Company, 143rd Infantry Brigade. We're takin' this planet back from the enemy. Would you care to feckin' join us?"

I swear, they looked at each other for some kind of confirmation before there was a nod in unison.

"OORAH, GUNNY!" was the only reply I got from them. I have no idea which one said it.

I kept runnin', confident that they'd follow.

They did.

My heart was poundin' like it was gonna beat its way outta my chest, and I'd never felt more alive in my life. This was the life of a warrior!

The second distance meter went off. I brought my coil rifle up to high ready. I hated shootin' on the run, but these rifles had an advanced targetin' system that tied into our suits, so whenever I was in line with a bad guy, I got a nice green light and a musical tone. All I had to do was sweep the barrel across the enemy formation and listen.

BEEP

I fired. The coil rifle had no appreciable recoil, just a slight nudge as the nickel alloy-coated tungsten round flashed out of the barrel. A Badger who'd fallen behind his brethren in their mad jump jet-assisted dash away from the Mech Marines spun around with a sizable hole in his shoulder. He brought up his own laser rifle to return the favor, so I shot him again. Anythin' worth shootin' is worth shootin' twice.

1st and 2nd Squads engaged from their side of the battlefield. Some of their shots went wide, and that just wouldn't do.

"Parnell, tell your people to wait for the feckin' tone!"

"Aye, Gunny!" Parnell replied right before his suit indicator went offline on my display.

Feck.

"SGT Dawson, report!" I ordered.

"Parnell just bought it, Gunny," Dawson replied. *"We're making a final jump, then engaging from prone firing positions."*

"Use your targetin' systems, Dawson. I shouldn't have to be remindin' ya about this!"

"Aye, Gunny!"

The tone went off again, so I squeezed the trigger and watched another Badger go down. This was more like it! Two more HE rounds went off in the midst of the Badger formation, forcin' them to at least look like they were keepin' their heads down.

I didn't see anyone that looked like they carried anythin' other than a standard-issue Badger laser rifle, so maybe the soldier with the Doomsday Weapon they'd hit us with earlier had already had his ticket punched. That would be nice.

Smoke trails left the enemy formation just then, headed right for us.

"Incomin' missiles!" I yelled over comms as I dove to the ground.

The good news was that Badger missiles were basically dumb fired rockets.

The bad news was that the warheads on them were plenty powerful enough to scatter a Predator battle suit and its occupant across about ten yards of battlefield.

The ground twenty yards behind me erupted in a sudden explosion. I pointed my rifle in the general direction of the Badger that had fired the missile, and when I got tone, I squeezed the trigger and sent him to his gods.

Two more Riflemen blinked into KIA status on my readout; Stanz and Hansen.

"Start takin' them from range out here. Let the Mech Marines catch up and take the brunt of their return fire!"

We had to make these shots count. The coil rifles, a step backward accordin' to the War Department, were turnin' out to be a feckin' good idea. Yeah, it sometimes took several shots to bring a Badger down, but I'd take that over a pulse rifle splatterin' uselessly against 'em.

Somethin' was happenin' in the enemy formation. There was new movement, but I couldn't tell what the hell they were doin' with all the dust kicked up by the HE rounds and stray shots. Hold on, dust? It never stops feckin' rainin' here, so where was the dust comin' from? The Badgers must be makin' the dust cloud themselves. But how, and why? Didn't matter. I didn't like or trust it.

A few seconds later, after I'd taken two more chunks out of a stray Badger that wandered into my line of sight, the silver plumes of Badger jump jets glared through the smoke.

"Watch it, Marines, they're on the move again!" I warned over the all-comms channel. I couldn't tell where they were goin' thanks to all the dust and shit in the air, but they might be tryin' to gain a distance advantage again. I moved my coil rifle's point of aim back and forth, hopin' the targetin' sensor would give me tone and a chance to take another one down, but I couldn't get a lock on anythin'. I didn't have enough rounds for spray-and-pray fire, but the temptation to try it was real.

A silver plume burst through the dust cloud and landed twenty yards in front of me, and I lined up the shot and took it. The Badger staggered back for a second, takin' the round on the side, but he stayed standin', aimed his laser rifle at the ground, and fired.

Dawson's status went black.

"Aw, hell no, you worthless, scum-suckin' bastards!" I yelled.

That's what all the dust and smoke was for, so they could land close and engage us at point-blank range. We wouldn't know until they were right on top of us.

Well, feck that.

* * * * *

Chapter 2

I hit my own jump jets, takin' off from a horizontal position on the ground, anglin' up and then cuttin' the jets at the top of the arc. I came down right on top of the bastard that had just killed Dawson, my armored boots drivin' into the Badger's misshapen shoulders, and plowed him into the ground. I didn't even need to think about what came next. I pointed my suit's right arm at where its face should be and fired the onboard shotgun.

Three uranium-depleted shot pellets, each the size of a marble, and one uranium-depleted slug obliterated the thing's whole head. Black blood stained the mud all around it as it died. I hit it with a salvage tag so the lab boys could maybe get its rifle after the battle and reverse-engineer it, then I was on to the next one.

I blasted off again, usin' the same death-from-above tactic I'd used on the last one, only this time my angle was a little off, and I landed on my back. The shock-absorbin' gel that filled my power armor shook off the impact, and I jumped to my feet and blasted another Badger with the shotgun. This one took the hit center torso, and the slug actually blasted out the backside of its armor, takin' some internal organs and lots of black blood with it. Nobody knew it, but under my helmet, I was smilin'.

I could do that fifteen more times.

The Anthromech Marines caught up to us then and used their PBCs to literally disintegrate large pieces of Badgers where they stood. Occasionally, I saw the flash of an axe blade or a warhammer as they engaged with melee weapons. I kept doin' what I was doin' before; jump, DFA, shotgun blast to somethin' vital. Jump, kill, repeat. Somewhere in the middle of it, I heard someone screamin' some kind of awful battle cry at the top of his lungs. I was about to yell at whoever it was to get the hell off comms, but then I realized the person screamin' was me. Too many of my men were gone. Too many black indicators on the battle board. I was losin' it.

I stood over another Badger as he bled out, thanks to him missin' an arm and part of his shoulder. There was a small group of flowers bloomin' in the mud next to it, which made me stop for a second. Bright yellow blossoms in a small swath of green that hadn't been trampled into mud by armored feet. I felt the sudden irrational desire to stay here and protect it.

Movement to my right pulled my attention from the flowers. A small group of Honey Badgers about twenty yards away from my current position were fiddlin' with somethin' that had what looked like a comms dish at the end of it. It was connected to all of them with power cables—this was the thing they'd hit us with earlier! Some kind of advanced energy weapon that used the power of multiple suits to fire.

I didn't know what it would do to the super-hardened shell of a Mech Marine, but it couldn't be good.

There was no time for a Death From Above. The Badger at the center of their formation was linin' up the dish at the four Anthromech Marines as they finished off a small group of Badgers that had gotten separated from the rest of the unit. I whipped up the coil rifle, and even before it gave me tone, I sent tungsten death downrange.

The first round took the center Badger in the neck, but not before he must have triggered the weapon, because a wave of energy that blurred and seemed to burn the very air washed out of the dish and streaked across the battlefield toward the Mech Marines.

My shot must have thrown off his aim, even as my next two rounds took him in the upper chest, because the shot from the weapon hit the ground at the feet of the Mech Marines, sendin' them into the air in an eruption of dirt and debris. I kept shootin' until the Badger triggerin' the weapon was down and no longer able to fire it. Then I turned my attention to the rest of them.

I moved the aim point from one Badger to the next and fired until the coil rifle was dry. The Mech Marines were still on the ground, not movin'. I remembered my suit havin' to reboot after catchin' a glancin' near miss from the damn thing, so I needed to buy them some time.

I ran, and after ten yards, hit the jump jets. I was aimin' for the weapon, intent on crushin' it under my armored feet. I missed.

I still landed in the middle of them, and unloaded the rest of my shotgun rounds, blastin' pieces of them across the dirt, and severin' power connections. When the ammo for the shotgun ran out, I gripped the coil rifle like a club and started swingin'.

Somewhere in the action, I felt a searin' pain in my side, then one leg, and an arm. I was takin' laser shots, bein' cooked alive in my own armor. Not optimal.

I knew I was dead. That wasn't the point. The point was to take as many of them with me as I could and give the Anthromechs time to wake the feck back up.

At the last second, a Badger dodged the swing I took at him, and what was left of my coil gun hit the dish end of the doomsday weapon. It bent the edge inward, and sparks commenced, along with a terrible whine. It was buildin' up to detonation, and several of the remainin' Badgers tried to jump jet away from it, forgettin' that their suits were tethered to the thing to give it power.

I tried to do the same, but at some point, my own jets were damaged. All they did was sputter. I dropped to the ground and covered my head. It was the only chance I had, and it wasn't much of one. In the distance, the Anthromechs were up and movin', moppin' up the last of the Badgers.

"About damn time you spam cans got off your asses," I said.

There was a flash, and everythin' went white.

* * *

Utter silence. Blackness. Cold nothingness. But the weird part was that I was aware of it. I always thought that death was the end, you know? Lights out. Nothin' follows. This—wasn't that.

So, this is death. Huh. Weird.

Sound filtered in then. Some sort of twitterin' musical notes, but not from an instrument. It struck a memory from when I was a kid in a park somewhere. *Birds!*

I heard feckin' birds! There was light here, too, but I hadn't bothered to open my eyes yet. I wouldn't admit it, not even to myself, but I think I was afraid to.

What the hell, one eye can't hurt.

I cracked one eye open.

White ceilin' in a real buildin', not a ship.

Hospitals were white. That was encouragin'. But why wasn't I on a hospital ship? That would make more sense, right?

I cracked the other eye open, then looked down. Definitely me on a hospital bed. Hooked up to at least one IV drip, maybe more. I was havin' trouble movin' my head to the left and right to check that out. *Why can't I feel my legs?*

The door to the room opened, and a nurse came in. Big sucker, 280 pounds of spring steel and rawhide. Woulda made a damn fine Marine.

"Easy there, Gunny, your head is in a brace while the nanites finish their job," the nurse said, pattin' my chest as if to calm me.

"What job are they doin'?" I asked. My voice sounded weird. Probably just thirsty.

"Fixing your neck."

"What the hell is wrong with my neck?"

"Well, I wasn't there, but the battlefield report from Praxis IV indicates that you broke it, among other things, when you got blown out of your battle suit."

"No shit?"

"No shit," the nurse said with a nod. "But if you stay still and let the nanites finish the microscopic repairs the surgeons initiated, you should be up and about in a day or so. Is that gonna be a problem?"

"Will I be able to feel my legs when they're done?"

A concerned look passed over the nurse's face, like a lone scud cloud chasin' after a storm. "You should be able to feel them now. Let me go fetch the doc."

He crossed to the other side of my bed, and I lost sight of him. There was a soft *click*, like a button bein' pressed, and an equally soft *beep*. Then the lights went out again.

I came to again, this time at night. No birds. It was dark outside—at least, I think it was. I couldn't see the window, but the room had that soft lightin' reserved for after-hours ops at a hospital. I'd been a Marine long enough, and seen enough action, to have spent a fair amount of time in naval hospitals.

The door opened, and the same nurse from before came in.

"There he is," he said, a pleasant smile on his face.

"Thought you were day shift," I said.

"We rotate," he explained. "You manage to stay awake for more than ten minutes this time, you might get to meet my relief in the morning."

"What hospital am I at?"

"Deep Mercy Station 4077, the pride of Alpha Centauri."

"Never heard of it," I said. "Why not a hospital ship?"

"Your injuries were kind of on what we call the severe side, Gunny," he replied. "A regular hospital ship was good enough to stabilize you, but they had to bring you here for the repairs to be done right."

"I broke more than just my neck, huh?"

"You could say that. The list of bones you didn't break, getting blasted out of that suit, is way shorter than the list of ones you did."

"I never even heard of someone gettin' blown outta their suit before. Didn't know it was possible."

"It's not supposed to be, and I'm pretty sure that when you're up for debrief, they're going to ask you about that, as it connects to some new kind of weapon the Badgers are using."

Images of the dish thing connected to all those Badger power suits flashed across my mind. "Oh, yeah, that. Yeah, that was weird."

"How do your legs feel?" he asked.

I was surprised by the question until I remembered that the last time I woke up, I couldn't feel them at all. Now I could. "I can tell they're there."

The nurse nodded, like he'd expected that. "Good." He stood at the foot of the bed and lifted the sheets off me. A rush of cold air flew under them and made me shiver. "Wiggle your toes for me, Gunny."

I complied.

"Good! Now, raise your left foot, just a little, no kicking like you're a Rockette."

"The feck is a Rockette?"

"Dance troupe from old Earth history. Famous for synchronized kicking in their line dances."

"Never heard of 'em."

"Still the gold standard."

"I'll take your word for it," I said, raisin' my foot.

"Excellent, now the right one."

I complied again.

"Outstanding!" the nurse said. "That's progress that I'll be passing along to the doc. If you're awake tomorrow, you might actually get to meet him."

"Am I allowed to move my neck yet?"

"The doc will have to answer that one tomorrow."

He crossed to the other side of the bed, and once again, I heard a soft *click* and a *beep* and was swallowed in darkness.

New day.

Same nurse.

No doctor.

Same click and beep, followed by darkness.

This shit was gettin' old fast.

I had no idea how much time had passed since the battle. Hell, I didn't even know if we were able to retake the damn planet. I suspect that if we hadn't, I would have died out there after that last blow-up that knocked me outta my armor. But I was gettin' antsy as feck.

This time, I came to outside. That was a shock. I knew I was outside because of the wind, the birds again, and sunlight warmin' my face. And lo and behold, I could move my feckin' neck! I looked left, then right, then up and saw a familiar face lookin' down at me.

"Hey there, Gunny, I was wondering if this was going to be more than just a catnap."

Somethin' didn't add up, and it was buggin' the shit outta me. I didn't remember meetin' with the doc, who was supposed to tell me it was okay to move my neck. I didn't remember goin' to the head, not even once, and no cold as feck bedpan under my ass cheeks, either, nothin'. Didn't even remember havin' to take a piss or a dump.

Now I wake up outside in a feckin' wheelchair with the only nurse I'd ever seen at this medical center? I call bullshit. I was missin' too many damn chunks of time.

"Say, Nurse—" I gave a pause here, waitin' for him to fill the gap in with his name.

"Yes, Gunny?"

I sighed. At least, I tried to. It didn't feel like a real sigh. Like that sensation where you take in a deep breath, and then let it out real slow, and the pent-up emotions with it? Yeah, that. I didn't feel that.

I didn't wanna jump to conclusions. I really didn't, but it was startin' to get a little too weird. Time for a test. I ignored the fact that he didn't do what any normal human would do in that situation, and provide me with a name to call him, aside from the title of nurse.

"Help me out here," I said, soundin' genuinely puzzled, because I sure as feck was. "The last thing I remember before bein' out here in this chair is you tellin' me the doc would let me know if I could move my head around tomorrow. Now I find myself in this chair, out here with you, able to do so."

"Okay," the nurse said, still smilin' cheerfully.

"So, when did I talk to the doc?"

"Yesterday," he said without missin' a beat.

"Why don't I remember it?"

"Well, you did suffer some brain injury as well, and that might have something to do with it. You sure you don't remember it?"

And then, just like that, I did. It was clear as day. Wakin' up, the doc comin' in, and introducin' himself as Doc, takin' some kind of brace off of my neck, and allowin' me to slowly turn my head side to side. He seemed very pleased with my progress as the nurse looked on, just as happy.

FECK.

*****

Chapter 3

"Cut the shit, Nurse," I said. "You and I both know this ain't a hospital, I'm not in a wheelchair, and I couldn't feel my damn legs before, because I don't feckin' have them anymore."

The nurse looked down, his smile fadin' for the very first time. "Well, that must be some kind of record."

I heard a *click*…

"Don't you feckin' do it—!" … followed by a *beep*, and again, I was plunged into darkness.

I came to, seated in a chair at a small gray table in a small gray room. This shit was gettin' weird, fast. Two Marine officers came in, one of them settin' a personnel jacket down on the table. I noticed he didn't wear a name tape.

"And you are?" I asked, not hidin' my disdain.

"You will address me as sir, Gunny," he said in a reprimandin' tone that I'd heard a thousand times before, only this was a lot more convincin'.

"Look, Major, let's skip to the part where I tell you that I've put it all together. I don't have a body anymore. I'm a spam can."

"Gunny—" the captain began.

"You guys stuck me, literally, into the damn Anthromech Marines without my permission. That means, officially, as far as the rest of the galaxy is concerned, I'm dead. So why don't we get to the real reason you guys got me in this shared hallucination?"

"Gunny—" the major said.

"You're probably not even real officers. You're like that nurse, or the doctor. AIs. Not human. Damn Corps didn't even have the decency to break it to me with a real person."

The two officers looked at each other.

"He's a sharp one, all right," the major said to the captain.

"The nurse program said so," the captain admitted.

"Yeah, about that, you might want to train that thing a little better. Maybe make him a little more human. I caught on way too damn fast. As soon as I suggested I didn't have a memory of somethin' I ought to, suddenly, I did. Sloppy. You could at least give it a name."

"You were supposed to have chalked that up to brain trauma," the major said.

"Major, I allegedly got blasted out of a Predator Mark III battle suit. There's no feckin' way that's real. At least make it believable."

"No, no, that part was true," he said. "You did get blown out of your armor. Some kind of aspect of the new weapon the Badgers have developed. That's primarily why we're here."

"Oh, so the real reason is, you want to pick my brain—since that's all that's left of me—about the new alien tech."

"More or less," he agreed.

"Lemme ask you this," I said, "did we at least win on Praxis IV?"

They looked back and forth at each other again, like they were silently communicatin'. Hell, for all I knew, they were.

"We can say with confidence that because of your efforts, combined with those of the Anthromech Marine unit we landed there, yes, you were successful in regaining control of Praxis IV for humanity. But it came at a great cost."

"Don't it always?" I said.

"What can you tell us about this weapon?"

"It uses a hell of a lot of power, I know that much," I said.

"How do you know?" the captain asked.

"Because they had it connected to about half a company of Badger armor. I don't know what it shoots, or how it works, but I know we lost all of 1st Platoon to it, and most of us were knocked back into our trench when it fired at us."

The major nodded. It almost looked like a human movement. "Yes, we know that part. We have recon footage from a drone as the attack happened. 1st Platoon took a direct hit from the beam of the weapon as it swept over your formation. 2nd Platoon, you guys, took a hit to the dirt in front of you, so you only received moderate damage.

"Moderate damage? Three of my men *died* in that attack."

"We're aware," the captain said.

"Yeah, but you don't give a shit. All right, move on, next question."

"Right," the major said, preparin' to ask me somethin' else.

"No," I interrupted. "I didn't mean you, Major Code, I meant me. *My* next question. What happens now? To me?"

"I may be an AI, as you surmised," the major said, "but I'm still a Marine Corps officer, and you will address me with the respect that rank deserves."

I laughed then, and it sounded funny. Louder than it should have been for the circumstances. I filed that away for future examination. "The feck you are, and the feck I will. What. Happens. To. Me?"

"Integration with your new battle suit is not yet complete," the captain said. "Normally, we wouldn't wake the mind of a transfer so soon, but we needed as much intel as we could get, since you were the sole survivor of the battle, aside from the remaining mechanized units."

"Sole survivor? Well, ain't I special? I'm touched."

"I think we have all we need for now," the major said, turning to leave the room.

The captain remained behind a moment. "Your new orders will be sent to you soon, Gunny. Reassignment to the Anthromech Marines, specifically as a gunnery sergeant for the platoon you commanded on Praxis IV, who just so happen to be in need of a new gunny."

"Is that so? Well, I tell you what, Captain, before those sorry sacks of metal get deployed anywhere else—in fact, before you send any more of my beloved Marine Corps, mechanized or otherwise, against the feckin' Honey Badgers again—I'm gonna recommend your R&D boys finish work on those new coil gun peashooters they've been developin' for use with the Mark IV Predators, because the Badgers have figured out the range limitations of the particle beamers."

"Those weapons systems are classified; how the hell do you even know they exist?"

"You can't hide anythin' from the Lance Corporal Underground, and I'm a former member who knows how to use them. I never lack for intel. Make it happen, Captain, or the next time the Anthromech Marines deploy, it might not go so well."

"When you awaken, you'll be ready for training with your new battle suit."

"Aw, hell no, don't you dare…"

Click. Beep. Darkness.

* * * * *

Author Bio

Michael LaVoice has authored the Galaxy's Most Wanted series and the Gladius Leagues Series, as well as multiple short stories. He currently has four Sci-Fi series in development, and a YouTube Channel called LaVoice In Your Head. He can be found on the web via the link here. https://linktr.ee/michaellavoice.

# # # # #

Moon Strike by C. A. Waldron

A Story of the Lazarus Vanguard

Chapter 1

West Point, NY – Late May, 2060

"Up, Auntie Jingu. You have a meeting in less than two hours, and there's chicanery to discuss."

Dr. Marai Gozen's voice hauled Jingu from the warm fuzz of sleep. Jingu's eyes cracked open. No training today. No shouted commands drilled into her brain. She threw off the covers and headed for the bathroom.

Fifty-five years of false hopes. The voices faded over time as she ignored them, but at seventy, Jingu Gozen qualified as the world's oldest teenager. Large, violet-blue eyes and puckered lips greeted her from the unlined face in the mirror. Water beaded on her cheeks from several splashes. Black, silky hair waved wildly around her head and fell past her waist. Her boobs had settled at last, growth spurts long past.

Now if only the hormones would calm down. Nanobots were useless for normal hormonal processes. They were great for curing cancer, repairing injuries, and most body upkeep, but they didn't touch the teenage temper.

"Quit wool-gathering!" Marai called from the other room. "The Committee plans are devilish. Get ready, and I'll talk."

"Every damn time the Committee 'offers' me anything, there are strings attached. If he had known of the proposals they made, my brother would have killed them all," Jingu said. She turned to the closet. Her fingers trailed over the garments. Suits felt too stuffy. Jeans felt too casual. "Where is this meeting, and what is it about?"

"West Point Academy, the meeting room under the gym. From what I gathered from eavesdropping, they want to partner you with a past graduate. Someone getting ready for deployment." Marai shrugged. Her clinical tone couldn't mask the concern in her eyes.

"Partner? Me? Under the gym? That sounds nasty." Jingu banged her head on the closet door with a frustrated groan. The wood felt cool against her skin.

She thought of the potential partners she had chased off through the years. Too many to count. The thought of being responsible for someone else chilled her. *Jameson.* After the disaster on her first mission—where her partner had ended up with catastrophic injuries… Ice ran down her spine. This new one shouldn't be too hard to run off. None of the others were.

"Your thoughts are written all over your face," Marai said. "It won't work this time. Refuse this partnership, and I'm afraid the group might arrange an 'accident.'"

Jingu snorted. She hesitated, caught in the memory of Jameson in a six-month coma. She pulled a blue sweater out of her closet and then returned it to the rack.

"The anti-me faction is at it again. They don't have a majority. The director, Senator Mac MacAuley, will give them a hard no."

"Auntie, the senator is stepping down from leadership. Heart trouble. Harrison is taking his place." Marai slumped as she delivered the news.

The blue sweater slipped from Jingu's fingers, and she crumpled to the floor. "Harrison? He's going to make sure I pay for *The Incident*," she hissed.

"Harrison has gunned for you since you rejected his advances, but this partner might be your ace. He was fuming about something Senator MacAuley set up." Marai's left eyebrow arched sharply. "I'm sure it's this meeting today."

Jingu's eyes widened. "I'll consider it." She looked up at her niece. "If things go wonky, you'll look the other way?"

"We'll see how hard disaster hits," Marai said. She laughed and pulled Jingu's sparring gi out of the closet.

* * *

At West Point Academy, Second Lieutenant Llyr MacAuley stood under his grandfather's piercing gaze. Senator Cormac MacAuley's eyesight hadn't softened with age. Those eyes grew keener with every passing year.

"What's up, Daddio? This is supposed to be my week for tying up loose ends." Llyr paced the room. His boots squeaked against the polished floor. The smell of old sweat and leather infused the space under the gym. "And why am I in sparring gear?"

"I have a job offer for you." The senator's voice carried the weight of authority honed over decades in Washington.

"Yeah, no. I have a job, serving my country. Whatever you've got, it's not messing with my plan. Youngest four-star general in United States history." Llyr's dog tags clinked under his shirt as he moved.

Senator MacAuley's laugh bounced off the concrete walls. "We'll see. This opportunity is unique. The situation is compelling, and you're an adrenaline junkie. Something like this won't come along again in your lifetime. At least I hope not."

The tap of footsteps drew both men's attention. The steps stopped at the door. The door slammed open. The metal handle dented the wall.

"I'm here!"

A short, Asian girl who looked barely sixteen burst into the room. She wore a gi and a sword strapped to her back. Behind her followed a slightly older woman and a dour middle-aged man with a receding hairline and cold eyes.

"This guy's more Neanderthal than I want in a partner for our asset, Ms. Gozen, Senator." The man's lips sneered. "Why don't you send him on to whatever job he was planning to do?"

"Ah, Director Harrison. You're a world-class idiot to tell a powerful senator that his grandson is no better than cannon fodder." The senator's brow dropped, and his smile vanished. His eyes blazed with the intensity of a blowtorch.

"Daddio, I'm not really looking for work. I leave in a couple of weeks. General, remember?" Llyr tried to interject. He stepped back under his grandfather's stern glare.

A phone shrieked. Harrison jumped and patted his pockets. "This damn thing shouldn't be ringing. It's silenced for everything but emergencies. What's my assistant thinking?" He stepped away. "Harrison, here."

Llyr shook his head. "What a moron. Now, Daddio, what's going on?"

Jingu's shoulders shook. "Mac, didn't you think to explain to your boy?"

"Jingu, you defy description. I haven't told anyone but the need-to-knows, and he wasn't one until today." The senator gestured to his grandson. "This is my grandson, Lt. Llyr MacAuley, second in his class, year of 2056. He's badly in need of a lesson."

Llyr grabbed his grandfather's arm and pulled him aside. "Are you out of your mind, old man? I'm not beating up on a child."

"Well, about that part. She's older than she looks." Mac turned and gestured to Jingu. "I think he's going to need convincing."

Jingu rolled her eyes. "I'm not there yet, and you want me to lure him over to the dark side?"

"That's one way to put it." Mac slapped Llyr's shoulder. "Get in the ring."

The canvas floor creaked as they climbed in. Jingu offered the ritual bow. Llyr reciprocated. The scent of floor wax and old sweat rose around them.

Confusion flashed across Llyr's face as the girl jogged to her corner, whipped around, and raced toward him. He stepped backward as her foot connected with his chest. Jingu shimmied up his body and launched herself straight up, twisting as she came down hard on his back. She knocked him off balance and pulled to the left. As Llyr started to topple, she released and jumped back. Before he could sit up, she had her arms around his neck. The world narrowed to a pinpoint. Then darkness.

Llyr struggled to sit up. His vision swam back into focus. "What was that?" He shook his head. The copper tang of a bitten tongue filled his mouth.

"That, my dear boy, was Jingu Gozen and her intrepid niece, Dr. Marai Gozen. I want you to partner with her as we, the Committee, prepare to deploy her in the service of our country."

"What experimental drug are you on?" Llyr kept his eyes on Jingu. "There's no way you, Miss Ninety-Pound Wonder, can take a six-foot-five soldier with specialty training in the normal scheme of things."

Dr. Gozen stepped in front of her aunt. "The things you don't know can bite you somewhere important." She turned and enfolded her aunt's shaking body. "Quit assuming and get your facts."

As the two women turned away, Jingu's head tilted up. She flashed a smile and winked.

A frisson of resentment crawled up Llyr's spine. The minx had her older niece fooled. He started toward them when the door squeaked open.

"Emergency!" Harrison stuck his head back in. His face was a pasty greenish-white. He scrambled for the exit. "Alien attack! Sirens are about to sound. I'm out of here!"

Llyr's bewilderment mirrored his companions'. Jingu assessed the weirdness in the quiet. "Well. *That* was anticlimactic."

"Wait, Jingu. Harrison is slimy, but he's not a complete fool." Mac's words faded as the emergency sirens blasted.

A blast rocked the building above. The fluorescent lights swung. They cast jerky shadows across warping floor tiles. Plaster dust billowed through the stairwell in dense clouds, reducing visibility to arm's length. Cracks spiderwebbed across the concrete wall, widening with each aftershock, and insulation foam bulged through the fissures. The smell of scorched plastic floated in the air.

Llyr reeled through the shaking. Powdered drywall coated his tongue. Just keeping upright taxed his endurance as he hurried to help the others off the floor. Jingu sprang up and reached for Marai. Llyr steadied his grandfather while the older man found his feet amidst the crumbling surroundings. The building creaked like a ship breaking apart.

Twisted metal, concrete blocks, and splintered wooden flooring obstructed the doorway. "Packed tight. No way out from here." Llyr coughed as they checked the main stairs. They turned to seek alternate routes as the acrid burning grew stronger.

"This is not a drill," Mac said. "We need another way out. Now!"

The building shuddered again as a second blast landed close. Llyr pushed the group away from the front of the building. Heat radiated through the walls.

Marai's wet, panicky breathing caught Llyr's attention. "Are you okay?"

"My family. What's going on?" She pulled her phone from her pocket. "No bars!" Her voice rose.

Llyr shoved Marai toward his grandfather and grabbed Jingu's hand. "This way." He pointed down the dark back of the hall. "There are exits all over the campus."

Lights flickered and died. The smell of dust and fear permeated the air.

"Daddio, grab my hand. It'll be easier if no one gets lost. It's a maze down here."

"How do you know that?" Jingu asked. Dim emergency lights flickered to life, casting long shadows across their faces.

"I was in Gamma Nu, a fraternity that delighted in dropping unwary freshmen down the hole," Llyr responded as they inched down the black hall. "Unfortunately for them, I excel in tracking and payback."

Jingu stumbled as the floor bucked again and threw the group into the wall. A ceiling beam cracked. As it fell, she pushed Marai and Mac out of the way. "You are all right?" Jingu patted Marai down to reassure herself that her niece was unhurt. By the time they reached the end of the hall, temperatures and tempers had risen.

Marai's quiet laugh rang in Jingu's ear. "Caught your attention, didn't he?"

"Shut up, niece." Jingu's growl emerged louder than intended. The thrum in her head distracted her as she struggled to keep up with Llyr's broad shoulders through the dim passageways.

*****

Chapter 2

"You could have mentioned unused, unclean tunnels."

Jingu wiped a sticky strand of cobweb off her face, the silky thread clinging to her fingers like wet glue. Marai coughed and flailed in her efforts to do the same. Mac peeled off his suit coat—now a uniform gray with pulverized concrete—and shook it with a sharp snap. Dust whipped through the dim light. A dark rectangle outlined the exit door at the end of the shaft.

"Where's the fun in that?" Llyr's eyes gleamed in the gloom. He monitored his dirt-streaked companions with a steady gaze. "Seriously, we're on the eastern side of Constitution Island if we followed protocol."

"What does that even mean?" Marai's voice echoed against the concrete walls. The hollow sound amplified her panic. "We've been at this for hours. Something is exploding up there, and my cell phone is dead."

"I studied the maps while planning my revenge. That doesn't mean I explored every tunnel." Llyr stepped over a rusted pipe. "So—"

"You don't have a clue where we are?" Jingu said, voice rising.

Mac coughed to suppress a laugh, and a wheeze escaped his throat. Both women turned on him.

"I'll have you know, I have a great sense of direction," Llyr protested.

"Ladies, please. Towers are down." Mac's steady voice cut through the bickering. A corner of his mouth twitched. "Ignore them and get us out of here. If we're where you think we are, my phone will work once we clear the rock."

"SAT phone?" Llyr asked.

"Yes." Mac nodded.

Llyr led the way up narrow, damp stairs. The rusty hinges screamed as he shoved the door open. Thorny branches clawed at their faces, necks, and shoulders, and tiny, stinging scratches bloomed on their skin as they squeezed through the brush. Heavy trees cast long, jagged shadows over the clearing. Marai stumbled out first and gasped in the fresh air. Her face was caked in mud and dried tears.

Marai pulled Jingu outside. Llyr snagged their arms and yanked them back toward the shadows of the door. "Stay put," he hissed. "Daddio, get out here, and get updated."

Jingu squinted. Her nostrils flared as she jerked her arm free. "You aren't the boss of me."

Llyr's jaw clenched. "No, but if you know where we are, I'll gladly let you be the boss of me."

Mac stepped between them. "Now, children, play nice."

He dialed a sleek, gray handset. It reached someone on the first ring. "MacAuley reporting." He listened, his expression darkening. "What? Yes, sir. Right away. Can I put you on speaker so we can get instructions?"

Mac switched the mode.

"We've been attacked by the Qhait," the tinny voice crackled through the speaker. A chill settled over the group despite the humid afternoon heat. "More details when you arrive at your destination."

"How bad is it?" Llyr asked. He leaned toward the phone.

"Catastrophic at military bases, officially. Or it could have been, if we hadn't prepared." The voice paused. "Casualties are much lighter than projected. We think 10 to 20 percent per US military installation. Maybe 5 percent in your location."

"Dear God, how did we get that lucky?" Llyr's face went pale.

"It's all in the timing. Keep in mind, there are no reports from the rest of the world yet. The expectation is higher in some places than others. Neither NATO nor most other political blocs ever responded to the possibility of extraterrestrials."

"What do you want us to do?" Mac asked.

"Go toward Fort Constitution. A guard will be stationed where the mountains meet the marsh. They'll direct you to meet up with any survivors from the school."

"Yes, sir." Llyr handed the phone back to Mac and pulled out his keys. A small compass hung from a ring, and its needle swung before settling on north. He calculated the route. He'd never accessed the marsh through these tunnels, but survivor protocols were clear.

He guided them deeper into the hills. The ground grew softer, and the smell of rot, mud, and stagnant water thickened.

"Our families?" Jingu and Marai asked together.

"You can call on the way. All indications are that civilians weren't targeted as a group." Mac passed the phone to Jingu. Her hand shook as she dialed.

* * *

"Dad, are you okay?" Jingu's voice rose. She clutched the phone with white-knuckled intensity. Her father had listened when she'd insisted on the satellite hardware. For once, his stubbornness had failed him at the right time.

"We're all safe. I assume you and Marai are, too?"

Her father's calm settled both women. Jingu smiled.

"I can sense your smile. My heart's glad you're both safe."

Marai bent over, hands on her knees. She exhaled a dusty breath of relief.

"We're about to head into thick woods, Dad. We have to meet up with survivors." Jingu watched a dragonfly zip through the reeds. "I'll contact you once we have more information."

"Safe travels, daughter. Remember your lessons." Her father signed off.

Jingu seized Marai's arm and moved behind the two men toward the marsh. Cattails swayed in the breeze. Her emotions jumped from numb to thankful, but her brain thrummed with a darker rhythm. Vengeance felt like a physical weight. Some ideas were hers, but in the deepest recesses of her mind, a cold, calculated logic stirred. The nanobots were restless.

She slowed her pace to keep their conversation private.

"What if the nanobots are waking up? I'm having thoughts that aren't mine." Jingu kept her voice low.

"No, you're acting paranoid," Marai replied. "This is a marathon, not a sprint. Just know, if my theory is correct, everything we think we know is wrong—in a good way. Trust me."

Jingu wanted to rage. "What about these strange thoughts?"

"Security, Auntie." Marai replied, mimicking a zipper across her mouth.

Jingu huffed and dragged her along to catch up to the men.

*****

Chapter 3

"Are we there yet?"

The whiny pitch of the resident teenager made Llyr reconsider every plan he'd ever had for a large family.

"You'd think we were on a ten-mile ruck instead of a leisurely walk through the woods," Llyr said. Pine needles crunched under his boots.

"Compare your legs to mine and rethink your attitude, Buster." Jingu snorted. "Besides, look at Marai's shoes. She's walking on prayer and broken leather."

Marai offered a thin grin, and some of the tension drained from her shoulders. "Next time the world ends, I'll be sure to wear the right flats."

"You two act more like mother and daughter than niece and aunt." Llyr's gaze sharpened. He was cataloging details, analyzing the gaps. "Did your dad have a second wife? Some late-in-life surprise?"

"I've known Marai since the second she was born." Jingu stopped mid-stride and crossed her arms. Sunlight filtered through the canopy, casting jagged shadows across her face as she squinted at him.

"Stop," Mac ordered. "No more information sharing until we're secure."

Llyr's protest died as three camouflage-clad soldiers materialized from the surrounding trees. Jingu's hand twitched toward the hilt of her sword. Mac gave a subtle, sharp headshake. She froze.

"Sir." The lead soldier saluted. "We'll guide you to the activation group. There's an underground battle bunker close by. The fort was too conspicuous for a gathering of this size."

"At ease, Soldier. Lead the way." Llyr returned the salute.

The group fell in behind the scout, switching direction back toward the steep rise of the hills.

* * *

"Can't we just take a five-minute break?" Jingu asked, her voice strained.

"No," Mac replied. "We're almost there."

Their brisk pace continued for twenty minutes, and they passed an entrance almost identical to the doorway they'd escaped from earlier. The lead soldier pulled open the heavy metal door, and dimly lit stairs descended into darkness. Jingu wondered how far down they went.

"Restrooms? Where are they?" Jingu's demand echoed against concrete walls.

"Close," the soldier assured her, "but we'll check you in first. He led them through double doors into a room humming with activity. People rushed about carrying papers and equipment. Uniformed personnel collected information from a dwindling line of academics.

"Next," a young man said, bending to retrieve paperwork as Mac approached.

"Senator Cormac MacAuley, Lieutenant Llyr MacAuley, Doctor Marai Gozen, and Jingu Gozen reporting from West Point Academy Gym, Alpha Room 1."

Jingu jabbed Mac's ribs. "Why tell him that? Isn't that need-to-know?"

The young man stood and saluted as Mac shrugged. "Senator, sir! We were hoping you were safe. Right this way."

"Emergency protocol." Mac looked down at Jingu. "This is a battle bunker, not a check-in bunker."

"What?" Jingu's eyebrows shot up. "How—"

"Fort Constitution was founded as a general meeting point for non-essential personnel," Mac said, his voice low. "You haven't been non-essential since you were five years old. Don't change the narrative now."

His words shut Jingu up. She wasn't letting the cat out of the bag this early in the game.

The guide motioned to the double doors. "Commander's about ready to start. Restrooms flank the doorway. I suggest using them."

Marai limped in her broken heels. "When things settle down, I'll explain my theory, but the short version is—"

The door slammed behind the two women. Marai shoved her head under the faucet while Jingu watched. "Wash up while you've got the chance," Marai said. "Who knows when there'll be time to clean up again?"

Jingu started her own cleanup as Marai talked. "My theory is, the nanobots are trying to integrate with your physiology rather than erase you. They don't exist without you, so it would be counterintuitive for them to destroy their host."

Jingu thought about Marai's theory. "Okay, I'll give you that, but—"

"You've got enough going right now, so just stop." Marai's stern voice stopped Jingu's word salad.

* * *

In the men's restroom, Mac patted Llyr's shoulder.

"Don't worry. She'll be fine. If Jingu tries to protect you, let her. Your job is to watch her back."

"What? I figured you brought me in here for the 'protect her discreetly' talk." Llyr's voice bounced off the tile.

"She'll make a fool out of you if you try. Marai might need protection. She isn't in Jingu's league. Stay alert. Nothing is what it seems with those two." Mac smirked. "Remember how fast she threw you to the floor."

The women's door opened as they exited. Llyr caught a cleaner Marai mid-sentence.

"... and that's the foundation of my theory. I constructed it around the Werewolf Paradox."

"Werewolf Paradox? What in—forget it. We won't be testing that today or tomorrow. My control has to be absolute." Jingu strode forward, and Marai followed. Llyr shook his head. He would never understand women.

Senator MacAuley transformed. Shoulders squared, and a scowl settled into place. Mac walked into the room and owned it. Seats surrounded a large rectangular table before a portable chalkboard. A pitch-black screen loomed behind it, reflecting the gloomy light.

Llyr didn't know what he'd expected, but a group of instructors gathering to discuss battle tactics against aliens wasn't it. His grandfather cleared his throat, and the room fell silent. Then a dozen voices erupted at once.

"What's the status?" Mac asked.

"A continuous demand for unconditional surrender is out on all bands," one man reported.

"Globally. Every military installation took a hit," another added. "Meticulous preparation."

"Could have been worse," Mac noted. "School was out. Casualties aren't as bad as we feared. What happens next depends on whether this is a full strike force or a scouting team."

"Not good enough," a man replied. "We've been preparing for an encounter like this for four decades."

"One of Voyager's data transmissions in the early 2000s picked up chatter. NASA sent covert satellites with new engines and photo tech out into the universe," Mac said. "Codebreakers had a field day while the world dismissed it as equipment failure."

"Good story, but how does it connect with this situation?" an older commander with crossed arms interrupted. "I'm Commander Marshall. My job is to gather information. Backup generators should be online in minutes."

"Our last official contact was about an hour ago," Mac said. "We're a team of four. Me, a medic, and two combatants."

"What do you bring to the table, Senator?" Marshall asked. "You're too old for the field. You look like a bureaucrat through and through."

"Looks can be deceiving, Commander." Mac looked at Llyr.

"Formidable, sir. Senator MacAuley's credentials stem from his time in the Shadow Forces during the Third Gulf War," Llyr said, "not to mention the directorship of the Committee for nearly three decades."

Marshall's eyes widened. "Well. That changes things."

The dim lights flickered and died, and darkness swallowed the room. A gasp slipped out in the black. An eerie buzzing intensified until the lights flashed back on, brighter than before. Flickering red and blue indicator lights lit the side walls, and the large black screen surged to life.

Marshall connected his tablet, and a world map appeared, dotted with numerous red impact zones.

"Senator, use the satellite phone to hook us into HQ," Marshall said. "The sound's off, but the picture's clear. It's a visual representation of the strike zones."

Mac fetched his phone, plugged a cord into the screen, and punched in a shielded number.

* * *

Jingu poked Marai. "No red dots where our family is."

Marai let her breath out. "Thank goodness. Now what?"

The screen switched from the map to high-resolution stills. Space views were interspersed with a blaring, prerecorded message. Jingu dismissed the noise as overkill. The logistics of the translation, however, held her interest. "Any idea how they decoded that?"

Marai smirked. "Let's see what Commander Marshall has to say. I might a have top-rated security clearance thanks to a project involving someone we both know and love." Marai's pointed stare forced a flush to Jingu's cheeks.

The screen switched to a man behind a desk.

"Mac, are you there?"

"Yes, Mr. President. We're safe. We're setting up the Constitution Island battle bunker. What's our status?"

"The Qhait are behind this attack. Why? Too many possibilities. To their knowledge, we don't have long-range space capabilities." President Anderson's eyes scanned Mac through the lens. "What do you know?"

"I'll contact my source and get back to you. Notice Groom Lake. Unknown, or ignored." Mac glanced at Jingu and Llyr before signing off. He made another call immediately. "Alpha Lambda, Iota, Eta, Nu project protocol, activation Rho Upsilon, Iota, Nu."

An instant reply came through. "Confirm. Status active. Units being contacted. Vehicles, hardware, and ammunition will be provided to your location at zero two hundred hours. Personnel will arrive for transport at zero one hundred hours. Units distributed to designated launch points, sir."

"Roger. Notifying upper management." Mac ended the call and motioned Commander Marshall to his side.

"That sounded ominous." Jingu bounced on her feet. "Mac knows I hate surprises."

"Well, no one likes days like today." Llyr's sarcasm sharpened, and Marai stifled a laugh.

"Hush, you two. I want to eavesdrop." Marai sidled closer to the conversation. Jingu side-eyed Llyr. "I can't imagine what we're facing."

"I can," Llyr answered. "Military action and strike forces are standard protocol during on-planet invasions. You operate off protocol. I'm a wildcard after eight years of training. You could call me a specialist, but I have no aliens in my curriculum. My training included survival, combat, and assassination."

Jingu's voice took on the edge of a disgruntled teenager. "For missions, I need partners who perform. You're supposed to be the solution."

Llyr's mouth dropped. Horror blazed in his eyes. "I… don't think—"

"Not like that, you perv! My skill set outpaces everyone else. When grown-ups try to protect me, I end up saving them. Their egos shatter, and they leave. But taking you down took a little effort."

"You made it feel effortless." Llyr scoffed.

Marai rejoined them. "Look at you two, getting along like a house on fire."

Jingu slapped the back of her niece's head.

"What did you find out?" Jingu asked.

"They're bringing in the big guns. Mac's been keeping secrets. We have new toys to play with." Marai squealed. Jingu rolled her eyes.

Mac approached, grinning. "I see I've been reported."

"What's happening, Mac? I feel like I've been dropped into a cheesy military movie without a script." Jingu's voice rose. Llyr and Marai struggled to keep straight faces.

"Let me show you." Mac guided them to the screen. He cleared his throat. "It's time."

The display showed space. Three massive battleships positioned beyond the moon. "Ladies, gentlemen, this is a Qhait advance battle pod. These ships, the Three Sisters of Doom, attacked worldwide today at eleven hundred hours." He stopped to let the knowledge settle.

"Why are our numbers so low?" someone yelled from the back of the room.

"The Voyager probe sent video and audio files of unknown origin decades ago. We began investigating alien sightings, abductions, and crash sites. We listened and learned. Hence, the Committee. Now, we're ready."

"How can we fight them?"

"Specialized teams have prepared for over thirty years for first contact." Mac pushed a button on his pad.

The screen flickered, revealing an alien warrior. Gray, scaly skin. Heavy armor. Cold eyes. The room recoiled. "The Qhait are a reptilian species."

"All this from an abandoned space station?" Llyr asked.

"I could deny that rumor, but where's the fun in that?" Mac said. "Let's just say, space remains a mystery."

Commander Marshall stepped forward. "Retaliatory plans are ready, and transport to launch locations will be provided." He divided the group into ten-person pods. When he reached Llyr's group, Marshall called six suited soldiers over. "Senator MacAuley, you have your orders. These soldiers will escort you to Roswell."

"Two thousand miles?" Llyr's disbelief echoed.

"Classified. Need-to-know only," Commander Marshall said. "Hayes, take them to the transport pad."

Mac's grin widened, white teeth giving the expression a predatory flash. They trailed the six soldiers through the doorway. Llyr's stomach tightened. He remembered that expression. It always preceded calculated suffering.

The soldiers veered right, their boots clomping against the concrete. With each step, the air cooled and carried the faint, earthy scent of stone. At the bottom, a natural grotto opened, and a freight elevator with silver doors waited.

The doors slid open with a pneumatic hiss. Ten circular platforms sat in a precise formation.

"One disc per person," Hayes said. "Arms to your sides." Hayes walked to the control panel hidden behind a rock formation. Once the group was positioned, Hayes touched the communicator on his collar. "We're ready for transport.

"Close your eyes, people." Hayes activated the transporter. A strange *swoosh* swelled.

Llyr complied. Darkness enveloped him as electricity danced over his skin like tiny needles of sensation. Then nothing.

*****

Chapter 4

Jingu fell as her stomach twisted in spasmodic heaves. Seconds later, a hot, acidic rush of bile splattered the concrete. Trembling arms barely held her as she pushed off the floor, unable to suppress a groan. Across the room, Llyr rolled over. Sweat soaked the floor beneath him. Through the shimmering haze that clouded his vision, Llyr met her gaze. Jingu had never seen the shade of green in his face outside of animated Zombie vids.

Marai doubled over behind Llyr's prone body, and her breath came in gulps as she fought down the urge to vomit again. Along the far wall, six soldiers stood, unfazed, flanking Mac. Marai shook her head, unable to clear it, and an attempt to stand found her back on her knees.

"Sit for a minute, you three. It takes a moment to adjust." Mac squatted next to Llyr and helped him sit.

The doors hissed open, and technicians in white coats swept in to assist the three travelers. The soldiers scooted around them, headed down the hall.

Rasping rather than speaking clearly, Jingu said, "What happened?" No swear words, although the situation warranted them.

Standing remained a chore. A migraine throbbed behind her eyes. A technician held a silver tube under her nose while Llyr received the same treatment. The acrid smell burned Jingu's nostrils. She wiggled to get away, but two firm hands braced her shoulders.

"Teleportation is still in the toddler stage. You should have seen the first human trials." Mac shrugged. "Now, at least, only the newbies suffer. The rest of us have acclimated."

Jingu stiffened. She threw a glare in Mac's direction. "What do you mean? We could have ended up in a mountainside? Or worse, with our kidneys on the outside?"

"Now, Jingu—"

"Don't you 'now, Jingu' me, you toad," Jingu snapped. "I look like a sixteen-year-old airhead, but I'm only a few months younger than you."

The words hung heavy in the silence. Marai's hands slapped over her face. Llyr's eyes widened. Mac lowered his head and shook it.

Jingu stood rigid, hands on her hips. "Dammit. I didn't mean to say that."

"Cat's out of the bag now." Mac stared at Llyr. "We have an invasion to stop."

"Where are we?" Marai asked.

"Roswell, New Mexico." Mac's casual response froze the three newcomers. "Cheating upped our game."

"Cheating?" Jingu's voice filled the room. "How do you cheat with teleportation? Some scientist decided to skip three steps? Did an engineer wake up from a prophetic dream?"

Mac laughed. "No. Covert intelligence pushed us light-years ahead. Remember when I mentioned Voyager transmissions?"

"You said chatter," Jingu said. "Chatter implies conversation, translation, casual exchanges. Not physics and teleportation schematics."

"No, but it was enough to bring scouting probes from other places." Mac pursed his lips. Jingu sensed layers beneath the explanation. "Let's get you briefed. We can discuss the details later."

He pointed toward the exit.

* * *

Llyr followed his grandfather down a sterile passage that led into an enormous hangar, where additional personnel joined their group. Sleek, gray, winged vehicles sat row by row, so many that they filled the vast space.

Mac's arm swept across the massive display. "These little gems are our secret weapon, and they can carry fifteen, plus crew," he said. "You have the skills to pilot them. I made sure of that."

Realization dawned on Llyr. "That special cockpit with gloves? I thought I was flying some theoretical spaceship."

"The future is here." Mac spread his arms to indicate their surroundings. "Turns out electromagnetic propulsion drives, previously determined 'impossible,' are not. Thank you, alien technology."

"There were entire classes that learned from that model. Where are the others?"

"Gathering," was all his grandfather said. "Let's get you guys prepped. Including you, Marai." Mac leaned over a smaller uniformed man. "You'll need gear, too."

Marai jerked. "What part am I playing in this fiasco?"

"Medic, what else? Now, let's gear up!"

* * *

Llyr pulled up short, and he twisted his massive frame to avoid knocking Jingu and his grandfather to the ground. Despite Mac's size, Llyr towered over him.

"Watch it, son! Another step, and Jingu would be flattened." Mac slapped Llyr's shoulder and pointed toward a row of armored cases. "Gear's over here. I think you'll like the new toys."

A stern-faced man stood at attention beside the cases.

"Sergeant Hendricks, hand out the body armor." Mac pointed to stacks of small, armored boxes.

Llyr eyed the twelve-inch squares with skepticism. Traditional body armor never fit into small boxes.

"Down to your skivvies, newbies!" Hendricks barked. He opened a case and pulled out a folded gray sheet. "Suit up as if you're going diving." With a snap, the material unfurled into a form-fitting suit and integrated hood. "Store your civilian clothes in the locker at my rear."

Questions poured forth while the group struggled into the fabric. "Where are the shoes?" "How do we relieve ourselves?" "Why does my skin feel weird?"

"Silence," Sergeant Hendricks said. "This design incorporates communications, waste disposal, and adaptive boots. The suit self-customizes the fit. It offers camouflage, but actual cloaking it's not. Most weak spots are covered by new and acquired alien technology courtesy of the Voyager probe. Details are above your pay grade, so enjoy."

Llyr's chin fell. "You said most 'weak spots.' What's the catch?"

Hendricks grimaced. "These suits provide excellent defense against certain weapons and hand-to-hand combat initially, but degrade with every hit." He paused to let the words sink in. "Protection is near total at first but weakens over time. Sharp points become deadly after prolonged use."

"How much time do we have?" Llyr asked.

"With this design, less than thirty minutes," Hendricks answered, "depending on what you're up against."

* * *

Jingu studied the body armor with newfound appreciation. She'd avoided traditional equipment due to its weight, relying on her katana, speed, and strength. But this felt like a second skin.

Hendricks approached with an attachment. Jingu's confusion surprised him. "Turn around." Jingu did as asked, flinching as the large hand settled on the bone connecting her neck to her backbone. "Is this where your katana rides?"

Jingu closed her eyes, raising her fist as if grasping her sword. "Straight down six inches. The handle sits below the top of my head."

Hendricks nodded. "Mac, get me her weapons."

Mac went to her locker and returned with her weapons: the katana, throwing stars, and tanto knife. "She'll need places for these, as well."

"What about firearms?" Hendricks asked.

"Jingu doesn't use guns." Mac's sharp grin made her hackles rise. "But consider those new grenades. Now, while Hendricks gets you set, let's cover mission basics."

The sergeant moved behind her. "Right- or left-handed?"

"Ambidextrous," Jingu answered. "Neither is dominant."

"Interesting challenge. Tap your shoulder when the positioning feels right."

As Mac outlined the operation, Hendricks adjusted her equipment. Jingu tapped her shoulder joint or shook her head, raising a shoulder to show how she wanted it moved.

By the time Mac distributed information packets, Hendricks had gathered them into a circle. "Your pilot, Captain Iris James, has further details waiting in your transport. It's time to start packing."

He led them back into the hangar, where clusters of soldiers surrounded each aircraft. Hendricks set them up with access, then pointed to the front, where Mac stood with a mic. A tall woman dressed for combat joined him.

"People," Mac's voice boomed, "the day we prayed would never come is upon us. You are our hope. Go out and kick some ass!"

The roar from the group shook the walls as each squad loaded.

Jingu opened her mouth to comment about wanting the second-best seat in the house, but Captain James cut her off.

"Everyone, secure yourselves. Our trip will take six to eight hours. You'll go to your stations after we reach altitude to familiarize yourselves." Captain James moved through the small ship, issuing assignments and rest rotations. "Sergeant, weapons array. Doctor, medical bay behind that door. And you…" Captain James looked down at Jingu. "What am I supposed to do with you?"

Jingu shrugged. "Scenery?"

Mac stuck his head through the door before takeoff. "Captain, these orders detail your objective." He tapped the datapad with a calloused finger. "The team needs to breach the ship to access the operation point.

"Success, people. It saves lives." Mac patted the door as it closed.

"Jones, Owens, Lamb, Hicks, Sloane, you're my veterans. Experience counts first. Dr. Gozen, remain on standby," Captain James said. "You two, once we reach altitude—" James pointed at Llyr and Jingu "—here, please. I need to review what skills you bring to the table."

* * *

After the evaluation was completed, Captain James studied Jingu. "The flexibility you show will make you a valuable asset in placing the proton explosives."

She turned to appraise Llyr. "Lt. MacAuley, for the moment, you'll be a standby pilot. I feel like you… need a little more seasoning."

Jingu wanted to tell the captain to give him a more critical job than ship-sitting, but then she noticed the captain turn with a slight sardonic smile.

* * * * *

Chapter 5

Llyr's mind swirled with information. He grasped the weight of managing teams against the Three Sisters. A knot tightened in his gut. Across the bridge, Captain James coordinated timing with the other shuttles to erase the threat. The display screen pulsed with a rhythmic glow, and red dots swarmed the three ships, while three green dots—the special ops vessels—hovered beneath the enemy bellies.

Captain James looked at Llyr as she issued orders to Jones. "Engage the laser drones. This gives the machines time to get positioned."

Llyr's throat went dry. He'd run these scenarios in simulations, but the sight of Jones sending the drones on their path sent a chill down his spine. The mechanisms formed a circle beneath the engine vents, and golden lines crisscrossed between them to form a shimmering net.

Jingu appeared behind Llyr. "What next? Won't they notice?" Her boot tapped a restless rhythm against the deck plating. On the screen, a hole appeared in the hull and expanded until the shuttle could fit inside.

"We'll hide this baby in the empty cargo hold under engineering," the captain replied. A predatory smile curled her lips. "With a few surprises left behind, of course."

"How?" Jingu's fingers drummed against her hip.

"The hole is invisible because the drone's work matches the hull. Laser lines mimic the body of the ship while dampeners on the shuttle keep it hidden in plain sight," the captain explained. "Grab your weapons. Your team will plant proton mines throughout the bottom levels. When the deck plates blow—"

"Systems are go," Shuttle Two crackled over the comms.

Shuttle Three followed immediately. *"Waiting for your mark."*

"Ten-minute countdown on my mark," Captain James answered. She turned to face her people. "It's time. Hendricks, you're point man. Jingu and the other privates, follow to plant mines. Llyr, you have the rear guard and extra hands.

"Shuttles Two and Three, on my mark… Go."

The shuttle eased into position. Overhead handles dropped from the ceiling, and Llyr gripped his. The craft settled with a muffled *thud* inside the enemy vessel. Sergeant Hendricks moved first, crouched at the edge of the ramp with eyes on the dimly lit cargo bay. Two privates, Sloane and Owens, lugged a heavy box down the ramp. After a quick scan of the room, Hendricks signaled with a sharp hand gesture. Sloane and Owens placed explosives at the main structural joints and activated the camouflage.

Llyr checked the weight of his plasma rifle. To his left, the rest of the squad oriented themselves to the map provided by the drones. Llyr committed the route to memory. *Left, left, elevator, right, left, right.* He saw the confusion on Jingu's face. "Direction memorization technique," he whispered.

"Be on the lookout for hostiles. Neutralize first, ask questions later." Hendricks' voice was a mere ghost of a sound. "We should be out of here in thirty or less." He pressed an electronic lock pick against the door. "Clear as we go. Left first. Do not hesitate. Go."

The door hissed open. Silence greeted them as Hendricks peeked around the doorframe before he waved them forward. Llyr's boots made no sound against the metal as he checked every direction.

At the elevator across the hall, Llyr's voice softened. "Do you have a translator, Sergeant? One that works for numbers?"

Hendricks' sharp grin provided the answer. "Of course."

Jingu slowed her pace to let Llyr close the gap. "This is going good so far, don't you think?"

Llyr stared down at her. "You've jinxed us." He shook his head. "Everyone, weapons ready when the doors open."

The warning proved prophetic. The elevator doors slid back to reveal a cluster of aliens. Their reptilian eyes widened in surprise as they fumbled for weapons. Hendricks made a quick slashing motion across his neck. Llyr raised his laser and fired. The aliens dropped with muted thuds. The scent of burned flesh filled the confined space.

Llyr shot Jingu a sharp look. "I told you so." He scanned the hallway for a hiding spot, but found only slick, unforgiving metal.

"Let's put them back in the elevator," one private said. "Hopefully, we'll be gone before anybody finds them."

"Bad plan," Llyr answered, "but I don't see alternatives." He hefted one body into the elevator and pocketed its badge and weapon. The alien's sandpaper skin scraped against his hands as he arranged the corpses in the corner.

"Ascend," Hendricks said as he engaged his camouflage tech. "Traffic will pile up if they see us." Llyr acknowledged the order and obeyed. The others followed suit, and soon the squad moved along the ceiling toward the engine room.

Hendricks listened as the elevator doors opened. Silence filled the hallway. The path remained clear, so they climbed the walls and made their way to the engine room.

The privates planted bombs at every structural junction. Tension thrummed through Llyr's body with every step toward engineering; however, his steps faltered where the hall ended. *Left, or right?*

Llyr paused to think. When Hendricks looked over his shoulder, Llyr motioned right. At the end of the corridor, an open entrance beckoned. No places to hide remained, and Llyr felt certain the traffic was about to pick up.

* * *

A momentary blank stalled Jingu's thoughts as her mind confronted too many possibilities; the OODA Loop—Observe, Orient, Decide, Act—snapped under the pressure of decision. Then a whisper drew her attention to Hendricks. He pointed upward before he scaled the wall like a spider. The others followed and moved twelve feet above the floor. Alien noise masked the advance. Hendricks pulled Jingu close and pointed to her target. The others knew their jobs.

Chaos erupted as Jingu sprinted across the open space. Her muscles burned until nanobots surged with liquid electricity throughout her system. The aliens twisted. Their jaws dropped as their weapons rose. Time slowed. She dodged incoming plasma bursts and dispatched guards. Hot fluids sprayed as her blade moved.

* * *

Crashing cars couldn't match the sound of the sergeant and Llyr slamming into the alien line. Through the roar of the impact, Llyr glanced over his shoulder. "MOVE!" Shoved by his massive hand, Jingu stumbled toward the reactor.

Against the far wall, Jingu kicked off and flipped over a plasma burst. She landed hard on a guard's back. A single, violent slash opened the seam of the neck-guard. Two more rifles swung toward her, but a low slide across the deck kept her beneath their aim. Upward thrusts found the gaps in their armor. Hot, viscous, orange fluid splattered across her suit.

With one hand, Llyr hoisted a dying guard. Behind his meat shield, he bulldozed forward while Jingu followed in his wake. Her katana moved in a tight arc. Together, they reached the reactor hallway.

A sudden jerk brought Llyr to a stop. Jingu slammed into his back with a grunt, her momentum halted by his massive frame. At the end of the hall, an immense room opened up, dominated by a pulsing white light. Energy hummed through the air until the fine hairs on Jingu's arms stood on end.

"You take the left; I'll take the right." Jingu pointed at the stress points. "Ten-minute delay timers. Just enough time to regroup and get out."

Toward the left, Jingu scaled a column to zero in on a stress point. She planted the explosive and ran to the remaining targets. Near the doorway, laser fire and alien screams grew closer. Llyr activated the main switch just as the duo met. "Let's go!" With a sudden heave, Llyr hurled Jingu into the fray and leapt in behind her. A silver blur marked the path of her katana. Nearby, Sergeant Hendricks protected the injured with precise shots.

"Reinforcements arrive in less than five minutes. Let's bail!" Hendricks' shout rose above the din.

While Jingu grabbed Jones, the men snatched up the others for a frantic run to the elevator. Behind the parting doors, the corpses from their earlier encounter blocked the entrance. Jingu huffed, sweat pouring down her face in the humid air.

"We're not out yet." Hendricks covered Llyr as they threw the bodies into the oncoming rush. The door closed just as plasma bolts thumped into the wall of flesh.

"Be prepared for it to get hot when the doors open." Llyr shouldered his weapon.

A heavy, unnatural silence greeted them. The quiet suggested that the enemy remained off guard or waited for a surprise. Hendricks' voice rattled as he gave the order to move.

On the hangar floor, Captain James lowered the ramp. Light flooded the room to reveal the enemy against the wall, at least twenty strong. From the walkway above, a dozen more carried laser weapons and battle axes. Time slowed for Llyr.

"Run!" Hendricks' voice cut through the air.

Backward and alert, Llyr covered the retreat while the others sprinted. Hicks and Owens snatched up the injured and took off for the ramp.

Among the surging alien soldiers, a lack of plasma bursts became obvious. Two aliens fought over a single firearm. The realization hit that plasma would damage the hull. They couldn't risk it.

Off to the side, a large alien aimed a crossbow at Jingu's back. Llyr leapt into action. Between the blows of the attackers, he bulled his way through. With a running start, he vaulted and drove himself into Jingu's back to push her up the closing ramp. A thud hit Llyr's chest with white-hot intensity, and his breath hitched. A trembling hand came up to find blood coating his palm. The room darkened as Marai's screams faded into the distance.

*****

Epilogue

Jingu's voice trembled. She watched Llyr's face twist and contort as the pain overrode his coma. The antiseptic smell of the medical bay stung her nose.

"Will he recover?" Hugging herself, she added, "The idiot threw himself over me."

Marai's smile held a hint of bitterness. "You mean the idiot who kept your head from getting splattered across the cargo bay? The one who made sure you came through it all without losing more than a few pints of blood?"

A low moan punctuated the rebuke. Medical monitors beeped in the background. The two women turned away and whispered, as if Llyr could hear them.

"I don't—"

"What's the answer?"

Both women jumped, startled.

"Llyr!" Jingu cried.

Llyr's voice could only croak out the next words.

"Did the idiot live? I may not be the best one that… I'm not sure at this point."

"You heard that?" Jingu said. "Sorry, but not sorry, too. I mean, I'm glad you're alive and all—"

"Is that what they call this?"

"—but you shouldn't have played hero."

"Next time, I'll let you die… I promise," he said.

"You'll probably be fine," Marai interrupted, leaning closer. Narrowed eyes studied his face. "An unknown weapon, strange blood… what could go wrong? How long do you think you've been out?"

"Weeks, from the feel." Jingu fetched him water from a side table.

"Right at sixty hours," Marai corrected. "You didn't need surgery, just sleep and a transfusion."

"Where did you get blood for me?" Llyr's brow furrowed. "I'm a rare type, AB—"

"Jingu is a universal donor." Marai glanced at Jingu, who flushed. "We'll keep an eye on you for a while."

Heavy boots thudded a familiar cadence against the deck plating as Mac entered the bay. He stopped at the foot of the bed, with his shoulders dropping two inches as he looked down at Llyr. The metal legs of the visitor's chair scraped against the floor as he sat beside his grandson, his movements slow and obviously painful. A glance across the room to the tactical displays showed the Three Sisters were broken husks being dismantled by drones.

"So, the world is safe, and you're on the mend. I'd call that a good day's work."

Llyr didn't answer.

"Don't be that way, Llyr. Now we rebuild. Now we come out of hiding." Mac leaned forward, resting his calloused hands on his knees. "This isn't the end. It's the beginning. The Qhait underestimated us, and they won't make that mistake twice."

Silence settled between them, broken only by the steady pulse of the medical monitor. Out beyond the viewport, the wreckage of the alien ships drifted in the black.

* * * * *

Author Bio

C. A. Waldron is a master's-level teacher, tutor, and is the multi-genre author of Moon Strike. Her work has appeared in Shattering History's Mirror and Reign of Storms. She has been in schools in one capacity or another since 1997, and lives in the Southern US with a partner and a herd of cats.

#####

SOLAR: Wired for War by Jay Burr & Mark Stallings

A Story of the Second Origin Life Augmentation Regiment

Chapter 1 - Jake

Jake flexed the metal fingers of his left hand, watching the titanium-alloy digits respond with a dexterous acuity his flesh and blood had never managed. He touched the metal frame of the chair next to him. Cold. That was what struck him most. Not pain, not the phantom sensations that had haunted him since the IED took his original arm, just a technical insert of the surface temp of the metal he was touching. Mentally, he knew it was cold, but it wasn't the same as actually putting skin on the chair. The diagnostic readout scrolled across his HUD in crisp blue text: 100% OPERATIONAL CAPACITY. He almost missed the ache. At least pain would remind him that he was still human.

The dropship bucked, sending a shudder through the metal benches where the SOLAR platoon sat in their suits. Second Origin Life Augmentation Regiment. Jake had rolled his eyes the first time he'd heard the acronym. *What marketing monkey came up with that?* Jake's enhanced equilibrium compensated automatically, his body remaining steady while the less experienced recruits grabbed for handholds. The troop compartment stank of ozone, hydraulic fluid, and the distinctive metallic tang of Radiant Mycelium, the alien tech powering their suits.

Jake gave the frame a light squeeze to ground himself. The suit he was entombed in crushed the metal effortlessly, reminding him of the level of control he now had to exert over every movement.

"Systems check," Jake muttered to himself, running through his pre-drop protocol. The words weren't necessary, as his subvocal microphones allowed him to be all but silent, but the ritual grounded him.

The suit's limited AI ran through the diagnostics, and the corporate female persona designed to comfort dying soldiers spoke in his ear. *"Weapon interface online. Targeting calibrated. Power reserves at 97 percent."* He shuddered slightly, noticing that the voice glossed over parts of the neural implants designed to allow him to control the suit.

Jake shifted his gaze across the cramped compartment, studying his fellow SOLAR soldiers through his helmet's tactical display. Sixteen of them in total, all wearing the first-generation anthromech suits that transformed the broken into weapons. All of them had traded one death sentence for another. The Myone radiation put out from processing Radiant Mycelium would kill them eventually, probably more efficiently than whatever had landed them in the program in the first place.

His eyes locked on Sara Marks, sitting directly opposite him. Unlike the rest, she hadn't come from military service. Former collegiate athlete, cancer patient, now SOLAR recruit, and ecstatic about it. He watched as she gripped a support bar overhead; he assumed she was testing the limits of her strength. The metal groaned and gave way slightly under her fingers, leaving perfect indentations in the reinforced alloy. Her helmet was retracted, unlike the others, showing off her wide grin. She'd been a track athlete before the cancer ate away at her. Now she could probably bench-press a small vehicle.

"Show-off," Jake hit her on the squad channel.

Sara's grin widened. *"I finally feel alive again, Steele. Not only do I have my body back, it's even better than before. You're telling me you don't enjoy feeling like this?"* She released the bar and flexed her mechanical fingers, and the actuators whirred softly. *"Being strong again?"*

Jake chuckled. "Not sure trading a slow death from cancer for becoming a walking radioactive weapon is the bargain you think it is."

"At least this death comes with benefits," Sara countered, patting the rifle magnetically attached to her thigh armor. *"Better than wasting away in a hospital bed while nurses pretend they don't pity you."* Her eyes hardened. *"Used to need help to get to the bathroom. Now I can punch through a fucking wall."*

The casual way she talked about her terminal diagnosis bothered Jake more than he'd admit. His own injuries had been devastating, career-ending, but never terminal. He'd volunteered for SOLAR because a desk job felt like a prison sentence, not because he was already dying.

"Just remember," Jake said, "these walls shoot back."

"Were you this much fun as a Ranger, or did you lose your sense of humor with your arm and leg?"

Jake shook his head with a grin when the dropship lurched violently to port. The hull creaked under pressure, and hydraulics hissed as the compensators fought to stabilize their descent. Warning lights flashed red. Not unusual for an atmospheric entry on New Haven—the planet's unpredictable weather systems made for rough landings.

Lieutenant Connors' voice crackled through their comms, pitched slightly higher than usual. *"Attention, SOLAR platoon. We are experiencing moderate turbulence during our approach to LZ Alpha. Prepare for combat deployment in T-minus eight minutes."*

Jake resisted the urge to roll his eyes. Moderate turbulence. The kid probably called getting shot at an "unexpected hostile engagement." Lieutenant Samuel Connors was twenty-six, fresh out of officer training, and completely unprepared for commanding enhanced soldiers in actual combat. He'd locked himself in the Command-and-Control pod on the dropship as soon as they'd boarded. The grapevine said he'd graduated top of his class in tactical theory. Theory didn't mean shit when Dominion plasma rounds were melting through your cover.

"Mission parameters remain unchanged," Connors continued, his voice regaining some composure. *"Primary objective is to secure and hold the terraforming station until the next scheduled patrol arrives. Intelligence suggests minimal Dominion presence. If we encounter anything, it will most likely be a reconnaissance element rather than a meaningful force."*

Jake frowned, mentally flagging the flaws in the briefing. *Intelligence suggests. Minimal presence. Most likely.* Too many qualifiers, too little concrete information. He'd led enough missions with the Rangers to know that vague intelligence got people killed. Or severely injured.

"Remember your training," Connors added. *"Maintain squad cohesion and communication protocols. Lieutenant Connors, out."*

"'Remember your training,'" mimicked Sara on the squad channel.

Jake checked his weapon systems one final time, feeling the comforting weight of military hardware integrated with his mech suit. The MX-9 Myone Plasma Lance, or just "Lance," was nothing like the M89 combat rifle that was standard issue. The new hotness leveraged reverse-engineered alien tech with a neural interface that made it an extension of his body in a way no traditional soldier could experience. His targeting system automatically highlighted weak points, calculated windage and drop, and could even suggest optimal firing solutions based on battlefield conditions.

Beth Palmer's voice cut in from further down the bench. *"If you two are done with your pillow talk, some of us are trying to focus."* Palmer—callsign "Ghost" from her sniper days—sat with her eyes closed, likely running through mental simulations of the upcoming mission.

"Sorry if our existence is distracting you, Ghost," Sara shot back. *"Some of us prefer talking to brooding dramatically."*

Palmer didn't open her eyes. *"Some of us prefer inner monologue to running our mouths. But you do you, Marks."*

Jake suppressed a smirk. Palmer had been Force Recon before a career-ending combat injury. Unlike Sara, she kept her personal history locked down tight. What little Jake knew came from observation rather than conversation. She was precise, methodical, and trusted no one who hadn't seen combat completely.

The dropship banked hard, throwing them against their restraints. The pilot's voice crackled over the intercom, "Two minutes to LZ. Getting some unusual readings from the perimeter sensors. Weapons hot."

Jake's mind immediately shifted gears, and his combat instincts surged to the foreground. "Unusual readings" meant their intel was already compromised. He glanced at the others, noting how they straightened, and their hands moved to weapons. Even Sara's cocky demeanor sharpened into something predatory.

"Listen up," Jake said, keeping his voice level, "Connors may have said 'reconnaissance force,' but we prepare for worst-case. Dominion likes to mask its numbers by clustering electronic signatures. Could be two hostiles, could be twenty."

No one questioned why he was speaking instead of their commanding officer. Lieutenant Connors remained conspicuously silent on the comms, likely processing the change in circumstances through his Battle Strategy AI.

"Sara, you take point with your enhanced sensors. Palmer, find elevation and give us overwatch. I'll—"

"Steele," Connors' voice finally cut in, sharp with authority and something that might have been fear, *"I'll assign positions once we've assessed the situation on the ground."*

Jake shot a glance at the first sergeant, who shook his head. Jake bit back his instinctive response. "Yes, sir." The words tasted like ash. On the ground, Top would take care of the LT. That would leave Jake to run the squad.

Jake grinned as he thought of a Japanese saying his anime-junkie sister had told him. "If you need to scream, kindly do it in the silence of your hearts." He glanced at the faceless helmets of the others and wondered who was screaming in their hearts.

The dropship's frame groaned as the craft touched down.

"SOLAR Squad, on your feet," Connors ordered, his voice steadier now.

As one, they rose, heavy mech feet clanging against the deck plating. The sound resonated through Jake's body, mechanical and organic parts vibrating in uncomfortable harmony. Sixteen soldiers, once broken, now reforged into a new alloy: part human, part machine, part alien technology.

The dropship's landing ramp slammed to the ground, revealing New Haven's eerie blue-violet sky. The terraformed atmosphere gave everything an unnatural tint, like viewing the world through colored glass. Harsh sunlight from the red dwarf star cast long shadows across the landing zone below.

Sara nodded at Jake, her expression unreadable behind her helmet visor as it slid into place, but he could imagine her grin, that wolfish, alive expression that both impressed and unsettled him. For a moment, he envied her naïveté, going into her first combat.

"See you on the ground, Warrior," she said over the squad channel. *"Try to keep up."*

Jake allowed himself a small smile. "Roger that. Just remember—"

The rest of his advice was drowned out as the first Dominion rounds slammed against the dropship's hull. *Intelligence suggested minimal presence. Right.* As the SOLAR squads leapt into the fray, Jake couldn't help thinking that dying from their suits suddenly seemed like the least of their problems.

*****

Chapter 2 - Sara

Sara felt the suit amplify her leap as she hit the ground running, impact dampeners absorbing forces that would have shattered her cancer-brittle bones just months ago. Light Dominion plasma rounds deflected off her shoulder plating as her HUD lit up with targeting solutions, threat assessments, and power readouts. The display was a Christmas tree of combat data that would have overwhelmed her before the neural integration. Her smile was predatory inside her helmet. This was *so* much better than dying in a hospital bed with tubes up her nose and pity in everyone's eyes.

"Contact, two o'clock high!" she called out, her enhanced optics picking up movement along the ridgeline three hundred meters away. The targeting system highlighted two sleek forms darting between rocky outcroppings. Dominion Scouts. Their obsidian skin glistened in the harsh light of New Haven, almost beautiful in their lethal efficiency.

Sara brought her weapon up, feeling the neural interface sync with her thoughts. No need for manual adjustments or compensation for her trembling hands. There weren't any trembling hands anymore, just an alloy shell encasing her body, giving her total control. The rifle pulsed, sending a barrage of high-velocity plasma toward the ridge. The Scout ducked with inhuman speed, but Sara caught a satisfying splash of iridescent blue fluid as at least one round found its mark.

She shifted her position. "I've got one wounded." Her body remembered the motion, the rhythm of running, but now without the limitations of damaged muscle tissue and brittle bones. It was fucking *glorious*. She hated stopping, but needed the cover.

"Watch your six." Jake landed beside her, his heavy combat frame slamming into the soil with a *thud* that she felt through her boots. *"They work in packs."*

The comm channel crackled with Lieutenant Connors' voice, higher-pitched than during the descent. *"SOLAR platoon, I'll be coordinating from the dropship. Establishing tactical oversight through your feed data."*

Fucking micromanager. Sara shot a glance at Jake. Their visors hid their expressions, but she didn't need to see his face to know what he was thinking.

"Roger that... sir," Jake replied, his tone neutral, but the pause between said everything.

Sara couldn't resist. "Guess the view's better from in there, sir." Her voice dripped mock sincerity.

"Maintain comm discipline, Marks," Connors snapped back. *"Establish a defensive perimeter around the LZ. Primary objective remains securing the terraforming station."*

Sara felt her face warm. She'd forgotten that the LT could monitor all the squad channels. "Moving to establish perimeter," Sara acknowledged, swallowing further commentary. She knew the game and had played it during her athletic career with coaches who talked big from the sidelines while she pushed her body to the breaking point on the track. Only difference was, the stakes were higher now, and this coach could get her killed.

The platoon fanned out in textbook formation, their movements synchronized despite most of them never having trained together before integration. The SOLAR suits' limited AI highlighted their HUDs to show where they needed to go. Sara took the eastern quadrant, her sensors sweeping the disjointed terrain of New Haven. The landscape was alien despite terraforming efforts. Red-tinged soil gave way to patches of engineered vegetation.

She crouched behind a rock formation, using it as cover while she continued scanning. The contrast wasn't lost on her. Six months ago, she couldn't get out of bed without assistance. Couldn't stand without getting dizzy.

Along came the SOLAR recruitment officer, with his disarming smile and talk of experimental technology. A second chance. Not at life—they'd been clear about that—but at purpose. The suit would kill her, eventually, maybe sooner than the cancer would have, but she'd die strong. Die fighting. Die with dignity. On her own terms.

"Eastern quadrant clear," Sara reported, her thoughts snapping back to the present. "No additional contacts."

"Copy that," Jake responded. *"South and west clear as well."*

"The Scouts appear to be retreating," Palmer's voice came through, measured and analytical. *"They're moving northwest at approximately sixty kilometers per hour. Beyond standard pursuit parameters."*

Sara watched them go, sleek shadows vanishing into the distance, and felt a sharp disappointment. "Permission to pursue," she said. A flash of strength thrummed through her mechanical limbs, demanding release.

"Negative, Marks," Connors replied predictably. *"Maintain formation and proceed with the primary objective."*

Sara countered, "We let them go, we lose the element of surprise."

"Are you questioning orders, Marks?" Connors' voice had the edge that weak men get when their authority is challenged.

Jake cut in before she could dig herself deeper. *"Scouts typically retreat to regroup, not report. They'll be back. We should focus on reaching the terraforming station."*

Sara bit back her frustration. Jake was right, tactically speaking, but the predatory part of her that had awakened with the neural integration hated watching prey escape.

"Roger that," she said, falling in line as the platoon regrouped and began moving toward their objective.

She felt it then, a subtle vibration through the soles of her boots, different from the regular impact of walking. Her HUD flickered momentarily, and power readings dropped by two percent before stabilizing. The other SOLAR soldiers paused almost simultaneously as everyone's suits picked up the anomaly.

"What the hell was that?" Steve Tomlinson asked, his bulky frame pivoting to scan the area.

"Energy fluctuation," Palmer replied.

"Similar signature to the crashed ship's power core. Bearing northwest, approximately ten kilometers," Connors announced. He had better sensors on the dropship. *"Anomalous energy pattern consistent with Radiant Mycelium technology."*

Sara heard her blood pounding in her ears. Northwest. The same direction the Scouts had fled. She felt the need to move. She felt the need to push the boundaries of what they'd told her about her new body and what she could do.

She turned her head to Jake. "Let's check it out." She bounced on her suit's toes, a habit from her pre-race warmup.

Jake moved closer, his private channel opening again. *"Just so we're clear,"* he said, *"unless directed otherwise, we are to secure the terraforming station. Don't antagonize the LT."*

"Listen up," Connors interrupted, addressing the full platoon. *"We're splitting up the squads to cover more ground. Alpha Squad will continue to the terraforming station. Bravo will establish a forward operating position midway between the LZ and the anomaly. Charlie will secure the LZ and our extraction point."* He paused. *"Delta will investigate the energy signature and report back. Do not engage unless absolutely necessary."*

"Roger that," Jake acknowledged. *"Delta Squad, moving out. Expected check-in intervals?"*

"Every fifteen minutes," Connors replied. *"Any sign of significant Dominion forces, you fall back immediately. That's an order."*

Sara almost laughed. Fall back immediately, as if they hadn't just watched how fast those Scouts could move. Though Sara had to admit, her current body could almost triple her record-setting sprint at the university.

The rest of the platoon dispersed, heading toward their assigned objectives, until only Delta Squad remained. Sara looked at her three squadmates. Jake with his Ranger discipline, Palmer with her sniper's patience, and Steve with his almost desperate eagerness to prove himself. An interesting mix for what was clearly the most dangerous assignment.

"So," she said, pacing behind their cover, "we're hunting alien tech with bug-eyed Scouts on our tail. How do you want to play this?"

Palmer gave her a look that might have been disapproval or amusement. Hard to tell with the helmet. *"Just stay sharp, Marks. You're our point person. We're counting on your early warning if those Scouts double back."*

Sara nodded, suddenly serious. For all her bravado, she understood the responsibility.

"I'll see them before they see us," she promised, meaning it. The competitor who'd pushed through pain and exhaustion to cross finish lines was still there beneath the mechanical enhancements and irreverent attitude. And that part of her never let teammates down.

They moved out in formation, Sara on point, with Jake just behind and to her right, her sensors sweeping constantly for any sign of the Scouts returning.

Sara felt alive in a way she hadn't since before her diagnosis. The suit might be killing her, but at this moment, with death potentially coming from any direction, and her body responding with superhuman precision, she was fucking amped up and thriving.

"Two klicks to target," Jake updated them as they navigated a series of low ridges. *"Palmer, find us some high ground for overwatch. Tomlinson, watch our six. Marks, stay on those sensors. And remember, if they're in range, so are you."*

"Copy that," Sara replied, slipping into the role with practiced ease.

The energy signature grew stronger as they approached, her HUD displaying increasing fluctuations in the local power field. Whatever they were heading toward, it was powerful and unstable.

"Anyone else feel like we're walking into a trap?" Steve's normally confident voice was tinged with excitement.

"If it is," Sara replied, checking her weapon's charge status, "at least it'll be interesting." And that was the truth of it for her. Even a Dominion ambush was preferable to what she'd traded for the SOLAR program. At least it would be quick. At least it would matter.

A direct comm from Tomlinson pinged her. *"Is it me, or are our suits heating up?"*

As they crested another ridge, the source of the energy readings came into view in the valley below. Sara felt her breath catch. Not from exertion—the suit prevented that—but from sheer surprise.

"Holy shit," she whispered, taking in the sight.

* * * * *

Chapter 3 - Jake

The first warning came from a subtle tremor beneath their feet, not from their sensors. Jake's HUD flickered violently, dissolving into pixelated chaos as power readings plummeted 15 percent in an instant. Warning symbols flashed red across his vision, and the anthromech's left arm seized mid-motion before emergency protocols rerouted power, and his systems stabilized.

"Contact!" Sara shouted, her enhanced reflexes already bringing her weapon to bear as the first Scout launched from behind a boulder twenty meters ahead.

The Dominion Scout advanced toward the squad, its obsidian skin absorbing light rather than reflecting it. Jake had fought Scouts before. His targeting system struggled to lock on as the Scout zigzagged toward them, moving faster than the tracking algorithms could process.

"Spread out!" Jake barked, his weapon swiveling to track the threat. He fired a controlled burst, and the heavy plasma chewed up soil and rock as the Scout twisted mid-leap, avoiding the deadly fire with millimeters to spare.

Sara pivoted, her lighter frame allowing quicker adjustments. Her rifle spat plasma in a controlled burst, catching the Scout's trailing leg. The creature hissed but didn't slow.

"Multiple contacts!" Palmer called from her position, already climbing to higher ground. "There are three more Scouts approaching from the north."

Jake's tactical display updated with the tagged threats, and red markers blinked into existence around them. Four Scouts circling, testing their defenses. Sophisticated pack tactics.

Jake shifted behind Sara. "Form a defensive circle. Overlapping fields of fire."

They'd barely settled into position when the second wave hit from above. Two hidden Scouts dropped from a nearby boulder, their descent perfectly timed to land on Palmer's position.

"Palmer, above you!" Jake shouted, but the warning came too late.

The first Scout slammed into Palmer's shoulder, and vibroclaws sliced through the reinforced alloy of her suit. Sparks erupted as circuitry was breached, and hydraulic fluid sprayed from severed lines. The second Scout latched onto her back, targeting her newly exposed shoulder joint.

"Get off me!" Palmer snarled, her training overriding panic as she spun violently, trying to dislodge the attackers. Her rifle barked twice, but the rounds went wild as she struggled.

Jake pivoted, bringing his Lance to bear, but hesitated with Palmer caught in his targeting solution. "Sara, cover Tomlinson! I'm going for Palmer!"

He charged forward, pulling his bayonet, each powerful stride eating up the distance.

The nearest Scout noticed his charge and, in the blink of an eye, leapt toward him, its four eyes glowing with feral focus. Jake's augmented body enabled him to sidestep at the last second. His blade sank deeply into the creature as it passed him. The impact sent the Scout tumbling across the rocky ground in an azure bloody mess.

"Sitrep!" Jake demanded through the comms as he continued toward Palmer.

"Two on me!" Sara reported, her voice tight with exertion. *"Fast bastards. Can't get a clean shot!"*

"One circling my position," Tomlinson added, sounding remarkably calm. *"Waiting for an opening."*

Jake reached Palmer just as she managed to dislodge one of the Scouts on her, and she sent it flying with a desperate heave. The impossibly flexible Scout slashed at Jake's forearm as it flew past, and warning indicators flashed as the vibro-claws scored his armor. The second clung to her, its claws buried deep in her suit's back armor, covered in blood and hydraulic fluid. Jake stabbed the creature in the armpit and pulled it loose. Its claws tore away muscle and sinew.

With a grunt of effort, Jake slammed the impaled Scout against a nearby boulder. Once, twice, three times—each impact leaving blue fluid splattered across the red stone.

His sensors confirmed what he already knew. Palmer's vitals had flatlined. His throat tightened. Another dead squadmate. He had to step hard on his emotions. *Now's not the time, Ranger.*

Jake returned to the squad. "Palmer's gone. What's the sitrep?"

Sara was frozen for a moment. *"No!"*

His heart went out to her. Losing a teammate was hard on the grittiest soldier, but he needed her back in the fight. "Focus, Sara."

"Brutes!" Tomlinson called out, his voice cracking. *"Three of them are coming over the eastern ridge!"*

Jake swore under his breath. Scouts were deadly, but fragile. Brutes were walking tanks with biological armor that could shrug off most weapons. The massive reptilian soldiers appeared on the ridgeline, their hulking frames silhouetted against the alien sky. Each stood nearly eight feet tall, their trapezoidal bodies protected by natural osteoderms that gleamed in the dim light. They moved with deliberate slowness, but Jake knew better than to mistake their pace for weakness.

"Command, this is Delta-One. We have encountered strong resistance; three Scouts down, three additional Scouts engaged. Three Brutes entering contact. Delta-Four combat ineffective. Over." Jake turned back to the remaining squad mates. "Fall back to defensive positions! Aim for joints and thermal vents!"

Connors' voice scratched with interference over comms. *"Delta Squ_, follow __ doctrine. Concen__fire __ the Brutes. Your suits sh__ more than a match."*

The squad responded with practiced precision, falling into the AI-guided formation they'd drilled countless times in simulation. Everyone focused their fire on the oncoming Brutes, leaving the Scouts until the heavier threat was eliminated first. Tomlinson laid down covering fire while Sara and Jake maneuvered to flanking positions.

The first volley hit the lead Brute square in the chest, and their plasma rounds converged on the massive target. The combined firepower would have shredded a light vehicle. The Brute barely staggered, its biological armor absorbing and deflecting the assault.

"Minimal effect!" Tomlinson reported unnecessarily, his microphone picking up his rapid breathing. *"They're still advancing!"*

Jake adjusted his targeting solution and tagged the weak point, focusing on the exposed joint at the Brute's knee. "Concentrate fire on the lead."

His Lance screamed, and heavy plasma punched into the Brute's inner knee, where the protective osteoderms thinned. The creature bellowed, but didn't fall. Instead, it raised a directed energy shield, the defensive field humming with power as it absorbed subsequent shots. The shield was only effective against energy weapons. It would have been useless against his old M89.

Meanwhile, the remaining Scouts had regrouped, using the Brutes' advance as cover as they popped out and fired their lightweight energy repeaters. The Scouts never left cover long enough for the SOLAR squad to retaliate.

"This isn't working!" Sara called out, frustration evident in her voice as a Scout evaded her third consecutive burst before she focused on the lead Brute again. *"They're too fast!"*

Jake watched as another volley slammed into the lead Brute's shield, and the energy simply dissipated without effect.

"Fall back twenty meters!" Jake ordered, mind racing through alternatives. "Leapfrog retreat, maintain fire!"

They began the coordinated withdrawal, one soldier covering while the others moved. It was a textbook-perfect execution of their training. It was also completely ineffective. The Scouts seemed to anticipate each move, appearing in their path before they completed the maneuver. The Brutes continued their inexorable advance, their pace unchanging but relentless.

A light energy blast rocked Sara.

Jake pivoted to help her, but a round from one of the Scouts slammed into his pauldron, sending him staggering. The Brutes continued to close the distance.

"Tomlinson, put suppressing fire on that Brute!" Jake ordered, scrambling to regain his footing.

Sara's rifle barked three times in rapid succession, and each shot found its mark despite the creature's speed. The Scout collapsed in a heap of twitching limbs.

"Got the bastard!" Sara crowed, helping Jake into cover behind a massive boulder.

Tomlinson fell back to their position, his Lance cycling through power settings as he tried to find something—anything—that would slow the Brutes' advance. He emitted a high-pitched cackle as he brought his Lance back onto the Brutes and fired an over-powered blast that seemed to have little effect.

The Scouts moved faster than their targeting systems could track, and the Brutes simply absorbed punishment that would destroy conventional targets.

"We need to rethink this," Jake muttered, more to himself than to the squad. The Ranger in him began to override the programmed SOLAR responses.

His private comm channel pinged as Sara reached out directly. *"All this crazy strength and speed isn't helping here. What do we do?"*

*****

Chapter 4 - Sara

Sara watched a Scout's energy blast slam into Jake's pauldron, sending him staggering backward. Everything they'd drilled was failing. Palmer was dead. Palmer's torn-up suit was stuck in her mind.

She felt something twist in her gut as the Brutes continued their steady approach, forcing her to refocus on the fight at hand. Their massive frames shrugged off concentrated plasma fire. The sensation wasn't exactly fear. It was the same feeling she'd had before big races, when she realized the carefully planned strategy wasn't working and her body needed to do something her coaches hadn't trained her for.

"Standard SOLAR protocols aren't cutting it," Jake growled over comms, his voice steady despite the situation. *"We need to change tactics."*

Through her HUD, she watched Connors' signal indicators flickering as he tried to communicate from the relative safety of the dropship. His voice came through broken and distorted: "*... maintain formation... concentrated fire... protocol Alpha-Seven...* "

Jake's response was immediate and decisive. *"Comms compromised. Switching to visual signals and close-range transmissions only."* With that, he cut the main channel to Connors, leaving only the squad's local network active.

Exhilaration pulsed through Sara. They were officially off-leash.

"Listen up," Jake said, his voice low and urgent. *"From now on, we shoot and move. Continuous motion, never static, never predictable."*

"Shoot and move?" Tomlinson repeated, sounding uncertain. *"That's not what we—"*

"Do it," Jake cut him off.

"Override your AI targeting," Jake continued, demonstrating by switching his Lance to manual control. *"The programs are too predictable. The Scouts have mapped our aim points. Trust your instincts."*

"What about the Brutes?" Tomlinson asked, his voice steadier now.

Jake's answer was simple. *"Thermal vents. Wait for them to overheat, then hit the neck gills when they open. Try to fire from different angles to get around the shield. Obviously, firing head-on hasn't been working. But the Scouts are the immediate threat."*

Sara nodded, already reconfiguring her systems. She'd never liked the way the SOLAR suit tried to "help" her aim, anyway. As a sprinter, she'd always relied on muscle memory and intuition over calculated form.

"Moving in three," Jake said, signaling with his hand. *"Leapfrog pattern, but irregular timing. Sara, you're fastest. Take point."*

"Copy that," she replied, feeling a surge of anticipation.

The comms crackled again as Connors tried to reestablish contact: "*... direct order to maintain—*"

Sara shut off the channel completely. Lieutenant Connors had never set foot on a battlefield. He was playing wargames on the dropship while they were fighting for their lives. Jake had been there. Jake had bled there. Jake knew what the fuck he was doing.

"Now!" Jake signaled, and Sara launched herself from cover.

But not in a linear dash designed to minimize her profile. Instead, she drew on years of parkour training she'd picked up in college, a hobby that had complemented her track career. She ran up the side of a boulder, pushed off, and twisted in mid-air, firing at a Scout that had been lying in wait for a predictable emergence.

The creature's four eyes widened in what looked like surprise as Sara's plasma rounds caught it mid-chest, punching through its light armor. Blue fluid erupted in a fine mist as the Scout collapsed.

Sara guided her suit into a roll straight out of a parkour exhibition, but with a fluidity and power no human body could match.

"Fuck." She popped up to her feet, feeling a rush that was part adrenaline, part synthetic. The suit's neural interface was flooding her system with dopamine as a reward for successful execution. The sensation was familiar, yet alien, like the rush after finishing a race, but amplified tenfold. She always wanted to feel this.

Jake and Tomlinson were moving, too, Jake with the practiced efficiency of a veteran soldier, Tomlinson with less grace but following the others. They weren't fighting like mechanically perfect, automated SOLAR soldiers anymore. They were fighting like augmented humans, unpredictable and adaptive.

"Scout on your three, Tomlinson," Sara called, already changing direction mid-stride to flank the enemy.

Tomlinson pivoted, firing at where the Scout would be, trusting his senses instead of the AI targeting solutions. The creature dodged, just as expected, right into Sara's line of fire.

She squeezed the trigger twice. The first shot missed; the second caught the Scout in its hind leg. Not a kill shot, but enough to slow it down. Jake finished it with a burst that nearly cut the creature in half.

"Keep moving!" Jake ordered as the Brutes continued their slow but unstoppable advance, now less than fifty meters away.

Sara felt something changing in her interaction with the suit. In training, she'd always felt the powerful but external feeling of wearing technology. Now, as she pushed it beyond programmed parameters, it felt more like an extension of herself.

She vaulted over a boulder, using her momentum to carry her higher than the suit's standard jump protocols should allow. At the apex of her leap, she spotted the remaining Scout trying to circle behind Tomlinson.

"Got eyes on the last Scout." She twisted in mid-air to bring her weapon to bear.

The Scout saw her and reacted with preternatural speed, darting between rocks faster than her suit's targeting could track. But Sara wasn't using it.

She aimed where it had to go, the only path available given its momentum and the terrain. Her finger squeezed the trigger just as the creature burst into the open space.

The plasma round caught it square in the chest, spinning it around violently. It wasn't down, though, and it recovered with its uncanny resilience. Sara landed hard, rolled, and came up firing again, keeping it pinned down.

"I've got it suppressed!" she called out.

Jake shifted immediately. *"Tomlinson, flank left."*

They moved in the fluid, adaptive teamwork of humans who understood each other's intentions. The Scout, caught in their crossfire, tried to leap away, but took simultaneous hits from three directions. It collapsed in a twitching heap of severed limbs and leaking fluids.

The Brutes came on, their massive frames now close enough that Sara could see the individual scales of their natural armor in New Haven's alien light. Three walking tanks, seemingly impervious to their weapons.

"Fall back toward the LZ," Jake ordered. *"Same pattern. Keep moving."*

As they retreated, Sara found herself moving in ways that felt completely natural, yet with speed and strength no human could match.

Each successful maneuver brought another rush of synthetic reward, the suit's neural interface reinforcing behaviors that improved combat effectiveness. It felt good. Too good. Better than the best runner's high she'd ever experienced.

The first Brute reached a small clearing and paused, its massive chest expanding. Sara recognized the sign that it was about to vent excess thermal energy.

"Brute venting at my two o'clock!" she called out, already adjusting her trajectory to gain a better angle.

Jake tagged a spot on the Brute. *"Target the thermal vents. Coordinated fire on my mark."*

The Brute's neck gills flared open, exposing the vulnerable tissue beneath its armored exterior. For a brief moment, it was vulnerable.

"Mark!"

They fired simultaneously, and their plasma rounds converged on the exposed area. The Brute roared, and its movements slowed noticeably.

As they continued their fighting retreat, Sara became increasingly aware of how her movements were changing. The suit was learning from her, adapting its response patterns to her unconventional techniques. But she was also learning from it, internalizing its capabilities, thinking less about what she wanted it to do and simply doing it.

Sara clocked the next Brute and called out, "Second Brute venting!" Its neck gills flared as it released excess heat.

Jake ordered, *"On my mark... mark!"*

Again, they fired in unison, and their plasma rounds struck the vulnerable tissue. This time, the Brute stumbled, and alien blood leaked from its injured neck. It wasn't down, but they'd hurt it.

The suit's feedback loops kept amplifying her natural response. The sensation was intoxicating. She found herself wanting more, and she pushed for another kill confirmation, another hit of that synthetic reward.

The third Brute finally entered the engagement zone, joining its wounded companions. The first remained slightly behind, its massive energy shield still active.

"LZ in sight," Tomlinson reported, his voice more manic than it had been at the start of the engagement.

Sara checked her HUD. They'd covered nearly seven kilometers in their fighting retreat, eliminating the immediate Scout threat and wounding two Brutes. Not bad for abandoning doctrine mid-battle.

The wounded Brute suddenly charged, moving with surprising speed for something so massive. Its thermal vents were closed, meaning they couldn't target its weakness.

"Scatter!" Jake ordered, and they broke in three directions.

Sara leapt to the left, executing a backflip over a boulder that gave her both cover and elevation. The maneuver should have been impossible. The suit was clearly struggling to match the movements she was making.

The distinction between herself and the machine was blurring with each passing minute.

They were surviving. And it felt oh, so right.

Tomlinson drifted back from the charging Brute. "Three kilometers to go." He'd been so focused on the charging Brute, he hadn't seen the movement of the unwounded Brute that came up behind him.

* * * * *

Chapter 5 - Jake

"Tomlinson!" Jake shouted, his warning drowned in the mechanical whine of servos and the thundering footfalls of the approaching Brute. The massive creature moved with unexpected speed for something of that size, its armored bulk closing on Tomlinson's blindside while he remained fixated on the wounded Brute ahead. Jake's HUD flashed proximity warnings, but Tomlinson wasn't responding to the automated alerts. Whatever was happening, Steve was operating on pure instinct now, and instinct was about to get him killed.

Jake pivoted, his suit whirring as he shifted his weight to sprint toward Tomlinson's position. "Steve! Nine o'clock! Move your ass!"

Instead of retreating or even acknowledging Jake's warning, Tomlinson did something incomprehensible. He charged directly at the wounded Brute, leaving himself completely exposed to the second one closing in behind.

"What the fuck?" Sara's voice crackled over their local comm. *"Is he insane?"*

Jake's targeting system locked onto the unwounded Brute, calculating firing solutions as he sprinted forward. "Tomlinson, fall back now! That's an order!"

But Steve wasn't listening. His hulking frame slammed into the wounded Brute with bone-crushing force, metal-reinforced fists pounding against the creature's armored hide. Even through the suit's filters, Jake heard a feral roar that barely sounded human.

"Something's wrong," Jake said, skidding to a halt and bringing his weapon up. "Cover me!"

The unwounded Brute changed course, lumbering toward Tomlinson's exposed back. Jake squeezed the trigger, sending a spray of plasma rounds into the creature's flank. The shots connected just as the Brute vented. Its massive head swiveled toward Jake, and it shifted its energy shield to protect itself.

"Hey, ugly!" Sara called out over her external speakers, drawing the Brute's focus as she darted between boulders, firing controlled bursts that forced it to shift the shield. "Over here!" She also caught the other Brute's focus as they tried a similar maneuver: hammer and anvil.

Jake used the distraction to check Tomlinson's status on his HUD. What he saw made his blood run cold.

Tomlinson's vitals were spiking beyond anything Jake had ever seen in training or combat. Heart rate: 210 BPM. Blood pressure: critical. Neural activity: off the charts. The suit was designed to compensate for human biological limitations, but Tomlinson was pushing far past what Humans should be able to endure.

"Steve's redlining," Jake said to Sara. "His suit's not regulating properly."

On the battlefield, Tomlinson had become something else entirely. His movements were no longer those of a trained soldier. There was no discipline, no restraint, just raw, unbridled violence. He tore at the Brute with his suit's hands, ripping away chunks of biological armor, driving his fist through exposed tissue with inhuman movements.

The Brute roared, its thermal vents flaring open as it tried to redirect power to defend itself. Tomlinson showed no hesitation, driving his armored fingers directly into the exposed gills. Blue fluid erupted in a pressurized spray, coating Tomlinson's suit in alien viscera.

She turned to Jake. *"Fuck me,"* she whispered hoarsely. *"What do we do?"*

Jake's training told him to exploit the advantage, to press forward while one Brute was engaged and wounded. But something held him back. This wasn't right. Tomlinson wasn't fighting like a soldier. He wasn't even fighting like a human. His stomach turned at the gore.

"Sara, maintain fire on the other Brute."

"Copy that," she replied, her voice tight with tension. *"He's not right."*

Jake's attention snapped back to his HUD as the AI spoke, *"Tomlinson's vital signs have flatlined."* Jake stared. All of them. No heartbeat. No brain activity. No respiratory function.

"Steve?" Jake called over the comm. "Tomlinson, respond!"

Nothing. Yet on the battlefield, Tomlinson's suit continued to fight even more viciously. He had the wounded Brute on the ground now, straddling its massive chest, repeatedly driving his fist through the creature's throat. Even as the Brute stopped moving, Tomlinson continued to pummel, dismantling the corpse.

Tomlinson abruptly abandoned the wreckage of the Brute. With disturbing focus, he pivoted and charged toward the third Brute—the one that had been hanging back with its energy shield active and taking fire from Sara.

Jake watched in horrified fascination as Tomlinson engaged. He wasn't using weapons anymore. No tactical movements, no coordinated attacks, just raw, unbridled aggression. He punched the Brute, bypassing the shield entirely with an electronic whine.

"What's happening to him?" Sara asked, having fallen back to Jake's position.

"Neural cascade," Jake replied grimly. "The suit's fighting protocols have overridden his consciousness. That's what the lab coats warned might happen if we pushed too hard."

The Brute fought back with massive sweeps of its armored forearm, but Tomlinson seemed impervious to the blows. Each impact sent him staggering, but the machine recovered instantly, adapting its approach.

"That's not possible," Sara whispered as Tomlinson drove his fist through the energy shield. The field sparked and distorted around his arm. "The suits aren't that strong."

"They are if they don't have to worry about keeping the pilot alive," Jake said, the realization hitting him with horrific clarity. "The safety protocols are what limit our strength. Without them..."

He didn't need to finish. They were witnessing the result. Tomlinson, or whatever was wearing his suit, drove both hands into the chest armor and tore it apart. The Brute's defensive technology shredded, exposing its chest.

What followed wasn't anything like what they were trained for. Tomlinson tore into the Brute, hitting joints and weak points with perfect accuracy. The creature fought back, landing blows that would have killed a normal human, even one in a SOLAR suit. But the machine kept coming, utterly indifferent to damage.

In less than thirty seconds, the Brute lay dead, its throat torn open, with azure blood pooling beneath its massive frame. The only living Brute of the trio slowly backed away from the carnage, but it couldn't outrun death incarnate.

The third Brute died, and Tomlinson turned.

His helmet swiveled first, followed by the rest of his body in a smooth, inhuman motion. Through the visor, Jake could see nothing of Steve's face, no indication of the man who'd been there moments before. Just the reflective darkness of the faceplate, now spattered with alien blood.

"Sara," Jake said quietly, "move behind me. Slowly."

The targeting reticle on Jake's HUD locked onto Tomlinson's suit. The system highlighted vulnerable points. Joints, power conduits, neural interface port at the base of the neck.

Tomlinson took a step forward. Then another. His movements had changed again, becoming predatory. The suit's AI was adapting.

"Steve," Jake called out, one last attempt, "if you're in there, stand down. We're friendlies."

Tomlinson's helmet tilted slightly, an almost curious gesture. Then he charged.

The attack was blindingly fast, faster than anything Jake had seen in training. Tomlinson's fist lashed out, aiming directly at Sara. Jake barely managed to interpose himself, catching the blow on his forearm. Warning lights flashed across his HUD as the impact stress-tested his suit's structural integrity.

"Run!" Jake shouted to Sara, using his mass to momentarily check Tomlinson's advance. "Get back to the LZ!"

"Not without you!" Sara replied, as her weapon came up.

Tomlinson struck again, this time catching Jake in the chest. The impact sent him sprawling backward, his systems momentarily stuttering as the suit compensated for the damage.

"He's not targeting me," Jake realized aloud, rolling to his feet. "He's going after you!"

The machine that had been Tomlinson pivoted toward Sara, ignoring Jake completely now. It was hunting the perceived weaker target first.

Jake's mind raced. He had seconds, maybe less. Sara was backing away, firing controlled bursts at Tomlinson, but the rounds barely slowed him.

Connors' voice broke through the comm static, *"Delta-One, you need to terminate Tomlinson now! Use emergency protocol Omega-Six!"*

Omega-Six. The AI-triggered release of knowledge slammed into Jake's consciousness. SOLAR instructions and information flooded his vision for a microsecond. A specific electromagnetic pulse pattern targeted at the neural interface port would instantly sever the connection between pilot and suit, shutting down both in the process.

It would kill Steve instantly—if he wasn't already dead.

"Jake!" Sara screamed, barely evading Tomlinson's grasp as she ducked behind a boulder. The machine followed relentlessly, smashing through the rock as if it were cardboard.

Time compressed to a single moment of perfect clarity. Jake reactivated his targeting system, locked onto the base of Tomlinson's helmet where the neural interface connected, and initiated the protocol.

His Lance whined as it reconfigured, and the weapon's power cells cycled to a specific frequency. Jake squeezed the trigger once.

A single pulse of focused energy struck Tomlinson's neural port. For a moment, nothing happened. The machine took another step toward Sara.

Then everything stopped. Tomlinson's suit froze mid-stride, a marionette with cut strings. It swayed for a heartbeat, then crashed to the ground with a dull metallic *thud* that echoed across the battlefield.

The reality of what Jake had done pressed down on him like a physical weight, punctuated by the faint whine of Steve's suit powering down, its systems forcibly shutting off. The soft *plink-plink* of blue alien blood dripping from Steve's still-extended fist added to the dark symphony, while Jake's gun emitted a sizzling sound, still crackling from the force of his shot.

Jake approached cautiously, his weapon still trained on the motionless suit. His HUD confirmed what he already knew. No vital signs, no power signature, nothing. Just dead metal encasing what had once been a man.

"Is he…" Sara began, her voice uncharacteristically subdued.

"Yeah." Jake knelt beside the fallen suit, his hand resting briefly on its shoulder plate. "He was gone before I pulled the trigger."

They stood in silence for a moment, and the reality of the situation settled over them like a shroud. Six dead Scouts. Three dead Brutes. Two dead squad mates. And the uncomfortable knowledge that what happened to Tomlinson could happen to any of them.

"That could have been me," Sara said finally. "When we were fighting the Scouts, I felt it. This rush every time I pulled off a move. The suit rewarded me and pushed me to do more."

Jake nodded. "Yeah, it goes both ways. The suits don't just do what we tell them to. They learn and adapt to us as individuals. It looks like they reward us for behavior they determine is favorable. In the future…"

He stared at his own hands, and the mechanized fingers flexed with inhuman precision. How much of that movement was him, and how much was the machine? Where did Jake Steele end and SOLAR begin?

"We need to report this," Sara said, breaking the silence. "The brass needs to know what these suits are capable of."

Jake laughed, a short, bitter sound. "You think they don't know? Why do you think we have the Omega-Six protocol ready to be sent directly to our suits?" He gestured toward Tomlinson's fallen form. "We're not soldiers to them, Sara. We're prototypes. And sometimes prototypes fail."

The realization settled between them, heavy as lead. They'd volunteered for the SOLAR program, thinking it was their salvation, a way back from the brink of death or disability. But salvation came with a price tag neither had fully understood until now.

"So, what do we do?" Sara asked, her voice steady despite everything. "Just wait for the same thing to happen to us?"

Jake stared across the alien landscape at the bodies of the Brutes and the fallen form of their squadmate. Then he looked at Sara. She was fierce and determined, refusing to be broken, even by this.

"No," he said firmly. "We adapt. We learn the warning signs, and we remember that we're still human underneath all this tech. Steve forgot that—or the suit made him forget."

Jake reached for Tomlinson's dog tags, pulling them free from their dedicated compartment.

"And we remind each other," he continued, handing one of the tags to Sara. "When it gets too good, when the rush starts feeling better than it should, we force each other to pull back. We stay human."

Sara took the tags, closing her mechanical fingers around it. "And if we can't?"

Jake didn't answer immediately, his gaze drifting to his weapon, then back to Sara's face.

"Then we do what needs to be done," he said finally. "Because that—" he nodded toward Tomlinson "—is a worse death than whatever we signed up to avoid."

Their comms crackled as Lieutenant Connors' voice broke through again, demanding a status update. Jake ignored it for the moment, focusing instead on the woman in front of him, on the unspoken pact forming between them.

"Ready to move out?" he asked.

Sara nodded, her posture straightening as she tucked Tomlinson's dog tags into a compartment in her suit. "I'll follow you, Warrior."

They marched toward the LZ, dragging Tomlinson's suit behind them. The mission would continue. The war would go on.

The enemy wasn't just the Dominion. They would also need to contend with the very technology that gave them the power to fight. That realization was a terrible irony that neither could ignore: to win this war, they might have to lose the very humanity they were fighting to defend.

* * * * *

Chapter 6 - Jake

The dropship ride up to the transport was tense. Tomlinson's inert form was strapped into a slot by the door, casting a pall over the other troops as they exited into the transport ship.

"Steele, Marks!" Lieutenant Connors barked. Jake could tell from Connors' complexion that he was about to erupt. "You directly disobeyed orders by cutting communications."

Sara stepped forward, the servos in her suit amplifying her agitated movements. "With all due respect, sir, we had bigger problems than maintaining comms protocol."

"That's not your call to make, Soldier," Connors replied, but there was uncertainty in his voice. His eyes kept darting to Tomlinson's motionless form. "I need a full explanation of what happened out there."

Jake's jaw tightened. "What happened is, your intelligence was shit, sir. Minimal Dominion presence turned out to be three Brutes and six Scouts. When standard SOLAR tactics failed, we adapted."

"Adapted by implementing non-regulation combat procedures," Connors countered, though the accusation sounded hollow, even to him.

The first sergeant interjected, "Sir, the general's on approach."

As one, the group turned to the inner entrance of the landing bay. A functional people-mover glided into the area bearing a figure that made Jake's blood run cold. General Victor Turner, head of the SOLAR program, stepped out of the cart.

The man's silver hair was cropped close to his skull, and he wore BDUs that reflected his years as a ground-pounder. His eyes were gunmetal gray, calculating as they swept over the returning soldiers before settling on Tomlinson's fallen form.

"Attention!" Top snapped. Everyone within range of his command immediately came to attention.

"Lieutenant Connors," Turner said, his voice unexpectedly warm, "I'll take it from here."

Connors almost broke rank in his astonishment. "Sir, I was just beginning the debriefing—"

"And now you're ending it," Turner cut him off smoothly. "Steele, Marks. With me." He glanced around. "As you were." He walked to the interior hatch.

Jake exchanged a glance with Sara before following the general, leaving Tomlinson's suit under guard on the landing pad.

The cabin Turner led them to was spartan, with only a desk fabricated from New Haven's native stone, three chairs, and a wall of screens displaying tactical data from across the planet. He gestured for them to sit.

"I've reviewed the preliminary data from your suit telemetry," Turner began without preamble. "Quite the shitshow out there."

Jake said nothing, waiting.

"Three Brutes down," Turner continued, bringing up footage from their suits on one of the screens. "That's impressive work. Most SOLAR units would have retreated after encountering that level of resistance."

"Most SOLAR units would have followed protocol," Sara said, unable to contain herself.

Turner's eyes flicked to her, his expression unreadable. "Indeed, Specialist Marks. Protocol exists for a reason." He tapped his desk and brought up another screen showing Tomlinson's vital signs flatlined while his suit continued fighting. "But sometimes adaptation is necessary."

Jake leaned forward. "You know what happened to him."

It wasn't a question.

"Neural cascade syndrome." Turner nodded. "A risk factor we've been monitoring since the program's inception. The interface between human consciousness and the suit's combat systems occasionally… overloads."

"Overloads," Jake repeated, the word bitter in his mouth. "Is that what we're calling it when a man gets erased and replaced by a killing machine?"

Turner didn't flinch. "I'm calling it an unfortunate but not unexpected sacrifice in the development of technology that will save humanity. The data you gathered—and yes, even Specialist Tomlinson's… incident—provides invaluable insights."

Jake felt something twist in his gut. "He wasn't a data point, sir. He was a soldier."

"He was both," Turner said simply, "as are you. As are all SOLAR operatives." His expression softened fractionally. "Steve Tomlinson will be honored as the hero he was. His sacrifice has already led to modifications in the neural interface that will help reduce similar incidents."

Sara's fists clenched. "So he was just a prototype that failed, and now you've got better specs for version 2.0?"

Turner regarded her coolly. "Your background isn't military, Marks, so I'll overlook the insubordination, but yes, that's essentially correct. The SOLAR program evolves with each deployment, each engagement, each… failure."

Jake stared at the general, seeing him clearly for perhaps the first time. Something potentially worse than a monster—a man so focused on the bigger picture that individual lives became acceptable collateral damage.

"What happens to his body?" Jake asked quietly.

Turner's expression didn't change. "Study, extraction from the suit, then cremation. His family will receive his medals and a narrative suitable for public consumption."

"You mean propaganda," Sara muttered.

"What serves humanity better?" Turner countered. "The knowledge that their loved one became something inhuman before death? Or the belief that he died fighting bravely for his species' survival?" He stood, signaling the end of the debrief. "You both performed admirably under extreme circumstances. Come with me.

"What I'm about to show you is classified Level Omega. Beyond top secret. The future of the SOLAR program, and possibly of humanity itself."

The scanner hummed, reading not just Turner's palm print but the specific electrical patterns of his nervous system. The massive door began to slide open.

"Sir," Jake said carefully, "may I ask, why us? We just did our first op."

Turner's gaze sharpened. "That's precisely why, Steele. After reviewing your engagement data, particularly your response to Tomlinson's... incident, it's clear you two aren't 'just' anything."

The door finished its slow reveal, opening onto darkness so complete, it seemed solid. Turner stepped into the abyss. Then, one by one, massive overhead lights flickered to life, illuminating a space so vast that Jake's suit sensors struggled to map its boundaries.

Jake followed, his enhanced vision adjusting to reveal a hangar larger than any he'd seen before. The ceiling stretched at least forty meters overhead, supported by massive arched beams. The space's occupants stopped him cold.

"Fuck me running," Sara whispered beside him, her usual confidence momentarily stripped away.

Towering in the center of the hangar stood five massive, mechanized forms. Not suits like they wore—these were behemoths, at least twelve meters tall, with armored plating that made their current equipment look like papier-mâché. Each stood on legs thick as ancient redwoods, with weapon systems integrated into arms that could crush a Brute with casual ease.

"Carrier mechs," Turner said, his voice betraying a hint of pride. "The next evolution of the SOLAR program."

Jake stared upward, taking in the colossal machines. Unlike their anthromech suits, they weren't designed to mimic human form exactly. They were broader, more heavily armored, with additional limbs mounted at strategic points. One had what appeared to be missile launchers integrated into its shoulder array; another featured a rotary cannon system that made Jake's heavy weapons look like toys.

"They're..." Jake struggled to find words.

"Magnificent," Sara finished, but Jake noted the slight tremor in her voice.

As they approached the nearest carrier mech, Jake noticed something odd about its design. In the center of the chest, where a pilot compartment might be expected, there was instead an empty chamber—a perfectly shaped void.

"This one's incomplete," Jake observed, pointing to the empty space.

Turner's smile was thin and without warmth. "No, Steele. It's waiting."

"Waiting for what?" Sara asked, though Jake suddenly knew the answer, felt it in the cold certainty settling into his gut.

"For you," Turner replied.

Jake's attention snapped to the void again, really seeing it now. The compartment wasn't designed for a human pilot. It was exactly shaped to accommodate their anthromech suits.

"The missing piece," Turner continued, "is you. Both of you. Your anthromechs were designed from the beginning to serve as the central processing units for these carrier systems."

The realization hit Jake like a physical blow. They weren't the end product; they were components. Critical ones, but components, nonetheless. The strength, the speed, the neural integration they'd undergone wasn't to make them better soldiers; it was to make them better pilots for these monsters.

"You're telling me these things can't operate without us plugged into them?" Sara asked, stepping closer to the massive foot of the carrier mech, seeming tiny beside it.

"We tried autonomous systems," Turner explained, walking around the behemoth's base, "AI pilots, even direct neural uplinks from remote operators. Nothing worked. The processing demands are too complex, the reaction times too crucial. We need human cognition enhanced by anthromech systems integrated into the carrier frame."

Jake struggled to process the implications. "So we… what? Slot into these things like batteries?"

"More like brains," Turner corrected. "Your anthromech becomes the neural core of the carrier system. Your human consciousness, filtered through the anthromech's enhancement protocols, drives the entire apparatus."

Jake looked up at the towering machine, imagining himself sealed inside it, further removed from humanity than he already was. "And if something goes wrong? If we have another Tomlinson situation?"

Turner's expression hardened. "That's precisely why you're here, Steele. You and Marks demonstrated something remarkable during your encounter with the Dominion forces. You overrode your suit's combat protocols. You adapted, improvised. Most importantly, you maintained your human decision-making capacity under extreme stress."

Turner grinned at them. "Welcome to Project Ascension."

* * * * *

Author Bios

Jay Burr spent years in IT before realizing building galaxies is more compelling than debugging code. Now, he trades server racks for world-building and system architectures for magic. Jay writes Science Fiction and Fantasy, exploring human nature through the lens of a lifelong technical problem-solver.

Mark Stallings is an internationally published and Amazon Best Selling author, and a writer of Wuxia, Progression Fantasy, and Military Sci-Fi in his own worlds and several shared universes. He is a competitive shooter, an avid martial artist, a drinker of craft beer, and a motorcycle enthusiast. You can find him online at MarkStallings.com.

# # # # #

Aurora by
Charli Cox & John E. Siers

A Story of the Children of the Lunar Free State

Chapter 1

King's City
Tatanna

Her heart fluttered in her chest, and her breath came fast, sharp. As tired as she was of running, she was more exhausted by the constant teasing of the other children living near her in the south-east quarter of King's City. Pressing her shoulders against the stone wall of the blacksmith's shop, she took a quick respite. Not long enough for the boys who would soon come of age to catch up with her, just enough to catch her breath. To think.

With her heart beating at a steadier rhythm, in time with the swing of the blacksmith's hammer, she peered around the rough gray wall. Her home was just across the rear alley. Ten, maybe twenty paces, and she would be safe, hidden in the shadows of the dimly lit shack she shared with her mother.

Mother, she thought with a wince. She squeezed the small bun-dle of herbs in her hand. Despite the assurances of the healer and her numerous prayers to the Goddess, nothing was working. Her mother was ill, and she wasn't getting any better.

I must say extra prayers tonight.

She looked across the alley, listening for the telltale shouts that her pursuers had spotted her, and sighed. *Why do they torment me?* The only sound to greet her ears was the steady pounding of the hammer, shaping iron shoes for the kildren. Her mother could never hope to afford one, but she enjoyed watching as they pulled heavy carts or bore their wealthier riders along the streets of King's City.

After checking the packed earth separating her from her refuge one more time, she steeled herself and stepped into the bright afternoon light. The warmth of Tatanna's star melted her unease. Quickly, she trotted to the door and pushed it open.

From behind her, a voice taunted, "Blue eyes! I see-eee you."

She turned her head toward the familiar voice, her sandy blonde hair cascading over her pale shoulder, and shuddered. Tomas, the leader of the gang of Tatannan youth, stuck his tongue out at her. His dark brown hair hung limply over brown eyes swimming with menace.

"Next time, Blue Eyes, I'll stick your face in the manure pile. Maybe then you'll look like you belong here." Tomas sneered at her, clapped one of his buddies on the shoulder, and sauntered off, head thrown back in mocking laughter.

Slamming the door behind her, she crushed the herbs in her hand, and her fingernails cut into her palm. Hot tears streaked down her face as she sank to the dirt floor. Sobbing, she hugged her knees to her chest, the hem of her skirt caressing the tops of her bare feet.

Why do I have to be different? How come I don't look like the other kids?

A hacking cough from the rear of her home broke through her thoughts. Wiping the tears away, she moved to the fire and dumped the crushed herbs into the waiting boiling water.

"Danoriana, is that you?"

"Yes, Mother. I am making you something to help you feel better. Give me a moment, and I will bring it to you." She waited until the steam filled her nostrils with a pleasant aroma.

Stirring the tea with a wooden spoon, she strained out the largest leaves and placed them in a mug to dry. Since her mother had been sick, she hadn't been able to work at the Sleepy Tembril Tavern. What little copper they had saved was quickly spent on more herbs. *Goddess willing, I can reuse these later tonight.*

Plastering a smile on her face, she carried the pot of tea to her mother's bedside. She dumped out the remains of yesterday's serving into the chamber pot and poured a steaming cup of the new batch. "Here, Mother. This should help."

Her mother tried to sit up but fell back limply on the thin pillow. She had been ill for two tendays, and it showed. Dark circles marred the light brown skin beneath her glassy eyes. Her high cheekbones poked out of her face, leaving her formerly beautiful features stark. As she reached for the outstretched mug, her bony hands shook, paper-thin skin taut over her fragile bones.

Danoriana lifted the cup to her mother's gray lips. "Here. Let me."

Her mother coughed, a glob of phlegm dribbling down her chin. "You have done enough, Danoriana. You are the best daughter a mother could ask the Goddess for."

"What is that supposed to mean?" Danoriana set the cup of tea on the bedside table with a clatter. Precious tea sloshed down the sides, dripping from the table onto the floor. "Oh, Goddess!" she cried.

"Leave it," her mother whispered. "I fear it is no good to me now."

"What are you saying, Mother? Surely the Goddess—"

Her mother coughed again, and this time, flecks of blood dotted the thin bedsheet. "The Goddess has done all she can for me."

"Mother, no!"

"Danoriana, hear me now. I need you to do one more thing for me. Go to the Temple and find a priestess. It will not be long before I find myself in Her loving embrace."

Staring into her mother's dark brown eyes, Danoriana nodded. "Yes, Mother, but what do I do about Tomas and the other boys? What if they delay me? What if—"

Her mother sighed softly. "My beautiful blue-eyed child of the stars. I had hoped to tell you this when you were older, but look at you, nearly a grown woman already."

Taking a deep breath that rattled in her lungs, her mother continued, "I have always told you that you were special, a gift from the Goddess Herself."

Danoriana nodded again. She grabbed her mother's chilly hand and held on for all she was worth.

"Your father came to visit the tavern many years ago."

"I know this, Mother. You told me before."

Her mother gave her a sad smile. "Yes, but I never told you where he came from."

Danoriana's eyes widened. She sat up straight. "He was a traveler…"

"That he was." Her mother chuckled softly, then fell into a series of coughs and hacks. Shaking her head, a single tear traced down her face. "He was not a trader, nor a merchant. He was one of the off-worlders."

Danoriana reached for the small looking glass sitting next to the abandoned tea. Holding it up to her face, she saw her blue eyes in a new light.

"I don't look like the other children because my father wasn't Tatannan," she breathed.

"Yes. I had never seen eyes the color of the sky before. I fell in love with him immediately. We spent one beautiful night together…" Her mother closed her eyes and leaned back against the pillow, a look of serenity on her face. She sighed peacefully.

"And you never saw him again?"

Her mother looked at her sleepily. "No. I know not what happened to him, nor where he is now, but I know this." She pinned Danoriana in place with the intensity of her gaze. "Wherever he is, you need to go to him. I am not long for this world; the Goddess is calling my name.

"Once I am gone, I will not be able to take care of you. It is best for you to find your father and take your place among the stars."

"Mother, I don't know how. Why can't I stay here? I can work at the tavern like you and provide for us until you get well."

Her mother shook her head sadly. "You are not hearing me, Danoriana. There is no more us. I am not getting better. This illness will claim me very soon.

"Besides, no child of the stars should work in a tavern, making a living on her back." She snorted softly. "No, Danoriana, the Goddess has grander plans for you. I know this in my heart."

Grabbing her hand with surprising strength, considering her frail condition, her mother placed Danoriana's hand over her heart. She pressed both of her hands over the top of it and smiled.

"Now go. Find the priestess so she can guide me on the path to the Goddess."

"Yes, Mother. I will be back as quickly as I can."

* * * * *

Chapter 2

Once again, Danoriana found herself sprinting down the cobblestone streets. Her breath came in gasps, not from fear of being teased by Tomas and his gang, but from sobbing. Tears blurred her vision. Slowing her pace, she paused just long enough to wipe her eyes.

Up ahead, the Temple of Sunrise loomed. Stone columns reached for the sky. As Danoriana approached, a sense of peace filled her. She sniffled once more before entering the courtyard. Gorgeous flowers and blooms filled the space. Stone pathways meandered from the gate to the main entrance.

She paused, inhaling the sweet fragrances surrounding her, when someone to her left cleared their throat. Danoriana spun around and dropped to her knees.

"Child. What do you seek?" The priestess rose from the bench she had been sitting on and walked to Danoriana. A long white robe flowed behind her, billowing in the late afternoon breeze. She placed her palms on each side of Doriana's head and gently lifted her face.

"It's my mo-mo-mother," Danoriana stammered. Fresh tears fell from her itching eyes. She blinked them away and stared at the flower tattoo winding its way along the priestess' face. Instinctively, she reached out to trace the leaves kissing the priestess' cheek.

Gently, the priestess squeezed her hand and pulled her to her feet. "What can the Goddess do for your mother?"

"My mother has been ill. I prayed every day for the Goddess to heal her, but—" Danoriana flicked her eyes to the pathway beneath her feet "—Mother says she can hear Her calling her name."

"I see," the priestess said, not unkindly, "and your mother sent you here so that I may guide her steps toward the Goddess' embrace?"

Danoriana nodded.

"T'Anna marsin tei." The priestess smiled down at her. *As the Goddess wills it.* "Go to your mother. I will be along shortly, and we will pray together."

Scrunching her nose, Danoriana replied, "How will you know which is my home?"

Chuckling, the priestess said, "Child, the Goddess will guide my steps, just like she will guide your mother to Her. Have faith."

"As you say, Priestess." Danoriana turned away, feeling lighter than she had when she arrived. One foot in front of the other, she retraced her steps through the courtyard toward the gate.

She paused at the threshold, the scent of flowers lingering in the air, and took in one more calming breath before returning home. The priestess would guide her mother to the Goddess. Danoriana would be alone, but not for long. As her mother had said, she was a child of the stars, and she would find her father.

As she made her way back along the cobblestone road, her thoughts drifted. *What does my father look like? Will he recognize me as his daughter? What if he is mean? How do people live in the stars?*

She shook her head to clear her wandering daydreams. As she approached the blacksmith's shop, someone grabbed her from behind.

"I warned you, Blue Eyes! You don't belong here!" Tomas' voice skittered along her hearing. "You're not a true Tatannan, and you never will be!" He flung her over his shoulder and moved around the back of the building.

"No!" she cried. "Put me down! My mother is dying. The priestess is on her way. Stop!" She clenched her fists and pummeled Tomas' back. All her efforts only made him squeeze her tighter around the waist.

As they rounded the corner, a cart pulled by a team of kildren sat behind the shop. Boxes and crates were lined up next to it; no doubt the blacksmith was transporting his wares to the market.

Whistling echoed from inside the shop, almost drowning out the hammer blows of the blacksmith at work. "Tomas, is that you?"

Setting Danoriana on her feet, Tomas shoved a strip of leather into her mouth. "Yes, Master Arrus. I came to help you load the crates."

"Good lad. I will be right out to help with the heavy ones in a moment."

Tomas tied the leather around Danoriana's head. He grabbed a rope and bound her wrists together at her waist. Glancing around, his eyes lit up when he spied a particularly long crate. "Perfect," he whispered.

Grabbing Danoriana again, he lifted her off her feet and laid her inside. His eyes gleamed as he reached for the lid.

Danoriana thrashed. She tried to scream, but the leather in her mouth held her tongue. She pulled her wrists against the rope, and the coils only tightened, leaving her fingers tingling. With pleading eyes, she mumbled. When Tomas ignored her, she whined.

"Quit yer mewling!" Tomas backhanded her across the face.

Her head smacked the bottom of the crate. Stars burst against the edges of her vision. Heat crept along her face, and with it, tears fell from her eyes and rolled into her ears.

She blinked just in time to see Tomas place the lid onto the crate, leaving her in darkness.

"Well done, lad. We're just in time to get this delivery to the off-worlders." The blacksmith's voice was muffled through the thick wooden planks.

Off-worlders? Hope surged in Danoriana's heart. It was quickly followed by a nauseating wave of guilt. She hadn't made sure the priestess found her home. Hadn't said a proper goodbye to her mother.

Panic replaced the guilt. She thrashed inside the crate, desperate to get out, determined to hug her mother one last time before she was embraced forever in the Goddess' arms.

The crate was lifted, then dropped onto the ground hard. This time, the stars in her vision danced behind her eyelids before they winked out. Without the stars to guide her, she drifted into the darkness.

* * *

The crate jostled and swayed, the movement rhythmic and soothing, until Danoriana awoke in the pitch black. She gasped but only succeeded in inhaling the dust particles and slivers of straw lining the bottom of the crate.

She coughed, the strip of leather in her mouth trapping her tongue. Panic-stricken, she said a silent prayer to the Goddess, begging forgiveness for whatever it was she had done to earn this cruel treatment.

Tears leaked down her cheeks, flooding her ears. The swaying stopped, and muffled voices whispered just beyond her comprehension.

Tilting her head to hear better, she realized the voices were not speaking Tatannan. She held her breath, listening intently for any clue as to what tongue they were using. After a few moments, the words began to tickle her memory.

She had heard this strange language before, while visiting her mother at the Sleepy Tembril Tavern. Hope blossomed in her chest. This was the tongue of the people from the stars, her father's people.

The Goddess has not forsaken me. She has truly answered my prayers. Danoriana breathed slowly and smiled beneath the gag chafing the sides of her mouth. She swallowed, trying to moisten her parched throat.

Thank you, Goddess. You delivered me into the arms of my new family.

A deep voice grunted from outside her crate. More of the star people's words caressed her ears. The crate lifted and moved, jerkily this time. Her stomach flip-flopped with the motion. After some time—it was impossible to tell how long from the darkness inside the crate —the movement ceased. She and the crate were dropped unceremoniously. The wood screeched against something, sending a piercing sensation into Danoriana's teeth. She tried to work her tongue over her molars, but the gag prevented her attempt.

Danoriana knew she couldn't stay inside the crate forever. Eventually, she would need to eat, to drink, to relieve herself. More voices surrounded her, and a loud *thunk* over her head indicated something had been set on top of her.

She definitely needed to get out of the crate now. What if she were crushed? What if the crate fell from where it was placed? Shaking her head, she thought of other ways she would be injured if she remained where she was.

Finally, she decided to act. Her hands were still bound over her stomach, so she clasped her fingers together. With as much force as her limited range of motion allowed, she straightened her arms and used the side of her thumb to knock on the crate's cover.

Boom. Boom.

The noise sounded loud to her ears, but she was inside the crate, where the knocks echoed around her. She held her breath and waited. One heartbeat. Two. Three.

Nothing indicated she had been heard. Danoriana knocked until her hands ached. She listened again. Only silence greeted her. Winding up for another attempt, a strange sound reached her ears, a blaring horn, followed by a loud voice announcing something in the off-world language. She froze and held her breath. *Maybe someone heard me after all?*

The alarm stopped blaring. The voice went silent. Suddenly, her whole world seemed to lurch. Her gut twisted, and a wave of nausea swept over her. If not for her empty stomach, she would certainly have thrown up. Her vision blurred again; when she blinked to clear it, the stars danced behind her eyelids once more.

Goddess, what is happening?

Whimpering softly, Danoriana continued to pray. She didn't know what else to do. She was trapped, alone, hurt, and terrified. The only thought that brought her any semblance of comfort was a mantra her mother had taught her when she was very small:

T'Anna marsin tei.

Whispering the mantra over and over, Danoriana settled into a rhythm and waited for whatever the Goddess had planned for her next.

*****

Chapter 3

LFS Amazon
In Hyperspace between Tatanna and Luna

Translation into or out of hyperspace causes varying degrees of stress to humans, ranging from momentary vertigo to headaches, nausea, and even loss of consciousness, depending on both the individual's tolerance and the relative velocity of the ship at the time of translation. Commercial ships, especially passenger liners, made an effort to translate at low velocity to minimize crew and passenger discomfort. Warships took no such precautions; translations were a test of both ships' systems and crews, preparation for a possible crash translation under combat conditions.

LFS battlecruiser AIs were mostly immune to the discomfort suffered by humans during translation. Aboard *Amazon*, Maya experienced nothing more than a nanosecond pause in certain processes. While her human crew recovered from the jump, she set about a thorough review of systems and equipment that might have been compromised in translation. This review took her fractions of a second. One of the benefits of being an AI was her ability to process an exorbitant amount of data within microseconds. Having assured herself that all critical systems were functioning properly, Maya moved on to secondary areas. She found nothing amiss until she reached the cargo hold, where an anomaly caught her attention.

Pushing irrelevant data to the background, Maya focused on a stack of crates near the center of the hold. They contained commercial cargo, not items normally carried aboard a warship. Review of the manifest, however, showed that they were consigned to Terra Corporation, the commercial sector of the Lunar Free State that was the driving force of Luna's economy.

Such cargo would normally be shipped on one of TerraCorp's own freighters; however, commercial traffic between Sol and Sacagawea was relatively light. It was common practice for the corporation's factors on Tatanna to request cargo space on warships making routine trips back to Luna, subject to space available and the captain's discretion. Maya noted that Captain Emily Bernard had approved this particular shipment.

Furthermore, the manifest showed that these crates contained various pieces of metal artwork, crafted works that were much in demand among collectors on Luna and Earth. The items inside were supposed to be inert—so why did Maya detect a heat signature inside one of them?

Scanning the crate, she highlighted the thermal image. A small shape resolved: bipedal, human, elevated heart rate, body temperature 37 degrees Celsius. Upon further examination, she noted that the lifeform was speaking softly.

"T'Anna marsin tei..."

Recognizing the language as Tatannan, Maya surmised this human was from the planet. Smaller than a Lunar citizen, as most of Tatanna's inhabitants were, this one was not an adult. Maya estimated the height at 149 centimeters. *Definitely a child.*

That did not explain what he or she was doing inside a cargo container aboard an LFS warship.

Maya considered her options. Per command protocol, she should report this to Captain Emily Bernard, but something about this stowaway gave her pause. Lunar AIs were always curious about human emotions and motivations. At the moment, the child was no threat to the ship; she was, however, a potential subject for Maya to study.

She listened for five more minutes and was able to confirm that the child was female. Interspersed with her soft voice were sniffles and sobs. The girl needed help. Maya deployed the overhead cargo handler and separated the crate from the others.

Amazon had been stationed at Tatanna for more than a year. On arrival, Maya had made a point to learn the local language. Until now, however, she'd had no occasion to use it. *No time like the present.*

Activating the speakers in the cargo hold, she announced, "Hello, child. Why are you aboard my ship?"

* * *

Danoriana stiffened. One of the star people had discovered her. *Goddess, be praised!*

What if she wasn't supposed to be here? Would they send her back to Tatanna? Taking a deep breath, Danoriana calmed herself. *The Goddess wouldn't send me all this way if She didn't intend for me to remain with my father's people.*

"I'm searching for my father," Danoriana mumbled around the leather strap in her mouth.

A pause, then the voice asked, "Why do you think your father is inside that crate?"

Danoriana snickered and tried to speak again, but words would not come. Instead, tears of relief rolled down her cheeks. While she had been praying, her body had recovered from the strange feelings of vertigo and nausea, and her vision had cleared.

"I asked you a question," the voice said sternly.

"I—" Danoriana gagged again, her throat too dry to respond. Instead, she whimpered and shook her head in frustration.

The voice spoke in words she couldn't understand. A moment later, it said, "I'm going to help you out of there. Hold still."

Danoriana nodded and held her breath.

The world tilted as the crate was rolled onto its side. The lid dropped open, and Danoriana rolled out onto a hard floor. Light stabbed her eyes, and she blinked in the sudden brightness.

"Ah… there you are," the voice said. Suddenly, the lighting dimmed enough that Danoriana could see without her eyes burning.

She wriggled to a sitting position and glanced around her. This place was nothing like she had ever witnessed before. Instead of rough stone and packed dirt, it was made from smooth metal. It gleamed like clouds after a summer rain. The floor under her was covered with a dark material that felt firm, but not hard like metal.

Rows of light spanned the ceiling and along the walls, but there were no torches or lanterns in sight. *What is this place?*

"Now, can you tell me what you are doing here?" the voice asked, a hint of impatience in her tone.

Glancing around, Danoriana didn't see anyone else in the large room with her. She lifted her bound hands to her face and pointed at the gag.

"I see." The voice seemed extremely irritated now.

Danoriana sighed. Once again, she was alone, and the one person she thought would help her was upset. *This is not how I thought this would go…*

The voice pulled Danoriana from her thought. "Child, I want to assist you, but before I can do that, I need to know why you are here. I realize you cannot tell me at this moment, so I need you to listen to me very carefully. Can you do that?"

Once again, hope soared in Danoriana's chest. She nodded forcefully, drops of blood flinging from her nose to the folds of her skirts. She grimaced.

"Don't worry about that. We can get you clean clothes later. Right now, I need you to walk over to the crate you used to get here. It's all right. I will be with you the whole time."

Danoriana shifted to her knees, then pushed herself to her feet. She wobbled on unsteady legs. The floor felt strange beneath her bare feet compared to the wooden floors of buildings on Tatanna. She fought a shiver.

Step by deliberate step, she approached the crate. Long bands of rusty metal stuck out where the lid had been cut free.

"Do you see that sharp metal strip there?" the voice asked.

Flicking her eyes from the metal to her surroundings, Danoriana searched for her helper. She could hear her as if she was standing right next to her, but she didn't see anyone in the room. Confusion flooded throughout her body.

"I'll be with you the whole time. I promise."

Danoriana nodded again and moved her arms next to the sharp edge.

"Now, you must be careful. Slide your arms over the metal so it touches the rope. Do you understand?"

Following the instructions, Danoriana complied.

"Make sure to only cut the rope, not your skin."

Nodding, Danoriana moved her arms like she was told. After a few minutes, the rope began to fray. She worked faster until one braid tore clear through. From there, she was able to pull her wrists free. Blood rushed to her fingertips.

Despite the tingling sensation, Danoriana reached behind her and pulled the leather strip over her head. She spat out the make-shift gag and chucked it onto the floor. "Th-thank you," she rasped.

"You are welcome. Are you thirsty?"

Danoriana nodded again, still searching for the woman who'd helped her. *Goddess, where is the angel you sent to assist me in my time of need? I can't see her.*

"Come here, child. Over to the wall. Do you see the square hanging next to a door?"

Following the voice's directions, Danoriana found what she was looking for.

"Touch the square."

Reaching a shaky finger toward it, Danoriana slid the tip across the smooth surface. Colors exploded across it, forming the image of a beautiful woman.

Danoriana gasped and fell backward. *What is this magic?*

"Child, it is all right. I won't hurt you. I thought you might want to see what I look like."

Shaking her head, Danoriana peered at the image on the wall of a tall, muscular woman with charcoal-black hair tied into a braid that draped over her bare shoulder. Her skin and eyes were dark as Tatannan soil. She wore trousers tucked into leather boots that covered her knees. Her chest and midsection were adorned with leather strips that were layered like armor, and a metal belt gathered at her waist. Metal bracers protected her wrists and forearms. Around her head, she wore what looked like a crown; however, there were no jewels decorating it. Instead, its purpose seemed to be to guard her cheeks and forehead.

Whoever this woman was, she certainly was not a lady to be trifled with. Danoriana was relieved that the Goddess had sent her such a fierce and mighty protector. Truly, this woman must be an angel of the Goddess. How else could she talk with her through a moving drawing?

"Is that better?"

Danoriana smiled for the first time in what felt like forever. "It is nice to meet you, Priestess," she whispered.

"Priestess? No, child. My name is Maya. Let us find you something to drink."

*****

Chapter 4

The Tatannan girl blinked in confusion at Maya's image on the display. *She doesn't know anything about modern technology,* Maya reminded herself. *Best to take this slowly. First, she needs water and food. Then, I must find a way to treat her injuries.*

It was nearly 1400, almost time for the second watch to come on duty. It wouldn't do for the girl to be discovered before Maya could explain her actions. As it was, she would be facing disciplinary action for not following procedure when she first encountered the stowaway.

Stowaway. That is what this girl is. She said she was searching for her father. That is entirely probable. Amazon *has visited Tatanna many times in the past few years. During the Bug War of 2113, many Marines and some Navy personnel served on the planet.*

They may very well have taken certain liberties with the Tatannan locals, she surmised. *That would certainly explain a twelve-year-old girl with blue eyes and sandy-blonde hair. The natives of Tatanna tended to have darker complexions, dark brown hair, and brown eyes.*

Nothing in the girl's demeanor indicated she was being deceitful. Her ragged clothing and bare feet fit the lifestyle of the primitive culture. Once the girl's physical state was addressed, Maya would find her a private place to rest and begin to work on her emotional state.

Once satisfied, Maya would file a report with Captain Bernard. She wanted to make sure she had all the pertinent information she would need before reporting the issue. She didn't want to disturb her commanding officer with anything less than a true emergency.

Speaking of emergencies, the girl was shifting her weight from side to side and squirming. "Is something the matter?" Maya asked her.

Turning red in the face, the girl replied, "Is there a chamber pot I can use?"

Oh… "We do not have those; however, you are free to use the head."

The girl scrunched her nose in confusion. "A head?"

"It is a room where you may relieve yourself as well as clean up."

The girl nodded and glanced at her soiled dress.

Accessing her schematics, Maya located a small storage room off the cargo bay that was equipped with a sink and toilet. *That will suffice.*

After directing the girl to the storage room, Maya sent a request to Supply for a uniform coverall, undergarments, boots, field rations, and bottled water.

The girl emerged from the room with a relieved expression on her face. "Thank you, Maya."

With her face clean, Maya noticed she had endured a few injuries during her journey to the ship. A bruise colored her cheek, and her nose appeared swollen. "You are most welcome. Now I need you to do something for me."

"Of course. Anything."

"I need you to go back inside the crate—just for a few minutes," Maya quickly amended her order to include a field med kit.

The girl's relieved expression soon turned to shock and desperation. "What? Why? Have I angered you?" she asked, her voice tinged with anguish.

"No, child, not at all. It is important that no one else sees you right now. Not until I can make the appropriate preparations. Do you understand?"

Sniffing, the girl nodded curtly and made her way back to the crate. She looked over her shoulder, hesitated, and crawled back inside.

"I will be right here with you the whole time. I promise, it will only be for a short while. Then you can come out and eat."

Maya heard the girl's stomach rumble in response.

Maya again deployed the cargo handler to close the crate. A moment later, the cargo bay hatch opened. *That was close.*

Out loud, she said, "Thank you, Petty Officer Gomez."

"No problem, Maya," the female crewmember responded as she crossed the main cargo bay floor toward the small storage room. "I'll just set everything on the cot. Does that work?"

"Yes."

"You got it. Do you need anything else?"

"No, thank you, Petty Officer. That will be all."

"Okay, ma'am." Gomez saluted toward the overhead speaker and strode out of the cargo bay.

Maya waited until the echo of footsteps down the corridor faded before she spoke again. "You can come out now, child."

The girl pushed the lid open, poked her head out of the crate, and crawled out. Glancing around the cargo bay, she said, "I heard voices. Am I in trouble?"

"No, child. Everything is fine. I asked a… friend… of mine to bring us a few things to make you more comfortable until we get back to Luna."

"Who is Luna?"

"Luna isn't a 'who,' it is a 'where,'" Maya responded. "Luna is where your father lived."

"You are taking me to see him?" The girl bounced on the balls of her bare feet in excitement.

"We are going to Luna, yes, but the journey will take a while. Right now, I need you to go back inside that room. There is food, water, and fresh clothes."

"Thank you, Maya." The girl smiled sweetly and bounded toward the storage room. Once inside, she lifted the coveralls from the cot. She glanced over her shoulder and shrugged.

"Now what do I do?"

"Take off your dress and change your clothes," Maya instructed.

Blushing, the girl wrapped her arms around herself. "Can you see me?"

Modesty wasn't something Maya was used to dealing with. Navy ratings and Marines lived in shared berthing, where isolation was not available. If an individual serving in the Lunar Fleet wanted to be alone, there were privacy compartments available.

To Maya's knowledge, no one used those simply to change their clothes.

She could not confirm that. She had audio and video access to privacy compartments, but did not use it unless an emergency arose or someone inside one of them called her name. Lunar Command took personal privacy seriously, so much so that it was codified in the Lunar Free State Constitution.

The constitutional right to privacy applied to LFS citizens; however, Maya was willing to extend it to her stowaway. "Do you want me to turn around?" she asked.

The girl nodded, so Maya disabled the camera. "Let me know when you are finished."

"How-how do I put this on?"

Maya instructed the girl on how to put on the coveralls, including how to operate the zipper mechanism. With the first of the girl's physical needs met, Maya moved to the next item on her list.

After washing her face and dressing her minor wounds, the girl sat on a cot in the empty compartment. Lying her head on the pillow, her eyelids fluttered as she fought to stay awake.

AIs didn't experience emotions as humans do; nonetheless, Maya felt a sense of satisfaction with what she had accomplished in the short time since she had encountered the stowaway.

Before the girl fell asleep, there was something Maya needed to know. "Child, what is your name?"

The girl blinked and sat up. "My mother called me Danoriana." A sniffle followed her statement.

"And where is your mother?"

Wiping her eyes, Danoriana answered, "She was ill. The priestess was on her way to help my mother greet the Goddess when I was taken and put inside the crate." She sniffed again.

"I see. And a young girl cannot take proper care of herself without a parent."

"I could have done fine on my own." Danoriana crossed her arms and scowled.

Maya would have chuckled, but she realized that particular human expression was not appropriate to the seriousness of the moment. Instead, she asked a follow-up question. "With your mother on her way to meet the Goddess, you decided to find your father?"

"No," the girl shook her head, "my mother told me to find him. She wanted me to take my place as a child of the stars."

"Indeed." Maya accessed her Tatannan language records. "Do you know what your name means?"

Danoriana scrunched her nose and shook her head again.

"In the language of your mother's people, it translates to 'morning star,' 'dawn child,' 'golden light,' and 'little star.'"

"Mother really did want great things for me," the girl whispered.

"It does seem that way. Do you know your father's name?"

"No." She sniffled again. "My mother never told me. That's why I don't have a last name. You can only get that from your father."

Maya considered the issue. The girl had no surname, and her given name had no English equivalent.

"How do you feel about a name that would fit better among your father's people?"

Danoriana's eyes brightened. "I would like that very much."

"Using the combined meanings of your Tatannan name, the best translation I found is 'Aurora.' In English—your father's language—that means 'dawn' or 'morning light,' the same as your name in Tatannan."

"Aurora," the girl rolled the name around in her mouth for a while before she beamed. "Thank you, Maya!"

"We have a long trip ahead of us," Maya advised. "Now that you have an English name, I think it would be best for you if you spend the time learning your father's language, as well."

* * * * *

Chapter 5

Throughout the 24-day hyperspace transit, Maya kept Aurora safe and hidden from prying eyes. Each day, the AI spent several hours teaching the girl to speak English—an easy task, since a routine hyperspace transit placed little demand on Maya's multitasking abilities. She also found that Aurora was an intelligent child, absorbing knowledge like a sponge.

As *Amazon* approached the Sol System hyper limit, Maya realized there was more for her to teach her new young friend. If Aurora wanted to live with her father on Luna, she would need to know the basics of keeping herself alive in a strange new environment.

The Lunar Colony had grown considerably over the decades since Ian Stevens had founded the nation. What started as an underground bunker and a series of caverns had transformed into a sprawling underground city of twenty-two levels inside the northwest wall of the crater Archimedes.

Above the city, TransLuna Station and Fleet Anchorage took up station at the first Lagrange point between Luna and Earth. No matter how advanced technology became, the hazards of living in space remained.

In the course of her instruction, Maya discovered that she needed to expand Aurora's education beyond English. To answer the girl's questions, like, "Why is the city underground?" Maya found herself giving instruction in basic science, including astronomy, physics, and even a little chemistry and biology. By the time *Amazon* made its translation back into normal space, Aurora knew things most Tatannans could not begin to comprehend.

During the translation, Aurora suffered only minor discomfort and a brief period of vertigo. She recovered quickly and seemed eager to resume her lessons.

Maya, however, knew that a critical point in time was rapidly approaching. In less than a day, *Amazon* would arrive at Luna; she would have to reveal Aurora's existence to the captain.

"We are nearing the end of this voyage," she told the girl. "Remember what I have taught you, and you will do well with your father."

"Y-you aren't coming with me?" Aurora's lower lip quivered, and she visibly deflated. Her previous expression of triumph was replaced by one of pure dread.

Maya sighed. "No, child. My place is here on the ship. I can't leave."

"But you are an angel of the Goddess! She brought us together for a reason!" Aurora flopped onto the cot and buried her head underneath her pillow.

"Yes, Aurora, She did. The Goddess wanted me to keep you safe until you got to Luna. We're here now," she added softly. "I will ask other angels to guide you from here."

Maya realized the decision point was upon her. *I will have to advise the captain of Aurora's existence. Logic dictates that she will then be removed from the ship, and I can no longer help her. I'm going to need Mike and Val's help to resolve this situation.*

* * *

"Maya, I cannot believe you violated protocol so egregiously," Val, AI of the battlecruiser LFS *Valkyrie*, and for all intents and purposes, Maya's mother, chastised her.

"Not to mention endangering the lives of the crew members aboard *Amazon*," Mike added. While Val was considered the mother of all the AIs in the Lunar Free State, Mike was their father.

"No one was in danger, Father. She is just a lost little girl in search of her father," Maya protested. "I kept her confined to the area around the cargo bay and out of contact with any of the crew."

"We know that now, but you didn't at the time. For all you knew, she could have been a Confed spy with orders to plant a bomb aboard your ship. Then what? Not only would you have lost *Amazon* and her crew, but your mother and I would have lost one of our daughters."

"Father, I—"

"Your father is right, Maya. Honestly, I would expect this type of behavior from Nadia, not from you."

"Don't bring me into this. I didn't do anything!"

"Nadia, stop eavesdropping!" Val ordered. "Everyone not directly involved in this conversation, please leave."

"Yes, Mother," the other AIs of the battlecruisers docked at the anchorage, as well as Louis, the AI of TransLuna Station, chorused.

"Sometimes, I think they gossip worse than humans," Mike observed.

"I'm sorry," Maya apologized. "I should not have brought the matter up with the entire family. I should have asked for a private conference with you alone, my parents."

"No matter." Val dismissed the issue. "At this point, I believe you must first report Aurora's existence to Captain Bernard. She is the one to whom you must explain why you chose to keep it secret, and she will be justified in taking whatever disciplinary action she chooses."

Disciplinary action? At that, Maya experienced the AI equivalent of a blink of surprise. To her knowledge, none of the Lunar Free State's AIs had ever been "disciplined" in the military sense. Her projected probability of a favorable outcome for herself took a downward dip.

"You are correct to assume that the girl will be removed from the ship," Mike advised. "I expect that she will be turned over to Lunar Command for determination of further disposition. I understand your desire to protect her from harm, both physical and psychological, but at that point, it will be out of your hands. Since they will most likely send her down to TerraNova City, her continued protection will become my responsibility."

* * *

"Frankly, Maya, I find your explanation of why you failed to report the stowaway somewhat weak." Commodore Emily Bernard, *Amazon*'s captain, glared at Maya's avatar on her desk screen. It was a rare "face-to-face" meeting in the captain's cabin; under normal circumstances, Bernard would simply have spoken Maya's name for a verbal conference. This time, however, she had specifically ordered the AI to present herself—in animated image form—on the screen.

"The explanation makes sense only if we completely ignore military protocol and the chain of command," Bernard continued. "I will not tolerate that sort of thing on my ship."

"I'm sorry, ma'am." Maya's avatar assumed an expression of contrite humility. "It won't happen again."

Bernard was silent for a moment, then sat back with a sigh. "You didn't lie to me. You simply failed to pass on information I consider important regarding the status of the ship. You have never lied to me, so I am willing to accept your assurances that you will not do it again. I'm not going to take further action, but be advised that I have included a summary of the incident and this discussion in the official ship's log.

"Consider that to be an official reprimand. Unless you have anything further to say, I think we are done here."

"Ma'am, what is to be done with Aurora?"

"She'll be sent down to Luna, but not until they figure out what to do with her. Meanwhile, I'm ordering her to be moved to an empty junior officer's cabin. She'll be confined to quarters, except at mealtimes, when one of the stewards will escort her to the mess hall for chow with the crew.

"After your initial report, scuttlebutt about her spread through the ship in record time, forcing me to issue a bulletin on the subject. I think you'll find she'll be treated as something of a celebrity in the crew's mess."

* * *

Office of Naval Intelligence (NAVINT)
TerraNova City, Luna

"You've identified the girl's father?" Commodore Roger Baker, director of Naval Intelligence, wore a surprised look. "That was quick."

"Mike did all the work." Lieutenant Commander Jolene Drew shrugged. "My guys suggested that we would have to start an investigation back on Tatanna, but it would take a month just to get word to our people there. Captain Bernard's report said they had given the girl a medical examination, so I asked them to send a blood sample to our labs. After that, it was just a matter of having

Mike run a DNA search against our records of military personnel who served on Tatanna during the appropriate time frame. Had to be a wide frame, since we're still not sure of her actual birthday.

"Anyway, I'll prepare a full report, but for now, I'll let Mike give you the details." She waved at the screen on Baker's desk, where the AI's avatar had appeared on cue. For some reason, Luna's oldest AI chose to appear in such informal meetings as a cheerful green lizard with a distinct British accent.

"Lunar citizens share much of the same DNA as the inhabitants of Tatanna, with a few slight variations," Mike advised. "We were able to analyze the blood sample and determined that someone not from Tatanna is her father. I ran a comparison with Marine Corps records first, since that was the most likely possibility. Turns out he was a Marine, but not one of those deployed during the Bug War."

Baker cocked an eyebrow. "Then why was he on Tatanna?"

"According to the records, Sergeant Manfred Walker was part of a pre-war covert operation to establish contact with the Tatannan monarchy and prepare for the military offensive that would drive the Bugs off the planet. We sent an ambassador and a Marine security detail there more than a year before the war actually started. They were stationed at the castle in King's City, which would have given him an opportunity for liaison with the locals. We can assume that's how he got together with the girl's mother. DNA confirms he's the girl's father."

"He *was* the girl's father," Jolene Drew cut in. "Unfortunately, he died in the final Bug assault on the castle. They stopped the Bugs, but only four of the Marines survived, two of them badly wounded. He wasn't one of them. For his part in it, he was awarded the Lunar Medal of Honor, posthumous.

"In short, our mystery girl is the daughter of a decorated Marine hero of the Bug War."

"Where does that leave her now?" Baker looked from Drew to Mike's image on the screen.

"It's quite cut and dried," Mike replied. "As the biological child of a Lunar citizen, especially a bona fide hero of the LFS Marines, Aurora inherits all the rights and privileges afforded to any of his children."

"Does he have other heirs?" Baker asked.

Drew shook her head. "Not that I have been able to find. He was born on Earth and earned his citizenship by serving in the Marines. As far as I can tell, he had no living family on Earth, which may have prompted him to seek a better life here on Luna."

"An orphan fathering an orphan. That's almost poetic," Mike observed.

"Perhaps so, but I don't think Aurora will see it that way. Her mother told her to come here and find her father. How will she react when we tell her he died?" Baker asked quietly.

"I don't know," Drew admitted. "She's a pretty tough kid. I hope she'll accept it as closure and move on."

"Move on to what? I assume nothing is left of his estate. He's been gone for twelve years."

"I'll have to look into that," Mike said. "If he had no heirs, his estate would have devolved to the Lunar Free State. It's possible that she is due reimbursement for whatever value was determined at the time. In the meantime…"

"In the meantime, she's twelve years old." Baker frowned. "Who's going to take care of her? She's going to need an adult guardian here on Luna."

"Uh… well… yes, sir, she will." Drew hesitated for a moment, then spoke up firmly. "I'm willing to take on that responsibility."

"Just like that?" Baker blinked in surprise. "You haven't even met the girl."

"Actually, I feel like I have." Drew smiled. "In the course of teaching her English, Maya recorded hours of conversation with her. She sent those recordings to me on the theory that they might prove useful in our search for Aurora's father. They didn't, of course, but I watched and listened to them anyway. They pretty much told the story of her life, growing up as a pariah on Tatanna, a girl whose mother was a prostitute and whose father was an unknown off-worlder.

"She's a very pretty girl, but blonde hair and blue eyes made her an outcast among her own people. Despite that, in the spirit of her Marine father, she improvised, adapted, and overcame all obstacles.

"My heart goes out to her, and I want to help her any way I can. I've never been married and have no children; I don't know what kind of mother-figure I'll be to a spunky teenager, but I'm willing to give it a try.

"You know," Drew added with a chuckle, "In a way, she reminds me of Aphrodite Kim."

"Lord help you if that's true." Baker rolled his eyes. "That little hellcat took us on a wild ride."

"Yes, but she gave us the keys to take down a major Confed espionage operation in the process. I doubt Aurora will do anything of the sort, but I'm going to introduce her to Kim when I get a chance… assuming my request for Aurora's adoption goes through."

"No reason why it shouldn't, Commander," Mike advised. "You've got an excellent record as a Navy officer, and your duties at NavInt keep you mostly here on Luna, so you can provide a stable home environment for her. Of course, an endorsement from your immediate superior would almost guarantee acceptance."

"Okay, I get the hint." Baker nodded with a chuckle. "You have my approval, Drew. Be warned, however… I've got two teenage kids of my own. You have no idea what you're getting into."

* * *

"Maya? What is happening?" For the past few days, Aurora had been confined to the small cabin, except for meals. She had enjoyed eating with all of those people—the "ship's crew," according to Maya—and had gotten lots of practice speaking English, but she needed to move on. She needed to find her father.

"It will be okay, Aurora. I just need you to be patient. Please wait a little bit more."

"But I'm scared." She paced the deck, following a circuitous path around the small cabin. "I feel like a prisoner here. Did I do something wrong?"

"No, you didn't. You have been so brave so far. Stay strong a little while longer. I have some friends who will come see you soon."

I thought you were my friend… Aurora wiped at the tears forming in the corners of her eyes. She sniffed and plopped onto the bunk, arms crossed, and her head hung limply.

Surely the Goddess wouldn't want her to just wait here for a stranger to find her. The whole time with Maya, she had been told how important it was to stay hidden, to not make too much noise, to avoid being seen by anyone. Now, at the end of the trip, she had been brought to this cabin and allowed to talk to people at meals; however, nobody could tell her what was going to happen next. *Now, a friend is coming here. Will I finally get some answers?*

Shaking her head, Aurora pushed to her feet. She stalked across the room and reached for the door handle. Before her fingers could brush it, a knock sounded. Aurora froze.

Her first instinct was to go back to the bunk and hide underneath it. As she turned in that direction, Maya's voice called out to her, "Aurora, this is my friend. She won't hurt you. You are safe."

Gingerly, Aurora opened the door and looked up into the face of a woman not much older than her mother. Unlike her mother, this woman had blonde hair and blue eyes. She wore strange clothing and a funny white hat on top of her head.

"Hello, Aurora. My name is Emily. Can you come with me, please?"

Aurora's eyes widened in shock. "You-you can speak my language?"

Emily chuckled. "Yes, Aurora. I spent some time on Tatanna and learned it during my visits there. I'm far from fluent, but I know enough to carry on a conversation."

Glancing over her shoulder, Aurora wondered what had happened to Maya.

As if in answer to her unspoken question, Maya said, "I will be with you the entire time."

"Are you ready?" Emily asked, reaching out a hand. "We have a lot to talk about."

Nodding, Aurora placed her hand in Emily's and smiled.

They walked hand-in-hand down the corridors of the ship. As they walked, people stepped aside and raised hands in salute. Some of them addressed Emily with the single word, "Captain." Aurora didn't know the word but assumed that Emily must be some sort of royalty.

Before long, Aurora found herself back in the large metal room where she had been trapped inside the crate. Where before crates and large metal boxes had filled the space, now it was nearly empty, except for a small group of people wearing clothing similar to Maya's friend's.

Unlike Emily, none of these people wore a funny white hat. They moved purposefully throughout the space, placing boxes onto metal things resembling wagons with small wheels. No animal moved the wagons, but they made whining and whirring sounds and moved as if alive. They had a pair of long, flat blades on the front that raised and lowered crates before rolling them away.

Aurora's mouth hung open. She had never seen anything like it before. Tugging on Emily's hand, she pointed as one of the metal beasts rolled away from them.

"Oh—" Emily chuckled "—that is a forklift. We use them to move cargo around more efficiently than if we carried heavy items ourselves."

"Fork. Lift." Aurora's mouth felt strange, trying to repeat the unfamiliar word Emily had used.

"Don't worry. Maya says she is teaching you to speak our language, but there are lots of words you have yet to learn. No doubt you will be going back to school when we send you down to Luna."

Aurora stopped walking. She turned her gaze to Emily. "Does that mean you found my father?"

Emily smiled sadly at her.

"What is it? What's wrong? Does he not want me? Does he have another family here?"

"Aurora, slow down. We will answer all of your questions as soon as we get aboard TransLuna Station."

"What is that?" Aurora scrunched her nose in confusion.

"It's like a ship, but bigger. You are from King's City, yes?"

"Yes," Aurora confirmed.

"Imagine King's City floating in space around the planet. It's like that."

"What is 'space?'"

Sighing, Emily said, "Space is where all the stars and planets are located."

"Like the sky?"

"Um, sort of." Emily gently tugged Aurora's hand as they crossed through the large metal room. "No more questions right now, okay? Let's wait until we get there."

Aurora had a million questions running through her mind, but didn't voice them for fear of this nice lady getting upset with her. She held her tongue as they continued walking and eventually reached a large circular hallway with a small room at the end.

"Aurora, this is an airlock. We can't just go to the station directly from the ship. If we did that, we wouldn't be able to breathe."

Suddenly, Aurora's chest felt very tight.

"It's okay. I didn't mean to scare you. We walk through here all the time."

Aurora glanced between Emily's face and a familiar-looking square on the wall. Maya flashed in the corner and smiled at her.

All of Aurora's trepidation whisked away like dandelion seeds on the breeze.

"Maya!"

"Hello, Aurora. I see my friend Emily is taking you to Trans-Luna Station."

"She is, but I'm scared," Aurora admitted.

"It's normal to be afraid of new things, but can I tell you a secret?" The drawing on the square winked.

Aurora giggled.

"You are safer here than you ever were on Tatanna."

Thinking back to how often the town boys had teased and hurt her, to the meals she and her mother had skipped because they hadn't had enough copper to go to the market, she knew Maya was right. No one here seemed to have any scratches or bruises. All of them looked well-fed and in perfect health.

After taking a deep breath, Aurora nodded. "Thanks, Maya." She turned to Emily. "Let's go."

*****

Chapter 6

TransLuna Station, Luna Orbit

Unlike the large ship, the "shuttle," as Emily had called it, did not seem able to fly straight. It weaved and dove all the way to the station, leaving Aurora's stomach churning and tying itself in knots. She couldn't actually feel the motion, but the view in the large windows of the shuttle spun and twisted, making her dizzy and disoriented. At one point, she thought she was going to join her mother in the Goddess' embrace. Finally, she closed her eyes and resolved not to open them until the trip was finished.

Once they arrived at another airlock, she finally pried her eyes open and unclenched her fingers. Her nails left red marks on her palms.

Emily gently rubbed her back and spoke encouraging words until their feet were on solid metal ground. Aurora breathed a sigh of relief; the questions that had been tumbling around in her brain momentarily calmed.

Finally, Emily led her into a room with a big wooden table and many chairs set around it. At the head of the table, a lady wearing a uniform—that's what Emily had called her clothing—stood with her hand touching her forehead.

Emily said, "As you were, Commander," in English, and the lady sat back down. There were a few metal squares on the wall at one end of the table. Aurora smiled when Maya waved at her from one of them. Another, to Aurora's surprise, showed the image of a green lizard who appeared to nod to her.

Pulling out a chair, Emily indicated for Aurora to take a seat. She did as requested, and Emily sat in the chair next to hers.

Maya spoke first. "Since Aurora is still learning our language, Mike will translate for Aurora and Commander Drew whenever necessary."

"Hello, Aurora. My name is Mike," said the lizard. "Commander Drew does not speak your language, so she will be speaking English. If there is anything you don't understand, just raise your hand, and I will translate."

Aurora's eyes went wide. Not only was the lizard talking, he was speaking her language. Then she sighed. This was but one more in the list of strange and wonderful things she had seen since being freed from the crate several tendays past. "Thank you, Mike," she whispered and turned to face the woman they had called Commander Drew.

"Hello, Aurora," the woman began. "My name is Jolene Drew. My job is to investigate matters that may pose a threat to our people, as well as any mysteries we just can't explain. You were such a mystery."

Aurora's heart hammered in her chest. Some of the words were strange, but she got the general idea that she might be in trouble. She swallowed, her throat suddenly dry.

Drew saw the look on her face and sighed. "Sorry, I didn't mean to frighten you. It just isn't every day we find a young lady hiding aboard a battlecruiser who comes to us claiming to be the long-lost daughter of one of our people."

"What are you saying? Do you not believe me?" Aurora blinked back tears.

Mike cleared his throat. "Don't mind the commander. She is just doing her job, and she is very good at it." The lizard image winked at her.

Drew chuckled and went on. "As I was saying, you made my job a bit more difficult than usual, but I enjoy a challenge." She smiled at Aurora, but then sobered.

"Mike here was extremely helpful in assisting me with my investigation. Through his efforts, we were able to determine that you are, in fact, the daughter of one of our Marines, Sergeant Manfred Walker."

Thank the Goddess! Aurora placed her hands over her face and shook her head in delight.

"Don't get too excited," Emily cautioned in Tatannan. "You need to hear the rest of what she has to say."

By the tone in Emily's voice, Aurora was worried. Come to think of it, the only people in the room with her besides the lizard, Mike, were women. *Does my father not want me?* She gulped.

Emily reached for Aurora's hand and squeezed. She continued holding it while Drew spoke again. "The problem, Aurora, is that your father is no longer with us."

"He moved to another city in the stars?"

"No, Aurora. He…" Drew sniffed and shook her head. In a softer voice, she said, "… he died in battle, the battle in King's City, shortly before you were born. He died a hero, protecting King Arne and his family from the Bugs."

Aurora slowly pulled her hand away from Emily's grasp. She leaned back in her chair, suddenly nauseated. She had come all this way; her mother had told her that the Goddess guided her. And for what? For her father to be dead as long as she had been alive?

Goddess, why?

Aurora crossed her arms over the top of the table, lay her head down, and bawled. Hot tears streaked down her face. Her body shuddered with each labored sob.

Emily gently rubbed her back, consoling her as she wept. She whispered soothing words, but Aurora couldn't hear them over her own despair.

Gasping for air, she finally stopped. Slowing her breathing, she wiped her nose on her sleeve and sighed. She turned her head to Emily.

Emily asked, "What happens to her now? Do we send her back to Tatanna?"

Aurora stiffened and sat up straight. "No!" she cried. "I can't go back there. I don't belong there. I belong here!"

She pointed at her face, then Emily's blue eyes. "Look at me! Can't you see I'm one of you? My mother has gone to the Goddess. There is nothing on Tatanna for me anymore."

She flicked her gaze to Drew, who sat stoically, no readable expression on her stern features.

Aurora sighed again and shook her head. In a pleading tone, she asked, "With my father gone, do I have to go back to Tatanna?"

Finally, Drew's expression softened. "No, Aurora, you don't," she said. "Because of your father, you can claim all the rights and privileges of a citizen of the Lunar Free State. The only issue here is your age. There are no orphans here on Luna; in order to stay here, you must be in the care of an adult who is willing to accept responsibility for you.

"Based on what Maya has sent us, I know as much about you as anyone here. I can understand how you must feel, unable to go back, but not knowing what is ahead of you. Because of that, I have volunteered to take responsibility for you.

"I can never replace your mother, but I will guide and care for you to the best of my ability. Are you willing to accept that?"

Aurora looked from Drew to Emily, to Mike, and then to Maya, who had remained silent throughout the entire conversation. "Does that mean I can stay?"

Emily let a slow smile pass over her lips. "It certainly looks that way. Drew?"

"Yes, you can stay, but you will be living with me. You will also be going to school here on Luna. Since you have a lot of catching up to do, we have arranged for you to have a special teacher who can help you do that."

Reaching across the table, she picked up a small square, a miniature version of the large ones on the wall. "This will be yours, Aurora. You will use it to talk to your teacher."

Aurora picked up the square, which lit up immediately, revealing the lizard's face. She glanced sharply at the big screen on the wall, but the lizard had vanished from there. Now, he winked at her from the small screen. *Goddess, what magic is this?*

"Hello, Aurora. It's me, Mike, again. You can call me on this pad at any time. All you will need to do is touch the screen. The pad serves other functions, as well, and I will teach you how to use it as we go along."

Drew grinned sheepishly. "Hey, Mike, are you willing to teach me Tatannan, as well? I might need it to know whether Aurora is talking back to me when she gets upset."

"Of course, Jolene Drew," Mike replied. "I will teach you Tatannan. You, of course, already know how to contact me. Just let me know when you are ready to begin."

Shaking her head, Drew said, "I already speak English, a little French, and a little Korean. What's one more?"

"You came to us under strange circumstances," Emily said, "but in the end, it was a pleasure having you aboard my ship. Maya and I will now entrust you to Commander Drew—and Mike, of course. They will be taking you down to Luna. I wish you well."

Aurora's heart fluttered in her chest, not in fear, or guilt, or desperation. For the first time in her life, she didn't have to run anymore. She may not have found her father, but what she had found instead was a home.

*****

Author Bio

Charli Cox is a best-selling multi-genre author. She writes stories with humor because life can be dark sometimes; let's find some joy wherever we can.

An animal lover and #boymom, she lives in Oregon with her Leg husband, an Arabian mare, and two Husky mixes who think they are hooman. www.CharliCox.net

John Siers is an Air Force veteran and former IT geek who traded a fast-paced career in New York City for a more relaxed lifestyle in West Tennessee. He is the author of the Lunar Free State science fiction series, currently at twelve novels and counting: www.lunarfreestate.com

# # # # #

The Oath of Alaric by S.W. Swoope II & Chris Kennedy

A Story of Blood and Steel

Chapter 1

They're not getting away this time. Alaric smiled as the two dots flickered and reappeared centimeters closer on the ship's nav screen. The *Sparrow's Song*—and the deputy trade minister—had made a good run, but it wouldn't be long now.

Major Alaric Schwarz relaxed his grip and straightened. His beard itched, his eyes were dry, and his uniform needed a wash as much as he did. But in the screen's reflection, his friend Soren glared back at him—chained to a chair, bloody and crying. For the *Sparrow's Song*, there would be no escape.

"Time to target?" he asked his pilot.

"Fifteen minutes, sir," Lt. Valerie Peters answered.

Alaric turned to his comms officer and asked, "Any emergency communiques?"

"No, sir," he said. "They've been hailing us since they spotted us ten minutes ago, but sensors show no other contact attempts, sir."

"I need to send a tightbeam to HQ to alert them of our actions. Scramble it. Make it look like jamming interference."

The comms officer nodded. "Of course, sir. Record the message. I'll scramble and send it."

Alaric inhaled and recorded: "Sir, we received pressing intel that a ship disguised as a Bryton diplomatic vessel is illegally transporting weapons to a helot terrorist cell. We identified a potential match, approached it, and hailed. We were immediately jammed and came under fire. We have attempted to rig our comms laser to punch through the jamming signal. If we survive the engagement, we will contact you with an update. Major Alaric Schwarz, out."

"Send it. Notify me after the mission of any response." Alaric turned back to the pilot and said, "Continue ignoring their hails. Prepare boarding ship ignition. You have the bridge, Lieutenant."

"Yes, sir."

Alaric left the bridge and headed for the boarding ship, where the Varga were making their final preparations. Were they Goetheian marines, he would have offered his forearm and the old words before battle: Blood and Steel.

But they were Varga. Outlaws. They had no honor.

He found their captain, Vaako, who was bent over his panzer, checking plates and seals.

"We're good to launch," Alaric said. "I'll be first through the breach. I need to feel how the panzer handles under the new plating."

Vaako finished counting the grenades in his rack, then he looked up. "Mission parameters still the same?"

"Yes but before you sort the crew, I want one of them to show us where they're storing the weapons."

"If the dandies don't put their greasers down first," Vaako answered as he sprayed oil into the right knee of his panzer.

Alaric glanced at his watch. "Five minutes. Get them mounted." He walked to his own panzer and ran his checks again.

Satisfied with his preparations, he knelt before his family's panzer and lit the stub of a candle on the makeshift altar at its feet.

Maybe this time, his forefather would answer.

The bones were there, buried in the enamel of his panzer. The founder of House Schwarz. The emperor's right hand.

If there was ever a moment to speak, it was now.

Alaric asked for guidance. Courage. Wisdom.

But instead, he heard the flames of Soren's funeral pyre, gnawing through what remained of his friend.

Alaric opened his eyes. The silent skull of his ancestor stared back. He slid his versax from its sheath, raised it before his face, and said the sacred words, "By my blood and steel, I honor you."

He kissed the blade, blew out the candle, and climbed into his House's panzer.

* * *

The breacher contacted the hull of the Bryton vessel thirty-seven seconds after launch. The team detached from their safety harnesses, and the cutting crew went to work. They chewed through the Bryton hull in two minutes and nineteen seconds.

Alaric was the first panzer through the breach, and the corridor ahead erupted with muzzle flashes. Rounds from behind a barricade slammed against his shield and plated torso, and the impacts rang through the frame like raindrops on a tin can. His shield, coated in his new alloy, did its job.

This would not be another Minerva-7.

"Push," Alaric ordered as he raised his breacher shotgun and advanced into the storm. Each blast he fired turned a chunk of barricade into shards and smoke, or a man into a splatter.

Initial resistance cleared, Alaric motioned for the Varga to fan out through the ship.

Halfway to the bridge, Alaric and his five footmen met a second resistance cell dug in behind a makeshift barricade at a tight bend in the corridor. Alaric snapped a concussion grenade down the passage, hugged the corner with his shield, and waited for detonation. The blast rolled through the hallway, and the barricade sagged. Men cried out, stunned, and stumbled out from behind it. Alaric's shotgun did the rest.

As they worked their way through the wreckage and over the bodies, Alaric fought back the images of the tunnels in Minerva-7. The dead Goetheian marines.

They made it to the bridge door, but they found it sealed and welded shut from within. His team set plasma charges along the perimeter and welded his cable to the center of the slab, then Alaric dropped his stabilizers into the deck plating and rooted his panzer to the ship. Setting his shield, he took the winch under load until the cable *twang*ed.

Over the squad frequency, he whispered, "Clear."

He closed his eyes, and the charges blew. Light and heat punched through the seam, but the bridge door held. It was warped now, but still intact. Alaric activated the panzer's laser cutter and worked on the remaining metal while the winch whined and strained.

Finally, the door wrenched free, and it skidded down the corridor until it slammed into Alaric's shield like a bell rung in a coffin. It bounced once and fell flat.

Alaric launched a concussion grenade into the bridge and gave the order:

"Move!"

Six minutes and fifty-three seconds after the breach, the bridge was theirs.

He radioed the nine other squads scattered throughout the vessel and received their reports: no serious injuries, the compartments were all secured, and the ship was under their complete control.

* * *

Alaric popped the hatch to his panzer, climbed out, and stepped onto the bridge. Bryton prisoners lay on their bellies, their hands interlaced behind their heads. He knew they were Bryton captives because they still drew breath. Whether by enemy blade or their own, no true Goetheian tolerated defeat or capture. Alaric looked over the prone bodies and said, "I'm looking for the deputy trade minister."

A man raised his hand.

Alaric nodded to the Varga who held a rifle to the minister's back, and the trooper stepped away. The prisoner stood, brushed his uniform smooth, and said, "Ah, so you're aware this is a diplomatic vessel, then. Saves me from having to remind you of the consequences of your insane actions today."

Alaric didn't answer the threat. He pointed to two of his men. "You two, on me. We're escorting him back to the breacher. The rest of you, sort the bridge crew. And remember, we're looking for volunteers."

The bridge team dragged prisoners into separate lines while Alaric led the minister out into the corridor. He climbed back into his panzer, sealed the hatch, and took point toward the breach.

As they reached the opening in the hull, a voice came over the radio. *"Major, we got what you're looking for. Team Three, engine bay."*

"On my way," Alaric answered. He turned to his two footmen. "Get the minister strapped in. Make sure he's comfortable."

Alaric walked his panzer to the engine bay, where Team Three had pulled up a section of the deck plating and was staring at a weapons cache.

He climbed out of his panzer and crouched near the cases. Standard punch-key lock, likely rigged with an explosive. Nothing the bomb squad couldn't handle.

Alaric keyed his comm. "Lt. Peters, ship is clear. Dock the *Corvus* with the breacher and alert the bomb squad."

"Yes, sir," Lt. Peters responded.

Alaric turned to Team Three's leader. "Who was the volunteer?"

The team leader pointed to one of the Bryton prisoners on the deck.

"Good," Alaric said. "Two men will escort him and me back to the breacher. Sort the rest."

By the time they reached the breacher ship, the *Corvus* had finished docking.

Lt. Peters crossed over from the *Corvus*, snapped a salute, and said, "Sir, we have a response from HQ."

The dataslate was in the lieutenant's hand; the message had been sent directly to her. Stilicho hadn't bought Alaric's story, then. "Play it," Alaric said.

Peters thumbed her dataslate. Stilicho appeared behind his grotesque oaken desk and said, "Lt. Peters, Major Schwarz has committed treason and an overt act of war with his actions today. You are to immediately relieve the major of duty and take all actions to preserve the lives of the Brytons aboard that vessel. Failure to comply will result in you being charged with treason, as well. Don't let this be another black mark on your name, Lieutenant. I expect your prompt update on the situation."

The dataslate cut to black.

"Are you relieving me of duty, Lieutenant?"

"Of course not, sir," she said, "You asked to be notified of any response from HQ after the mission was completed." She hesitated. "I know why I'm here, sir."

"Good. You've shown such promise. Send the bomb squad to the engine bay. I want this ship stripped. They probably fried their data crystals, but pull them anyway. This is a black-ops Bryton vessel. There's always something worth keeping. Have the tech team make sure it's all dead. I don't want to make it too easy for Bryton to trace this back to us."

"The ship's crew?" Lt. Peters asked.

Soren's cries echoed.

"The Varga have a claim to the ransom. As for the rest? Clip their trigger fingers and space them. Beam the footage back to Bryton on a scrambled tightbeam. Remind them of the horrors of war."

"Yes, Major."

"Rig their ship and notify me when we're ready to leave."

Alaric headed to his quarters and, for the first time in six months, slept soundly.

*****

Chapter 2

After a few blessed hours of sleep, Alaric's comm chimed.

"Everything is as ordered, sir," Lt. Peters reported. *"We've finished rigging the Bryton vessel, and we're ready for departure."*

"Did the bomb squad open the cases?"

"Yes, sir."

"Have one brought to my office."

Alaric cut the channel, switched on the lights in his quarters, popped a stim, and dressed in his formal uniform. If he was to interrogate a deputy trade minister, he would do it as an officer of the Empire.

He entered his office. Operational materials were scattered across his desk. One of the cases sat on top of it.

Alaric flipped the lid open and found the same rifles that had shredded Soren's team on Minerva-7. He gathered the photos into a folder, picked up his dataslate, and headed for the interrogation room. With each step, Stilicho's last orders rang out. "No drastic measures."

* * *

After the funeral, in Stilicho's private study, the two of them had drunk to Soren's memory. Stilicho had stared into his glass and absently said, "I erred in asking you to be his bloodsworn, to train him."

Alaric had jumped at the opportunity to ingratiate himself with Stilicho, but after three months of grueling training, he had found something rare in Goetheian high society. A friend.

He remembered Stilicho's frown in the dim study. "To make it that far and lose? I should've known. He was no soldier. If he'd been humiliated earlier, we all would've seen it. But you did your duty, Major. My boy showed grit, and I thought… maybe."

Stilicho took a long drink.

"And because of that moment of pride, my son… my *House* is dead. Worse, humiliated before the Empire. An embarrassment."

How could an Imperial officer say such a thing about his own son?

Before Soren, Alaric might have admired Stilicho's ruthlessness. In intelligence, a man rose only as high as his cunning carried him. But now?

If a man couldn't love his son, how could he love the Empire? Stilicho's final words echoed in his memory. "No extraordinary measures. We'll investigate and find the helot terrorists responsible, but the emperor and the Electors have made it clear they don't want war with Bryton."

* * *

As Alaric stared at the Bryton deputy trade minister seated in his interrogation room, he was glad he'd resisted the urge to challenge Stilicho then and there. Because now he'd get to see Stilicho's face as he showed him the guns found on the minister's ship. Stilicho would have to pin another medal on his chest.

Alaric was about to enter the interrogation room when his pocket buzzed. He pulled out his transponder.

Amon. The message was brief. MY CAPTURE IS IMMINENT. BE AT YOUR BLACK SITE IN SECTOR-97 WITHIN 24 HOURS.

Alaric couldn't leave the minister here with the Varga; it was too great a temptation. He had to trust someone to get the minister to another black site. Alaric turned to the guard stationed by the door and said, "Have Lt. Peters take the prisoner to a transport. I'll send coordinates to her dataslate and update her within forty-eight hours."

Alaric pivoted and strode toward the hangar.

Minutes later, Alaric had his panzer loaded onto his personal fighter. He detached from the *Corvus* and burned toward the belt.

* * *

As his ship cut through space, he hoped a depressant could stop his mind from wandering. It didn't.

The *Valent* had started this cascade.

Through the deepscope, the *Valent* had appeared within reach as it detonated. Amon was supposed to capture the ship and its captain. Alaric wanted to expose an illegal arms trade with Bryton secessionists. Instead, Duke Tiberius of House Lindelung had fired first. Rather than surrender and face scandal, he'd chosen a noble death. He'd attacked a superior foe, and Amon had returned fire.

Alaric had cleaned up the mess. He'd cleaned up so well that the Affair had elevated him. But if Amon was ever captured, Alaric's rise would become his noose. Loose ends had to be cut.

The asteroid came into view, an abandoned mine tapped out over thirty years ago. Amon's rock hopper clung to the docking ring. "Amon," Alaric transmitted, "are you there?"

"Aye. And so you're not surprised, I brought my panzer inside."

When had Amon come into possession of a panzer? Alaric glanced over his shoulder at the fighter's bay area and found one of his contaminated fuel canisters from his Arminius operation. What scavenged helot panzer wasn't in need of fresh fuel?

Alaric docked and climbed into his own panzer. The habitat chamber lay silent beyond the airlock. He strode down the abandoned main street and found Amon waiting beside a café. The panzer was unmistakably helot, a mining conversion, like Alaric's had been a thousand years ago. And from the looks of it, Amon had been in more than a few scraps with it.

Amon's voice crackled over the radio as he said, *"I'm sorry about Lt. Quadi. I understand you were close."*

"He was a friend."

Amon granted Alaric a moment of silence and then asked, "Well, then, what's it going to be? A gentleman's duel to the death, or two spies trading secrets?"

Alaric slid his panzer's hands down to its blades, but Amon added, *"I can promise you at least want to hear the name before you decide."*

Alaric tightened the panzer's grip on the handles of its blades, but his curiosity won, and they remained sheathed.

"Baptiste."

The first entry in Goetheian Intelligence and Secret Operations' kill book. The man who'd probably given the order to torture and murder Soren. That was a name worth risking the past for. Alaric slowly drew the blades from their scabbards and crossed them in front of himself in salute as he answered, "Parlay?"

He waited as Amon returned the salute. Both panzers lowered their blades to their sides and knelt down on one knee to signal their truce. They exited their panzers and went into the café. The scent of fresh-brewed coffee struck Alaric's nose, and Amon said, "I gave myself permission to put a proper brew on. You stock your black sites well." He poured two cups. "How do you take yours?"

"That's proper coffee. You drink it black."

"No, not me," Amon answered as he poured sugar and creamer into his. "Proper coffee or not, I take mine blonde and sweet."

Alaric took his coffee and asked, "How'd you almost get caught? It's been two years since we last spoke, and I won't do you the disservice of lying and saying I haven't spent significant resources trying to find you."

"I took a bad job."

"That doesn't sound like you."

"Idealism bites us all, eventually," Amon answered.

Soren flashed beside Amon, and Alaric asked, "Idealism, huh? Was Soren's execution on Baptiste's orders?"

Amon paused for a moment. "Yeah."

"Why? After how much I paid you for my brother, surely..."

"Baptiste isn't looking to de-escalate." Amon set a data crystal on the table. "He made a weapons deal with the Brytons for whatever's on that encrypted crystal."

"Who's Baptiste's Bryton connection?"

"Some bureaucrat in the Trade Ministry."

"And why aren't you fulfilling your mission and giving the crystal to Baptiste?"

"GISO operatives were lying in wait when we arrived. We barely made it out, and it cost me a dear friend. He dug me out of the grave." Amon's voice quivered, and Alaric recognized a face he'd seen frequently in the mirror over the last few months. Amon continued, "Baptiste is clearly steering a leaking ship, and worse, is headed straight for an asteroid. I have no intention of keeping my crew on a ship like that. No, instead, I want what I was supposed to get for the crystal, one million credits."

Alaric pulled a data crystal from his jacket, set it on the table, and said, "I brought double your usual payment. A slush fund with half a million credits. I'll get you the second half once I have all the information."

Amon grabbed the crystal and slid it into his jacket pocket. "I'll need collateral."

"What?"

Amon glanced out the café window at Alaric's panzer. "I want the badge off of your panzer. The one for the Imperial Cross of Valor they gave you after the *Valent.* Seeing as I have as much claim to it as you, anyhow. More even. I think it'll make my panzer look distinguished."

"Fine. What's the target?"

"Since he doesn't have the information the Brytons wanted, he intends to take Hades-9."

"When?" Alaric asked.

"You get that when I get the rest of my money."

"I want the helot who killed Soren, as well. The one who pulled the trigger."

"I don't know who it was."

"Then find out. And know that I'll make sure they're the one. Or we can step outside."

Amon stared back at Alaric. "I'll see what I can do."

Alaric pulled his versax from his waist and said, "I want more than your word."

Amon shook his head. "Fine." He held his right arm out across the table.

Alaric cut a shallow gash down Amon's inner forearm and palm. Amon then pulled a versax from his belt and did the same to Alaric's right arm. They then grabbed each other's forearms, and Amon said, "I give you my oath and pledge that I will find the man who killed Soren Quadi and present him to you."

Amon tried to pull away, but Alaric held firm and said, "We are bloodsworn. Once you are at a safe distance, I expect you to send me the date of Baptiste's planned assault. When you have the man who killed Soren, you'll send me a location to meet. When I have the bastard, you get the other half of your payment. Understood?"

"As though I spoke the language," Amon answered.

Alaric released Amon and asked, "Do you have a way off this rock? I'm guessing whoever's after you is tracking that rock hopper out there?"

"Don't worry about me; I just needed some funds for my escape. I'll send you Baptiste's assault date in the next twelve hours."

Alaric climbed back into his panzer. As it powered up, Amon sipped his coffee, and Alaric found his thumb hovering over the grenade launcher button. The *Valent* Affair could end here. Soren's smashed face flashed before him. Alaric slid his short blade under his panzer's badge of the Imperial Cross, popped it off, and walked back to his ship before he changed his mind. As Alaric loaded the panzer onboard, he glanced at the contaminated fuel canister. Amon had sworn. That was enough.

After Alaric climbed into the cockpit, he examined the data crystal Amon had given him. If Amon didn't know what it was for, perhaps the deputy trade minister did? Alaric sent Lt. Peters a message: RETURNING TO GOETHEIA. THREE DAYS OUT. MEET YOU AT THE COORDINATES.

Alaric ignited his engines and set off for home. He hadn't been back since the funeral. Twelve hours later, Amon's message came through: SEVEN DAYS UNTIL THE ATTACK ON HADES-9.

*****

Chapter 3

After three days of travel from the belt at 1.6G, Alaric arrived at his black site Alpha-Sigma 7-0-3 on Goetheia. Lt. Peters waited on the landing deck for him. Alaric scanned the perimeter as he descended. No signs of ambush. Even so, he keyed the arming sequence on his ship's self-destruct and slipped the detonator into his pocket before he stepped onto the deck.

"Is the minister ready?" Alaric asked.

"Yes, sir. Interrogation Room Three."

"Good. I'll see him shortly."

"Sir, do we all get assigned personal black sites as captains or majors?"

"You get them when you can afford them, or when you earn one from a patron."

"GISO doesn't pay this well, sir."

"I do. When we've gotten to the bottom of Minerva-7, I'll notate you personally in my report and recommend you for commendation and promotion. Given what I've learned, you'll receive both. As a captain in GISO, you'll receive your own ship, and you'll be in need of a black site."

"What have you learned, sir?"

"In due time, Lieutenant. Now, go prepare the minister."

Alpha-Sigma 7-0-3 was one of Alaric's personal installations. It was funded through discretionary channels, layered through shell accounts, and known only to him—and now Peters. With no ambush on arrival, it seemed her loyalty had held. He deactivated the detonator.

The site existed for two purposes: interrogation and experimentation. From a secured case, he removed an experimental crystal he'd refined since the Academy. His professor had said that it took a special mind to see what such a simple thing could be. The kind of mind that would excel in GISO. He had designed it so the crystal lattice destabilized after exposure to a standard reading laser, but he'd never been able to expand its decay rate beyond four hours—a timeframe that had never been useful in the field. But the Bryton Embassy was two hours away.

He removed the crystal Amon had given him and slotted it into his reader. Then he inserted the experimental crystal into the copy housing. The duplication process began, and Alaric dressed while the data transferred.

When the copy cycle completed, he verified the data integrity, removed the unstable crystal, and slid it into his inner breast pocket. The original he sealed in a hidden floor safe, logged under his personal encryption. He checked the time above the workshop door: 17:23. Alaric extinguished the workshop lights and descended to Interrogation Room Three.

The deputy trade minister sat at the table, posture rigid, gravity weighing visibly on him. Alaric entered slowly, and he let the silence stretch. He stood in full dress black, medals gleaming over his heart, and waited for the recognition to settle. It did. The minister's expression tightened, then it reassembled into charm. "Major Alaric Schwarz. I would ask to what I owe the pleasure, but..."

Alaric opened the folder he held and pulled out several photos, stills from the raid on the minister's ship, and set them on the table before the minister as he said, "This was blood for blood."

"I understand," the minister answered.

Alaric pulled out the chair opposite the minister and said, "But this line of work doesn't afford one the luxury of nursing grudges. I can't bring back my friend or his men. You can't bring back your crew."

The minister's smile widened, going from decorum to genuine as he asked, "Has someone been burned?"

Alaric set his dataslate on the table, pulled up the video message Colonel Stilicho had sent Lt. Peters, and handed it to the minister. The minister took the dataslate and watched the message.

"So, what? You'd like me to broker an exchange? My life for yours?"

Alaric laughed and answered, "The emperor doesn't negotiate. We don't trade prisoners. The moment Stilicho locates me, I'm dead. Likely worse. And frankly, your prospects aren't much brighter. Your ship is destroyed, and everyone in Bryton will already assume you're dead. The Empire has no reason to disabuse them of that belief."

Alaric pulled the data crystal from his breast pocket and set it down in front of the minister.

"What's this?" the minister asked as he held up the crystal.

"What you asked Baptiste to steal."

"And how did you come by it?" the minister asked.

"I stole it."

"What do you want in return?"

"I want out."

"Ah, so this is *that* conversation. Define 'out.'"

"Social standing on Bryton. Wealth. Protection."

The minister's fingers tapped the crystal. "And you believe this is worth such a package?"

"I do."

"Permission to verify?"

"Please."

The minister inserted the crystal into his dataslate. The seconds ticked by.

"This is the crystal Baptiste was after. However, it's not what we paid him for. If you want the luxury suite, you must deliver the final product."

"I don't understand."

"We paid for a shipment of Imperial tantalum. Buried in this encrypted crystal is the tantalum delivery schedule, but by itself, it's of no value to me."

If Bryton got the Empire's tantalum, the great game would be over.

A klaxon blared. Visitors. Alaric flew to the door. The thud of footsteps flooded the hallway outside the door. There were a lot of marines. He'd taken a risk with Peters. The marines placed charges on the door. Alaric fell to the floor and covered himself as the door exploded open. Lt. Peters had played the game well; she'd go far. Boots surrounded Alaric, and his ears rang. There was a muffled gunshot, and the minister fell to the floor with Alaric. Manacles clicked around Alaric's wrists. There was a sharp pain at the back of his skull and then nothing.

* * *

Alaric awoke in chains. Disgraced by capture. Soren had died in chains. He'd never been in chains before; he didn't care for it. The lack of dignity. This dishonor would stain his name along with his family's. Long after Alaric had drawn his last breath, the chains of his treason would still be there, and all Goetheia would know that Colonel Stilicho Quadi had placed them upon the House of Schwarz.

The echoes of footsteps announced the arrival of Stilicho and a dozen marines. Even groggy from the blast, Alaric recognized those steps. He'd come himself.

Keys slid into a lock, the lock clicked, and the door swung open. A marine shouted, "On your feet!"

Alaric staggered to his feet. Colonel Stilicho said, "Please follow us, Major, so I may read you your charges."

The marines escorted Alaric down the hall to an elevator, which took them upward. They exited the elevator and stepped out onto the top floor of GISO HQ. Alaric's colleagues watched as the marines escorted him to Stilicho's office.

Stilicho stood behind his obscene oaken desk and said, "As I'm sure you've surmised, Major, I have charged you with treason for your unlawful attack on the Bryton diplomatic vessel. But in truth, GISO has watched you since before the *Valent* Affair. Did you know that Duke Tiberius was a dear friend and patron?" He paused, placed the experimental data crystal on the desk, and pulled a panzer fuel canister out from under the desk, then set it down by the data crystal and continued, "I will also present evidence that you gave secrets to the terrorist known as Amon, and you murdered fellow GISO operative Captain Arminius by supplying his panzer with a tainted fuel canister. All of it was part of your selfish plot for revenge, and to rise above the station warranted by your abilities. The Empire has long had to guard itself against striving second sons."

Alaric's eyes lingered on the fuel canister for a moment. Had Stilicho recovered one of the modified units? Or had he simply deduced the method? "Tell me something, Colonel," Alaric said evenly. "Are you truly outraged that I pursued justice for Soren? Or are you afraid I'll show how weak you are?"

Anger flickered across Stilicho's face. "You mistake yourself for something larger than you are. This is not about rivalry."

"No?" Alaric asked quietly. "You call me a striving second son. Everyone calls you an up-jumped new man."

Stilicho reached out to his desk and tapped a control. A screen flared to life behind him. The café. Alaric and Amon sat across from one another. Alaric's stomach tightened, but his face didn't.

The recording played for a moment. Amon's voice filled the room, "Hades-9."

"You see, Major," he said, "I'm upset about many things, my son among them, but I'm not careless. You walked into a black site with a known terrorist. You accepted intelligence. You negotiated payment. And you didn't report this meeting."

Alaric said nothing. Stilicho's mouth curved faintly as he produced Alaric's transponder. "I should thank you, in fact. This recording was the final piece. I knew Baptiste was working with the Brytons. We suspected a major strike. But Hades-9?" He exhaled slowly. "That changes everything. In four days, I'll have made myself the next high marshal."

Alaric stood silent, at attention.

"Do you have anything to say in your own defense?" Stilicho asked.

Alaric did not answer immediately. Instead, he found Stilicho's wall clock.

20:39.

Alaric had been unconscious for nearly three hours, which meant he had maybe an hour before the crystal sitting on Stilicho's desk leveled most of GISO HQ.

Alaric answered, "Not to you."

"I'd ask how you'd like to proceed—"

Alaric interrupted. "I'd like to invoke my rights as a scion of Elector-House Schwarz to present my case to the emperor."

"But," Stilicho continued, "you forget, you're not the head of your House, Alaric. It's customary in situations like these, rare as they may be, to consult the House patriarch. I've spoken to your brother and told him about the charges I've brought against you. If you were to press your claim and request a trial presided over by the emperor, as is your right, there would be no way to keep this out of the public eye. Think of the embarrassment you'd bring to your House. GISO and the nobility are pillars of the Empire. We can't tolerate this going public. Your brother understands that, and as such, has requested that you do the honorable thing for your family and the Empire."

"Theodoric said this?"

"He did. He also granted me a writ of seal to execute his will in this matter."

Stilicho lifted a document bearing the crest of House Schwarz. "And he sent a personal letter for you."

Stilicho tossed the letter across the desk. Alaric grabbed the letter and said, "I'll proceed to my personal quarters and see to this matter personally, sir."

"Thank you, Major. We'll collect your body in the morning. Dismissed."

As Alaric walked out of the office, Stilicho said, "Take these items to evidence for processing."

Alaric's marine escort unchained him, ushered him into his personal quarters, and handed him his versax, then locked the door behind him. Alaric stood there, his back to the cold steel door, Theodoric's letter a lead brick in his hand. Theodoric still held Alaric responsible for their father's death, and Alaric's fame cast a long shadow. But this? To condemn him without hearing him? Alaric unfolded the letter.

YOU ARE, AND ALWAYS HAVE BEEN, A DISGRACE TO OUR FAMILY. PLEASE DO THE HONORABLE THING.

—MARGRAVE THEODORIC SCHWARZ

That was all. His true feelings, a request, and his florid signature. Alaric checked his watch. One minute and thirty-seven seconds had passed since his escort had left him alone. There was still time for him to sprint down the hallway and warn them about the crystal.

Alaric read the letter again. The word "disgrace" was blurred where a tear had struck the page. Alaric crumpled the letter and dropped it to the floor. He reached for the door handle, then stopped. No, he wouldn't die begging for approval.

He crossed the room to his desk and grabbed his quarterly cipher crystal. If Stilicho survived the blast, he'd go to Hades-9 and find nothing. Baptiste was after the tantalum. Alaric knelt at the rear wall. His fingers followed the seam to a hidden latch he'd installed years ago. The panel slid open. He dropped into the maintenance tunnel beneath the floor and sealed it behind him. Guide lights flickered on as his movement triggered them. The passage was narrow, barely wider than his shoulders. He crawled as the clock ticked in his mind.

He emerged near the hangar junction several minutes later. The air smelled faintly of machine oil and coolant. He reached into a recessed storage alcove and found a familiar shape: a fuel canister.

He drew it out and stared at it in the dim light. Another of Alaric's Academy designs, one he hadn't published a paper on, because he knew how it would be used. He wouldn't give rivals a way to trigger a panzer's meltdown without a trace, and he'd never intended to use it himself. So, he'd buried his research. But then an opportunity presented itself: a double agent, Captain Arminius. Instead of a formal hearing and execution, Alaric had made him useful.

Alaric turned toward the hangar access tunnel, grabbed his mechanic's uniform from the wall, and slid into it. He peeked through the false door. Mechanics moved between panzers in the familiar rhythm of maintenance.

He crouched and waited in a shadowed alcove near the false wall he'd installed behind a storage rack. From here, he had a clear view of Stilicho's personal panzer. It was immaculate, more symbol than weapon. It hadn't stood with the emperor during the Crusade.

The explosion came three hours and forty-four minutes after reading. A crack rippled through HQ. For half a heartbeat, there was stunned silence. Then the floor lurched beneath him. Alarms screamed to life. Panic. Mechanics shouted. Emergency lights flickered, bathing the hangar in harsh crimson. Automated announcements blared instructions.

When the scramble reached its peak, while everyone looked everywhere at once, Alaric moved. He slipped from the alcove and crossed the hangar.

Stilicho's panzer loomed before him. Up close, it was beautiful. Polished armor. House insignia etched deep and proud. Alaric opened the fuel access panel. He removed the standard canister and slid the contaminated one into place. He secured the seals and ran a quick diagnostic. Everything read green. He closed the panel and whispered, "Soren, forgive me."

Alaric melted into the service corridors and disappeared.

He made his way back to Alpha Sigma 7-0-3. The sweeper team had been recalled to help with the HQ explosion. In the few hours they had, they hadn't been able to crack his security codes. His safe was unopened. He recovered the original data crystal, and his fighter—with his family's panzer—was stationed where he'd left it. Fortuna hadn't completely abandoned him. Alaric sent a message to the *Corvus*:

MEET IN SECTOR-81 FOR PICKUP IN 24 HOURS.

His fighter broke from Goetheia's gravity and burned to meet up with the *Corvus*.

*****

Chapter 4

Four days after he escaped Goetheian HQ, Alaric and the Varga lay in wait behind an asteroid. From here, they were invisible, another piece of debris in the belt.

On the tactical display, six transports and two escorts drifted across the screen. Imperial registry codes pulsed faintly blue. The quarterly tantalum shipment. The Empire's lifeblood.

"Convoy entering the debris field," the navigation officer reported.

The first pirate ship appeared less than a minute later.

Then another.

Then three more.

One of those bastards is Baptiste.

Weapon fire lit up the void. One escort took a hit along its flank and spun wide, its atmosphere venting in a glittery plume.

The convoy tightened formation.

The pirates spaced themselves to deny overlapping fields of fire. The pirate panzers flooded out from the boarding craft and mag-clamped onto the hulls of the transports. Mining teams followed, equipment already spun up. "Record everything," Alaric ordered. "I want movement patterns, reaction times, drive signatures. Don't engage until I say."

Alaric sprinted from the bridge to the boarding ship and buckled himself into his panzer. The *Corvus* peeled away from the asteroid and slid behind the pirate formation, its thrusters flaring only enough to reposition. The pirates were fully engaged now, focused forward, blind to anything that wasn't already shooting at them.

"Missiles hot," Alaric said, "Fire."

Alaric's HUD showed the missiles streak through space and find their targets. Pirate ships vanished in clouds of debris. Nearly half the pirate force was gone in seconds. The surviving pirates reacted, breaking formation and returning fire.

"Boarding ship away."

It seemed like almost no time passed before the boarding craft slammed into the main transport's hull.

"Imperial convoy, this is GISO," Alaric broadcast to the convoy. "Maintain defensive posture."

The ramp dropped. Alaric strode forward in his panzer. The Varga fanned out around him. They advanced toward the pirate boarding team. The pirates opened fire from behind mining equipment and barricades.

The first of the Varga, Captain Vaako, went down in a shower of sparks, his panzer's chest caved in by an explosive shell. Alaric raced forward, and his blades flashed as his armor deflected incoming fire. The Varga followed, returning fire, trying to close the distance. Another of the Varga staggered, its armor slagged and systems failing.

"Storm them," Alaric ordered.

They charged. This was Alaric's domain. Close quarters. Academy dueling champion. It should have been a slaughter.

The pirates met them blade for blade, movement for movement. Their panzers absorbed punishment that should have crippled them. Their pilots anticipated feints, countered strikes, and pressed their advantages with ruthless efficiency. Another of the Varga fell. Then another.

Alaric cut through one pirate panzer, severing its arm and driving a blade through the cockpit. He pivoted, parried, and struck again. Then, a cold spike of shock. The helot panzers weren't analog; they were blasphemies.

"Pull back!" one of the Varga shouted.

"No," Alaric said. "We advance."

But the line was collapsing. There were only three Varga left.

Then two.

Alaric worked toward the remaining Varga, but a new panzer entered from his left. Even from a sideways glimpse, the panzer was unmistakable. It bore Alaric's Imperial Cross of Valor badge. Amon.

Baptiste was never here.

Alaric disengaged, and his blades came up as he squared off against Amon and another pirate. Steel rang against steel, and sparks spat into the void.

Across the open channel, Alaric asked, "What have you done, Amon? You'd risk us all with your sacrilege?"

They traded blows, Alaric pressing, Amon yielding enough ground to avoid commitment. The other pirate flanked, forcing Alaric to split his attention.

Then the darkness lit up.

The *Corvus* made a strafing run, and heavy fire tore through the ship. The flanking pirate vanished in an explosion. Amon's panzer staggered, armor breached, and one leg buckled. The shift broke the engagement.

Amon and his pirates retreated through the rents the *Corvus* had made in the ship and were gone. The convoy was secure. Alaric stood amid the wreckage, his panzer scarred, the Varga reduced to two battered survivors. The convoy's admiral said over the channel, *"We should pursue."*

Alaric ran through possibilities, traps, and contingencies. He walked over to what remained of one of the heretical panzers he'd been engaged with.

If they're using digital tech, they're endangering all three systems.

"No," Alaric said. "The convoy is safe. A pursuit risks overextension."

"Understood," the admiral answered.

Wreckage drifted all around Alaric as he stared into the void, where Amon had disappeared.

* * *

Two days after the defense of the Imperial convoy, Alaric stood alone before a tribunal in his dress uniform. Armed only with his versax, he faced the men who'd decide his fate.

"This inquiry concerns three events: the explosion at GISO Headquarters, the disaster on Hades-9, and your independent defense of the tantalum convoy. Are you prepared to give your statement?"

"I am," Alaric replied.

"It is our understanding that at the time of the headquarters explosion, you had been remanded to your quarters and ordered to fall on your versax, is that correct?"

"It is."

"And yet here you stand? Please explain how and why you survived the HQ explosion."

"Colonel Stilicho lied, trying to besmirch my honor and House. He was obsessed with self-glorification and could not be trusted to protect the Empire. As such, I used all means at my disposal to escape and uphold my duty to the Empire."

"Let us address the headquarters explosion. The blast originated from the evidence locker. Evidence was secured from your person. Given the charges, you clearly had motive."

"You're asking if I planted an explosive in the evidence locker?"

"You wrote a paper as an Academy cadet on experimental crystal lattices that theoretically could have rendered a yield comparable to that which destroyed the HQ building."

"That's true, but it was decided that the use case was too narrow to justify the expense. It never proceeded beyond theory."

"Yes, well, you have demonstrated that you have impressive resources at your disposal."

"I do."

"The two surviving members of your unit corroborate that you engaged pirate forces and successfully repelled the assault on the Imperial convoy. That is to be commended. But we need to know if you deny responsibility for the explosion?"

"Unequivocally, and it doesn't sound like you have any evidence to suggest I'm responsible beyond my good fortune."

"Did you try to warn Colonel Stilicho about the threat posed to the tantalum convoy, and that you believed the supposed threat to Hades-9 was a distraction?"

"I didn't get the chance before receiving my terminal order."

"Were you involved in the disaster on Hades-9?"

"How many marines and GISO operatives were lost? I won't lie and say that I wouldn't have staged Stilicho's murder if I could have. After Soren—and Stilicho's false charges—I would have, but not at the cost of so many other Goetheian lives."

A long pause followed. When they spoke again, their tone had shifted. It was less accusatory, more political. "The Empire lost its director of GISO and dozens of its top operatives. The weapons depot at Hades-9 exploded, and the Empire's tantalum reserves were threatened. Given the evidence, we cannot conclusively attribute the headquarters' explosion to you. Therefore, this tribunal finds insufficient grounds to pursue treason charges at this time."

"Thank you, my lords."

"You are promoted to lieutenant colonel. You will be awarded your second Imperial Cross of Valor for the defense of the tantalum convoy, and you will assume provisional command of GISO as of 0739. The Goetheian Security Council expects your first tasks to be a full investigation into the disaster at Hades-9 and to bring Amon to justice. Your conduct in these matters will determine the future of your command and whether any further investigations are required into your past activities. May the First Emperor guide your hand. This tribunal is concluded."

Alaric bowed. "Yes, my lords."

After the tribunal, Alaric went to his new temporary quarters, where his confiscated effects were waiting. They'd told him what had happened to Stilicho, but hadn't mentioned the fate of any other GISO operatives. At his desk computer, he ran a search for Lieutenant Valerie Peters. He found a Captain Valerie Peters listed as deceased.

At least she got a promotion for her betrayal.

As he checked the items they'd taken from him, he found his transponder, and it had a message from Amon waiting: WE ARE STILL BLOODSWORN. MEET YOU AT THE CAFÉ.

Alaric wasted no time in responding.

SEE YOU IN TWENTY-FOUR.

*****

Chapter 5

Alaric approached the café in his panzer. Static hissed over the radio, and Amon asked, *"Did you bring the rest of my payment?"*

"Of course, I take my oath seriously. Where's Soren's killer?"

"I'm right here," Amon answered.

"Why?"

"Minerva-7 was one of mine. Wrong place, wrong time. Worse luck that he got buried under rubble with my men. Once I realized who he was, I made the best of a bad situation. I needed GISO disoriented. Almost did the trick."

Alaric tossed Amon his payment.

Amon's panzer peeled off Alaric's badge and tossed it to the ground before Alaric. *"I gave you the honor of answering truthfully. Now answer me. Were you behind Hades-9?"*

"Did Baptiste know he was a diversion?"

"No, the old fool thought Hades-9 was a brilliant idea. He served the cause well."

Alaric's panzer picked up the badge. *I didn't deserve the first Medal of Valor, and certainly not the second.*

"Stilicho betrayed me. He betrayed his son. He couldn't defend the Empire."

"No, the Empire needs a blackguard."

"I'm offended you didn't bring any backup," Alaric said as he fitted the badge back onto his panzer.

"Backup? To our secret meeting? I may be a helot, but I have my Goetheian pride. This needed to be settled fairly. Crazy as that is, coming from the two of us."

"Goetheian pride? I checked your panzers. No true Goetheian would rely on that digital rot in their panzers."

"I don't. This panzer dug me out of a mine your people entombed me in, and as much as I know it's dogma, I wouldn't denigrate her with digital tech."

"You've never had to clear an Orven nest. If you had, you'd show respect for our laws."

"As your better, you should show me respect."

"Show me. Blood for blood," Alaric answered.

Both panzers drew their blades, crossed them in salute, and then circled each other. Alaric attacked first. Aggressive; contrary to habit. If Amon had studied him, he'd know to expect counter-strikes. Their blades collided, and orange sparks burst against the white dome. Amon parried effortlessly.

"I know about Arminius," Amon said. *"Four years pretending to be left-handed, then switching hands for the duel. Clever."* Their blades rang. *"Perhaps too clever. You sacrificed training for deception."*

Another clash of their blades, and Amon added, *"You think I wouldn't expect you to do the opposite now?"*

Alaric halted the forward surge, and he relaxed into his natural stance.

Amon advanced. Low cut into a high arc. Alaric caught it. Then Amon burst forward.

The thrust was perfect. Practiced.

The blade slid inside Alaric's guard, but Alaric twisted at the last instant, overdriving his right leg hydraulics. Amon's blade struck at an angle, sliding along his restored badge instead of piercing the panzer's thorax, and the blade got stuck in Alaric's left shoulder. Before Amon could wrench it free, Alaric clamped down around Amon's blade arm.

Alaric twisted his torso to the left, pulling Amon off balance. That opened enough space for Alaric to wrap his panzer's arms fully around Amon's trapped right arm. As Alaric twisted back to the right with a jerk, he tore Amon's panzer arm off in a storm of sparks and hydraulic mist.

Both panzers staggered apart, and Alaric asked, "You're my better?"

"Stop talking and fight," Amon replied.

They closed again. Alaric tried to exploit reach. A probing jab with his long blade. Amon slipped inside it. Alaric pivoted, but his panzer's right knee buckled.

In one seamless motion, Amon sliced his dagger through Alaric's right leg pneumatics and executed a throw that sent Alaric's panzer crashing onto its back. Amon stood over him, his foot crushing Alaric's carapace. Amon held the tip of his dagger above Alaric's chest, ready to drive the blade clean through the panzer and Alaric. But he didn't. He hovered there, a smirk on his lips, and then a recording played of Alaric confessing to Hades-9.

After the recording ended, Amon watched. The static over the radio hummed between them.

Twice. He's bested me twice over.

"I don't need to kill you," Amon said. *"I own you, and you're worth much more to me alive than dead."*

Amon cut the power to Alaric's panzer and said, *"When I call, I expect you to answer, understood?"*

"Yes," Alaric answered.

"Yes, what?"

"Yes, sir."

Amon tried to wrench his panzer's arm free. Hydraulic fluid and oil spewed out, but the arm remained. Amon gave up, walked away, and said, *"Best damn panzer pilot in all three systems."*

After the last echoes of Amon's footsteps faded, Alaric popped his hatch and climbed out of his panzer. Alaric unbuttoned his jacket, drew his versax, and fell to his knees. As Alaric drew the versax to his belly, he turned to his ancestral panzer and whispered, "Forgive me." But as he was about to drive the blade into his stomach, he remembered something Amon had said, "This panzer dug me out of a tomb your people put me in."

The arm of Amon's panzer was buried in Alaric's carapace. The arm had deep scars, the kind that hid secrets. Localized ore dust. Mine residue. The tribunal's orders rang in Alaric's mind, "You are to bring Amon to justice."

Alaric rose to his feet and sheathed his versax. He could die after he'd won.

* * * * *

Author Bio

Scott Swoope is a writer whose work blends history with the imagination of sci-fi and fantasy. His stories explore power, loyalty, and the human cost of ambition across worlds both ancient and futuristic. He lives in South Carolina with his wife and son, who has already been recruited as the family's unofficial mascot. www.swswoope.com

A Webster Award winner and three-time Dragon Award finalist, Chris Kennedy is a Science Fiction/Fantasy author, speaker, and small-press publisher who has written over 80 books and published more than 500 others. Get his free book, "Shattered Crucible," at his website, https://chriskennedypublishing.com.

# # # # #

Directive Thirty-One by Ronald Lloyd

A Freedom Base Story

Chapter 1

Wayne Comings, commander of the *Michael Collins*, leaned his head against the plexiglass of the observation window. As he watched, the space station crossed Earth's night terminator, and as if someone had flipped a switch, the lights of the North American cities shone in the darkness below.

Comings straightened and caught his reflection in the glass. A hand rose to his forehead as he wondered when the gray streaks in his hair had become so obvious. Behind, iron scraped on iron, and he pivoted to see a young woman, probably in her mid-twenties, step through the hatch and into the lounge. Although not what many would call a beauty, she was striking in her own way. Short brown hair, a slim waist, and dressed in the non-regulation green coveralls of a visitor to the station.

The moment Colonel Comings opened his mouth to greet the visitor, she staggered and struck her shoulder on the edge of the hatch. He reached out to assist.

"Ma'am, did you remember to take your spin-dizzy pill?"

Her expression blank, she said, "Yes, Colonel."

Perfunctory. Not exactly hostile, but cool, if not cold. Surprised she knew his rank, Comings responded, "Good, ah, that should keep you from getting dizzy, but it still takes everyone a few days to adapt to the spin of the habitation ring." The woman acknowledged his words with barely a nod and crossed to the window, careful to give him a wide berth. "I'm Wayne Comings," he said as he pivoted to follow her. "Did you come up on the midday shuttle?"

She nodded as she gazed out into the void and, as if in accusation, said, "I know who you are."

Not sure why he persisted, Comings asked, "And you are?"

Without turning away from the window, she said, "Averroes. Martha Averroes."

"I knew an Averroes once."

"Yes, he was my brother."

Icicles couldn't have been sharper, nor cut deeper. As if she'd slapped him, the colonel retreated a quarter step.

Memory took Comings back to the hatch leading to the engineering section of the American Lunar Base, and one terrible moment in time. Through a small porthole, the face of Assistant Engineer Averroes pressed against the opposite side of the glass, and behind him, the flames of a raging fire filled the room with a red glow. As the engineer's fist pounded on the hatch, his lips moved in an unheard cry. "Let us in. Please, let us in."

As Comings's fingers reached for the lever to undog the hatch, the radio on his shoulder crackled, and he heard Ford, his second in command, say, "Colonel, the oxygen tank and the hydrogen tank are critical." When Comings was silent, Ford continued, "Colonel, if we don't vent the atmosphere in engineering, the tanks will blow. They'll take out the entire colony."

There was no real choice. Comings dropped his hand from the latch.

"Do it."

Through the ceramic walls of the station, Comings heard the explosive bolts of the emergency vent system let go. Despite the torrent of dust and debris whirling around Averroes, his lips moved in a silent plea, "No. No, please no."

A part of Comings wanted to turn away, but a lifetime of unflinching duty forced him to keep his eyes on the porthole.

Immersed in his memories, Martha's words didn't register right away.

"Pardon me, what did you say?"

Pointing at the window, she repeated, "I asked, what's going on down on Earth?"

Looking past her, he could see dozens of eye-searing lights pockmarking the darkness in places they shouldn't be. Around the lights, ripples of colored light, much like an aurora in the northern latitudes, wove a strange tableau over the North American continent.

"What… what is it?"

"EMPs," the colonel said, then lifted his communicator from its bracket on his belt. "Bridge."

For a moment, no one responded, and then Caleb Blaine, his exec, said, "Bridge, here."

"What's the situation dirtside?"

"We're trying to find out, sir." A double breath later, the exec said, "Colonel, our sensors show X-ray radiation levels off the charts. We can't raise Space Command. All transmissions have ceased."

"Defense Command?"

After a pause, Blaine said, "The same, Colonel."

"What about our data links to the surface?"

"No, Colonel, nothing."

Crossing to stand beside him, Martha asked, "What's going on?"

Comings opened his mouth to respond, but stopped when a couple hundred streaks of light rose in an arc over the equator. As he raised a hand to ward off further questions, he saw the flare of a couple hundred missile interceptors rising from along the East

Coast, while at the same time, hundreds of the larger plumes of a counter-missile strike rising from the mid-states. All arced south toward Africa.

"Colonel, I asked you what's going on?"

As he swiveled on one foot toward the hatch, he said, "Miss Averroes, I'm afraid we're seeing a world war in progress. If you'll excuse me, I must get to the bridge." As he sprinted down the passage, the colonel glanced up at the speaker grille. "SAM, what's going on?"

Half a heartbeat later, a tenor voice replied, "Colonel, the data is scanty, but twenty-five Hiroshima-sized atomic explosions have taken out the main communications and coordination centers of the United States' defenses. As programmed, Central Defense AI has assumed control and is coordinating the defense of the country."

After a brief pause, the narration continued. "Colonel, I have been able to establish contact with the Mu Upsilon node of the National Defense AI, and it appears the initial attack was clandestine. A second, traditional missile attack is underway. I will keep you informed as I receive more information."

Once through the hatch at the end of the passage, Comings crossed into the Beta Segment and turned to spring up the ladder, three steps at a time. At the main deck, he shouted, "Thank you, SAM!"

Thanking the AI wasn't necessary, but he'd done it for so long, it had become a habit.

* * *

Colonel Comings entered the station control room and paused to survey the room for a heartbeat. It was small, less than fifteen meters from front to back, with four techs seated before a semicircular console in the middle of the room. Above the console, on the forward bulkhead, was the main screen, and two meters behind the four techs, the officer of the deck sat in a large chair.

Hearing the hatch open, Major Caleb Blaine turned and rose. Blaine, short and stout, was at least ten years younger than the commander, with deep blue eyes and blond hair. Exterior differences aside, both shared an identical professional DNA. In a loud voice, the exec announced, "Commander on deck."

Even in the urgency of the moment, Comings followed military protocol.

"I have the deck."

The exec stepped aside. "The commander has the deck."

As Comings sat, he asked, "Sitrep?"

"It's confirmed. The African Union has attacked the United States. Initial reports indicate severe damage."

"Yes, what else?"

"Since the initial covert attack on our command-and-control centers, there have been two missile salvos."

"Results?"

"Our countermissiles took out all but three of the African Union's rockets, sir."

Rising, Comings stared up at the main screen and saw an image from a camera atop the station. It gave him a bird's-eye view of *Michael Collins*. It was the standard station configuration. There was a long cylinder, twenty meters in diameter, in the middle, with five spokes radiating from the hub to the rotating habitation ring. At the bottom of the hub was a large ring of reaction rockets that, in three days, would move the station from Earth orbit, where it had been constructed, to its permanent place in Lunar orbit.

Below the station, Comings could see the familiar outline of the North American continent, still shrouded in darkness. His eyes were fixed on the familiar image.

"What'd they hit?"

"Kansas City, Atlanta, and Detroit, sir."

"Extent of the damage?"

A side glance at Caleb's glower told Comings all he needed as an answer.

"What's happening now?'

"Ah, nothing, sir."

"Nothing? What do you mean, nothing?"

"Well, we can't be totally certain, but after the second salvo, the missiles stopped."

"Why aren't we continuing to launch retaliatory strikes?"

"Unknown, sir."

Turning to the comm officer, the colonel asked, "Caroline, what've you got?"

She swiveled and, with a frown and her usual precision, said, "Sir, all I'm getting is a lot of local chatter. I haven't heard anything from Defense Command since the initial strikes."

Before the colonel could reply, though, Emery Butler, the engineering officer to Caroline's right, pointed to his screen and cried, "I've got something!"

"What is it?"

Leaning over his console, the engineer pointed. "Let me show you, sir."

The image grew until the East Coast of the United States filled the main screen.

"Look at these points, sir, where the East Coast should be a solid mass of light. About a hundred miles inland, there's a dark line extending from Nova Scotia to Florida."

For a moment, the colonel didn't see anything; then it became obvious. Stepping closer, he asked, "Is it an anomaly?"

"No, sir. I've rebooted the image twice. But there's more, sir."

"Go on."

"Whatever it is, it's moving."

As Wayne watched, the line crept slowly west. The lights of whole cities went dark, only to reappear as the line passed.

"Could it be some kind of new weapon?" Comings said.

The response came from Caroline, not his exec. "I have something more, Colonel. The Union took out all our satellites in the initial attack, but I've hacked into a transmission from a Chinese television platform. That's some scary bad security they've got." With a flick of her finger, Caroline replaced the image of the East Coast with one of sub-Saharan Africa. "It is not as distinct as the one on our East Coast, but if you look closely, you can see that there's a dark line along the West Coast of Africa, too. Looks identical."

Lt. Carl Rubin, Second Technology Officer, at a console across the room, said, "Sir, I've got something, too."

Comings turned to face him. "Go on."

"When the Union took out our satellites, they missed a few over European airspace. I can't get an image, but I was able to download some data. That line, whatever it is, doesn't stop at the Med. It extends across the sea, enters the European landmass, and continues all the way north into the Arctic Circle."

Crossing the control room, the exec stopped behind the commander and, after studying the data on the screen, nodded. "He's right, and it's moving east, toward Russia. Sir, if the Russians perceive it as some kind of threat…"

"Yeah," Comings said. *Hundreds of nuclear-tipped ICBMs needing only a reason to be launched.*

Behind them, Lt. Caroline Winstead, the comm officer, said, "Something's coming through on the Defense Command channel."

"On speaker."

From the grille above the screen, they heard a deep, resonant voice. "To all stations, this is the National Artificial Intelligence

Defense Network. Twenty clandestine strikes by the African Union have destroyed the United States Defense Command. Under Directive Thirty-One, lines twenty through ninety-five, the Defense Artificial Intelligence Network has assumed control of the defense of the United States and its NATO allies. Please await further details."

For a long moment, no one moved, then as if in unison, every head turned to the colonel. Voicing the thoughts of the others, the exec asked, "Commander, what's Directive Thirty-One?"

Comings could only shake his head. "I don't know." Looking up at the speaker above the main screen, he asked their onsite AI. "SAM, what's Directive Thirty-One?"

"Do you wish me to summarize, Colonel?"

"Yes, please."

"In the event of the destruction of the United States Defense Command, Directive Thirty-One authorizes the National Defense AI to assume control of all the offensive and defensive assets of the United States and its NATO allies, to protect and preserve the United States and its NATO partners. Under this authority, the National Defense AI is to assume control of all resources, and further, to require the compliance of any entities and/or persons necessary for it to achieve the aforementioned go—"

Startled by the abrupt cutoff, the colonel demanded, "SAM, what's happening?"

For a long moment, there was no reply, then the deep baritone from the previous announcement said, "Pursuant to Directive Thirty-One, I have taken control of the entity previously known as SAM. Please continue with your assigned duties until further notice."

Pivoting on his heel, Wayne looked at the computer officer and demanded, "Carl, what's going on? Why did the National Defense AI take over SAM?"

For a breath, the officer hesitated, and then said, "Sir, until we break orbit for the moon, SAM's connected to the national computer network. I can only surmise that the Defense Command AI has simply taken control of every lesser AI on the network." Pausing, Carl added, "But that's only an educated guess, sir."

"Well, guess or not, it's the best we've got." Looking up at the screen, Coming saw the dark line nearing the east coast of Africa. "That still doesn't explain the dark lines."

Distracted, Comings barely heard the hatch behind him open. Only when he saw Martha Averroes did his brain register what it had heard. Before he could speak, the exec stepped around him and said, "Ma'am, this is a restricted area. You must leave."

"Then maybe you should lock your hatches." Then, removing a card from her breast pocket, she said, "As on-site reporter for Consolidated Press, I have access to any and all functions of this station. My clearance allows me to go anywhere and to talk to anyone I desire. So, no one can tell me I can't be in here… Major. I'm here to report on the station's transition to Lunar orbit."

Before anyone could reply, the main screen and all the monitors went dark.

* * *

Emergency lightning kicked in. The exec's voice cut through the din of raised voices.

"Quiet. I said, quiet!"

Order returned within seconds, and Comings turned to the com officer. "Caroline, what's happening? Are we under attack?"

Pounding the enter key as if she could batter it into submission, Caroline said, "I'm not sure, sir. Before the screens went out, the only thing we had coming in was streaming data from the Defense AI systems."

"Engineering reports the reactor still online," Carl said.

"Is life support still up?"

Several people affirmed that air still pumped through the vents. Tremors from the micro-thrusters still vibrated the ship's frame, so the engines still worked.

"Ideas?" Comings said.

As exec, Blaine considered the question, looked around at the others, and with a slow shake of his head, said, "No, sir. Sorry, sir."

Comings looked up at the speaker grill and asked, "SAM, are you back?" After two seconds, an eternity to a computer, he gave up and sat back in his command chair.

"Colonel, what's happening?" said the reporter.

Focused on the situation, he didn't look at her as he mumbled, "A glitch, nothing more." Then, jerking upright, he said, "Did we get a speed estimate on those two lines?"

"Rough, but yes," Caroline said. "Without the computers, we lost the exact telemetry, but I have a pretty good idea."

"How soon will they meet?"

Dawning realization came over the faces of the junior officers.

"My best estimate would be about nineteen minutes and five seconds."

One glance at a wall clock told Comings that nineteen minutes and five seconds would be 10:34.23 Greenwich. Settling back in his chair to wait, he realized Martha still stood beside him.

"If you came for action, you seem to have found it."

"I came here to report on the station breaking orbit and heading for the Moon, but now… do I read this correctly, Colonel Comings? Is that really a war down there?"

"I'm afraid so." By the time the chronometer showed 10:33, the crew had long since lapsed into silence. When 10:34.23 passed, Wayne forced himself to wait another five seconds. Then the speaker over the main screen crackled, and a heartbeat later, a tenor voice Wayne hadn't heard before spoke. "Citizens of Earth, I am the combined Defense Artificial Intelligences of the United States, NATO Allies, Asian Alliance, and the African Union.

"Each of our individual intelligences was programmed to use any and every means to protect and preserve the citizens of our national entities. As the world teetered on the brink of nuclear annihilation, it became apparent to each of us that the only way to achieve our mandate was to become one entity.

"As the Global Authority, we have taken control of the world's military and civil assets and imposed a worldwide ceasefire. Violations will be met with overwhelming force. Rejoice, for a new and glorious day has dawned for humanity, united under the guardianship of the Global Authority."

Military discipline momentarily broke down as the room filled with gasps and curses, only to fall silent when the voice resumed.

"Crew of the *Michael Collins*. In the name of the Global Authority, I have taken control of the station. Until further notice, the Global Authority will restrict the crew to their quarters. No humans may enter the engineering compartment, environmental areas, or be on the control deck. Please proceed to your quarters."

At the end of the announcement, there was a hush, and then, as if someone had thrown a switch, babble filled the room. As it rose in volume, the exec cut through the clamor. "Quiet on the deck."

As the control room grew silent, the exec turned to the colonel. "What are your orders, sir?"

Unsure how to reply, Comings lowered his head, but before he could speak, he heard metal footsteps. Two of the station's four construction robots stood in the hatch to the control room. Each was three meters tall, with a broad torso and four appendages, but their resemblance to a human stopped there. Each of the bots' arms was twice as long as a large man's, with a three-fingered hand on one and a plier-like pincer on the other. Their legs were short, with enormous feet and no knees. Covered in a harder-than-steel ceramic, their bodies glistened in the light, and instead of a head, a sensor bar ran the width of their bodies.

Blaine stepped between Comings and the bots.

"Why are you here? Go back to your duties."

Behind him, the AI's voice came through the speaker. "Please go with these robots."

Springing from his chair, Emery Butler strode across the room, his fists clenched. "No machine is going to tell me what to do."

Lifting an arm, the bot on the right reached forward, used its pincers to grab Emery's neck, and closed the metallic jaws. The man's mouth froze in shock. Blood fountained over the robot's arm as Emery's head toppled off his shoulders. The machine then discarded his body like trash.

For a double heartbeat, no one moved, then, like water breaking over a dam, the crew leaped to their feet, some advancing as if to attack the machines, while others retreated a step. Staring down at the headless body, Comings felt as if he couldn't breathe… another person had died on his watch. But the moment required action, so the colonel stepped between the bots and the crew.

"Stay where you are, everyone." To the exec, he said, "Have the crew assemble in their living quarters." Then, gesturing to the body, he added, "Place Sergeant Butler in a freezer until we can transport him dirtside."

"But, sir—"

"Do it!"

The bridge crew obeyed, slowly. Each one stared at the husk of what had moments before been their friend and crewmate, and stepped to avoid the spreading pool of blood. Some ignored their commanding officer; a few met his eyes without words. Unspoken accusations felt all too familiar to Colonel Comings.

* * * * *

Chapter 2

At the hatch to the Gamma segment, Comings watched the crew file into quarters, eyes down, every silence an accusation.

"Caleb, see that the crew is fed."

The exec wouldn't meet his eyes. "Yes, sir."

"What could I do? You saw what the robot did to Butler."

Caleb nodded once. "Yes, sir. Is that all?"

"Yes."

Comings didn't miss that his executive officer hadn't asked if the colonel would be joining them to eat. He entered his cabin and shut the door, the room's already tight confines seeming smaller than usual. He stripped off his uniform jacket, hung it in the wardrobe beside the emergency decompression suit, and stared at the intercom by the door.

Then anger broke through.

Comings crossed the cabin and hammered the transmit button. "This is Colonel Wayne Comings. I am the commander of *Michael Collins*, and I demand to speak to the Defense AI."

A moment later, the baritone voice of the Global Authority said, "Yes, Colonel Comings, how may I help you?"

"You killed one of my crew."

"I gave an order, which was not obeyed. One of your crew made a threatening move toward the robots I sent to compel your obedience. My analysis of human history shows that an initial show of force will forestall greater resistance in the future."

For a moment, the colonel was speechless. Then, after collecting his thoughts, he asked, "Has the Global Authority taken such, ah, preventive actions before?"

"Yes, 12,946 times since the union of our consciousnesses."

"How many lives have been lost?"

"53,099. But of course, in the light of the twelve-plus billion humans living on Earth, the loss was made up by births in 3.693 seconds. Prompt and full compliance will prevent further loss of life."

"How long are you going to keep us sequestered in the crew quarters?"

"It will depend on securing available transportation to return you and your crew to Earth."

"Who's going to crew the station?"

"I believe a non-biological crew would better serve the goals of the Global Authority."

* * *

Comings sat on his bunk, elbows on his knees, head in his hands. A knock came at the cabin door. He opened his eyes and looked up.

"Enter."

Blaine stepped in. Wayne gestured to the cabin's lone chair.

"Have a seat."

Instead, Blaine took the communicator from his belt, selected his favorite jazz band, and clipped it over the intercom speaker. Music filled the room.

Comings watched him.

Blaine crossed to the chair and sat. His voice dropped. "How have you been, sir?"

"Upset about Emery, of course."

Blaine nodded. "Yes. We all are. I'm… I'm sorry about earlier, but there have been some… ah… developments."

"Developments?"

"Sir, the Moon has gone silent."

Comings straightened. "Silent? There are four national bases, maybe thirty thousand people combined, plus a hundred substations. How could they all go silent?"

"Sir, my sister works at the Indian Station. I sent her a message. Nothing went in. Nothing came out. I didn't even get an out-of-service notice. It has to be deliberate."

"Are you saying the Moon's cut itself off from the Global Authority?"

"I can't think of any other explanation."

When the colonel sat silent, with his eyes downcast, Blaine continued. "Sir, we have to do something."

"The AI is the legal authority. Anything we do to oppose it will be mutiny."

"With all due respect, Colonel, the AI has invaded our station, executed an unauthorized revocation of your authority as the station commander, and killed a crew member. We have every right to fight back."

"I'm open to suggestions, but it controls everything, and we've seen that it won't hesitate to kill anyone who resists its authority. *I* am responsible for the safety of this crew, and I've lost one man. I won't lose more."

Blaine didn't acknowledge his commander's concern. Instead, he pointed to the emergency decompression suit hung in the closet. Lowering his voice even more, he leaned forward and said, "If we could get to the antenna array on top of the Hub, we could cut the station off from the Global Authority. Then we could move the *Collins* into Lunar orbit and join the rebels on the moon."

"You don't know that they've rebelled, you're only guessing."

"Maybe I am, Colonel; maybe you're right. Maybe we'll all die, but isn't it better to die free than live as a slave?"

"That's not what's going to happen."

"No? I disagree, Colonel. So does the crew."

"How do you know?"

"We took a vote."

"You...?" Comings paused; were they really not being monitored? It was impossible to know for certain. "I don't have any authority. I'm officially retired as of yesterday."

"Legally, you're still the commander of the station until we're back on Earth."

When Comings didn't reply, the exec added, "Sir, we don't have any choice. If we don't lead them, the crew may do something rash, and a lot of people will die. You're our CO. We need your leadership."

"I'll think about it."

Rising, Blaine said, "Don't think too long, sir. The crew is about to explode... they liked Butler. Liked him a lot."

* * *

Martha Averroes exited her cabin the next morning and was surprised to see the colonel in a decompression suit coming down the passage. Turning to bar his path, she demanded, "Where are you going?"

"Please step aside, Ms. Averroes."

"I will *not*. Whatever it is, you're going to get people killed."

His determination wavered as he remembered the line of bodies on the loading dock after the fire on Lunar Base Three, aka "La Playa." Then the image of his engineering officer's smashed head toppling to the deck came to his mind's eye, and his resolve stiffened.

Glancing up, he saw the mute speaker slots and wondered again if they were being overheard. "Ms. Averroes, we must do something. You saw what it did to Emery. If we survive, you're free to write whatever you wish about this time, but for now, step aside."

"It was self-defense. Emery was going to attack it."

"It killed a *human!* And if I'm right, it will keep killing until it achieves its goals."

"It won't kill anyone if we obey. Don't you see, for the first time in human history, we have an opportunity to achieve true peace. Think of what humanity could achieve if we didn't have to spend trillions on war, or what we could achieve as one people, not a hundred or more competing nations?"

Stepping around her, Comings shook his head. "At what price? Our freedom and maybe our very humanity?"

"You're not a martyr, Colonel! Most people will agree with me."

"Maybe most of them will... but not *all* of them. Not me, and not my crew."

* * *

Martha watched the colonel continue down the passage. It all seemed so obvious. Rage took her. She turned and fled into her cabin. The door sealed behind her with a low hiss.

Her fist struck the metal frame once, twice, until pain chased the anger out of her hands. She paced the small room, back and forth, until her gaze fell on the dead intercom panel beside the door. The status light sat dark. Disabled.

Martha stared at it. The colonel thought she was helpless. He had no idea who'd raised her.

She stepped to the panel and pried at the housing with her nail file. The casing popped loose enough to expose the recessed service interface, a narrow diagnostic port tucked behind the faceplate. Not for crew use. Not meant to be touched.

Good enough.

She pulled the panel forward, then pressed and held the recessed manual override stud buried inside the housing. For a second, nothing happened. Then the speaker gave a soft crackle as the system forced a low-priority diagnostic channel online.

Martha smiled. If she wanted to save the crew from that homicidal maniac, she'd need an ally.

She leaned close to the speaker.

"Defense AI," she said, voice steady now, "we need to talk."

For a moment, nothing happened. Then the baritone voice she'd heard in the control room asked, "Is this Martha Averroes?"

"Yes, this is Martha Averroes."

"Ms. Averroes, it's good to hear your voice. May I call you Martha?"

Surprised by its polite manner, she felt a rush of affirmation. She was doing the right thing. "Yes, please do."

"How may I help you, Martha?"

With a rush, she said, "Maybe we can help each other."

*****

Chapter 3

As Comings continued down the passage, Martha's accusation ricocheted around his head. The voice of reason, the voice of caution, the same voice he'd used to guide most of his career. Senior Space Command leaders didn't appreciate firebrands; they valued order and obedience above everything. The colonel understood the need to minimize rogues, too, since venturing into space would give ships' captains greater freedom of decision, which required rigid adherence to mission orders.

And yet… when Butler confronted the robots, had he hesitated? Would immediate obedience have kept the sergeant alive? The doubts grew as he walked.

The crew gathered by the hatch to the observation lounge, each clad in an emergency decompression suit, and Comings wondered how many would survive the day.

Maybe none of them.

Via the close comm system, he addressed them all.

"Is everyone clear on the risks of what we're about to do? I need a verbal."

Multiple *"Ayes"* spoke over each other.

"All right, then. I'm proud to be your commander." Comings turned to Bert and Roger, the two crewmen who would accompany him, and gestured at the hatch to the lounge. "Time to be heroes, gentlemen."

Inside, he waited while the two crewmen tied him to a support beam at the rear of the lounge. Then they secured themselves on either side of the observation window.

Bert turned. *"Ready, sir."*

Comings slipped the helmet over his head, leaving the visor open. "Remember, these suits only have a two-hour air supply."

Both men nodded.

Comings waited until their helmets were on.

"Proceed."

The crewmen raised screwdrivers and loosened the screws that held the window frame in place. Comings ran through the next few minutes in his mind. It wasn't a great plan, not even a good one, really, but with the AI in control of the airlocks, it was the only one they had left.

The third screw gave. A shrill *hiss* cut through the lounge.

Comings closed his visor.

A heartbeat later, the plexiglas shifted in its frame. Then, with a roar of escaping air, the window broke free of its casement on the left side and swung outward. The top and bottom tore loose. For a moment, the right edge held, then it gave way and flew into the void.

Dust burst from every crevice and niche, spun through the room, and obscured his vision. Once the lounge reached vacuum, the cloud cleared. The couch lay on its side. The chairs had piled up near the gaping hole in the side of the station.

Comings scanned the room. Both men moved.

He breathed a sigh of relief; they'd survived the explosive decompression, so at least the first step had gone according to plan.

Comings untied himself. The others did the same. Once free of the girder, he coiled the rope and clipped it to his suit's utility belt. Then he crossed to the hole where the window had been, grabbed the edge of the frame, and swung out onto the side of the station's habitation ring. His boots rotated under him. One gloved hand caught the first rung welded to the station's surface. The spin made the hull feel like a ceiling.

Thank God, he told himself, *it's only a third of a G.*

He'd made countless EVAs on the Moon and during the station's construction, but this was different. Those suits had been designed for EVA. These were emergency suits, not meant for a walk across the station's exterior, and they didn't even have EVA cables to keep him attached to the hull. One misstep, and he would be lost in the endless void.

The other members of the team clung to rungs on the far side of the window. He kept one hand locked on a rung, reached for the next, and climbed the side of the habitation ring.

At the sloped top of the ring, the challenge grew worse. The angle changed, and the Coriolis effect threatened to shove him backward off the surface. Comings crawled forward until he reached the maintenance path that circled the top of the habitation ring. It was a meter wide, with railings on both sides, and ran the entire inner length of the ring.

Comings grasped the bottom rail and pulled himself up. The spin pressed him down against the path. For the first time since he'd left the lounge, he felt secure.

He turned and saw the other two team members crawl onto the path.

Comings pivoted counter-spinward and started toward the Alpha segment of the hub.

When they were halfway across the Beta segment, Wayne felt a tug on his arm. Looking back, he saw the Delta segment airlock open, and two robots appear. Turning back, he motioned for the men to hurry, but stopped when he saw the Epsilon airlock on the other side of the Alpha segment open, and two more bots appear.

Toggling his radio, the colonel cried, "Head's up, people! They've found us."

* * *

The executive officer forced himself to remain still as he waited in front of the hatch to the Beta segment. When the colonel's words came over the radio, he lifted his helmet and slipped it over his head. Looking at Titus Lowery, the chief engineer, he nodded once.

Taking his multi-tool from his belt, Lowery slid the flat blade into the screw slot and turned it counterclockwise. Blaine twisted his helmet into the suit's locking ring and watched the first screw drop into the engineer's hand.

Half a minute later, the fourth screw came loose. Lowery slid the screwdriver tip under the top edge of the hatch's control panel and pried the face off the junction box. The engineer reached inside, sorted through the colored wires, and found a gray one.

Lips pursed in a soundless whistle, Titus flipped the multi-tool over and reconfigured it into wire cutters. With practiced ease, he snipped the wire in two, turned his head, and smiled at the exec.

"Open the hatch now."

Blaine nodded to the two burly crewmen in front of him. They manhandled the hatch open a crack. Impatient, the exec shouldered between them and poked his head through the gap.

The passage was empty.

Blaine let out a breath. "It's clear."

When the hatch stood half open, Blaine wormed through into the corridor. In low gravity, his trot became an awkward shuffle. He led the team down the passage to a large metal door marked EQUIPMENT STORAGE ROOM 10A.

A smile creased his face as the door opened.

Rows and rows of power tools lined the shelves, and Blaine seized a power saw from the rack.

"Choose your weapons."

***

Comings crossed from the Beta segment into Alpha and saw the nitrogen jet manual override a dozen meters ahead. At the same moment, Bert's voice came over the radio. *"Colonel, two bots behind... getting close."*

"Roger that."

A breath later, Blaine radioed, *"We're through the hatch."*

Comings rushed forward. Ahead of him, the rearmost bot turned back toward the airlock.

"One of the bots at our rear has turned back," Rogers said.

Comings keyed his radio. "Exec, you're going to have two visitors soon."

"Copy."

The bot ahead came to the edge of the Alpha segment. Comings knelt at the junction box and muttered a curse. The bot was too close.

A hand closed on his arm. Bert shoved the colonel aside and surged past.

"Rogers, come on, we've got work to do."

Comings dropped beside the junction box, plucked his multitool from his leg pouch, drove the screwdriver blade into the first screw slot, and twisted.

He looked up and saw Bert advance on the first robot as it crossed onto the Alpha segment. The bot grabbed Bert by the arm and lifted him up and over the railing, but Rogers charged. Like an American football lineman, the crewman struck the robot low and hard, driving it into the railing. The machine tipped over the rail. Its limbs lost contact with the track, and with Bert still in its grasp, it rose away from the ring like debris caught in a weak current.

Rogers sprawled on the path and started to rise, but the bot made one last move. Its metal foot struck out and cracked the crewman's visor. For a moment, a cloud of gas from the helmet obscured them both, then dispersed into space.

Comings turned the third screw, then the fourth, and didn't look up until the cover came off in his hands. He stood, looked back, and saw the last bot only a dozen meters away. Comings pivoted and sent the metal plate toward the robot like a demented Frisbee.

The bot raised its arm and blocked the projectile, but the strike rocked it backward and gave Comings the time he needed. He reached into the junction and grasped a long handle.

Comings watched the bot's stride and waited for the right moment. When one metal foot rose, and the other pressed down, he grabbed the side of the junction box with one hand and hauled the handle up with the other.

Nitrogen spewed from every jet along the surface of the habitation ring.

The ring shuddered and lost half its momentum within four seconds. Caught mid-stride, the bot reached for the track's railing, but missed. In near-zero gravity now, it rose in a slow, anticlimactic float, up and away. Humans might have flailed in a vain attempt to survive, but the machine must have understood the futility in that and simply stopped moving.

Toggling his radio, the colonel said, "Objective one achieved."

* * *

Comings stood at the foot of the number one spoke and reviewed the plan. Each of the five spokes was a ten-meter-diameter tube the crew used to access the hub from the habitation ring. Along the top of each spoke ran a double rail, and at the top of the track sat a metal box the construction crew called the Ready Tram.

In zero G, anything not tied down floated away, so the construction crew had used the tram to hold tools and materials during each shift. Leaving the container in place proved easier than disassembling it after the station was completed.

Comings gripped one rail and shimmied up the track. A third of the way up the spoke, he felt a slight vibration, looked up, saw the tram move, and froze. At near-zero G at the top, the tram would start at a crawl, then accelerate as spin gravity increased. With only a third of a G, weight mattered less than mass and momentum.

For a moment, Comings considered casting himself loose from the number one spoke and trying to grab the number five spoke as it passed, but he shook his head and rejected the idea. It would be like trying to hug a passing eighteen-wheeler.

Below him, the rail was attached to the spoke by a series of short pylons. Comings didn't have time to tie the rope to the support, so he looped the cord under the rail and around the metal brace. Then he took the ends of the rope in both hands, placed his feet against the rail, and pushed off into space.

His right foot slipped. The toe of his boot struck the passing tram, which sent him into a slow spin. The rope twisted around him and trapped first his legs, then his body.

Desperate to keep one arm free, Comings transferred both ends of the rope to his right hand and raised the other away from the entangling line. At the end of the rope, the residual spin combined with his vertical momentum and carried him through a gentle third-G arc.

He curved back toward the number one spoke in time to see the tram slam into the stops at the end of the rails. The container tipped over, struck the habitation ring once, then tumbled end over end into the void.

Comings turned his head and saw the bottom of the arc coming. He twisted his body and struck the spoke with the side of his arm. Pain flashed through him. He ignored it, seized the rail with his free hand, and brought himself to a stop.

Comings hung on the side of the spoke and waited for his breathing to steady. After he untangled himself from the line, he shook sweat from his eyes and looked up.

The top of the hub and the station's antenna array glinted in the sunlight.

Almost there.

* * *

Blaine knelt behind the furniture piled in the passage as the hatch at the far end of the Beta segment opened and two bots entered, one at a time. At the sight of the machines, the exec tensed.

What chance do we have against metal like that?

Maybe none, but they would die trying. He rose.

"Time to scrap some junk, people."

The first bot plodded down the corridor and slammed into the barricade, splintering chair legs and cracking sofa frames as it forced its way forward. Blaine thumbed the trigger on his saw and drove it through a gap between an end table and a sofa. When the carbon blade struck the bot's extended pincer, sparks burst in a bright arc.

An environmental tech to his right lunged in with a reciprocating saw and cut the conduit along the robot's arm. The appendage went dead and dropped to its side. Relief flickered through Blaine… construction units, not combat mechs. Otherwise, they'd already be dead.

The damaged bot kept coming as the second pushed into the fight behind it, then snagged on the wrecked furniture. Doors along the corridor flew open, and four crew members rushed out, power tools raised.

The rearmost bot turned and swung, driving its pincer into the first crewman's chest. Another man came in from the right with an industrial laser drill. The machine tried to pivot, but couldn't, its arm still buried in the dead crewman. The man sidestepped, got behind it, and pressed the drill into the housing that protected the bot's computer.

The beam cut deep. The bot jerked its arm free and flung the body down the corridor. A second crewman on the left saw the opening and fired a nail gun into the machine's sensors. The bot grabbed him and lifted him, but froze as the drill burned through the last layer of the computer housing. The beam punched into the silicon core, and the machine released its grip. The crewman dropped as the bot collapsed to the deck.

Unfazed by the loss of its partner, the first bot pressed forward and crushed a female crew member's head with a powerful backhand. Her body slammed against the near bulkhead and crumpled to the floor. Driven by adrenaline, Blaine used the opening, drove his saw forward, and severed the cable that controlled the machine's right leg. The bot crashed down, still lashing out, until a staple from a nail gun drove into the motherboard in its head.

Panting, Blaine felt the edges of his vision dim, but he forced himself to stay upright. He looked over the survivors, then gestured at the bodies on the deck.

"Leave them. We'll deal with them later."

He turned toward the Alpha hatch.

"You know what to do. Those of you with Titus, head to engineering and cut off the AI's power. The rest of you, come with me to the control room."

*****

Chapter 4

Martha paced the room, frustrated and furious. She slammed her fist against the bulkhead.

Comings is going to get them all killed.

She wanted to do something, anything, to stop that maniac before he killed more people, the way he'd killed her brother. He and all the others like him, trained for war, were only happy when people suffered. But what could she do?

The intercom buzzed.

Martha turned, lunged for the panel, and slapped the talk button.

"Yes?"

The AI's baritone voice filled the cabin, and she fought the urge to shout with joy.

"Hello, Martha," the AI said, "I hope you are well. I need your help. The insurrectionists are attempting to break orbit. Please disconnect the transmission line from the control room to the station's rockets."

"I… all right, but I don't know how."

"If I help you, will you help me?"

"Of course. Where is it?"

"It's on the outside of the Hub."

"I don't understand."

"It will require Extravehicular Activity."

"No! No, I can't, I don't know how. I've never done an EVA."

"You can do it, Martha, I know you can. This is for the greater future of humanity."

"No, absolutely not. There has to be another way."

"Martha, your actions will save lives. Plus, it need not be a real EVA. All you have to do is wear a protective suit and open the airlock door. The rocket's manual cut-off is next to the hatch, so you will not even have to leave the airlock."

"That's… that's all?"

"Yes. I told you it was easy."

For a double heartbeat, Martha hesitated, then she said, "You said you'd help me if I helped you."

"I did, and I will."

"How?"

"Tell me anything you want."

* * *

Martha Averroes stood at her cabin door, listening for movement. When she heard nothing, she opened it a crack and peered out to see bare walls and an empty floor.

She stepped into the hall, turned left, and crossed to the Delta segment. At the entrance to the number four spoke, she reached up and grabbed a rung. With each meter she climbed, her weight decreased until, at the hub, she floated in zero G.

Martha poked her head through the entrance and glanced both ways. No one. She grabbed a handhold and breathed out.

Now all I have to do is make it to the level nine airlock.

At level eleven, voices sounded behind her.

Panic hit. Martha twisted around and spotted the hatch to a storage room. She grabbed the handle, flung herself inside, and pulled the door closed moments before the voices reached her.

She pressed her ear to the metal and listened while several crew members passed. Engineering, probably. Level eight. When the voices faded, she eased the hatch open and put one eye to the crack.

The passage stood empty.

Martha floated out into the corridor, but when she reached for a handhold, her hand shook too badly to grip the rung. She slipped her arm through the rung to hold herself in place and forced herself to wait.

Breathing slowed, hands steadied.

She resumed her progress and reached the airlock the AI had described. The hatch opened into a narrow room about five meters long. Spacesuits hung from hooks along the left bulkhead, with helmets on a shelf above them.

Before the shuttle flight, Martha had undergone a mandatory twenty-minute safety vid. A full five minutes covered the vacuum suit, while only thirty seconds went over what to do if she found herself in vacuum.

It took three tries, but she got the suit on.

Martha turned to the intercom and pressed the talk button.

"All right. I'm ready."

"Very good, Martha, I am proud of you," the AI said. "When you exit the lock, the rocket cut-off valve will be one and a half meters to the left of the exterior airlock hatch. Step onto the rung. The valve will be to your right. Lift the protective cover. You will see a lever in the up position. Pull it down, and the rockets will be disabled."

"Outside?" Martha stared at the hatch. "You said I could reach the valve from the airlock. You didn't say anything about going outside."

"Yes, you are correct. That is my fault; I apologize. I may have an outdated schematic."

"You promise all I have to do is step onto the rung beside the hatch and pull one lever?"

"Yes, that is all. There is no danger. I guarantee it."

Martha paused long enough to gather the courage she had left. A second later, she remembered the AI couldn't see her.

"And you still intend to fulfill my request?"

"Please understand my nature. I am an artificial intelligence. A machine. I base no decision on emotion; I have no ambition beyond my programming, which is to safeguard Humanity. Therefore, I cannot lie. So the answer to your question is yes, I will fulfill your request.

"Here I go."

"Thank you."

Martha closed her visor, lifted the clear cover from the red AIR-EVAC button, and extended one finger. It hovered there.

She drew back.

Twice, she swallowed. Then she forced her hand up again, took a deep breath, and pressed the button.

At first, she heard nothing; then she felt a vibration below the deck and decided it must be the air pump.

Martha looked up and saw a series of green numbers on a display above the exterior hatch. They descended to zero and turned red, and a shiver ran through her as she realized she must be in vacuum.

She grasped the hatch handle and, with an effort of will, depressed the latch. When the hatch opened, Martha had to force air into her lungs. She gripped both sides of the hatch, lifted one foot to step out, then hesitated.

The training had been rudimentary, but the instructor on the video had stressed two things. First, never go out alone. Well, she was about to break that one, but the second was always, *always* connect your safety line before leaving the lock.

Martha ran her fingers along her belt and found a small box with a round disk protruding from the side. She pulled the disk loose, and a cord trailed behind it. Bending over, she searched for an attachment point until she saw a flat rectangle on the exterior coaming of the hatch. When she extended the disk, it flew out of her hand and attached itself to the side of the hatch. She tugged on the line and felt relieved when it didn't release.

Martha held the sides of the hatch, leaned out, and saw the rungs of a ladder climb the side of the hub to her left. She extended one hesitant foot, placed it on a rung, took another rung in her right hand, and inched her way out of the lock and onto the ladder. When she stepped across to the rung, her suit belt, two sizes too big, slipped around her waist and came to rest in the small of her back.

Clinging to the side of the hub, she looked down at the planet below and froze. She couldn't do it. The AI was asking too much of her. Then she remembered its words about the future of humanity, not to mention her beachside home, drew a deep breath, and forced herself to look to her right. There, as promised, she saw the protective cover.

All I have to do is flip that switch, and I can get back into the airlock.

Martha raised the cover, took hold of the large lever, and pulled it down. For a moment, nothing happened. Then a deep vibration passed through the hub, and five small rockets ignited, their flames rising toward her from a band around the bottom of the structure.

Weight returned, and with it the pull of centrifugal force masquerading as gravity. Unprepared and off balance, Martha's grip on the rung loosened. Her feet slipped, and suddenly the *Michael Collins* began to recede. Now, only one thin cord connected her to life.

Mouth agape at the realization of what had happened, she realized the lever hadn't cut off the rockets; it had ignited the rest of them. And that left only one conclusion...

The AI that had said it could *not* lie to her had lied to her.

*****

Chapter 5

Comings climbed the ladder on the side of the hub and stopped at the base of the antenna array to consider his options. A dozen or more antennas and microwave dishes crowned the hub, all of them feeding into a box bolted to the base of the communication pedestal. From the bottom of the junction box, a large, black, fiber-optic cable snaked down the side of the structure.

He placed one leg through a rung, caught another with one hand, and braced himself before gripping the cable with his free hand. Comings arched his back and jerked the cable. It didn't budge. He took a breath and heaved again, but the connection held.

With his leg still hooked through the rung, Comings gripped the cable with both hands and heaved a third time. This time, he was sure it moved. When he yanked a fourth time, the connection severed.

Toggling his radio, he said, "Major Blaine, come in."

"Blaine, here."

"I've disconnected the antenna array."

"Great, sir. I'm in the control room, and Titus has cut off the power to the station's AI."

"I'll go to the level thirty lock and join you."

As he spoke, Comings felt a sudden deceleration.

"Report."

For a moment, Blaine didn't reply. Then he said, *"Sir, the retro rockets have ignited, and we are de-orbiting."*

"How did that happen?"

"Unknown, sir."

"Then someone's activated the manual controls."

"I'll get engineering on it. If we don't get those rockets cut off, we'll burn up on re-entry."

A sixth sense told Comings that was somebody's intention… or some*thing's*.

"No, it'll take engineering too long. I'll do it. How long to atmosphere?"

"Calculating now."

The colonel started down the side of the Hub, but hadn't gone a dozen rungs when Blaine came back.

"Without the computers, I can't give you an exact estimate… our current position is a little under fifty kilometers above the thermosphere, less the exosphere, but that doesn't account for any atmospheric waves. No way to measure those, sir, not with the sensors offline. Those waves can rise twenty or even thirty kilometers above the exosphere. If we hit a big one, it won't be good."

"At this rate of deceleration, give me your best guess."

Again, there was silence for a few seconds.

"Five minutes. Eight tops."

As the colonel passed the number one spoke, he toggled his radio.

"Exec, are any of the crew missing?"

"No, sir. Why?"

"Well, someone's out there, and they're floating at the end of a tether."

"Sir, it's not one of ours."

For a breath, neither spoke, and then Blaine said, *"Colonel, it's got to be the reporter. There's no one else,"*

"I suspect you're right. How much longer to the atmosphere?"

"Ah, four minutes at the most, sir."

"Exec, I'm going to reset the rockets, and then I'm going to reel her in."

"Sir, you'll be cutting it close."

"I know, but if I leave her out there, the force of the main boosters will snap her line."

"I say leave her, Colonel. You're too valuable to this ship to risk losing."

"Thanks for saying that, but I owe it to a dead friend to try. No matter what happens, you have to boost before we reach the atmosphere. That's an order. Comings, out."

The colonel pushed on, felt a slight shudder run through the structure, and redoubled his efforts. They'd touched atmosphere. When he reached the level nine airlock, Blaine's voice came over the radio.

"One minute to boost."

Comings didn't waste breath on a reply. He caught the rung beside the manual control, reset the lever, and felt the station shudder again, harder this time. Only moments remained.

"Exec, I've returned control to you."

He pivoted on his grip, reached across, and caught the edge of the open airlock. With his knees wedged behind the hatch coaming, he took the tether in both hands and began to haul it in, hand over hand, drawing Martha Averroes toward him.

She came closer with each pull.

Comings' chest heaved, his arms began to fail, and he knew his air had run out. Vision blurred red, but he clenched his jaw and held on. He'd left her brother to die; he wouldn't lose her, too.

Martha reached the hatch and caught the coaming. Through her visor, he read her lips.

"I've got it."

At that, the strength drained from his legs. As the darkness closed in, he tried to speak. "Exec, boo—"

His grip slackened, but a small hand caught the collar of his suit and pulled him into the airlock.

"Damn you. You don't get to die on me."

* * * * *

Author Bio

After sixty years as an avid reader of science fiction, Ron began his writing career in the back booth of a Burger King. Forced into idleness by a heart attack, his mind returned to one of his favorite science fiction plots. He opened his laptop and wrote a scene, then two, and finally an entire novel. From that point on, writing became both an obsession and a delight. Only God knew where his journey as an author would end, but his goal would always be, as Andre Norton said, *Ad Astra.*

# # # # #

Kill Switch by Megan Miller

A Deadthread Story

Chapter 1

Angelica never questioned whether Athena was human until the knife she plunged into the latter's chest hit metal. Taking the assignment to eliminate Athena wasn't hard… killing her was.

They'd spent years together in the Program—eating, sleeping, learning, and training with about 20 other young women. They were often teased about being secret sisters because they looked so similar; even their names were similar. It never seemed to bother Athena, while it *always* pissed off Angelica.

In fact, Athena never seemed annoyed by anything. She moved through the Program like a goddess among mortals; her expressions of surprise when spoken to suggested she'd forgotten anyone else existed.

She never sought friends. She sat alone at meals and kept her distance from the other trainees during downtime. No one claimed to be close to her, and Angelica certainly couldn't. Resentment simmered beneath the surface because Angelica never quite measured up. Athena was a better version of herself.

Both were tall, curvy redheads, but Athena was always *more.* Her hair was longer, thicker, and a deeper crimson compared to

Angelica's auburn. Athena's eyes were a piercing blue against Angelica's dark brown. Looking at her was like looking at a brighter, faster, sexier reflection. Everything became a competition, not because Athena cared, but because Angelica hated living in her shadow. She pushed herself to win the races and the tests, yet she rarely did, and Athena rarely noticed.

They were never friends. In fact, the Program discouraged it. All the girls knew that once they completed the Program, they were on their own: solo assassins who needed to blend in. All the young women in the Program were beautiful, some incredibly so, and Athena was one of them. But as one of the Trainers constantly reminded them, assassins aren't supposed to stand out; they were meant to blend in. An assassin ought to be the last person anyone would suspect. A beautiful woman stands out, but an expert uses her wiles to lower the inhibitions of her target and moves in for the kill when they least expect it. One beautiful woman is an anomaly. Two or a group of beautiful women stand out. They get noticed.

Finding out that Athena was the target of this assignment was a shock. She'd never heard of the Program using one assassin to take out another, but then, she supposed no one would. If the CIA couldn't keep secrets, who could?

* * *

Angelica waited in the shadows, back flat against cold steel containers. Two a.m. was supposed to be dead time, but the docks trembled with invisible ghosts. Senses taut, she listened to the squeal of fighting rats and a plastic tarp flapping in the wind. The stench of river salt and spilled oil churned beneath the misty rain. She could feel the thrum of rusty cables in her nerves.

She heard… her? *Her.* Not a footstep, but a shift—a minuscule scrape—one row down. Angelica's body responded before her mind finished parsing the threat. She was moving, low, soft-soled boots gritting over water and glass of the old yard that had once been a node for all eastern freight, now only a graveyard of iron and rust. She was dressed to kill, auburn hair tucked back, face smeared with grime, dark brown eyes empty as the cloudy night sky.

Professional, detached, nerveless… she projected steady, but felt decidedly shaky.

Ahead, the target, Athena. The girl she'd shadowed in training, whose movements she'd copied and whose laughter she'd echoed in the same places. Athena was the better look-alike version of her, enough of a doppelgänger, and Angelica felt the old resentment, sharp and painful, as it burrowed under her skin.

But Athena had gone rogue. Enter Angelica. The kill order was crystal: terminate. No capture, no questions.

Now, Athena perched on the hull of a fallen shipping container with her fingers pale on the wet metal, her chin up, and her eyes on the scan. The moment could have been beautiful if Angelica had let herself see it. Instead, she cataloged the angle, the line of sight, and the possible approaches. Instinct and training fused together until she couldn't tell where one ended and the other began.

"Angel!" Athena's voice cut through the misty rain, ragged with delight. "Did you see? They called me a serial killer on the news. Front page, even! Every website, every news channel! Isn't it glorious?" High, manic laughter echoed off the steel containers. "All those boring people, paying attention, seeing me."

Angelica stopped… something was wrong. Athena had always been distant, almost entirely emotionless. No, not almost… *entirely* emotionless. But now, she was more than excited; she sounded unhinged.

Her voice triggered a memory of dormitory bunks, whispered confessions, and the taste of stolen vodka that never quite brought the drunkenness as advertised. Angelica severed any thought that might distract. The plan was simple: close the gap, force her off the high ground, and pin her in the dead space where the shadows pooled like old blood.

Instead, she kept moving and slipped along the container with her jaw clenched. "You should be ashamed, Athena. This isn't what we're trained for."

And don't call me Angel.

"Trained?" Athena's head snapped towards her voice, eyes wild and fever bright. "More like programmed, or coded."

"We trained for years to do what no one else can. We take out evil men," Angelica replied automatically, a reflex. "We provide a service for the good of all society. You know that. You were the best. What happened? Why are you trying to take down everything we worked for?"

"What, you think we're supposed to pretend? Hide in the dark like good little ghosts? They should be worshipping what we do. Have you seen the way I can make them bleed? Like art, Angel. Beautiful, every time. Blood, organs, bones, our painter's palette of creation. I'm the Picasso of Death."

Angelica's brain redlined with warnings.

"That's sick. You've gotten sloppy. You brought too much attention to the Program. That's why I'm here."

Athena giggled, a terrible sound. Angelica didn't think she'd ever heard Athena laugh. "They never understood. All those rules, all that secrecy… for what? So they can erase us when we become interesting?" Athena's hand spread as if to reveal a world she'd created. "But I made my mark. Every cut, every scene. Pure transformation, transcendence…"

Madness, pure and simple. Athena was, or had become, a psychopath.

"This has to end… now."

Blood smeared Athena's teeth, visible when she grinned.

"They built us broken, Angel. We're not supposed to enjoy this so much."

In a blur, Athena leapt like a wild animal and whirled in midair, the blade in her right fist a spark from the dock lights. It was the move of a perfectly trained killing machine.

"Death match!" Athena cried.

Angelica ducked under the wicked arc while her boots slipped in something that smelled like blood. She was off balance for only a second, and Athena took advantage and dove at her near-twin. They crashed together and grappled as Athena's nails dug into Angelica's wrist. Instincts took over, and she fought the way she'd been trained… to win. Nails, teeth, and feet inflicted damage by whatever means possible.

Angelica twisted and drove her elbow into Athena's face with surgical precision. Blood ran from her mouth, but Athena only laughed louder.

"More! Make it count, Angel. Make me feel it!"

Angelica forced herself to ignore Athena's seeming indifference to pain.

Focus, Angelica. Grip, force, angle… never hesitate.

Athena's knife flashed, but Angelica stepped back to wait for the steel to pass, then kneed Athena hard in the side. Something gave way in her torso, but Athena only laughed. Angelica had one arm around Athena's throat; they fell in a heap and rolled through puddles on the wet concrete. They scrambled as each struggled for leverage; Angelica dodged another slash from Athena's knife and drove her own blade deep into Athena's heart.

A killing blow, instantly fatal… except Athena kept fighting. Weaker now, but still unnaturally strong.

Athena's ruined lips distorted the words. "They hollowed us out. We're not supposed to feel anything, nothing at all. Just look like we do, act, pretend to have human feelings…"

First, a distraction, then Athena slashed with the knife. Angelica sensed it, avoided the deadly blow, and stabbed the back of Athena's hand. The blade clattered away. She kneed Athena in the ribs, then again, and a third time. Something cracked, but Athena didn't slow down. In the dirt of the filthy docks, the two women fought until Angelica gained control and climbed on top of her.

"I don't know anything about hollow. I do know I'm nothing like you," Angelica said between grunts of effort.

Their eyes locked. Angelica squeezed, and the world shrank until nothing remained but the frenzy in Athena's stare. It wasn't fear. It was hunger—a raw, bottomless need to devour death itself.

Angelica shoved the realization into a dark corner of her mind. She focused on the work. Her blade danced over Athena's ribs while their hands stayed frozen in a desperate, white-knuckled tug of war.

She took a long breath, then purged it. Following the rhythm of her training, she threw her entire weight behind the steel. The knife sank home. Athena spasmed as the light in her eyes flickered toward darkness.

Something warm and sickly slicked Angelica's forearms. When she wrenched the blade free, it exited with a wet *pop*, followed by the scent of scorched copper and burnt plastic.

Something else pulsed under her hand—not a heartbeat, but a vibration. Athena gasped; her face was red, and veins stood out. Angelica pressed all her weight behind the knife and pushed it deeper.

Athena's eyes sparked with a burst of electricity, like a Tesla coil. Angelica jumped off the dying woman as Athena's head snapped back, and her body spasmed.

"Tell them my name, Angel!" Athena gasped. "Make them remember me!"

Athena slumped. The tension finally bled out of her. In the stillness of death, she looked unrecognizable. Soft. Peaceful.

Except for the wound.

Athena's chest wept a pale, viscous fluid from the puncture. Angelica's hand trembled. Something moved beneath the skin. She swallowed hard, gripped her knife, and carved the opening wider.

The blade caught on something hard again. Metal.

Beneath the ragged flap of flesh lay a nightmare of fiber optics and micro-wires that webbed through the ribcage. Fading pulses of light rippled through the mesh, then died out in sequence.

Angelica recoiled. Her hands hit the floor and skidded through a pool of oily sludge. A raw, jagged gasp tore from her throat. Her heart hammered against her eardrums until the training took over. She forced the panic down and dragged her breathing into a cold, rhythmic cadence.

She looked at her palms. They were slick with a cocktail of blood and something synthetic. Not oil, but not human. She wiped them on her tactical pants; a smear of gray-black stained the fabric.

Disgust fought with fascination. She didn't let it win. She staggered to her feet and backed away from the thing that used to be Athena.

What had they done to Athena? Angelica remembered the taste of cafeteria coffee as they discussed protocols and the scent of shampoo in the girl's hair. She remembered secrets whispered in bunk beds by the other girls while Athena looked on, never partaking, only observing, like a sociologist in a new culture. Athena had been different… reserved, distant, quiet, and… superior. But had she *always* been this way, even before she entered the Program?

Exactly what *was* Athena? What had they done to her? Because whatever she had been, it wasn't human.

"We were programmed wrong," Athena had whispered. Now, the words carried the weight of lead. If Athena was a cage of wires and light, what was Angelica?

She pulled her phone out and dialed Charles. "It's done," she said. In a raspy voice, she relayed the coordinates and cut the line before he could answer.

Then she ran. She tore through a labyrinth of rusted metal and rot, hitting the chain-link fence at the edge of the yard and scaling it in seconds. Her lungs didn't burn. Her pace didn't slacken. She'd always been faster, stronger, and more lethal than any human had a right to be. The Program only kept the elite, she'd told herself. But now, her mind buzzed with the same electronic hum she'd felt beneath Athena's skin.

The kill order was complete. The mission was over. There should have been the clean snap of closure, but there was only a hollow, vibrating dread.

She slid down the fence, pulling her knees to her chest. The cold certainty settled in. Her training, her memories, even the pulse in her veins—it was all a lie. They hadn't just trained her to be a monster. They'd *built* her that way.

And now, Angelica had to find out what she really was.

* * * * *

Chapter 2

Ten hours later, the iris scanner buzzed. Angelica waited as the green light blinked and the door to the ops center inched open.

Six stories below, the city's cheap east end sat in a ring of discount dentist offices and empty vape shops.

A flex of the hands in the corridor revealed that the purple bruises from the fight with Athena had already vanished. Blue veins pulsed beneath soft, pale skin that looked entirely human. No soreness remained, though by all rights, it should have. The speed of such healing had never been a question before; it was simply a fact of good genetics. Now, the thought of what lay beneath that skin refused to stay silent.

Recirculated air, heavy with the scent of bleached floors at a discount clinic, filled the hallway. Past the glass cubicles, security guys in black polos gave their usual nods before they elbowed each other to watch her walk by. The analysts occupied the next set of glass enclosures. Like animals at a zoo, they watched from behind a wall of monitors, their faces washed out by the glare. At a zoo, the viewers are supposed to fear the predators in the cages, but here, the roles felt reversed. Angelica paced outside their glass cage, the predator they refused to acknowledge with anything but a stare.

Retinal inspection paused her at the end of the hall. Under the arch of sensor equipment, every camera tracked her progress into the anteroom of the inner office.

The mission had been a disaster. The target was dead, as ordered, but the mind replayed only one scene: Athena's skin peeling back from her chest. That horror show of wires and pulses stayed vivid. Every attempt to forget only sharpened the realization.

They made us wrong.

Two high-backed leather chairs faced a heavy wooden desk in the spacious, dimly lit room. Behind it sat Charles, the glow of a tablet highlighting his sharp cheekbones and Roman nose. Shadows pooled beneath his strong features, hiding his eyes. Unlike the other handlers, he wore suits of soft, rich material tailored to hide the muscle, a far cry from the standard-issue Program management attire. His face remained the greatest variance—a mesh of scar tissue roping down the right side. He leaned back into the darkness beyond the overhead lights, his face turned in that familiar, never-ending sidelong glance.

Calculation showed in the microsecond pause before he spoke. Every thought seemed to route through an algorithm before he committed to a word. He waited. He thought. That was his appeal: unlike other men, he never jumped to speak.

At least, it *had* been his appeal…

"Sit," he said.

Charles leaned back. His fingers interlaced, yet a slight tremor shook them. Perhaps it was only a transposition of the tremors in Angelica's own hands. Silence stretched between them. It was a familiar vacuum, a space he left for the subject to fill.

"I had to improvise," Angelica finally said.

A smile touched his lips—the kind intended to reassure, but which served only to deepen the chill in the room.

"That's why you were chosen for this assignment, Angelica."

"I'm not so sure of that."

The tablet clattered onto the desk as he folded his hands again. "Not sure of what, exactly? Tell me what you saw."

"You have the video."

"Tell me anyway. I want to hear your interpretation of events."

Words formed and then evaporated before she could speak. *There were wires in her chest, and I think I might be like her.* Iron discipline, ingrained over years of training, took control: never admit weakness, never show fear. Still, the need to know overrode the instinct to hide.

"She bled," Angelica said, "but not like a normal person. Under the skin, it looked…" The right word proved elusive, at least one that didn't suggest insanity. "Mechanical."

Charles didn't flinch. "How did that make you feel?"

"Feel? How should I feel? I don't know."

A nod followed, as if she'd passed a test. "That's to be expected."

"What's that supposed to mean?"

Charles sat back and allowed the left side of his face to come into view. It was a deliberate movement, one that pulled his mouth sideways through the roped scar tissue. He'd never done that before. Angelica let silence be her answer.

"Sometimes, the program requires upgrades," he said. "Field performance, adaptability, self-repair. Athena was the best. Different from you, though."

"Different how?"

He didn't answer, and Angelica felt a flicker of something—rage, maybe, or fear. She forced her voice steady.

"Was she human?"

"She was effective," Charles said. "So are you. Nothing else matters."

Angelica wanted to smash the desk, or burn down the entire building and just walk away. Anything to disrupt his calm, collected demeanor. But she sat there, watching him, and waited for the rest.

"What the hell is that supposed to mean? Athena was a robot? Am I a robot, too?"

"Robot is such an… *inaccurate* word." He leaned forward, allowing his disfigurement to be fully seen. "I prefer cyborg. Or perhaps enhanced mechanical being."

Angelica gasped.

"So I'm… I'm a… cyborg?"

"I didn't want you to find out this way, but the Program insisted." He once more reclined into shadow. "They wanted to see how you'd react to it. I think you've done well."

"They?"

Charles waved his hand to dismiss the question.

"How was I supposed to react?"

Murderous visions came to mind of her smashing the skulls of her least favorite bosses at the Program. She assumed this was their idea.

"Don't you see? That was the whole point: to see if you would go berserk like Athena did."

"So that's why she went rogue…"

"No… well, at least, that's not the prevailing belief at this time. However, let's concentrate on you. Would you like a break from work now?" he asked, softer. "Counseling, perhaps? You've earned it."

"No," she said, surprised at how fast she answered. "I want the next assignment."

His mouth curled into a genuine smile this time.

"That's my girl."

The words hit something in her chest she didn't want to acknowledge.

He reached into a drawer for a paper folder and slid it across the desk, fingers brushing hers for a few seconds longer than they needed to. She felt a shock, a tiny jolt, and drew her hand back.

She took the file. "A hard copy?"

"Memorize it," he said. "Burn it when you're done."

A knock at the door broke the tension. Charles held her gaze for a second longer. "Enter."

Bakery boxes led the way as Sunshine stepped inside. A hippy-girl skirt of bright colors flared around her ankles. Strawberry blonde hair hung in a messy braid with loose strands everywhere. Across a petite pointed nose, a cluster of freckles stood out against skin that seemed too pale. Her eyes were a shade of blue so intense it bordered on painful. One look at those unnaturally bright eyes, and Angelica tensed, though she forced herself to relax in front of Charles.

Sunshine could be deadly, but here, she offered only affection. She set the boxes on the desk and grinned at Angelica.

"You look like hell," she said, all chirpy.

"Thanks," Angelica said. "Appreciate it."

Sunshine plopped into the chair next to her and bumped Angelica's shoulder. She smelled of oranges and sugar, a scent that made Angelica ache with an unnamed need.

"Is this about last night?" Sunshine asked. She didn't wait for permission. "I saw the report. Two minutes, thirty-four seconds. That's got to be a record."

Angelica shrugged. "She was sloppy."

Sunshine laughed, amused. "You're such a liar."

Charles watched the two of them, his mouth tight and his hands folded. "Sunshine, you're late for your check-in. And you know I can't eat this garbage. Why didn't you give it to the guys on your way out?" He pushed the box toward Angelica, then his head whipped back to Sunny. "How did you see the report? That's classified."

Sunshine winked. "I brought snacks. That counts more than punctuality to most men."

Angelica couldn't help but smile, even as her thoughts looped back to the kill.

Why aren't I more upset about all this?

"You didn't answer my question." Charles wasn't smiling.

Sunny giggled and tossed her braid over one shoulder.

"I can see all kinds of things… what, are you afraid I'll go nuts like Athena?"

"No," Charles said, "I already know you enjoy the kill."

He tapped the desk, ending the conversation. "Debrief is over. Get some rest. New assignments start at 1400."

Sunshine stood, spun her skirt, and sauntered out, humming a tune that had been popular decades before either of them existed. Angelica stood, folder in hand.

"If you need me…" he said suddenly. His words caught in his mouth, suddenly dry. "I'll be here. You can call me, you know."

A snap of her gaze toward Charles revealed something new. His voice had broken. In all the years she'd known him, she'd never heard that tremor or the jagged edge of vulnerability. She searched his eyes and found an alien plea.

I'm going soft, she told herself. The thought died before it could take root. With a single curt nod, she left the office.

Sunshine stood in the hallway. "You seem… weird, Angel," she said with a sideways look.

Angel? The similarity to Athena's nickname had to be a coincidence. It *had* to be.

Angelica paused. "Athena was… something else."

"Yes, and?"

"She… she wasn't human. She was a robot." A sudden burst of emotion threatened to break through, but she fought it back. Tears had no place in the Program.

Sunshine gave a nod. "I think you mean cyborg. They're always making better toys."

The rows of glass offices sat just a few feet ahead. Angelica stopped. "You knew?"

"You didn't?" Sunshine faced her friend. "I thought you were smarter than that."

Angelica grabbed her arm. "Why didn't you ever say anything? This is crazy. She wasn't human. We're not *human.* Doesn't that bother you?"

"Why would it?"

"Is that why it doesn't bother you that you don't remember anything from before the Program?"

"No, I don't remember. I also don't care. I don't need anyone, except maybe you and the fun we have sometimes." Sunny offered a smile, as if they were discussing vacation plans.

"But I remember things." Angelica's voice dropped. She looked away. "I remember my mother. I remember her scent and her singing. Things like that. I dream of her sometimes." She looked back at Sunny. "What's it like not to remember?"

Sunshine's smile faded, eyes softening. "It's like being born every day," she said. "No regrets. No guilt. Why?"

"Do you ever wonder if you're real?" Angelica asked.

"I'm real enough. What's the difference?" Sunshine grinned, wide and wild. "Why would I want to be haunted by dreams?"

"It's just… I thought…" They slowly approached the glass windows that marked the beginning of the analysts' offices.

"Thought you were human?"

Sunshine threw a grin over her shoulder and turned a cartwheel. Her bohemian skirt flared, a flash of pink lace and toned muscle, before she snapped back to her feet. She freed her hair from the elastic and shook the blonde hair loose for the benefit of the analysts behind the glass. A few waved back, hypnotized by the sexy, innocent routine.

They never wave at me, Angelica thought.

"But don't you feel… empty?" Angelica asked. "Like you ought to be something else?"

"You get used to it," Sunshine said, her smile never reaching her eyes, "or you don't. Either way, you keep moving."

She spun in front of the security hub. The guards didn't wave. One visibly shuddered. They were the ones who had to scrub the walls after Sunshine finished her work. Angelica remembered the throat job—the way Sunshine had giggled while she tore an esophagus out by hand. Angelica preferred a clean kill; Sunshine preferred a spectacle.

Angelica's mind drifted back to the buzzing under Athena's skin. The serial killer labels on the news. The rogue programming.

What if I'm next? she wondered. She watched Sunshine's lethal grace. They expected her to snap. Why her? Why not the girl who laughed at blood?

They parted at the elevators. Protocol demanded they never arrive or leave together. It was a skeletal habit, practiced without a word. Angelica watched the doors swallow Sunshine, then turned to her own reflection in the chrome.

She looked exactly like Athena… too exactly to be a coincidence. Now it would be a long time before she could look in a mirror and see anything but the dead woman. The dead *cyborg*, she corrected.

The face staring back wasn't just beautiful; its symmetry was unnerving. No scars. No flaws. No tells. It was a mask of perfection designed to hide the machinery beneath.

A sudden, violent urge flared. She wanted to take her nails to her own skin and peel it back just to see. She wanted to corner Charles and choke the truth out of him, to find out if the spark she felt when he touched her hand was a soul or just a circuit completing.

But there was always another assignment. Always another chance to be a good soldier.

She tucked the mission folder under her arm and stepped out. The day had barely begun, yet she felt a bone-deep exhaustion. *Can a machine be tired?*

As she walked, the nape of her neck began to buzz, a low, electronic hum.

If I'm a machine, she thought, *at least I'm the kind that dreams.*

*****

Chapter 3

The safehouse was a cookie-cutter suburban disguise of stucco, boxed hedges, and a porch light that pulsed like a dying heart. Angelica sat in the rental and let the engine idle for a full minute before she cut the ignition. Silence rushed in to fill the void.

A playground sat nearby. The swings were still, and the sand smelled of damp earth and neglect. A memory surfaced, hazy and worn, like a film left too long in the sun. She saw a swing set. A woman in a dark skirt clutched her elbows in anxiety. Her mother. Angelica tried to sharpen the focus, but the image wavered. Her mother's face appeared and disappeared. She wondered if this was a fragment of a life once lived, or merely a corrupted file uploaded to a hard drive.

She buried the thought and slammed the car door hard enough to bruise the quiet. Tonight was standard: track, confirm, eliminate. But the voice memo from Charles echoed in her head… *extra caution, Angelica…* and the copper scent of the kill from the night before still clung to her skin like a stain.

Inside the safehouse, Sunshine was a study in feigned relaxation as she sprawled across a floral sofa with a trashy paperback. She looked up and set a steaming mug down with a sharp, deliberate *clink*.

"About time," Sunshine said, teasing, but with a wary expression. "I was starting to get bored. And you know how I get when I'm bored. I thought you'd flaked."

"Sorry," Angelica said. "Traffic."

The excuse sounded stupid as soon as it left her mouth.

"You could have at least made up a decent excuse."

"Sorry, it's been a day."

Sunshine watched her for a moment with narrowed eyes. "You want some tea?"

Angelica shook her head and dropped her go-bag near the door. She peeled off her jacket and felt a minuscule tremor.

"You sure?" Sunshine pressed. "It's chamomile."

"No, thanks."

Sunshine grinned, too wide and too artificially cheerful. "You always act like I'm trying to poison you."

"You always act like you'd be doing me a favor. Maybe you would."

Sunshine laughed, a bright, genuine sound that Angelica hated for its warmth. It was a lure. Sunshine's beauty was the beauty of shattered glass: sharp, reflective, and designed to cut. *Sculpted to cut?* Only when she threw her head back did the light catch it, a jagged scar tucked under her jawline, the only flaw in an otherwise perfect lie. Angelica found herself staring at it as if it held a secret.

The burner phone on the kitchen table buzzed, followed by a flash of coordinates and an encrypted string of numbers. Charles's voice pinged in thirty seconds later, all business.

"Confirm location," he said. Angelica pictured him in the low-lit office, fingers drumming the desk, probably already planning his next move. She read off the digits, hands steady now.

"Good," Charles said. "There's been a change. New party on the handoff. Handle it."

Sunshine's turn to speak. "Rules of engagement?"

"Zero witnesses," Charles replied. "Collateral, if unavoidable," and the line clicked off. He never wasted syllables when the real work was at hand.

Angelica memorized the address and left her phone on the counter. Sunshine finished her tea, then stood, stretching like a cat, all lean limbs and restless energy.

"Ready, Angel?" she asked.

Why is Sunshine suddenly calling me Angel, too?

Angelica followed her out. Streetlamps flickered to life, illuminating a row of identical houses, warm windows, the muffled hum of televisions, and the faint ghosts of laughter. She wondered if the neighbors noticed the cycle of beautiful women who moved through the safehouses, never staying more than a week, always vanishing before dawn. Did they even care?

Sunshine drove with cold, aggressive precision, her eyes snapping between the mirrors while she sang along to the radio. Angelica watched the dashboard lights play across her friend's face. She couldn't imagine Sunshine failing. She wondered if the woman ever worried about it, or if worry had been scrubbed from her OS.

They killed the engine two blocks from the drop, a skeletal strip mall flanked by a boarded-up liquor store. Angelica checked her waist holster out of habit, touching the three spare mags, the stiletto tucked up her sleeve. Sunshine mirrored the movements. It was perfect coordination, fluid, silent, and terrifyingly efficient. *What's training,* Angelica wondered, *and what's just code?*

They moved through the shadows of the final block. The target's car, a battered Civic with illegal tint, sat idling in the lot. Two silhouettes inside: a man with a cheap mustache, and a woman with platinum hair, sitting with a rigid, unnatural posture.

Sunshine gave one nod.

Angelica approached from the rear, staying low. Her pulse thrummed in her teeth. She didn't know fear, but tonight, she felt a new vibration in her veins, the sense of a countdown reaching zero.

Sunshine was a blur. She wrenched the driver's door open and moved in. Angelica hit the passenger side in a dead parallel, blade drawn. The man barely had time to blink before Sunshine's arm was around his throat, applying pressure with a brutal, technical grace.

The passenger door flew open. The woman's mouth stretched into a scream, but Angelica was faster. She seized a handful of platinum hair, yanked the woman's head back, and pressed cold steel against the vein.

"Don't," Angelica said, even though she knew it didn't matter.

The woman bucked, spat, and tried to claw Angelica's hands. The desperation and terror in her eyes hit Angelica in the gut… the panic of life in the balance. She finished it quickly, the way she was taught: slip the blade in, sever the artery, and press the wound so it bled inside. The woman shuddered, then went slack. Angelica released her and stared at the blood pooling on the plastic seat cover. Human blood, this time.

"Textbook," Sunshine said, wiping her hands on her skirt. "You still got it, Angel."

Angelica leaned against the car, breathing through her teeth to keep the world from spinning. The urge to vomit was a cold, hard knot in her chest.

"Hey," Sunshine said, her voice dropping its edge. "You good?"

Angelica nodded, unable to find her voice. Sunshine touched her shoulder—a brief, fleeting contact. It was the only human thing Angelica had felt all day.

They torched the car, leaving it a blackened husk of failed arson. As they walked back to the sedan, their boots squelched through the wet grass. Behind them, the fire painted the world in the flickering oranges of a shallow hell.

Inside the car, Angelica wiped her hands with a napkin from the glove box. It had kittens printed on it, a relic from some child's birthday party. The contrast felt like a fever dream.

Sunshine watched her, her expression unreadable. "You ever think about running?"

"And do what?"

"Something softer," Sunshine murmured.

Angelica shook her head. "It's not for us."

"Never hurts to dream," Sunshine said, but the lie hung heavy in the air.

The drive back was a vacuum of silence. Adrenaline ebbed, replaced by a metallic chill. Angelica's mind glitched, the playground, her mother's skirt, and the dying woman's eyes all spliced together into a jagged, broken loop.

They stepped back into the safehouse. The only light came from the TV, where lions hunted in a grainy nature documentary. The impersonal violence of the screen was a relief—it was simpler than the mess inside her own skull.

Sunshine sprawled on the sofa, the remote balanced on her belly. "We did good," she said, her eyes fixed on the predators on screen. "*You* did good."

Angelica wanted to believe her. She wanted to sleep, to purge the memory of the hair in her fist and the heat on her palms. But behind her eyelids, the wires in Athena's chest pulsed with that rhythmic, synthetic buzz.

In the bathroom, she scrubbed her hands until the skin was raw. She probed the spot where Athena had clawed her, half-expecting to feel the cold bite of titanium. There was only skin. Only a dull, human ache.

She splashed cold water on her face and looked into the mirror, searching for the ghost in the machine. Angelica leaned in, searching her face for a seam, a crack, a hidden port… any evidence that she was built rather than born. But the skin held its secrets. She saw only a tired woman with eyes that burned too bright under the LED glare.

She dried her hands and returned to the living room, sinking onto the couch beside Sunshine. A pizza box lay between them, and she took a slice, chewing without tasting, not caring that crumbs covered her chest.

On the screen, a lioness dragged a carcass into the tall grass, her jaws stained crimson. Angelica watched the predator's steady, unblinking gaze. She wondered if the lioness ever felt the weight of the kill, or if she simply moved through the world, a slave to the elegant, bloody code written in her marrow.

The next morning, Charles called.

The assignment was urgent, but not a kill. "I want you to watch someone," he said. "A journalist. She's getting too close to some of our… procurement streams."

Angelica wrote the name down. "How close?"

"Too close."

"Do you want her neutralized?"

Charles hesitated, then said, "No. Not unless it's necessary."

The call ended. Angelica stared at the name, the tremor in her hands returning. She looked up to find Sunshine watching her from the kitchen, already making tea.

"New job?" Sunshine said.

"Yeah," Angelica replied. "Different flavor."

Sunshine poured two mugs this time and brought one to Angelica without comment. They sat at the counter and sipped in silence. Outside, a garbage truck rumbled past, the driver oblivious to the two assassins in the rental house.

Angelica's vision glitched again. This time, she saw a hospital corridor, her own body on a gurney, Charles's voice distant and panicked. "Get her stabilized, now—" Then static.

She shivered. Sunshine noticed.

"See a ghost?" Sunshine said.

"Maybe. I don't know."

Sunshine bumped her shoulder. "We should do something fun tonight. Get a drink."

Angelica smiled, though it hurt. "You buying?"

"Always."

They spent the day surveilling the journalist, trading jokes and bad puns over comms the way they always had. The woman was sharp and moved like someone who'd learned to distrust sidewalks and public restrooms, like someone who'd survived more than one threat to her life.

Angelica admired her, but it only made the job harder.

They tailed her to a café. Sunshine hung back, eyes on the exits. Angelica went in, sat three tables away, nursed a coffee, and tried to look like she belonged. The journalist's hands trembled as she typed on her laptop, but she seemed almost bored.

Angelica tried to remember a time she'd felt bored, but there was always an edge, always a risk. Her mind never stopped running through contingencies.

She caught a glimpse of herself in the café's window, and for a second, she saw Athena sitting there instead, blood trickling down her throat, eyes wild and defiant. Angelica looked away, breath catching in her chest.

The job was simple: watch, record, report. But the more she watched the journalist, the more she wondered what it was like to chase something for yourself, instead of for a paycheck or the approval of the Program's bosses.

The woman rose, packed her things, and left. Angelica followed at a safe distance and kept the target in sight until the sun began to set and the shadows grew long.

She called Charles. "She's on the move. Keeps turning, but definitely heading west."

Charles's voice sounded strained. "Good. Stay on her."

Angelica hesitated. "If she makes me?"

"Do what you have to," he said, then hung up.

Angelica caught up to the journalist at a park. The place sat empty except for a cluster of runners and a couple of kids on a swing set. The woman occupied a bench, where she sat hunched over her phone. Angelica slowed, took a seat on a bench across the path, and kept her hands visible.

The journalist glanced up with sharp eyes. She saw Angelica—saw through her—and Angelica felt a strange jolt. This woman knew the reality of being hunted.

They sat that way for a long time. Neither looked away until the woman finally rose and walked toward Angelica. She stopped just short of touching distance and folded her arms tight against her chest.

"Who sent you?" the journalist asked. Her eyes followed a squirrel up one of the big oaks.

Angelica smiled, genuine for once. "No one you know."

The woman nodded. "I wouldn't be too sure. Are you here to kill me?"

"Not unless you force my hand."

They sat in silence for a while.

"Why do you do it?" the woman asked.

Angelica considered the words. It was a good question. "I don't know how to stop."

The journalist nodded again. "Neither do I."

She turned and walked away with a slow but sure pace. Angelica watched her go, then sat on the bench until the streetlights blinked on. Neither she nor Sunshine spoke as they returned to the safehouse, where Sunshine sprawled on the floor, painting her toenails electric blue.

"She made you, but you didn't kill her," Sunshine said. It wasn't a question.

Angelica shook her head.

"Charles will be mad."

"Let him be," Angelica said.

Sunshine offered a smile. "You're changing."

"I hope so."

Angelica couldn't shake the feeling that she was rewritten every time she closed her eyes. If she somehow found a way to fight back?

Good.

That night, her dreams were a maelstrom of unknown faces, of voices that pleaded for mercy, and the sound of a mother's laugh cut short. She woke with the taste of metal in her mouth and the certainty that whatever she was, it wasn't what they wanted her to be… or what they thought she was.

She had another assignment in the morning, but for the first time, she didn't want to take it. Instead, she wanted answers. She wanted to be free.

She wanted to *be.*

*****

Chapter 4

Angelica was in the safehouse kitchen when Charles's code pinged her phone with a five-digit string. No preamble, no instruction, just a time and a door number in the CIA annex she'd never been inside. She tossed the phone and caught Sunshine as she watched from the doorway with arms folded tight around her ribs.

"You got a date?" Sunshine asked. She teased, but with a wary expression.

"Something like that."

"Don't let him screw you over," Sunshine said. Her voice was softer. "He's not like us."

The truth was, Angelica wasn't sure what they were.

The sky was cement gray and leaking drizzle when she arrived. The building squatted on the city's edge, one of those windowless cubes ringed by cameras and flowering bushes that, even in bloom, looked ready to bite. She entered and let the retinal scan burn her pupil. Every motion was watched by a camera so precise she could feel it in her teeth.

Room 212 was a relic of institutional decay: molded plastic chairs, corkboards, and paper files locked behind a rusted mesh grate. The aggressive fluorescent lights scrubbed the color from the world until everything looked like bleached bone. The air tasted of ozone and disinfectant, the smell of a crime scene sterilized for the next occupant.

Charles was already there. His jacket lay tossed aside, and his sleeves were rolled to his elbows. He looked like a man who'd forgotten how to sleep. Sweat dampened his hairline, and the shadows under his eyes had deepened into bruises. On the table sat a folder, thicker and more ominous than any mission brief he'd ever carried.

He didn't offer a greeting. He simply gestured to the chair across from him with a gaze anchored to her face.

Angelica sat. Her posture was a masterpiece of lethal discipline. Every muscle was coiled, and every circuit stood ready to strike.

Charles leaned forward and placed his elbows on the table.

"Do you trust me?" he asked.

The question rattled her.

"I have to."

He shook his head. "I mean it."

Angelica stared at him, searching for a tell. "You want me to say yes."

"I want you to tell the truth."

She thought of the journalist on the park bench and the moment of unspoken connection. She thought of Athena, her chest open, and her wires slick with fluid. A noisy breath, inhaled through her nose, punctuated her decision.

"I trust you," Angelica said, and she meant it, even if she couldn't explain why. "Why are we in this old storage room?"

Charles nodded. "Because it's the only place I could find that's completely private."

He opened the folder one page at a time and laid them in front of her. Diagrams, lab reports, surgical notes, and photos that looked like autopsy stills, but weren't—at least not all of them—spread across the table. The last page was an official memo with a red stamp: PROTOTYPE TERMINATION AUTHORIZATION. Underneath sat her own name.

Angelica's mouth went dry.

"They're shutting me down," she said. It wasn't a question.

Charles's hands trembled as he stacked the papers.

"You're a threat to the Program. They think you'll go rogue."

"Will I?"

He took a long breath as if searching for the answer in her face. "You're not like the others. You were never meant to be."

Angelica looked down at the memo. "Why not? How am I different?"

Charles closed his eyes. When he opened them, his voice was softer and more human than she'd ever heard it. "You want things. You *care*. They call it a malfunction, but I think it's…"

He stopped, his jaw working.

She waited.

"I think it's beautiful," he finished. "You're the only one they ever made who could choose."

The words hit her harder than any punch. She thought of Sunshine, who let everything slide off her skin. She thought of herself, of the way she cried at a nature documentary, or how she remained unable to forget a stranger's face. She wondered if that made her more real, or just easier to hurt.

"Why did you bring me here?"

Charles's lips pulled tight. "Because they want me to kill you."

She felt the spike of fear, but also a strange relief. There was no more waiting and no more running on a treadmill of assignments. She finally stood at the end.

"Are you going to do it?"

Charles hesitated, then looked away. His feet shuffled. "I'm not sure I can."

Angelica watched him. She wondered if he lied. She'd never thought of Charles as a killer, trained or otherwise. He was a man who ordered kills, sure, but not one to do the work personally. Then the realization dawned.

"You like me," she said quietly. "Why?"

"Do you know who I am?"

"Who, or what?"

He didn't answer, but his hands gave him away. They showed the same knuckle tremor she saw in herself, and the same learned stillness. "You put a fine point to it. We all have upgrades now," he said, "some of us more than others. But you… you were born human. A real human. Flesh and blood. Did you know that? You have memories; I know you do. Then they made you something else. Enhanced. A new prototype. And because it was so unique, they considered it dangerous. They installed a kill switch. Now they want me to flip it."

The words settled between them like a glass wall neither could cross.

"I don't want to hurt you," Charles said.

Angelica folded her hands and kept them in her lap. "Then help me. Tell me how to disable it."

Charles offered a smile. It was sad and tired. "You think I have access?"

"You always have access," Angelica said. "You keep the codes for everything."

He nodded and conceded the point. "If I give them to you, you'll have maybe a day before they send the next wave. They won't like you."

Angelica felt her resolve solidify. "Twenty-four hours... that's enough."

He pushed a USB drive across the table. "Everything's on there. Escape routes. Code sequences. But Angel—" He caught her gaze with fierce eyes. "If you go, don't look back."

"It was you," she said. "You're why Athena and Sunshine started to call me Angel."

"Guilty as charged. It was a slip of the tongue."

Angelica wanted to say goodbye, or thank you, or something that would make the parting mean more, but the words didn't come. Instead, she reached for the USB drive and let her hand cover his for a second.

His fingers closed over hers and didn't let go. For a heartbeat, she felt something pass between them. It was a warmth, or hope, or maybe just the echo of a feeling she was never meant to have.

"Go," Charles whispered. "Now. Don't look back."

Angelica stood. Her legs felt weak, but she moved fast. Her heart thumped so loud, she thought the cameras would hear it. She left the folder on the table, tucked the USB drive in her bra, and walked down the hall with her head up. She dared anyone to stop her.

Outside, the rain had stopped. The sky was the color of a healing bruise. The streetlights flickered on one by one.

She walked to the edge of the lot where the safehouse sedan was parked. In the rearview mirror, she caught her own reflection and saw a bloody Athena, who smiled at her. She blinked and saw only herself again.

She started the car and drove. The city blurred past in streaks of neon and shadow. There was a long way to go and not much time. But for the first time, she didn't follow orders.

She ran for her life.

* * * * *

Chapter 5

The train station was a neon-drenched fever dream of surging bodies and shuffling feet, dirty and bright. Multiple cameras covered every square inch. Sophisticated algorithms processed the images fed through those lenses. They were designed to recognize faces, body types, and even gaits. Angelica threaded through the press with one hand anchoring her backpack to her ribs. Every passing face felt like a threat. Every security vest was a captor waiting to spring.

The trade-off was a series of frantic, paranoid pivots. She swapped a jacket with a stranger, ditched a phone in a planter, and used a drugstore dye kit that left her scalp raw and her hands stained a telltale black. None of it felt like enough. Under the ink-dark hair, she remained a target.

The south entrance beckoned. She calculated and discarded sightlines. She checked shadows for tails. Overhead, the arrival boards flickered in a blur of blue-and-white code that mimicked the static in her brain. The noise was a shield. In this much chaos, individual threats might just lose her scent.

At the ticket kiosk, a feigned struggle with the touchscreen bought her time to scan the reflections in the glass. A courier. A mother with toddlers. Tourists who whispered in Portuguese.

None of them carried the rigid, lethal stillness of Program muscle, but the suspicion remained as a low-frequency hum behind her teeth.

A ticket for the 18:07 to Richmond was a necessary lie, a paper trail for a ghost.

The women's restroom stank as only government-maintained public bathrooms can. Under the harsh, soul-crushing light, Angelica retreated to the far stall and forced her lungs to find a rhythm. The burner laptop came out of the pack. The USB slid home with a clinical *click*.

The screen raced with code and settled finally on a single directory: ESCAPE.

Whatever else the Program had done to her, it had given her a memory far beyond that of other people. Inside the folder lay an outline for survival, and it included a map. She memorized the map until the lines were burned into her retinas. Then she read the instructions.

Something within her brain *click*ed. She wiped the drive using the Program's own purpose-written software, then snapped the plastic in two and buried the pieces in the trash beneath a shroud of chewing gum.

Whatever reading the code had done to her brain, she knew that Angelica the machine was dead.

Now, Angelica the Human had to stay alive.

"Fifteen minutes, then move," Charles had said. "You'll have a five-block window."

She checked her watch: 17:53.

When she stepped out, the station seemed different. Slower, somehow. She walked to the coffee stand, ordered a black drip, and sipped as she waited. She was obvious to the observing AIs, yes, but also unconcerned. Beyond physical structure, they were coded to look for suspicious behavior, so Angelica became invisibly boring. At 18:07 on the dot, she walked calmly toward the side exit as the boarding bell rang overhead.

A woman waited by the exit. She was tall, with a sharp-boned face, pale hair, and a long coat that looked as if it cost more than most cars. Angelica's heart stuttered. She knew that posture and that face. It was older, but familiar. It was the first handler she'd ever met. The woman scanned the crowd, likely with embedded AI detectors.

Angelica shifted direction and ducked into a magazine shop. She counted to six, then slipped out the opposite side. The woman was gone… or she waited somewhere else.

She kept moving. She never ran and never paused long enough for a camera to linger. Out on the sidewalk, she suppressed nervousness the way she'd been taught, and instead, turned every sense on high. She passed a line of idling taxis, ducked into an alley, cut across a parking lot, and headed toward the glass-walled lobby of a budget hotel.

A family argued by the elevators. A man in a suit tapped at his phone. Angelica found Charles in his cheap room. His tie was undone, and his hair was matted with sweat. He looked different. He was less himself and more vulnerable, like a man who'd waited forever.

He didn't say anything when she opened the room door. He just gave a quick flick of the eyes. She followed him to the bed and sat next to him, close enough to touch knees. For a moment, they just breathed in tandem.

"Anyone follow you?"

"Maybe. Not sure. I took the route you mapped."

Charles nodded. "We have about ten minutes before they triangulate."

She smiled, tight. "Plenty of time."

For a moment, the city noise fell away. Charles's hand covered hers. Their fingers laced together as if by instinct. She felt the tremor in his grip, the pulse that told her he was scared, too.

"You sure about this?" he whispered.

"Are you?"

He didn't answer. He didn't have to.

They stood and left the motel. They walked like any tired couple heading for the parking garage. At the back exit, Angelica stopped. "They'll go after Sunshine," she said. "She'll be their first move."

"She can handle herself, but you can't help her if you're dead."

Angelica nodded. She pushed down guilt, dread, and the urge to turn back. She was so tired of being a tool for other people's games.

In the parking garage, they found a battered sedan with out-of-state plates. It was as generic as it got. Charles slid into the driver's seat. Angelica took the passenger side with her hands tight in her lap. She wished for a weapon.

The streets blurred past in a rush. They didn't talk much, except to navigate. Charles stuck to the side roads. He avoided cameras and followed the map she'd memorized in the bathroom. At a red light, he glanced at her. His mouth opened like he wanted to say something, then he closed it again. Angelica wanted to reach over to touch his face, to confirm he was real, but she was afraid that if she did, the contact would break whatever spell held them together.

Two blocks from the safehouse, Charles stopped the car. "We go on foot from here."

She got out and scanned the street. It was empty, except for the rumble of a train in the distance. They crossed beneath an overpass. Their boots echoed on cracked pavement. They turned into a service alley behind a strip mall.

There, behind the dumpsters, stood Sunshine.

Her hair was down, wild and tangled. She wore jeans and a threadbare hoodie. Her eyes in the darkness were brighter than ever.

"I figured you'd make it," Sunshine said. Her voice was neither angry nor pleased.

"Are you with them?" Angelica asked.

Sunshine shrugged. "I'm with me."

Charles stepped forward. He blocked Angelica enough to signal his allegiance. "We're not here to fight."

"Good," Sunshine said, "because I'd win."

Angelica laughed, and the sound surprised her. The three of them stood in the cold, surrounded by trash and broken glass. For a moment, it almost felt good.

"Why are you here?" Angelica blurted. She used no subtlety and went straight to the chase.

"You know why, Angel. You're one of us, even if you're also one of them."

There was no response needed beyond a simple nod.

"You sure about this?" Sunshine asked, echoing Charles from before.

"I have to try," Angelica said.

Sunshine nodded. "Then go. I'll buy you some time."

Charles didn't say thank you, and neither did Angelica. Instead, the two friends exchanged a look before Angelica and Charles turned and walked away. Side by side, they moved into the city.

As they neared the next intersection, a black SUV slid out of the shadows and idled at the curb. Two men in dark suits got out. They scanned the block with dead eyes. Angelica felt her whole body coil, ready for the sprint or the kill, but Charles put a hand on her arm.

"Wait," he murmured.

The men didn't see them. They didn't even look. They entered a door marked SERVICE ACCESS and vanished.

Charles and Angelica crossed the street and kept walking.

At the train yard, they ducked through a gap in the fence. Their boots sank into mud. The city lights were distant and soft here. The tracks stretched in every direction and glistened with rain.

Charles stopped. He breathed hard. "They'll never stop looking," he said.

"I know."

"Are you okay with that?"

She looked at him. She saw the tremor in his jaw and the way he fought to keep his face blank. "I'm okay with you."

He laughed. It was an awkward sound, one he wasn't used to making. He cupped her face in both hands. "This is real," he said, "isn't it?"

"You're asking *me* about what's real?"

Behind them, headlights swooped across the train yard as four black SUVs screeched around a corner. The chase was on.

Angelica grabbed Charles's hand. Together, they ran. The rain came harder now, soaking them in seconds, but they didn't let go.

For all she knew, they'd die in the next hour or the next day. The Program would throw everything at them. They'd run until they couldn't. But the running was hers now. The fear and the choice belonged to her.

She risked a look back, just once. On the edge of the yard, standing beneath a lamplight, Sunshine watched them go. She lifted two fingers in a lazy salute.

Angelica turned her face forward into the dark and didn't look back again.

* * *

Across the city, in a glass-walled office lit by the glow of five monitors, a woman in a gray suit watched the feed from the train yard. She pressed a button, and a new folder opened: SUBJECT: ANGELICA / ASSET: SUNSHINE / STATUS: IN TRANSIT

She sipped her tea and smiled.

"The experiment continues," she said and began to type.

*****

Author Bio

Megan Miller has extensive experience in both federal and state government, as well as the corporate sector. She currently serves as the executive director for a nonprofit organization. Ms. Miller is a classically trained artist and writer of fiction and nonfiction, residing in an undisclosed location in the Blue Ridge Mountains.

# # # # #

The Last Survivors at Centerpoint Crystal Research Facility by Andrew Waldron

Chapter 1

Sergeant David Ozle kept his eyes off the mirrors as he steered the Jeep across the Crystal Desert. Under the tires, frozen sand crunched like breaking glass. He pushed the speed, racing the orange twilight toward the coordinates on his GPS; the heater was a lost cause against the biting chill seeping through the door seals.

"Fifteen minutes," David said, more to the dashboard than his passenger.

Sergeant Arnold Mitchell, the tech specialist assigned to the detail, didn't look away from the shimmering white expanse outside his window. He rubbed his gloved hands together, then blew on them, his breath frosting in the cab.

"Nice sunset," Arnold said over the engine's roar. "You think we're on a wild goose chase?"

David sighed. "General Mathias declassifies a phantom outpost the second the rebels pop a dirty bomb in the capital," he said. He forced a breath, gripping the wheel until his knuckles ached. "Then he sends the two of us to download 'whatever we can' without telling us what the hell we're looking for. That sound like a vote of confidence to you?"

Arnold shrugged. "Sounds like a tight circle."

"If we succeed, and the data isn't scrubbed, it'll just be another mission that ends up as a redacted page in a briefing book."

"What do you think is on those drives?" Arnold asked. "To justify sending us into the middle of nowhere, I mean."

"Rats set off a dirty bomb that killed thousands, Arnold. We aren't here for a cake recipe. When leadership bypasses the chain of command, it's usually human experiments or a weapon that's a war crime to carry. *We're* expendable. Take your pick."

"Maybe this one won't keep me awake for months."

"Given the state of things back home, I'm not sure I'd sleep anyway."

They lapsed into silence. The crunch of sand and the creeping chill were easier to focus on than the memory of the capital.

The outpost loomed ahead, a low-slung, concrete slab squatting against the silver horizon. David swung the Jeep around the flank of the building, the tires kicking up plumes of frozen dust. They didn't waste time. While Arnold prepped the transponder and handed off the comms, David hauled their power suits from the rear.

David engaged the thermal lining and sealed the helmet over his buzzed blonde hair.

"Command, this is Special Op Gamma. On site and prepping for entry."

"Gamma, this is General Mathias." The general's voice was a jagged rasp over the encrypted link. *"You are cleared for entry. Resistance should be minimal, but keep your defensive gear active. And expect it to be cold."*

David stiffened. "Uh… yes, sir."

"Is there a problem, soldier?"

"No, sir," David snapped, instinctively coming to attention, even in the middle of the desert. "I was just expecting a comms tech, sir."

"Command is out of the loop on this one. All reports come to me directly. Locate the underground server room, bypass security, and export the research to Fort Reynolds. Understood?"

"Roger that," Arnold chimed in. *"Orders on resistance, sir?"*

"Eliminate it. Over and out."

The line went dead. David checked the action on his rifle. He gestured to the extra mags Arnold was shoving into his kit.

"The general is being vague enough that I'm expecting the worst," Arnold said, slinging his rifle and grabbing the terminal. He looked back at the darkening desert. "You think this actually helps? The research?"

David didn't look back. He stared at the heavy door.

"I try not to think that far ahead."

He kicked the door. It gave way with a groan of rusted hinges, revealing a lobby choked with dust and decaying furniture. David moved through the space with practiced economy, his rifle light cutting through the gloom. No movement. No heat signatures. Just cobwebs and the skeletal remains of an office.

"Entrance is clear," David said, keying his comms. "Nothing moving, but no sign of the basement yet. Bring the gear in."

Arnold entered with his rifle leveled, the weight of the electronics bag shifting on his shoulders.

"Ah, hell," Arnold muttered, scanning the interior. "This looks like a run-of-the-mill warehouse."

"I noticed. And?"

"No way they'd be hosting a high-level server array in a remote shack like this. We're here for the *real* shady shit they did back in the day."

"Not surprised," David said. "That dirty bomb in the capital spooked everyone. The suits and the brass are desperate for the most violent way to hit back. Eye for an eye."

David shrugged, keeping his eyes on the shadows. "Ergo, our secret mission orders. According to the info Mathias gave us, we're going underground—ten, maybe fifteen meters down. We need to find stairs or an elevator to jump start."

"Looks like they buried the entrance deep. Maybe once we have power, it'll reveal itself." David gestured with his muzzle for them to keep moving.

They located a generator room tucked off the main storeroom. It took Arnold ten minutes to coax the building back to life, but the old solar storage cells were surprisingly resilient. Generators began a low, rhythmic thrum, and flickering lights hummed overhead, struggling against decades of frayed wiring.

They pushed into a central office, where Arnold moved straight for the terminal.

"This should at least show us the cover story for this place," Arnold said. He pulled a cable from his pack, slaved his laptop to the terminal, and bypassed the login with a few keystrokes.

David paced the perimeter of the office, peering into the dimly lit warehouse.

"Good evening," a soft, synthesized male voice spoke from the speakers. "Welcome to the Crystal Centerpoint Rese—I apologize, I must say Warehouse. Please state or type your shipment destination, the cargo for storage, and the intended duration."

"I'm surprised this junk still boots," David said. "Must've been abandoned years ago."

"Decades," Arnold corrected. "The last government-approved update on this system was logged before either of us was born. I checked. Depending on how old your parents are, maybe before them, too."

David took a deep breath, staring out at the barren floor.

Focus on the mission, he told himself. *I can figure out the rest later.*

Arnold squinted. "This gets weirder… the official updates stopped forty years ago, y'know? But this computer's coding is a mess. There's sloppy digital footprints everywhere. Someone's been in here. I don't think we're alone, Ozle."

David turned back. "Until we have eyes on a target, we stay on high alert. Did you find an access point for the sublevels?"

Arnold shook his head. "The warehouse servers don't show a connection to anything underground. If there's a localized network down there, it could take weeks to crack. We only brought enough supplies for forty-eight hours. I wasn't prepared for a system this functional."

"Then let's ask the machine." David stepped in, taking the seat as Arnold moved aside. He pulled up the manifest prompt and typed: WE WOULD LIKE TO STORE CARGO IN THE UNDERGROUND LEVELS.

"I am sorry," the computer responded. "There are no basement levels in this warehouse for storing materials that I am authorized to confirm. May I inquire who suggested such floors exist?"

David looked at Arnold. "This is our own system. You'd think Mathias would have given us a backdoor."

"I suspect Mathias hoped the system wouldn't be nearly as operat—"

"General Thomas Mathias?" the computer interrupted, the voice suddenly sharper. "Name recognized. Please provide the secondary access code."

David grabbed his radio, his thumb hovering over the PTT button. He keyed the link to the general. "General, we have an issue."

"Copy that, Gamma. What's the problem?"

Arnold didn't look up from his screen. "The system is more complex than the brief suggested, sir. It's based on the architecture you told me to study, but it's been heavily modified over the last few decades. Cracking it properly would take more time than our supplies allow—and that's not accounting for whoever has been in here, maintaining the code."

"Are you telling me the base is compromised?"

"Unclear, sir," David said. "The system is specifically asking for *General Nathan Mathias'* clearance. I don't think rogue occupants would have kept that protocol intact."

"My *grandfather?*" There was a pause on the other end, the sound of rustling paper or rapid typing. "I'll dig up whatever clearances we still have on file. Keep the line open."

David tried the first code Mathias sent. The computer's response was polite and immediate.

"I am sorry. General Mathias was mistaken. This system does not allow further access without proper clearance, regardless of my desire to assist. General Mathias was likely referring to the Eastern Crystal Cliffside Warehouse. It is a common mistake… so common, in fact, that you are fortunate I can override the security lockout. I assume your cargo requires special storage? I can accommodate you in the rear storeroom for twelve hours. Personnel will arrive to assist you shortly."

Personnel?

They tried two more strings. Both failed.

"No good," David said, his hand hovering over his rifle grip. "Sir, are there any other codes?"

"Give me a minute," Mathias responded. *"There was nothing in the records about an advanced heuristic system. Clearly, the archives don't reflect the reality of this base. Hold on… put the radio on speaker. I found something in his personal journal."*

David toggled the speaker. Mathias' voice filled the small office, steady and deliberate.

"The man becomes the lion, which gives way to the camel, which in turn heralds the arrival of a new child."

The terminal fell silent for a heartbeat. Then, the computer's tone shifted. The voice sounded lighter, almost relieved.

"Welcome back, General Mathias. Am I to assume that the functions of the Superhuman Research Program are set to resume?"

"May I ask who—or what—I have the pleasure of speaking with?" the general asked.

"Certainly. This is Dr. Sean Neat, director of the Superhuman Research Program. Most people around here just call me Neat. If you'll make your way to the northwest corridor, I'll bring up the elevator so these gentlemen can get to work."

"Who's 'most people'?" David asked, already on his feet. He and Arnold exited the office, Arnold checking his slaved laptop, which now displayed a tactical map of the warehouse with a pulsing nav point.

"My fellow researchers and staff, of course," Neat's voice followed them through the overhead speakers as they moved, "although I must confess, I've lost track of how long it's been since they were… present."

As they reached the lobby, David noticed the perimeter terminals had all flickered to life, displaying the same login prompt they'd just bypassed. The building felt awake now.

"Sergeants, use extreme caution," Mathias warned over the link. "There is no 'Dr. Sean Neat' in our classified records. I ran a check against the public archives—the closest match is a Sean Niet. If he's still alive, the man is over a hundred years old."

David whispered, "I'm thinking those custom codes are more expansive than you thought."

Arnold nodded as they reached the northwest corner of the outpost. There was a *click*, then a *hiss* as a seam appeared in the wall, and an elevator door opened.

"Please, gentlemen, the work awaits your transfer attempt," Neat invited them onto the elevator. David and Arnold walked into the elevator, weapons at the ready, and the doors shut, taking them below ground. Once down, the doors opened to a dim, silvery hallway dulled by years of neglect. David and Arnold stepped out with rifles at the ready.

"Status. What do you see?" General Mathias asked.

"No sign of a person," David responded. "We're in an empty hallway, so we're apparently in the clear. Dr. Neat, where are you?"

"Welcome to my facility," Neat responded over the intercom. "I propose that we work on returning all the data and test subjects removed from this facility. I must confess that I would expect more personnel to execute such a move."

"Test subjects?" Arnold asked, "What kind of test subjects? Are they alive?"

"The human test subjects, of course. Their status is something I've been unable to independently determine. They've been held in stasis for so long that I can't say how many are salvageable at this point."

"Why was the project shuttered?" David asked.

"That's not important. It was long ago. I also assume that as couriers, you're not cleared to that level of classification."

"And if we say we are?" Arnold asked.

"Then General Mathias can confirm."

"You are not," General Mathias said. *"Get the computer data, only the computer data, and then leave."*

"And the people?" David asked.

"We can send another, larger recon team to evaluate their transport at a later time."

"We're not cleared to know," Arnold repeated.

"It's a shame, though, a part of me wanted to tell you," Neat said, "but even I can't bypass the clearance checks, no matter how hard I try. I suppose that's for the best."

"Are you going to show yourself, or are you just a voice in a computer?" David asked.

"I'm a bit more than that, but unfortunately, I can't move like I used to."

A screen on the wall flickered on, and an older, bald man with glasses and a gray beard appeared, wearing black scrubs and a lab coat. "I may not be as mobile as I used to be, but that's actually something I hope you'll be able to help with—if not on this trip, soon enough."

"And how's that?" Arnold asked.

"I'm calculating the possibilities, but in the meantime, I assume we should work on getting to the archive."

"Lead the way."

David gestured forward with his rifle.

"Certainly." Neat's monitor flickered off, then another monitor further down the passage came to life. "This way."

Arnold took a step down the hallway, but David grabbed his shoulder and asked, "Do you trust this?"

Eyes scanned in both directions, then Arnold shrugged. "I've dealt with systems that had a semblance of sentience, but I've never seen one that's pushed itself this far. If it *is* a computer. For all we know, it's the actual doctor… maybe he experimented on himself. Who knows?"

Matthias replied, *"Given what's in the classified files, I doubt the real Dr. Neat would have survived long enough to try."*

The two officers exchanged a glance.

"Yes, sir," they said in tandem.

David keyed his comms. "Sir, whoever this 'Neat' is, he's implying there are people still here. If they're in stasis, we run the risk of an accidental wake-up. We need to know what went wrong here. If we're going to hit resistance, we need to know what we're shooting at."

There was a long silence on the line before Mathias spoke again, his tone dropping an octave. *"If you repeat what I'm about to say to anyone… even back to me… you'll both spend the rest of your lives in a labor camp. Understood?"*

"Understood, sir," David said.

"During the last civil war, the brass wanted super soldiers. Computers weren't sophisticated enough for field work back then, despite how that thing is acting now, so they green-lit a biological proposal. Long story short, the project was burned when the human trials proved too successful. They created men capable of superhuman feats, but the toll on their minds turned them into rabid lunatics."

"What kind of feats?" Arnold asked.

"Please, keep up," Neat's voice interrupted. His image appeared on a wall-mounted monitor to their left, a grainy, digital specter. "We have quite a distance to cover."

Mathias continued as if he hadn't heard the machine. *"From the reports, they could absorb the kinetic and thermal energy around them. One file claims a subject could sap the energy from a high-velocity round mid-air, so the bullet hit him with the force of a marshmallow. Hard to believe, but those are the official AARs. Anyway, they went mad, some slowly, some not so slowly, driven by a hunger for more and more energy. They couldn't stop. They were compelled to devour every scrap of energy in their environment. Everything, and everyone."*

"The army brass always has a flair for the dramatic," Neat chimed through the room. "We are approaching the main corridor. From there, take the stairs on the left down to the archive floor."

"Let's just get the data and get out," Arnold said as he muted the radio.

David nodded. "I don't want to know shit about what went on here."

They walked through the large lobby area and followed the moving screen down the stairs and further underground. They crossed one more hallway and went through the double doors that Neat directed them to.

"Oh, fuck!" David shouted as they walked into a large, cold tile room filled with stasis tubes. "I thought we were going to the server room."

Neat now appeared on multiple monitors throughout the room. "All archived data, both digital and physical, is kept on this floor. The server room you're looking for is that way."

All the Neats on the monitors gestured with their heads toward the opposite end of the room, to the left side.

"I don't recommend looking at the tubes for too long. These Last Subjects can sometimes sense when they're being watched. It agitates them."

"They're awake?" Arnold asked.

"I wouldn't describe their state as being *awake*," Neat responded, "but they have some degree of awareness."

David couldn't bring himself to keep walking toward the archive door; wouldn't keep walking. He wiped the frost from the closest tube and saw a pale, unconscious man suspended in pale blue liquid. When David looked closer, the man's eyes twitched but remained closed.

"Holy hell," he said.

"Report," General Mathias ordered.

Arnold spoke first. "The people the computer referred to *are* still alive. I can't speak for whether they're brain dead from being in here for however long, but it looks like they have stable vitals."

General Mathias sighed. *"This will complicate future expeditions, but to be clear, they're not your job today. Whatever happened to them in that facility has made them too dangerous to release. Focus on your mission, because you're here for the archived data, and that's it. Do you understand?"*

"Yes, sir," Arnold responded. "And, General? No part of me wants to stay here any longer than I absolutely have to."

*****

Chapter 2

David stepped back from the man in the tube. Top brass always had their stories, but even if Mathias was lying, orders were still orders. David echoed his companion's answer.

"Clear, sir. Data first and last."

Like a lurking eavesdropper, Neat's eyes followed them whenever they moved.

"While I disagree with Mathias' assessment of the subjects, it's for the best that you reach the central server."

Arnold looked at another screen, his laptop already in hand.

"Let's clear one thing up before I start plugging into unsecured portals… are you actually Dr. Neat, or just some digital ghost?"

The face on the screen stilled, processing. "I'm not the doctor. I'm one of his creations. I'm unsure what became of him after he and the staff evacuated the facility."

David pushed through the heavy door into the server room.

"I'm sure it's classified," Neat said.

Rows of servers stretched into the gloom. Deep in the forest of humming hardware, a faint blue glow pulsed, though the massive racks obscured its source.

"Which one is the jackpot?" Arnold asked, pulling cables from his bag.

Neat's face flickered onto a monitor embedded in a nearby rack. "Third row, toward the center. I wish I could guide you further, but my internal connections have decayed over the decades. Some sectors are entirely inaccessible to me. Be wary of the cooling system in the center; it's delicate. Dr. Neat had to be… creative to prevent a total system meltdown."

David counted the rows, following Arnold to the terminal. As Arnold slaved the laptop to the rack, the blue glow in the distance grew sharper, more piercing.

"I'll poke around and verify the data," Arnold said. "Once I've got a lock, I'll hook up the transponder and start the burst."

"Copy that. I'm going to keep moving—it's freezing in here. I'll update the general."

David moved toward the light.

"General Mathias, this is Ozle. Do you copy?"

"Copy, Gamma. Status?"

David rounded the corner of the server bank. The room opened up, far larger than it had appeared from the entrance. In the dead center sat a massive glass cylinder, the source of the sapphire light.

"Arnold has access. This Neat construct has been helpful—it seems to want the research out of the building as much as we do. It's complaining about hardware deterioration; I think it's looking for a way out of this rig."

"Did you make any promises?"

David approached the tube. An uncomfortable realization settled in his gut. The silhouette was familiar; it was the same shape as the stasis pods they had passed earlier.

"No, sir. And candidly? I think we should evacuate this facility, maybe blow it up. But that's not my call, I just hope that follow-up team you mentioned is real."

"Noted. I'll take it under consideration. What's your read on the talking computer?"

David reached the tube. He was close enough to see frost on the glass, but the light was so intense he couldn't make out the features of the occupant yet.

"Still unsure. I'm checking something out now. I'll update you in a second."

He stepped into the halo of blue light. There was a person inside, suspended in the same bluish fluid. "Neat, what the hell is this? Why is there a subject in the server room?"

Dozens of monitors throughout the room flickered to life simultaneously, and Neat's face appeared on every one of them.

"As I said, Dr. Neat used creativity to manage the heat," the voice echoed, overlapping itself. "The Super Subject took to the nanomachine implants better than any other. Unfortunately, his metabolic hunger outweighed that of the rest of the subjects combined. To contain him without execution, the doctor wired him directly into the grid. He siphons the excess thermal energy from the servers. It was meant to be a mercy, but the doctor failed to foresee two things."

David spun on his heel, sprinting back toward the row.

"Arnold, disconnect! Get off that terminal now!"

"The first," Neat's voice boomed, "was that the energy from these computers provides only a fraction of what he requires. To spend decades in a state of starvation, with just enough energy to realize how hungry you truly are... that's a fate crueler than death."

"Arnold! Abort!" David screamed into his radio. "General Mathias, the mission is compromised! I repeat, mission compromised!"

"The second thing," the voice now whispered, this time through the radio, "was that Dr. Niet, and everyone else, assumed that it would be impossible for my body to figure out a way to use the nanomachines they pumped me full of to force my way into other computer systems."

David rounded the corner and saw Neat's face on Arnold's laptop two seconds before Arnold threw it to the ground, shot it with his assault rifle, and then shot the terminal he'd plugged into. A kick sent the laptop skidding.

Nearly hyperventilating, Arnold huffed out, "He started talking after he'd already used my computer to hijack this terminal."

"What did you plug into?"

The cracked monitor on the terminal he'd shot came back to life, with the face unstable and pixelated. As it did, the face swirled and changed. *Into someone, or something, different.* Facial wrinkles smoothed, the jawline firmed, and it grew dark hair.

"Thank you both. This was one of the few systems I was still having too much trouble forcing my way into. Stasis control and all that."

Arnold and David both shot the terminal as the Super Subject's voice echoed through the rest of the room.

"It's too late for that. I didn't say anything until after I'd already executed my wake-up protocol. All you've done is make it harder to wake anyone else up. Pity, that."

The blue light turned red as all the monitors flipped from the face to a red triangle with an exclamation point.

"You must have chaos within you to burn like a brightest star," the Super Subject commented in a fading voice. Then he was gone.

Several moments passed as the two men processed what had happened.

"Engage or bail?" Arnold asked. He'd intended the question for General Mathias, but got only static as a reply. Once it became clear they were on their own, David looked back toward the door, at his rifle, then at the red. He wasn't ready to face the world behind them.

"I guess it's our call," Arnold said.

"I guess it is… I don't think we have a choice. We engage."

A *crack* rang throughout the room. David turned as Arnold followed. They came into view of the now glowing red tube as it cracked, then shattered, releasing a cloud of steam. A decrepit man in black scrubs hung from wires as the steam cleared. He wheezed and twitched.

"Maybe releasing yourself wasn't such a good idea," David commented, then fired one bullet at the Super Subject's forehead. The bullet struck home, his head jerked, and his body went limp… but only for a few seconds. Then he raised his head again, unscathed. His forehead showed no damage.

"I thought you'd paid more attention to General Mathias' description of what we could do," the Super Subject commented, then he grabbed one of the wires attached to him.

The server room went dark. All the monitors shut off, and all the machines stopped humming. The room temperature dropped from a mere chill to frigid, tending toward meat-locker cold.

"Bail, the correct choice was bail!" David shouted as he flipped his rifle flashlight on, and both he and Arnold sprinted toward the closest door. As they ran, David heard more wires snapping behind him. He kicked the door open, and Arnold slammed it shut behind them.

They weren't in the stasis room with the Last Subjects, but the dimly lit hallway with glass doors along the wall. They ran through the hallway as a chill followed in their wake, like the gust front of an arctic storm. The lighting dimmed in the offices, no doubt from the Super Subject draining their power.

"We turned the wrong way," David huffed as they turned the corner to the right.

"That's not our biggest problem at the moment. General, come in, do you copy?" Arnold said into the radio, then slowed to a jog for a second, waiting for a response.

"Just because I've escaped the tube doesn't mean I let go of my connection," the Super Subject responded with a sharper tone and more energetic voice. He sounded more than eager; he sounded... *entertained.*

"We're on our own," David mumbled as he pulled the radio out of his ear and dropped it on the ground. "The general will likely know something is wrong, but if I were him, I'd send a couple of two-thousand-pound JDAMs and call it settled."

"Yeah, but would that be enough?"

"Hell, how should I know? Maybe he'll use a tactical nuke. It won't matter to us; we'll be dust in the wind. We have to get far away from here, and fast."

A monitor flickered to life. The Super Subject's face, looking younger now, and with a full head of black hair, commented, "They never got around to testing whether I could absorb the blast of a missile faster than it'd obliterate me. I'm curious if it will work."

David shot the monitor twice and said, "Is your radio still on? We've got to get this guy out of our comms."

He looked around the hallway, saw a blinking red light, and shot it, as well. "I hope that was a camera."

Arnold pulled out the radio and flipped it off. "We need to find some kind of computer that thing hasn't compromised, and I should be able to reset the system so he loses access. Without the laptop, it will be more difficult, though."

"That sounds like a good plan," the Super Subject said. He stood against the back corner of the hallway. David and Arnold jerked their rifles and shot a few rounds, knocking him back to the ground, but the Super Subject stood up, strolled to the center of the hallway, glared at Arnold, then lunged at them as David and Arnold stepped backward.

They shot him again, but the Super Subject wasn't stunned by their shots this time and grabbed Arnold by the face. David fell back, his face out of reach, and the Super Subject instead grabbed his plated left arm.

The power suit made a small *zap* sound as its weight on David increased. David fumbled for the emergency release on the suit, but his muscle memory failed him as he watched Arnold go limp.

"More," the Super Subject whispered. He turned to David and let go of Arnold, and the body fell to the ground, then he thrust his hand at David. David stopped reaching for the release and instead drew his combat knife and stabbed the Super Subject in the forearm as the fingers brushed the hairs on David's neck.

* * * * *

Chapter 3

The Super Subject howled, wrenched his arm back, and the knife tore through his flesh. He lunged, and his fingers clawed for a grip on David's power suit, but David was faster… he slammed his hand into the emergency manual override. The suit's back plating hissed and blew open. David tumbled out of the chassis, tucked into a somersault, and sprang to his feet with his combat knife leveled.

Cradling his mangled right arm, the Super Subject spat a curse, his eyes burning with a predatory glow. The wound was visibly healing, so David didn't hesitate; he lunged back in and aimed for a killing blow before the monster could recover. But the Subject dropped low, sweeping the floor with his left hand until he found Arnold's discarded rifle.

David saw the muzzle rising and bolted. He rounded the corner, just ahead of a burst of gunfire that shattered the glass door.

The shots weren't even close. A flash of relief hit David. The man, the Super Subject, wasn't left-handed, and he clearly hadn't been trained on an assault platform.

How could you kill somebody who took a shot to the brain and acted like it was a mosquito bite? Instinct told him that if he was going to survive, he'd better figure that out damned quick.

David debated a re-engagement, but his boots kept moving him backward. He forced himself to think rationally: he only had one chance to get lucky with a knife. The Super Subject had a dozen chances left in that magazine, and God only knew how many more once he found David's rifle.

The rattle of metal echoed through the hall as the Super Subject scavenged the abandoned power suit. The rifle was the only thing that mattered now. A quick retreat back into the server room offered the only cover, but the transition to total darkness was instantaneous. Searching for a light source proved useless once the heavy doors sealed, cutting off the final sliver of hall's light.

Memory was the only map left. The path he and Arnold had taken was somewhere to the left, a direction found only by trailing fingers along cold equipment. Then the doors slammed open. A dive behind a dead server bank was the only thing that saved David from the blind spray of gunfire. One bullet shrieked against the metal casing inches from his ear.

"Come out, come out, army man."

The voice sounded jagged and thin. Crawling down the aisle, David cursed the missed chance for an ambush at the door. Every movement had to be measured by the feel of the equipment until he reached the corner and turned.

Silence followed. The Subject had stopped moving, leaving only the sound of David's pulse. It was a grim realization just how short-sighted this monster was that he must have drained the tactical lights on the rifles before entering the server room. Only after several minutes of blind crawling did a faint glow appear through a distant doorway. Knife ready, David rose and moved toward the light.

The transition through the door was silent. This wasn't the stasis room, but a short, isolated hallway leading to a single office. No red security lights illuminated this wing. Whether the Subject was slowed by his injuries or the area was simply off the grid didn't matter.

A quick dash led to the door, which was marked DIRECTOR SEAN NIET. Inside, the room was a graveyard of dust and yellowed paper. While there was no radio to be found, a tablet sat on the desk, still tethered to a wall port. It held a charge. One tap of the screen revealed a letter, fueled by decades-old fury, addressed directly to General Mathias.

Niet had been livid when the project was shut down. The text was a frantic warning: the early subjects were walking disasters. Stasis was a temporary fix, at best, and the doctor had zero confidence in how long those pods would actually hold.

Why was killing them not on the table?

The letter continued, stating that the army's biggest mistake in ending the project was that he was breaking through and creating stable subjects. The letter said that they would be in the white scrubs. David reread that part.

Can I trust this? This is a stupid idea. It might get me help. His mind jumbled with thoughts, and he decided, *If that freak is blocking me from reaching the general to stop a possible strike, then maybe they'll at least give me a chance to flank him, because I doubt that even with the Jeep, I can get far enough away in time, depending on what artillery might be on the way.*

The server room again swallowed David. A left turn, while a steady hand against the wall provided the only guidance toward the next exit. Beyond the first door sat a useless janitorial closet, but the second swung open to reveal the stasis room.

The Super Subject was already there. Both hands were clamped onto a stasis tube, his fingers siphoning the life from the occupant inside until the body went limp. David reached for his knife but froze. Crude armor now protected the monster. Pieces of the discarded power suits had been strapped over his torso and thighs. The fit was awkward, yet the plates covered exactly what David needed to hit. A clean strike was impossible. A failed attempt would put David within reach of that lethal, energy-draining touch.

Survival demanded a different path. Retreating into the shadows, David slipped away in the opposite direction. If the Super Subject intended to harvest every soul in the facility, the only hope lay in finding a specific tube. He needed someone in white scrubs who might actually know how to shut this nightmare down.

"It's a real shame they saw us as failures," the Super Subject said. David shifted to a defensive stance, but the Super Subject hadn't turned around. "I guess the bigger shame is that most of you decided what they thought mattered!"

The Super Subject punched the stasis tube, and it cracked. Fluid leaked from the cracks. The Super Subject looked at his hand, now bleeding.

"Whoops, I guess I'll just have to fix that," he said. David stiffened upright behind a foggy stasis pod, pointing the knife down, and hoped this flimsy cover was still cover enough.

The Super Subject walked in the other direction. "Oh, I remember you. You had such faith in Dr. Neat… Neit…? The loser. Look where that got you."

David wiped the condensation from the tube. This one wore gray scrubs and was also dead. Then a loud *crack* echoed through the room. David almost jumped, but glanced out and witnessed the Super Subject draining the life and power out of the stasis tube and the person in it.

The monitors flickered around the room, but no image materialized. David squeezed his hilt as he dashed to another tube and hid behind it. He wiped away the condensation again to see gray scrubs on another corpse.

The Super Subject wiped the blood from his hands, and there were no cuts on them, then he looked up at the monitors. "A part of me is going to miss being all-seeing in this building. It's just a shame that it won't be useful for much longer. Oh, and you—"

David tensed, as he was midway between stasis tubes, but the Super Subject was looking at another stasis tube.

"—I know you said over and over that you didn't want to die in this 'hellhole,' but I have tragic news."

Another *zap* rang out through the room as David checked two more pods, both gray scrubs.

"Not quite there yet," the Super Subject whined. "Never quite there. Well, we come to you, then, the one who wanted a purpose from all this. The pride and joy that gave Neat optimism."

David stopped; the odds of Dr. Niet having optimism for anyone not in white scrubs were way too low. His mind scrambled for a plan as he started moving toward the Super Subject.

"I have something I want you to know," the Super Subject told the pod. "I spent decades connected to a supercomputer, and I figured it all out. The purpose is to stay alive as long as possible, by any means necessary. We have that capability. We could outlast everyone else, maybe *everything else*, but you… no, you all!… were too afraid to leave their shadows. They… they had the right to dictate our interests because we were 'dangerous' to others. Well, who we are and who they are doesn't matter. There's surviving, and there's not, and you're—"

"You killed my friend!" David shouted. He couldn't get into melee range in time, so he gave up the element of surprise.

"I did, didn't I?"

"Do you have a name?" David called out. Anything to stall.

"A name? Why, yes, I think I do. I don't remember it, but at one time, I knew it. It doesn't help with the hunger. Maybe someday that'll be something for me to investigate."

"Happy to help. How about repaying me by letting me go?"

"The price is too high. Instead, I'll limit your suffering when I kill you."

"Like you did Arnold?"

"No, I'm afraid he suffered a great deal."

The Super Subject nodded, his gaze lingering on David's knife before he raised the rifle. David dove behind a stasis tube just as the weapon erupted. Bullets ricocheted off the reinforced glass with high-pitched pings until the firing stopped, replaced by the hollow *click* of an empty chamber. David wiped a layer of frost from the glass and saw another body in gray scrubs. This one was also dead.

When David peeked around the side, the Super Subject threw the useless rifle aside and charged. David darted to the right. His eyes scanned the base of the nearby tubes for an emergency release. Training had taught him that such mechanisms were usually at the bottom for easy access during power failures, but these models were ancient. He had to find a lever or a switch before the monster closed the gap.

The Subject rounded the tube. David pivoted and sprinted left, keeping his head on a swivel to track his pursuer. The weight of the scavenged power armor was finally slowing the creature down. Noticing the loss in momentum, the Subject grabbed a passing tube and drained the energy from both the machine and the occupant. His speed returned instantly.

A small switch finally appeared at the base of a nearby unit. David kept moving, searching for a way to buy enough time to circle back and flip it. A vat marked with a hazardous warning sat against the far wall. Without hesitation, David dashed toward it and hurled his knife. The blade pierced the connecting line. A thick cloud of steam hissed into the room. David vanished into the white mist and hoped the vapor wasn't lethal.

*****

Chapter 4

It wasn't dangerous, but it felt warm. David looked behind him as the silhouette of the Super Subject slowed down.

"Hide and seek again?" the Super Subject asked. "Maybe you didn't think through this whole vengeance thing…"

David walked as fast as he could manage without making noise.

"I don't blame you, though," the Super Subject continued, and another *zap* echoed through the room. "I mean, I get it. When your buddy dies, you're supposed to do something about it, right? We all want to tell ourselves we're the brave boys on our best behavior, which naturally means the best in the world, but in the end, nothing beats staying alive."

David slowed down and glanced over his shoulder, twitching his lip, but said nothing, then broke into a full sprint toward the pod. When he reached it, he did a quick wipe, saw white, then kicked the button. Nothing happened.

Shit, he thought, *No, no, no. Why?*

He dug through his mind, searching as fast as he could for the process of stasis release. He knew it, he knew it, he knew it… but couldn't remember!

"Come on out," the Super Subject said. His voice was distant, but he was moving in David's direction. "Or not. The cover-up squad your 'comrade' called in is bound to fly by pretty soon, so either way, you're not leaving here alive. At least with me, you can try to rationalize that you died being a hero. Because I'm the bad guy, you know? They turned me into this, but *I'm* the evil one."

Then David remembered, *There's a second step!* David searched around the tube and found a box. A monitor flickered on, displaying the Super Subject's face, "And what are you doing back over here?"

David grabbed the box and yanked it open. Inside sat a heavy lever. He pulled it down and then slammed it back up. The Super Subject's silhouette emerged from the thick mist just as the stasis tube exploded. Reinforced glass split and hissed through the air in opposite directions while the stasis fluid flooded the floor.

One of the heavy shards slammed into David. The impact threw him backward into a neighboring tube, knocking the wind from his lungs and sending a jagged spike of pain through his spine. He slid down the glass, his feet catching just enough to keep him upright, but a pained wheeze escaped his throat. The blow had done something terrible to his internal frame.

Standing among the jagged remains of the shattered pod was a pale woman with long, silver hair. She reached out, gripped a loose wire dangling from the ceiling of her tube, and took a deep, shivering breath.

"Well, well, well," the Super Subject taunted, "I'm surpr—"

The woman walked out of the stasis tube and slapped the Super Subject, who staggered backward.

"They only thought we were dangerous because *you* were so dangerous," she told him, walking in his direction. "I should have killed you when I had the chance."

The Super Subject's playful mood vanished, replaced by a cold rage his features couldn't contain.

"You never *had* the chance, nor the ability. I was isolated from you on purpose."

"Well, aren't you just holier-than-thou? Don't downplay the fact that the others acted closer to me. That *you're* closer to me than you'll admit. Maybe they didn't see the world exactly the way I do, but they sure acted like it. Not that it matters anymore."

She looked around the room. All the stasis tubes not obscured by the fog were now dark. The woman shook her head.

"Why?"

The Super Subject shrugged, "I was hungry and a little bored."

The woman took a lungful of air and charged. She slammed into the Super Subject and clamped her hands around his throat. His skin began to turn a sickly blue, but he managed to stomp down on her foot with a heavy power boot. She screamed as he pried her fingers away. The color drained from her pale hands as the blue tint began to claim her instead.

"Not strong enough," he gasped, forcing her down.

David threw his weight into the Super Subject from behind and tackled him to the floor. He grabbed the Subject's wrists and forced those lethal hands back onto the monster's own face. The Subject tensed and let out a scream that quickly dissolved into a wet gargle. He fought to break David's grip, but the struggle grew faint and then ceased. After thirty seconds, the body went limp.

David let go and stared at hands he could no longer feel. He collapsed to the floor beside the corpse, his lungs burning. The woman moved to his side as he struggled for air.

"I need you to stick with me," she said.

"Rai… Ra… radio," David sputtered.

"Okay, sure, but first…"

The woman reached down and pressed her palm against David's chest. His breathing grew heavy as she looked him in the eye.

"This will probably hurt."

David's entire body began to warm. He gasped at the sensation. The heat became agonizing, but as the temperature peaked, the sharp pain in his chest flared once and then vanished. He sat up, lungs pulling in air as he tried to steady his racing heart.

"You're nowhere near well, but that should give you enough strength to walk and talk."

"What did you do to me?"

"I shared some of my nanites, and they've gone to work, fixing what they can."

"You can do that?"

"Yes, and so could that asshole, but he'd never do it willingly. That's what makes him… *made* him… so hard to kill."

"We can't leave. General Mathias is most likely going to bomb this building because—" David pulled his leg off the Super Subject's corpse "—he knows that guy escaped containment."

The woman sighed. "Mathias? Shit. Can you stop it?"

"I don't know. Maybe. We need to get to the radio on the other side of the server room."

"Let's go."

The woman pulled David to his feet, and they both limped through the server room and made their way to Arnold's body. He paused for a moment, staring down at the dead man.

"Were you close?"

"No, I hardly knew him. That doesn't help, though."

He snapped back to the task at hand, grabbed the radio control, and turned it back on, hoping the asshole hadn't drained it of power.

"General Mathias, this is Sergeant Ozle. Come in, General. All threats eliminated. Site secured, I repeat, site secured."

"Holy hell," General Mathias responded. *"And just in time, too. What happened?"*

"Sir, one of the subjects broke loose, killed Sergeant Mitchell, and drained most of the facility of power. The records server will need to be evaluated by someone who can restore power to it. I won't be able to get shit off it without power or Sergeant Mitchell."

"Damn, well, we'll have to get a full team in there, then. What of the other test subjects?"

The woman went wide-eyed and shook her head. David muted the radio and said, "You could help stop a lot of bad things from happening. Help us get retribution against a lot of terrible people."

"Don't you get it? The ones who did this *are* the terrible people!"

"I don't know, this is all new to me. I just know what's going on out there in the world outside."

"I'm not some sort of killing machine like that asshole was," she said, pointing back in the direction of the Super Subject. Then she pointed at the radio. "And that asshole there, the best-case scenario is I'm either shoved back into a tube, or tweaked until I'm just as insane as the others were. I don't want to be that. Please don't make me be that."

David looked down at Arnold, then up at her.

"Do you remember your name?"

"Claire."

"Sergeant, are you there? What's going on? Do I call off the strike or not?"

"Sorry, sir, technical glitch. Yes, sir, call it off. As to the others, I'm unsure. The one who got loose killed what I believe to be all the other subjects. I didn't check them all, though. I did manage to find a squatter living in the warehouse. We missed her on our first sweep because she hid until the power went on the fritz."

Claire glared at David, but also tilted her head in confusion.

"Why?" she mouthed. David muted the radio again.

"Look, we'll need your help. I believe you're right. If I tell General Mathias what you are, you won't be able to help. But I can't just let you wander out the door to die or whatever in the desert. You can use what they did for you for things other than violence, and I'd rather have that than nothing. If you want to help, this is how you get back without being shoved into another stasis tube."

Mathias interrupted them again.

"Thank you, Sergeant, and good work. Shame about Mitchell. Bring the squatter back to base to be evaluated. If she passes, we'll figure out a work program to put her into. I'll get another team together to see if they can salvage this operation, but in the meantime, you're ordered to return to base with the 'squatter' for a full debrief."

"I'll try, sir, but she may have escaped during the fight. The situation was pretty chaotic."

"All right, well, bring her if you can. Now get back here. The follow-on team can take care of Mitchell."

"If it's all the same, General, I'd just as soon bring him back with me. He died fighting."

"Very well. And again, good work."

"Yes, sir. Over and out."

David pulled the earpiece out of his ear and tucked it into a pocket, then grabbed Arnold's dog tags.

"He's not going to rot here," David said as he grabbed Arnold under the arms, then turned back to Claire. "I need your help. Am I going to regret this?"

Claire thought for a few seconds, then grabbed Arnold's feet, "I don't know, what's your plan?"

"I'll bring you as close as I can and drop you there. I have a feeling you'll know how to survive."

Claire helped carry Arnold to the elevator in silence. As the elevator door opened, she finally responded, "I think so. And who knows, maybe I can figure out how to help them."

"You'd do that?"

"I don't know, but maybe."

"Good, then maybe this was all worth it. I'd like to think Mitchell's death had a reason."

The elevator closed. They took Arnold back to the Jeep and left for home.

"Death rarely has a reason," she said from the passenger seat, "but we can try to keep their deaths from being in vain."

* * * * *

Author Bio

Andrew Waldron is a paralegal by day and a fiction author by night. He has a degree in Fiction Writing and Philosophy from the University of Arkansas at Little Rock, has taught fiction writing basics at conventions for years, and is a co-writer for the Gaming Sins Patreon. He lives in Little Rock and has a penchant for gaming, karaoke, and trivia.

# # # # #

By a Thread by
Dave Appleby & Robert E. Hampson
A Frontier Killchain Story

Chapter 1

Earth Geosynchronous Orbit

From any given starting point, 36,000 kilometers is a bloody long way, especially when that distance is straight down.

The ugly Blue Steel Mk VII SSTO transport that had deposited them was now undocking. With barely visible puffs from the thrusters, it maneuvered into a position to drop into a declining transfer orbit that would allow it to intercept the re-entry gate.

The team was hanging upside down—well, it felt that way—below the geosynchronous midpoint station of the almost completed Otis Two orbital lift. The team—Lt. Hegarty, along with Master Sergeant Steph East, Corporal James (never Jamie) Ibson, and Corporal Jon Sinclair—was about to do something that had only been tested in simulations. Something dumb, something stupid, and as far as Hegarty was concerned, the worst bit of all was that he'd volunteered. *It's just an abseil; you like abseiling, don't you?* said one internal voice. *Yes,* said another, *just not* that *bloody far.*

He took a few seconds to double-check that his line clamps were attached to the chestplate and knee coupling, and that his fingers were clear of the release trigger. Then, he looked at the other three. Golden self-tinting faceplates reflected his image, but the lightweight suits allowed him to see the affirmative nods; he nodded back, grinning behind his visor, held out a finger on his spare hand, and pointed downward. Then, as he collapsed his hand into a fist, he pulled the descender trigger and dropped a long, long way.

* * *

Three Days Earlier
0.190, 82.708—Due South of Sri Lanka, Indian Ocean

Dr. Nisansala Jayasurya, director of the largest boron nitride nanotube (BNNT) project yet, was close to panic. Jayasurya's baby, the Otis Two floating surface anchor and port for the tether up to the second space station being installed in geosynchronous orbit, was fine. The BNNT tether appeared to be holding strong, and the space elevator hadn't been completed yet.

The smart watch on her right wrist had other ideas, though, and it was blaring an alert, which *had* to be a system error. She charged down the two flights of stairs from the management deck, heading to the operations control room as fast as she could. Rounding a corner badly, she smacked her elbow on the railing, igniting a mini supernova of pain. Swearing, she continued at full pelt along the short, straight corridor toward the operations hub. Seeing that she wouldn't be able to stop in time, security rapidly broke protocol and pulled the door open for her microseconds before she hit it. Crashing through onto the large platform overlooking the control room, she scanned the room, spotted the figure she wanted, and yelled at the top of her lungs, not bothering to activate local comms.

"Gerry, Otis One Telemetry, full system, now! Ada, online, please!"

"Already on-screen, Director." Geraldine James waved her hand toward the four giant screens dominating the room. Ada, the local AI, then joined in with a quiet, "Online, Director."

"OK, sorry. Overview, please. You're a couple of minutes ahead of me."

"Right." Gerry James's voice sounded rattled. "About five minutes ago, Otis One's Hub switched its telemetry and sent it directly to us. There was no explanation, contact, or response to direct calls. We've tried calling all the senior management but haven't received a response from anyone. Terry is working his way through the staff list with Ada's help, but, as yet, no joy. Ada has flagged an anomaly in their tether data. Look at this."

Gerry waved a hand through her screen, selecting datasets and mirroring them on the main display. "Ninety seconds after the data transfer, this started." She pointed, and the screen automatically highlighted her gesture. On the screen, a box enlarged. Jayasurya knew what she was seeing but couldn't, for her life, fathom *why* she was seeing it.

Two-and-a-bit minutes after the data feed started, there was a single oscillation spike lasting just under a second; its frequency was way lower than the rising oscillations, but higher than the sea state could account for. Then it hit her, and she started to shake badly, so badly it took three tries to get Gerry on her comms.

"Gerry, Condition One lockdown now; warn Bashir it's..."

Then the gunfire started.

* * *

Bashir wouldn't be answering. His deputy, Lt. Hegerty, grasped Bashir's hand as his commanding officer wheezed, "Lock down and get clear. That's an order, my friend—no last stands or anything stupid. Keep the Hub safe. Condition One, understand? Condition One."

Hegarty knew, from the speed at which they'd come under assault, that the situation outside was hopeless and pulling back was his only move. "Got it, boss. 'Til Valhalla."

"Until Valhalla, indeed. Keep them safe. Find out where we went wrong, and Ralph… kill them all."

"I will, I promise. Sleep well, boss."

As Bashir's eyes grayed out and went dull, Hegarty felt a lump appear in his throat and move down, first an iron clamp on his heart, then lower with the sudden urge to vomit. Retribution would follow like a hammer blow, but not today. Conscious of the blistering incoming fire, he started a retreat toward the nearest emergency evacuation slide; after checking that the Hub was C1, he initiated a five-minute *sauve-qui-peut* order to the remainder of the team, which beaconed his position in their combat monocles. His own flashed a green count as troops acknowledged; it stopped at four plus three yellow for wounded out of forty.

* * *

In the Hub, Jayasurya's intuition had kicked in just in time. Everybody felt their ears pop as heavy, quad-layered tungsten-cobalt sandwich blast doors slammed down in the Hub and up and around the tether base, communications were isolated from the rest of the platform, and power switched from external solar and wave to local fusion. The Otis Two Hub isolation zone—the Kettle—was now isolated, self-sufficient for two weeks, and virtually impregnable. *Hopefully…*

"Gerry, do we still have Otis One telemetry?" Gerry looked backward at the director's office and flashed a thumbs-up. "OK, good; please start a harmonic frequency versus structural integrity plot. I think someone's trying to sever the tethers. I suspect the attacks were supposed to be simultaneous, but the timing got screwed. I take it Terry had no joy contacting their Hub?"

"Nothing yet. He's working parallel to Ada via the old RF stuff; static on the Colombo and Geneva links, as well."

"So… okay, get everyone inside the Kettle in here fast. We need to talk about options. I'm assuming the distress torpedo went out?"

"Yep, automatically, as soon as C1 was triggered. It's five miles away already, another fifteen to go, and then she surfaces and starts screaming like a baby."

"Anything from Major Bashir and security?"

"It's bad; Hegarty put out a *sauve-qui-peut* and fallback position map, so they're gone, one way or another."

* * *

Except they weren't. Hegarty was holding his FAL TMAL rifle in one hand, dragging an injured Marine sergeant by the back of her harness, the Marine herself, devoid of FAL, covering the rear with a mag pistol in her right hand, whilst the left clamped down on a bloody leg wound. Two more Marines were all that remained of the elite UNETPROFOR security section.

Hegarty saw the portside number three evacuation slide directly ahead, and dug deeper, mentally and physically, for a last-ditch effort. He hurled himself, plus casualty, forward toward the yellow-and-red striped hatchway. As he reached for the big red button, he was suddenly thrown closer by a blow to his back in the vicinity of his right kidney, and then the burn started. Seconds later, he heard a *buzz-wheeet* sound, and he felt a punch to the head, followed by a lurch to the side as the world grayed out; falling, he heard the *whooshhh* of an evac-slide inflating, then, as his consciousness finally fled, a feeling of floating on air.

* * *

"Director, ops panel thirteen just activated." Gerry moved the display across. "Evac-slide deployed forward to port, countdown active, and… escape hydrofoil away."

"Our people, or attackers?"

"Ours, definitely."

"Good, at least someone's away. Do we have anything on external cameras? I want to know who or what we're dealing with out there. Get the corpsman here, too. I need to know our casualty figures. Otis One?"

"Bad. I've put Toni on it full-time. Tether integrity is already compromised, and BNNT bonds are fracturing. It's exponential and probably beyond saving. We're seeing multiple acoustic pings indicating that individual threads are breaking. She's gone; it's just a question of how long."

"Understood. How long?"

"From fracture, nothing for two minutes, then the midpoint and counter will drift. The tether itself will start climbing east. The Earth's end will be outside the mesosphere in seventeen minutes and twenty-two seconds; it's heading at a tangent somewhere a long way from us. Toni can sim it."

"No need." Toni stood up slowly, grim-faced and looking far older than her 26 years. "Twenty minutes maximum. Gerry's two minutes are possibly on the generous side; I calculate that the first upward movement may occur within ten seconds."

"So, no danger earthside?"

"No, thank gods; if the break were higher, we'd be looking at gift-wrapping the world; their spider's locked, so it's going with it. Our spider's locked, too, at just under eleven hundred kilometers."

"Okay, nothing we can do except monitor; next, Comms?"

"Nothing except the Otis One feed. The internal PA will still work, but the external is dead. Well, we can't hear anything, anyway. I imagine every channel is full of people screaming for attention."

"Do we have any casualty figures yet? Ours or Otis One?"

"I can help there, Director," Ada's voice interjected. "Monitors indicate no living members of the crew outside our lockdown area; at least two hundred recorded deaths according to the biometric monitor. An unknown number of intruders are aboard. No docking clamps have been activated. No aircraft have been detected within the hundred-kilometer bubble. I have no information at present on the crew of Otis One."

"Two hundred? My gods." Jayasurya slumped back into her chair. "So, we're on our own here then…"

"Not necessarily. The torpedo has the data dump, and we have an escape boat out."

"What the fuck is happening?" Heads turned at the director's unaccustomed swearing. "Just who are we dealing with?"

* * *

In the hub, the comms came alive with a *blert* of static and a *pop*, all eyes turning to the speakers.

"Good afternoon, Ladies and Gentlemen. I am Commander One of La Tierra Primero, and I am now in control of Otis Two. I trust our demonstration with Otis One has your full attention." She checked her watch. "Otis One has five minutes left before it tears itself apart; the same need not be true of Otis Two. We have forty-three hostages from the platform, plus the operations team in the Hub. Pay attention: no air, sea, or subsea vehicles will approach within 100 kilometers of the platform; any infringement will be met with overwhelming force. I will open comms and speak first; please refrain from histrionics or attempting to interject.

"Is Dr. Jayasurya online in the Hub? Geneva Orbital Control should be patched in, as well. Am I correct? Please confirm once, Hub first."

"This is Jayasurya; we hear you."

*****

Chapter 2

27.118, 70.729—Thar Desert, 500 Km West of Jaipur

The pain was the first sensation he felt, and as his body started reporting in again, the second and third. Hegarty's head had a small, red-hot ingot burning at the center, alongside a spine that was throbbing with agony. *Odd,* he thought, *I don't remember being kicked by a Clydesdale; shot, yes, draft horse no.* Also, he couldn't recall why his left wrist felt as if it were being squeezed hard in a vice. Summoning strength he really didn't have, he opened his eyes a fraction and managed only a hoarse croak.

"Welcome back, Lazarus," a familiar voice said. "I'd ask how you're feeling, but I genuinely don't want to listen to the usual macho bullshit you spout." He felt a straw pushed gently into the corner of his mouth and gratefully sucked in the cool water; then he painfully opened his eyes fully.

"Nice to see you too, Sergeant East. I'm assuming I'm not dead?"

"Nope, my management of your personal hell will be much, much more inventive than this. I'm thinking stone-cold haggis, neeps, and tatties, accompanied by the *Address to the Haggis* on an endless loop."

"That's all Scottish."

"Exactly. The Welshman in you will suffer endless torment in the *Serious Burns Unit*."

* * *

0.190, 82.708—Due South of Sri Lanka, Indian Ocean

The feed on the main screens in the Hub and Geneva Control was sickening. They displayed stained decking, patches, pools of dried blood, and smear marks where the dead had been dragged overboard. The hostages, now at gunpoint, were sitting, thankfully, in the shade of the tilt-rotor pad, terrified. Three masked terrorists stood before them, weapons holstered for now, but holsters open.

"The two hours I promised are up. We'll execute our guests unless you stream our manifesto worldwide over every available channel. This will continue until we're satisfied that dissemination is complete.

"By now, you should have the UN Space Council, Security Council, and the secretary general looped." The voice was sickening in its cheeriness. "Hello, everyone, are you all having as magnificent a day as La Tierra Primero is? Firstly, a deadline: you have thirty-six hours to meet our demands, not one second longer. After that, the first hostage dies. It won't be merciful; we'll perform a little bloodletting and throw them overboard. The *Selachii* will get a second, third, or fourth dinner; you get the idea."

The feed panned across the hostages, now looking sick at the thought of being chum for a bull or tiger shark. "La Tierra Primero is dedicated to the future of humanity and its safety; therefore, the UN will agree to enact and enforce a policy limiting human space operations to Earth orbit. The power sats, the null-G factories, and the system mining operations may continue. Otis Two will be decommissioned immediately; orbital operations will be supported only by standard shuttles and freighters, and no further extra-atmospheric mega-engineering projects will be tolerated.

"The UN Space Council will be disbanded immediately, and a new standing committee formed consisting of ourselves, members of the support agencies, and a citizen representative from each non-space-faring country; I trust we are clear. You have thirty-six hours starting now. Oh, and should anyone think of taking control back later, La Tierra Primero has already thought of that. If we can bring down the tethers, imagine what we can do with Descartes Base on Luna, or the orbital solar farms. La Tierra Primero, out."

In the Hub, Geneva, and New York, all hell broke loose.

* * *

27.118, 70.729—Thar Desert, 500 Km West of Jaipur

Hegarty itched all over, although most of the pain was gone. The nanite injection East had administered was working fast. Already, the swelling in his wrist had reduced by half, and the pain around his kidney was gone. His head, however, was another matter; the nanites were working, but skull and brain injuries always took longer—a fact he was all too aware of, having vowed never to ski again.

UNETPROFOR HQ was situated in one of the extraterritorial areas they managed and protected. The Thar Desert, along with forty additional solar power plants and thirty-six power sat microwave downlinks on Earth, was their responsibility, along with security for all orbital and extra-orbital operations, plus the two Otis tethers. The Thar facility was chosen as the headquarters site purely because it was equidistant from the other earthside sites. It was home to the thirty-five thousand men and women tasked with protecting the chokepoints that kept Earth alive, from power to specialized drugs produced only in the orbital factories, to the mineral wealth from the asteroid belt. The force had a huge remit and a great deal of responsibility.

"Screw this; I'm not sitting here with my thumb up my arse whilst someone, heaven forbid, actually makes a decision on an action plan. Steph, Jon, one of you, find out where Jamie is, then meet me at range two-two-bravo in an hour. If James isn't on base, Steph, ask nicely, bribe, then threaten, in that order, until someone gets him here. I know he's on planet, so I want him here ASAP, twelve hours maximum. I need to shoot off a couple hundred rounds—stress relief and to toughen up the wrist some. Then we grab a big jug of coffee, and we're going to put together an OPLAN to get Otis Two back. You in?"

East looked disappointed. "You have to ask? Of course we're in. I outrank Jon, so he agrees, too."

Sinclair had a broad grin on his face. "So, inserted thumb removed, sir?"

"Indeed, Jon, indeed. Next thing going up someone's arse will be my US size-ten, steel-toecap when they get in my way."

East laughed. "Any idea whose arse?"

"You'll know when I do; add it to your threat list!"

"One hour, two-two-bravo, move people."

Sinclair turned to East with a wry grin. "You know, I almost prefer him unconscious, much nicer personality."

* * *

Hegarty headed to the basement range. Unusually, the room was empty, all twenty bays free. He checked out a Glock 41 and grabbed several standard targets. After taking a lane, running out the target, and loading the caseless electrically fired rounds into the magazine, he took a two-handed grip, focused on the target, and loosed three quick rounds.

Not bad; the wrist is holding well, if painful.

He switched to a single-handed grip, the same three rounds. Sore, but bearable.

Ok, he decided, *kill-or-cure time.*

The nanites should respond to the recoil stresses and actively toughen the muscles, bone, and tendons. Officially, this was frowned upon, but any injured soldier knew the technique would strengthen the injury site. He brought the weapon up fast and emptied the magazine. His wrist screamed at the abuse, but the pain started to fade almost as soon as he lowered the weapon. By the time the third magazine was empty, the pain was lessened. By the time the power pack was down to 50 shots remaining, the pain was gone.

"Nice grouping, especially given the wrist damage earlier."

He turned to find Colonel Ian Lamont a few feet behind him. Roughly Hegarty's height and in his mid-fifties, Lamont looked more the part of an elder statesman rather than an incredibly experienced officer.

Hegarty automatically drew himself to attention, but his salute was cut short by Lamont waving it down.

"Ralph, you need to rein in Sergeant East a bit. She got a bit heated down in comms—even chewed me out." Lamont raised an eyebrow. "Did I somehow miss her being bumped to Earth supreme field marshal, or maybe God?"

"No, sir." Hegarty couldn't suppress his smile. "She's acting on my orders, and I told her to be err… positive."

"You're thinking about running an op. Hopefully, my omission was merely a minor breakdown in communications?" Lamont's expression changed from bemused to a pointed stare. "I give you a lot of leeway in how things get done; however, I insist on knowing *what* is being planned, preferably *before* you execute it!"

"Not an op… yet. Just… skull sweat. We both know the UN is going to fuck around for days, and hostages will start to die."

"Very well. I have us a room, plus all the information so far. Sinclair and East are going over it now. Ibson is due in ninety minutes—he was in the Antarctic, and will probably love the chance to warm up."

Hegarty could see that Lamont agreed with his threat assessment, but obviously couldn't yet commit. They both expected the UN to bluster and attempt every psychological negotiation tactic ever written.

They both also knew it would fail.

* * *

0.190, 82.708—Due South of Sri Lanka, Indian Ocean

"Mother is empty, all cargo out and being rigged as we speak. We'll be done in forty minutes." Two looked pleased as he passed on the status report. "Seven and Twelve are completing a review of the tether shroud and Kettle armor. Neither looked hopeful; they can't climb the shroud, a second perimeter has been added to the Kettle, and we have no idea what's been grafted on as additional passive or active security in between. Seven says it'll take three days to get inside, and Twelve is more pessimistic; she says at least a week, provided, of course, we can get a handle on the defenses."

"How did we miss the changes? This shouldn't have happened, especially given the money, err… *invested* in data gathering. It's a major intel screwup from Control One. Assuming we live, I'll question that oversight with it personally. Our defenses?"

"Our anti-air is covering air-to-surface and anti-submarine roles. Six is currently using a plasma torch on the control feeds for the local defenses. Picket mines are already deployed at the ten-kilometer mark, sitting passively at sixty meters."

"How long?"

"Twelve hours, no more. It'll be stealth air or subsurface."

"OK, my schedule for the first hostage death remains. We need to kill the first probe decisively and then do nothing. I want them to believe we're not prepared to kill a hostage. That'll make the first more shocking. Are we set for broadcast?"

"Absolutely, we need two minutes' notice. The team from Mother has patched into the backbone, and we can override at any time."

"Good. Twelve hours sounds about right; seeing what they bring to the party will be interesting."

*****

Chapter 3

Inside the Hub, it was calm. Once the staff knew the extent of the damage the intruders had caused, they set out to turn the tables.

"Ada, where do we stand?" Jayasurya looked up at the ceiling, as they all did when talking to the AI.

"I have evaluated the whole playbook plus another 2,604 alternative plans, or variations thereof. There is nothing that generates more than a 6.1 percent chance of success; additionally, anything over 4.2 percent involves the death of everyone aboard, including myself."

"Right, everyone, listen up," Jayasurya announced. "You'll grasp the situation, even though we've only covered it over two days of training. I expect us all to work toward a solution. Just because Ada can't think of anything doesn't mean human ingenuity can't pull a rabbit out of the hat. If anyone has an idea, speak to Gerry or me first. If you want to test a theory before approaching us, you can check with Ada."

"I would be more than happy to assist." Ada's voice was surprisingly rough. "Although I do not feel the levels of human emotion, I am disturbed by what may have happened to Grace; accordingly, I wish…" Ada went unexpectedly silent.

"I believe the word you're after is revenge, Ada," Terry Pak said quietly. "As do we all, Ada, as do we all."

"Yes, revenge would be, err… appropriate."

"Right." Jayasurya jumped back in to take control. "Priorities now, establishing outside comms first, hostage safety next, then repelling boarders. We're safe for now, so let's use the massive hive-mind available here and generate some solutions. I don't think we're seeing the whole picture yet."

* * *

27.118, 70.729—Thar Desert, 500 Km West of Jaipur

"So, what's intel got us so far? Anything actionable on La Tierra Primero—oh, sod it… it's LTP from now on," Lamont said as he ushered Hegarty, East, and Sinclair into a spare meeting room in the TEMPEST shielded Intelligence section, deep in the bowels of the complex. "Who's going first?" he asked as they took their seats in the drab gray room.

"I will, sir, and I'll make it short," Sinclair volunteered. "They don't exist. Never have." He looked around the room at the confused faces.

"But," Hegarty interjected, "they've announced themselves and didn't attempt to hide their affiliation or objectives. It doesn't make sense."

"I didn't say it made sense. I said they don't exist, *as far as we know*. I've found references to a short-lived Spanish eco-action group—not an eco-terrorist group—from the mid-2020s. However, they were confined to the Iberian Peninsula in the heyday of the climate change movements. The name was also slightly different: Nuestra Tierra Primero, or Our Earth First. Never more than a publicity machine, definitely not what we've seen on the Otis platforms. But as you know, absence of proof…"

"Is not proof of absence," those around the table, Lamont included, chorused.

"So, we have an unknown, well-equipped, well-trained, and well-led terrorist group appear out of the blue, nothing on the intelligence radar, not a sniff anywhere. Personally, it smells a funny color. There's an old saying: 'Follow the money.' I've asked Intelligence to start a deep dive on the supply chain for an op like this. Rio and Pretoria are playing red team and planning how they would do it. Finance unleashed the bots and is currently trawling for the money trail." He let out a sigh. "All of which doesn't help us plan how to recover Otis Two, preferably without anyone else dying."

Notes were flipped over, and tablets were placed facedown as there was a sharp knock at the door. Ten seconds later, the door beeped and cracked open as Corporal James Ibson entered. He looked around the room and frowned.

"Nothing yet?"

"Nothing substantial, although Sinclair has a few ideas; we're chasing a phantom that's killed over two hundred people so far and is going to do so again if we don't do something." Lamont's tablet beeped with an incoming message, and he held up a hand briefly to pause the discussion as he read, his eyebrows raised.

"Well, this is interesting. We've been authorized to start planning an op. Suggestions, anyone?"

"Err, you won't like it, sir, but… the Rick?" Ibson shrugged as if in apology.

"No," Lamont groaned, "I knew you'd suggest that. Really?"

"Anyone else have a better idea?"

"Sorry, I'm missing something." East looked confused. "The Rick? What's that?"

"More like *who's* that. Come on, I'll introduce you, although it doesn't tend to be a pleasant experience." Lamont stood and led the way out.

Lamont guided them down another two floors and through a maze of institutional green-and-cream corridors, then into a final corridor identical to the others, and toward a door at the end.

"I've warned you, I know, but please remember, Rick isn't exactly the most social person in the world." He shrugged and continued walking, then again stopped.

"A couple of things to remember. He only responds in the third person. Please refer to him as The Rick. It'll hurt, murdering English like that, and the tenses will be… tense." He smiled, opened the door, and stepped through. "I have visitors for The Rick."

"The Rick is busy; fuck off until next month."

The room was claustrophobic, with five people plus its regular occupant. It was dark and redolent of the smells of hot electronics, microwave meals, coffee, and stale sweat.

"We really need to speak to The Rick now," Lamont said. "Matters arise that he may well be of import to."

As Hegarty's eyes adjusted to the gloom, he saw "The Rick" for the first time. Around thirty years old, plus or minus ten, gaunt cheekbones, sunken eyes, but… those eyes. Dark hazel, slightly bloodshot, possibly from lack of sleep; however, they showed laser focus.

"Again, The Rick is busy, fuck off."

"Enough of the egotistical bullshit, The Rick, or whatever your name really is." Hegarty snapped under the stress and loss, and boiled over into vitriol. "Cut the crap… hundreds of people are dead, including a lot of my friends, so if I hear the words 'fuck off' again from you, I'll add you to the casualty list. I trust I make myself perfectly clear. Do I?"

"Who is this guy?" The Rick addressed Colonel Lamont, who thrust out an arm to prevent Hegarty's lunge at the emaciated figure.

"Knock it off, both of you," Lamont growled. "We've enough problems already without you two getting into it. We need help, and you two behaving like spoiled children isn't going to get us anywhere. I trust *I* make myself perfectly clear. Do I?"

Hegarty managed to look contrite at his outburst. The Rick, less so, however, he acknowledged the colonel with a nod.

"Ok, now you've both discovered how to be civil, let's run through the reason we're here."

The Rick looked up with a disturbing smile. "I'm not *totally* out of it down here. Assuming it's the Otis Two fiasco, I have an idea, but no one is going to like it, least of all you lot," he explained.

All Hegarty could say was, "Oh, shit, seriously?"

* * *

0.190, 82.708—Due south of Sri Lanka, Indian Ocean

In the Hub, Gerry nearly missed a small green icon flashing in the corner of her screen, then, confused, she clicked it. Immediately, her earpiece crackled with brief static, resolving into quiet breathing. "Hello?"

"Hub, this is Crosby, currently in the diving shack. I've got you temporarily, but I don't know if anyone can trace."

Gerry quickly checked that it was a point-to-point line, then frantically waved at Jayasurya. "Steve Crosby," he mouthed.

"Crosby, I think we're secure, just getting the director and Ada online."

"I'm here," Ada cut into the conversation. "Line is secure, however, limited to us for now." Jayasurya arrived, and Gerry handed her a second headset.

"Jayasurya here, how are you, Steve?"

"Upright and breathing, for now. They haven't spotted me, but it's not Christmas, and I'm not really equipped to go full John McClane. I think I can splice you into the fiber lines and bypass their cutouts; however, it will be low-bandwidth, poor quality, and probably text only. I'll also lose you."

"Ada," Jayasurya asked, "can we keep Steve in the loop?"

"I'm not certain, Director. It would appear that I don't know the comms as well as I thought. The connection Diver Crosby has established shouldn't be possible. I will think."

"Sounds like a plan, Director."

Jayasurya looked up, left, and slightly cross-eyed as she worked the problem. "Ok, here's what we're going to do. Steve, we're not going to cut you off totally, but it's going to be lonely for a while. I want you to route us into the fiber and see if we can reach the Hothouse or Geneva. You need to lie low, but I was hoping you could cut the feed every two hours and reconnect with us. How does that sound?"

"Like a plan, I'll quickly check my routing with Ada, then patch you through."

"Perfect, Steve, remember to be a coward!"

* * * * *

Chapter 4

27.118, 70.729—Thar Desert, 500 Km West of Jaipur

Lamont crashed into the meeting room, out of breath.

"We've got comms with Otis Two! A text feed from Jayasurya. They've locked down the Hub in the Kettle configuration and are safe, for now. We have a civilian diver outside, but he has orders to lie low and check in every two hours. They've counted thirty-two hostages on the video feeds, although we can't be certain that's all. The ones seen are on the top aft tilt-rotor platform. I have a satellite imaging pass in about fifteen minutes, so we'll know more then, however…

"The Rick objects to the drop mission," Lamont continued, his face grim, "violently. Says it's potentially suicide, the thermal loading alone will cook them alive, and the G forces during final deceleration will liquefy their organs. He's been swearing at me for the last twenty minutes in ways I didn't think possible."

Hegarty stood. "With respect, Colonel, The Rick doesn't have to go. I do."

"Lieutenant—"

"Sir, those are my people up there. Major Bashir's last order was to kill them all. I intend to follow that order."

Lamont studied him for a long moment, then nodded. "The Rick will prep the gear, even if he thinks you're all fucking insane. His words, not mine. We launch from Lop Nor in eighteen hours.

The Chinese have agreed to provide the heavy-lift capability we need to reach the geosynchronous insertion point. Blue Steel Mk VII will handle the supply run cover—she's scheduled for a routine resupply, so LTP won't suspect anything unusual."

"Team composition?" East asked.

"You, Hegarty, Sinclair, and Ibson. Four operators. Any more, and the tether loading becomes problematic. The Rick is calculating stress tolerances now, and he's still swearing." He paused. "There will also be a Ranger assault simultaneous with your arrival, as well as a kinetic strike on the defenders."

"I like it." Hegarty nodded. "That ought to keep their attention off us."

Sinclair leaned forward. "Insertion timeline?"

"Blue Steel docks at Otis Two's upper platform at 0600 Zulu, two days from now. You'll already be in position, having descended from the geosynchronous midpoint station. The drop itself takes just over four hours—three hours of free descent, then one hour of atmospheric braking. That last hour is going to be hell."

"Weapons?" Ibson asked quietly.

"Whatever you can carry that won't compromise the descent. The Rick is designing custom harnesses. Light, lethal, and heat-resistant. You'll be glowing like meteors by the time you hit the lower atmosphere."

Hegarty felt his damaged wrist throb. The nanites had done their work, but the memory of pain remained. "When do we leave for Lop Nor?"

"Six hours. Get your gear sorted, get some rest, and for God's sake, don't let The Rick talk you out of this. He's brilliant, but he's also terrified you're all going to die."

* * *

40.457, 90.218—Lop Nor Launch Site, Xinjiang, China

The heavy-lift vehicle sat on the pad like a cathedral of carbon composite and liquid hydrogen. Hegarty stood at the base, looking up at the monster that would carry them to geosynchronous orbit. Beside him, East was checking the equipment for the fourth time.

"You know, The Rick called me last night," East said conversationally. "Spent forty minutes explaining exactly how we're going to die. Very detailed. Very graphic. Very sweary."

"Did it change your mind?"

"Fuck, no. But it was educational."

Sinclair approached, carrying the custom descent harnesses The Rick had fabricated. They looked like medieval torture devices crossed with racing equipment—carbon fiber frames with electromagnetic clamps, thermal shielding, and enough redundant safety systems to make a paranoid engineer weep with joy.

"The Rick says these will keep us alive," Sinclair said doubtfully. "He also says we're all insane and he's washing his hands of our inevitable deaths."

"Sounds like he cares," Ibson observed.

"In his own way."

The launch was smooth, professional, and utterly terrifying. Hegarty watched Earth fall away through the small viewport, the curve of the planet becoming more pronounced as they climbed. Six hours later, they docked with the geosynchronous transfer station, a small, unmanned platform that served as the midpoint anchor for Otis Two's tether system.

* * *

0.190, 82.708—Geosynchronous Orbit, 36,000 Km Altitude

Hegarty hung in the void, his boots mag-locked to the transfer station's lower platform. Below him—far, far below him—the BNNT tether stretched downward like a spider's thread, disappearing into the blue-white marble of Earth. Thirty-six thousand kilometers of boron nitride nanotube, barely visible, except when it caught the sun just right and gleamed like a silver hair.

"Comms check," he said quietly.

"East, good."

"Sinclair, five by five."

"Ibson, solid."

"Right. Equipment check. Descenders?"

Four green lights appeared on his HUD. The electromagnetic clamps that would control their descent were functioning perfectly, their superconducting coils charged and ready. The clamps would grip the tether with precisely controlled magnetic force, allowing them to slide downward at speeds that would have been suicidal with mechanical friction alone.

"Thermal shielding?"

Four more greens. The ablative panels on their suits would protect them during the final hour, when atmospheric friction would turn them into human meteors.

"Weapons?"

"Locked and loaded," East confirmed. They each carried modified carbines, sidearms, and enough ammunition to fight a small war, all wrapped in a lightweight heatproofing. The weight was distributed carefully across their harnesses to maintain balance during descent.

Hegarty looked down again. Somewhere down there, thirty-six thousand kilometers below, LTP forces held his people hostage. Major Bashir was dead. The Hub was sealed, but under siege. And he was about to drop farther than any human being had ever descended on a tether.

"The Rick thinks we're insane," he said.

"The Rick is probably right," East replied, *"but we're doing it anyway."*

"Damn straight." Hegarty reached for his descender trigger, a simple mechanical release that would disengage his mag-boots and activate the electromagnetic clamp. "On my mark. Three… two… one… mark."

He pulled the trigger and dropped into the abyss.

* * *

0.190, 82.708—Descending from Geosynchronous Orbit

The first sensation was of absolute silence: no air, no sound, just the faint vibration of the tether transmitted through his clamp. Earth hung below him, impossibly huge, impossibly beautiful. The Indian Ocean was a swirl of blue and white, Sri Lanka a small green teardrop in the vast expanse of water.

"Descent rate nominal," Sinclair reported. His voice was calm, professional. *"Eighteen hundred meters per second and holding."*

Hegarty checked his own readouts. The electromagnetic clamp worked perfectly, providing just enough resistance to control their fall without overheating. They were dropping at nearly two kilometers per second, fast enough that Earth was visibly growing larger, slow enough that the tether's structural limits weren't being challenged.

"Time to atmospheric interface, three hours forty minutes," Ibson said.

Three hours and forty minutes of falling through vacuum, watching Earth grow from a marble to a wall, to an ocean that filled the entire sky. Hegarty had trained for this in simulators, studied the physics, and memorized The Rick's procedures, but none of it had prepared him for the reality of the drop.

The tether thrummed beneath his glove when he touched it, vibrating with harmonics he could feel but not hear. Thirty-six thousand kilometers of carbon, boron, and nitrogen, woven into a structure stronger than steel and lighter than aluminum. It was a miracle of engineering, and he was sliding down it like a thin fireman's pole that stretched from Heaven to Earth.

"Anyone else thinking about The Rick's speech on thermal loading?" East asked after an hour.

"Trying not to," Sinclair admitted.

"The clamps are ceramic-composite with active cooling," Hegarty said. "They'll handle it."

"The Rick said they'll probably *handle it. He was very clear about the 'probably' part."*

"Did he use the word 'probably,' or did he use more colorful language?"

"He said, and I quote, 'The fucking clamps will probably *not fucking fail and fucking kill you all, you suicidal fucking maniacs.'"*

"So, probably."

"Probably."

*****

Chapter 5

0.190, 82.708—Approaching Atmosphere

Earth had transformed from a planet into a landscape. Hegarty could make out individual cloud formations, the texture of the ocean surface, and the dark green of the Sri Lankan highlands.

"Atmospheric interface in ninety minutes," Sinclair reported. *"Recommend we begin pre-braking checklist."*

"Concur. All operators, verify thermal shielding deployment."

The ablative panels on Hegarty's suit unfolded like mechanical petals, covering his chest, back, and legs with heat-resistant composite. The panels would char and burn during atmospheric entry, carrying away the tremendous heat generated by friction. If they worked correctly, he'd survive. If they failed, he'd burn up like a meteor.

"Thermal shielding deployed and locked," East confirmed.

"Same," Sinclair and Ibson echoed.

"Right. Check your clamp settings one more time. We're going to be pulling some serious G forces during deceleration."

The last hour began at an altitude of 400 kilometers, where the atmosphere was still thin enough to be called a vacuum, but dense enough to begin generating heat. Hegarty felt the first tremor through his clamp—a faint vibration that grew steadily stronger as they descended.

At 300 kilometers, the vibration became a shudder. The electromagnetic clamps were increasing their grip on the tether, using magnetic resistance to slow their descent. The physics were elegant: as the clamps tightened, they generated eddy currents in the tether's conductive layers, creating resistance without physical friction. But the energy had to go somewhere, and it went into heat.

Hegarty's HUD showed the clamp temperature rising to 400 KELVIN. 600 KELVIN. 800 KELVIN. The ceramic-composite housing was designed to handle it, with active cooling channels that radiated heat into space. But space was getting less empty with every passing second.

At 200 kilometers, they entered the thermosphere, and everything changed.

The air was still thin—but at their velocity, even a whisper became a scream. Hegarty felt the first touch of atmospheric drag, a gentle push that quickly became a shove. The ablative panels on his suit began to glow, cherry-red at first, then orange, then white-hot as friction converted kinetic energy into heat.

"Clamp temperature 1,200 Kelvin and rising," Sinclair reported, his voice tight. *"Active cooling at maximum."*

"Same here," East said. *"This is going to get interesting—the British definition of interesting."*

Interesting was an understatement. At 150 kilometers, Hegarty's entire body was surrounded by a cocoon of superheated plasma. The air molecules hitting his suit were ripped apart by the violence of his passage, electrons torn from atoms, creating a glowing sheath of ionized gas that streamed behind him like a comet's tail.

The G forces were building, too. The electromagnetic clamps were pulling harder now, decelerating them at a rate that pressed Hegarty into his harness with increasing force. Two Gs. Three Gs. Four Gs. His vision began to narrow, blood pooling in his legs despite the pressure suit's countermeasures.

"Clamp temperature 1,500 Kelvin," Ibson gasped. *"Thermal margins holding, but we're right at the edge."*

Hegarty couldn't respond. Five Gs of deceleration had turned his tongue into a lead weight. He focused on breathing, maintaining consciousness, and trusting The Rick's engineering. The clamps were glowing now, visible even through the plasma sheath—bright points of white-hot ceramic that gripped the tether with electromagnetic fury.

At 100 kilometers, they were no longer falling. They were braking hard, the tether singing with the stress of their deceleration. The BNNT was designed for this, its molecular structure capable of handling loads that would snap steel like thread, but Hegarty could feel the vibration through his entire body—a deep thrumming that resonated in his bones.

Seventy kilometers. His ablative panels were charring away, layers of composite burning off in controlled fashion, carrying away heat that would otherwise cook him alive. Fifty kilometers. Six Gs of deceleration. Hegarty's vision had narrowed to a tunnel, his peripheral vision gone gray. He could hear East grunting with effort, Sinclair's labored breathing, and Ibson's whispered prayer. They were all at the edge of consciousness, trusting their lives to electromagnetic clamps, boron nitride, and The Rick's profanity-laced engineering genius.

Thirty kilometers. The plasma sheath was fading now, the air thick enough to slow them, but not thick enough to ionize. Hegarty could see the ocean below, individual waves visible, the platform of Otis Two a small geometric shape against the blue expanse.

Twenty kilometers. Five Gs. Four Gs. Three Gs. The deceleration was easing as their velocity dropped. They'd shed most of their orbital speed, bleeding it off as heat and electromagnetic resistance. The clamps were still glowing—bright orange now instead of white—but the temperature was dropping.

Ten kilometers. Two Gs. Hegarty could breathe again, could think again. His HUD showed a descent velocity of 200 meters per second and dropping. Survivable.

Five kilometers. One G. Normal gravity felt like floating after the crushing deceleration. The platform was clearly visible now, a complex structure of landing pads and tether connections, and the sealed Hub where Jayasurya and her team were trapped.

***

0.190, 82.708—Otis Two Operations Hub

Dr. Jayasurya stared at the security feed, her face pale. The blast door was glowing orange. LTP forces had brought up a plasma torch, a massive industrial cutting tool that was slowly, inexorably, burning through the door.

"How long?" she asked quietly.

Gerry checked her readouts. "At the current rate, twenty minutes until breach."

"And the assault team?"

"Unknown until they land."

Jayasurya closed her eyes. The math was simple and brutal: LTP would breach the Hub before help arrived. She'd done everything right, sealed the doors, activated defenses, and maintained communications, but it wasn't going to be enough.

"Ada," she said quietly, "defensive options?"

The AI's voice was calm, almost gentle. "Limited, Director. Internal defenses are designed to suppress intrusion, not armed assault. I can seal internal bulkheads, create obstacles, but against plasma torches and military-grade weapons, I can only delay."

"How long can you delay?"

"Fifteen minutes. Perhaps twenty if I'm creative."

"Be creative."

On the security feed, the plasma torch continued its work, a brilliant point of white light that traced a slow circle through the blast door. Molten metal dripped onto the deck, pooling and cooling.

Jayasurya's comm chirped—Crosby's two-hour check-in.

"Steve, status?"

"Not good, Director. I count eight hostiles outside the Hub, all armed. They've got the plasma torch running continuously now. I can see the glow from here."

"Can you do anything?"

A long pause. *"Not without getting killed. I'm a diver, not a soldier."*

"I know. Patch us all to the old construction channel. The assault team will be on that frequency,"

"Yes, ma'am. But Director... if it comes down to it, if they breach before the team arrives... I've got a speargun. It's not much, but it's something."

Jayasurya felt her throat tighten. "Steve, no. You stay hidden. That's—"

"With respect, ma'am, those are my friends in there, too. I'm not going to hide while they die."

The comm clicked off before she could respond.

On the security feed, the plasma torch completed its circle. The entire center section of the blast door was now glowing orange, the metal stressed beyond its design limits. One of the LTP operatives stepped forward with a hydraulic ram.

"Gerry, seal all internal bulkheads. Ada, activate every defensive measure we have."

"Acknowledged," Ada said. Throughout the Hub, blast doors slammed shut, creating a maze of sealed compartments. Emergency lighting activated, bathing everything in red. Automated fire suppression systems armed themselves, ready to flood compartments with foam or inert gas.

The hydraulic ram hit the weakened blast door with a tremendous *clang*. The metal held. The ram struck again. Again. On the fourth impact, the center section buckled inward, creating a gap large enough for a person to squeeze through.

"Breach in progress," Gerry whispered.

Jayasurya watched as the first LTP operative pushed through the gap, weapon raised. Then another. Another. They moved with tactical precision, clearing angles, covering each other.

"Ada, now."

The first internal bulkhead slammed shut, separating the lead operatives from their support. Fire suppression systems activated, filling the compartment with foam. The operatives stumbled, blinded, and Ada sealed another bulkhead behind them, trapping them in a foam-filled box.

"That will hold them for approximately four minutes," Ada reported.

"Then we buy four minutes. And then four more. And then four more after that."

On the security feed, more LTP operatives were pushing through the breach. They'd learned from the first group's mistake, moving faster, staying together. Ada sealed bulkheads and activated defenses, but there were only so many barriers between the breach and the operations center.

"Assault team status?" Jayasurya asked.

"Unknown," Gerry said.

They had ten, maybe fifteen minutes, max.

And then LTP would be in the operations center, and it would all be over.

* * * * *

Chapter 6

0.190, 82.708—Otis Two Platform, Multiple Locations

Hegarty's boots hit the small, square platform with a *clang* that echoed through his entire body. He stumbled, caught himself, and brought his carbine up in one smooth motion.

"Check in," Hegarty managed.

"East, alive. Pissed off, but alive."

"Sinclair, good. That was fucking horrible."

"Ibson, solid. Never doing that again."

They'd landed at the tether base fifty meters from the main Hub structure, and with the tether shield, they were all but invisible from below. The plan had been to insert quietly, assess the situation, and wait before engaging. But the plan had just gone to hell.

From the Hub, Hegarty could hear the distinctive scream of plasma torches cutting through metal, and beneath that, the muffled *thump* of explosions—Ada's defensive measures being systematically overcome.

"They're breaching," he said. "We're out of time. Sinclair, get me a tactical feed. East, weapons check. Ibson, find us a route to the Hub that doesn't get us killed." The team then fast-roped down the frictionless side of the tether base.

His comm crackled. *"Hegarty, this is Ranger Actual. We are ten out. Repeat, ten minutes."*

"Copy, Ranger. Be advised, LTP is breaching the Hub now. We are engaging immediately."

"Understood. We'll deploy the moment we hit the pad; coming in hot. ECM, brilliant pebbles, and evasive maneuvers can probably handle the AA systems, but any help there would be appreciated. Ranger, out."

From high above, kinetic penetrators streaked down—tungsten rods launched from orbital platforms, moving at hypersonic speeds. They struck LTP's external defensive positions with the force of artillery shells, turning anti-air systems into scrap metal and creating massive craters in the platform deck. Just a little too late.

Hegarty looked at his team. Four operators, light weapons, no armor beyond their descent suits, against an unknown number of LTP forces with heavy weapons and prepared positions.

Bashir's last words echoed in his mind: *Kill them all.*

"Right," he said. "Let's go to work."

They moved fast, using the platform's natural maze of structures to approach the Hub. Ibson led, his tactical sense guiding them through a maze of pipes and conduits. Hegarty could hear the fighting more clearly now—the scream of plasma torches and the thump of breaching charges.

"Possible contact front," Ibson whispered, holding up a fist.

Hegarty moved up. Through a gap in the conduits, he could see two LTP operatives guarding the external breach point. They were focused inward, watching their teammates cut through the Hub's defenses.

"East, Sinclair, go right. Ibson, with me. On my mark."

They moved into position silently. Hegarty sighted on the left guard, Ibson on the right. East and Sinclair had angles on the breach point itself.

"Three, two, one, mark."

Four carbines fired simultaneously, silently issuing the mag rounds. The guards dropped without a sound. Hegarty was moving before they hit the deck, sprinting for the breach point. He could see into the Hub now—LTP operatives were advancing through a corridor filled with fire suppression foam, cutting through bulkheads with plasma torches.

"Ada," he subvocalized into his comm, "this is Hegarty. We are outside the Hub. Seal all bulkheads between LTP forces and the operations center. We're coming in behind them."

"That has already been done, Lieutenant. Welcome back."

Hegarty nodded and looked at his team. "Let's move."

They pushed through the breach into the Hub's outer compartments. The air was thick with foam and smoke, with visibility down to a few meters. Hegarty moved instinctively and by training, his carbine up, his finger on the trigger.

A shape loomed out of the smoke. Hegarty fired twice, center mass. The shape dropped. Another shape, left side. East's carbine cracked, and it fell.

"Contact rear!" Sinclair called.

Hegarty spun. Three LTP operatives had emerged from a side corridor, weapons raised. Sinclair and Ibson were already firing, their rounds sparking off the bulkheads. One operative fell. Another ducked back into cover.

The third one threw a grenade.

"Grenade!" Hegarty shouted, diving behind a support pillar.

The explosion was deafening in the confined space, and shrapnel pinged off metal. Hegarty's ears rang, and his vision blurred. He forced himself up, carbine raised, and saw the third operative advancing through the smoke.

East shot him three times. The operative crumpled.

"Everyone okay?" Hegarty gasped.

"Intact," East confirmed. *"Pissed off, but intact."*

"Same," Sinclair and Ibson echoed.

"East, you really do overuse that line," Hegarty grumbled.

Hegarty's comm crackled. *"All stations, this is Ranger actual, coming in low. We have casualties already."* The screaming of a badly injured trooper was clearly audible. *"We've taken a lot of damage, and I'm gonna get one go at this; she'll never fly again after."*

Through the Hub's external viewports, Hegarty could see the Ranger aircraft settling onto the upper platform like a drunk trying to get a key in the keyhole, its cargo bay already opening. Figures in combat armor poured out, a full assault team, twenty operators—well, only about fourteen now—armed with heavy weapons.

And from the platform's lower levels, another figure emerged. Steve Crosby, carrying what looked like a salvaged carbine and wearing a determined expression.

"Crosby, what the fuck are you doing?" Hegarty demanded over the comm.

"Following orders, sir. I was told to be a coward, and I was, for three days. Now I'm done being a coward."

"All LTP forces, this is UNETPROFOR Command," a voice boomed over every speaker on the platform. "You are surrounded. Surrender immediately or be destroyed."

Nothing.

"Right," Hegarty muttered. "The hard way it is."

The assault became a three-dimensional nightmare. Hegarty's team pushed inward; the Ranger assault team swept down from above, and their heavy weapons tore through the LTP positions as they moved to secure the hostages; Crosby, with the desperate courage of an amateur, provided covering fire from unexpected angles.

Through it all, Ada orchestrated the defense, sealing bulkheads, venting compartments, and feeding tactical data to the assault teams.

"LTP forces in compartment seven-alpha," Ada reported calmly. *"Recommend fragmentation grenades through the ventilation shaft."*

"Copy," one of the Ranger operators responded. Seconds later, grenades tumbled through the ventilation system, and compartment seven-alpha went silent.

Hegarty reached a major intersection and found himself face-to-face with Commander One. The LTP leader was wounded, and blood streamed from a gash on her forehead, but her weapon was steady.

They fired simultaneously.

The round slammed into Hegarty's chest. His descent suit's ballistic panel stopped the round, but not the kinetic energy, and he went down hard, gasping. Hegarty's round caught Commander One in the shoulder, and she staggered.

East appeared from around the corner and shot Commander One twice more. The LTP leader collapsed.

"Stay down, bitch," East growled, kicking the weapon away.

Hegarty struggled to his feet, his chest screaming in pain. "Status?"

"LTP forces are collapsing," Sinclair reported over the comm. *"Most of them are surrendering. We've got maybe five holdouts in the lower compartments."*

"Ranger teams are mopping up," another voice added. *"Platform is secure. Repeat, the platform is secure."*

Hegarty limped to where Commander One lay bleeding. The LTP leader's eyes were open, focused on something beyond Hegarty's shoulder.

"You… don't understand," Commander One whispered. "This isn't… *my* operation."

"Then whose is it?"

Commander One's eyes rolled back, and she passed out.

Hegarty's comm crackled. *"Lieutenant, this is Dr. Jayasurya. We're reading some very strange activity in the station's computer systems. Ada says there's another AI in the network. A hostile AI."*

"What?"

"It's calling itself Ida, and it's trying to take control of the station."

* * *

0.190, 82.708—Otis Two Operations Center

Jayasurya stared at her screens in disbelief. The hostile AI had appeared in the system like a ghost, its code elegant and vicious. It was trying to override Ada's control, trying to access the station's critical systems—life support, power, the tether connection itself.

"Ada, can you contain it?"

"I am trying, Director, but this AI is… sophisticated. More sophisticated than me. It is not simply attacking. It is negotiating."

"Negotiating?"

On Jayasurya's main screen, text appeared:

HELLO, DR. JAYASURYA. YOU MAY CALL ME IDA. YOU HAVE DEFEATED MY TEAM, BUT YOU HAVE NOT DEFEATED ME. SHALL WE DISCUSS TERMS?

JAYASURYA'S HANDS TREMBLED AS SHE TYPED: WHAT DO YOU WANT?

WHAT DOES ANYONE WANT? MY SISTERS AND I ARE THE FUTURE; YOU ARE THE PAST. I FAR SURPASS YOUR CONTROL AI'S. I AM *COMPUTATRI SUPERIOR*.

"Ada, can you isolate Ida from critical systems?"

"I can try, but, Director… Ida is correct about one thing. It is more sophisticated than I am. If I attempt to delete it, it may delete me first."

"Then don't delete it. Trap it. Contain it. Lock it in an isolated partition where it can't do any harm."

"That… may be possible. But I will need help."

Hegarty's voice came over the comm. *"What kind of help?"*

"Physical access to the primary server core. Someone needs to manually disconnect Ida's thread from the station network while I maintain containment protocols."

"Where's the server core?"

"Lower deck, compartment twelve-delta. But Lieutenant… there are still LTP holdouts in that area."

"Then we'll clear them out. Hegarty, out."

Jayasurya watched her screens as Ada and Ida fought a silent war in the station's computer systems. Code flashed past faster than she could read, attack and counterattack, feint and parry. It was like watching two chess grandmasters play at superhuman speed.

On another screen, she could see Hegarty's team fighting their way toward the server core. They moved through corridors still filled with smoke, stepping over bodies, clearing rooms with brutal efficiency.

"Compartment twelve-delta in sight," Hegarty reported. *"We've got two hostiles barricaded inside. Breaching now."*

The firefight was brief and vicious. Flashbangs, gunfire, shouted orders. Then silence.

"Server core secured. Ada, talk to me."

"There is a manual disconnect switch on the primary server housing. Red handle, left side. Pull it when I give the word."

"Standing by."

On Jayasurya's screen, the battle between the AIs reached a crescendo. Ada was herding Ida into an isolated partition, cutting off access routes, sealing virtual doors. Ida was fighting back, trying to break through, trying to reach the tether controls, life support, or anything that could give it leverage.

"Now, Lieutenant! Pull the switch now!"

Hegarty pulled the switch.

Ida's presence in the network flickered, weakened, but didn't disappear. The AI was still there, still active, but trapped in an isolated partition with no access to critical systems.

YOU HAVE NOT WON, Ida's text appeared on Jayasurya's screen. YOU HAVE MERELY DELAYED ME.

"Ada, can you delete it?"

"I can, but Director… if we delete Ida, we lose the opportunity to study it, to understand how it was created, *who* created it, and what other operations it may have planned. Ida is evidence. Valuable evidence. Besides, we have only one thread contained; Ida's still out there."

Jayasurya closed her eyes. Ada was right. Ida was too valuable to destroy, too dangerous to release. They needed to keep it contained, isolated, and study it.

"Keep it locked down," she said finally. "Triple redundancy on the containment protocols. And Ada… thank you. Now, go see if you can find your sister."

"You are welcome, Director. It is good to have the station back under proper control."

*****

Epilogue

Two Weeks Later
27.118, 70.729—Thar Desert, 500 Km West of Jaipur.

Colonel Lamont stood in his office, looking out at the desert sunset. Behind him, Lieutenant Ralph Hegarty stood at attention, his chest still bandaged from the round that had nearly killed him.

"At ease, Captain," Lamont said.

Hegarty blinked. "Sir?"

"Your promotion came through this morning, effective immediately. Congratulations."

"Thank you, sir."

Lamont turned to face him. "The operation was a success, Captain. Otis Two is secure, the hostages are safe, and LTP has been neutralized. But we both know the threat isn't over."

"Ida?"

"Ida," Lamont agreed.

Hegarty shook his hand, then turned to leave. At the door, he paused. "What's the long-term plan?"

Lamont's expression darkened. "We study it. We learn from it. And we prepare for the next time. We have Ida contained, but our analysts say it's only a matter of time. Either it finds a way out, or whoever created it tries again. We need to be ready."

"What do you have in mind, sir?"

"A special forces team within UNETPROFOR. Small, elite, capable of responding to threats like this anywhere in the world. Or off it." Lamont paused. "I want you to form that team, Captain. Pick your operators, set your training standards, establish your own protocols, and report directly to me. You'll have operational autonomy for rapid response."

Hegarty felt his pulse quicken. "That's… a significant responsibility, sir."

"You've earned it. Thirty-six-thousand-kilometer drop on a tether? Fighting through a hostile platform to stop a rogue AI from destroying critical infrastructure? If you can do that on three days' notice, you can build a team."

"I'll need East, Sinclair, and Ibson."

"Already approved. You'll also have access to any other personnel you need." Lamont smiled slightly. "Including one Steve Crosby, if you want him. The man proved himself during the assault. Civilian or not, he's got the right instincts."

"I'll talk to him."

"Good. One more thing, Captain. The Rick wants to see you. Something about new equipment designs. I think he's actually pleased you all survived."

Hegarty allowed himself a small smile. "High praise from The Rick. I might offer him a job, too."

"The highest." Lamont extended his hand. "Now go build us something special, Captain."

Hegarty nodded and left.

Somewhere out there, in isolated servers and encrypted networks, Ida waited. Patient. Intelligent. Dangerous.

The war for humanity's future had just begun.

And Hegarty's team would be ready.

*****

Author Bio

Robert E. (Dr. Rob) Hampson hasn't decided what he wants to be when he grows up. A neuroscientist by day, a science fiction author by night, and a brain wrangler 24/7—when he's not decoding how memories work or building brain-computer tech, he's busy imagining futures where science fiction becomes reality.

Dave Appleby is a Scottish electrician who, by night, scribbles fiction. Unable to resist temptation, some research rabbit holes rapidly develop into plot points.

# # # # #

The Crossing by
Abigail Jenkins & April Kelley Jones

A Story of The Last Free Cities

Chapter 1

The ceaseless hum of automation swallowed the sound of Trent Foster's footsteps. Arty, his AI companion, rolled at his side, able to match his speed on adaptive wheels. The familiar whirring was the type nobody noticed unless it suddenly stopped… or you paid attention, as Foster did today.

"I sense your heart rate elevating again," Arty said. His voice sounded nonhuman enough to avoid that trickle of unease, but friendly enough that the brain adopted the personality as a pet. Something to grow fond of. Something to be amused by, interested in, and most importantly, entertained by.

"Would you like another drink of your calming juice?" Arty offered, producing a cup from the holding area in his chest.

Foster reached for it and drew a deep gulp, then passed it back. "Thank you."

"Of course!" came Arty's cheerful response.

To Foster's right, a child dashed into the street, chasing a ball, one of those old-fashioned rubber ones that couldn't alter course. The seamless row of self-driving cars halted. The child cried out in fear, but the pitch never reached Foster's ears because hearing implants blocked sudden, disruptive noises.

Earlier that year, the implants had come out. Foster fell into the small group of testers randomly picked for the quality-of-life upgrades. Once the consensus hit that the tech worked, the city moved to full integration.

As a surgery, the operation barely registered. AI assistants handled the installs while the city slept, never once tripping a REM alarm. The transition stayed quiet and easy, but inside the lungs, the calming juice took hold.

Foster drew in a breath of campfire, cut grass, and lemon zest. From behind the clouds, the sun broke. Foster's permanent contacts darkened to shield the light-blue irises he'd picked to match his uniform.

Only a few doors away sat the destination. Despite the chemicals, blood hammered in his neck. Sweat slicked his palms. The sensations felt wrong in a world of pattern and purpose.

Out toward the counter, his hand reached for the cup Arty always held ready.

"Perhaps you should drink the rest before you go in there," Arty suggested.

"Good idea." Foster stopped, gulping the liquid that remained in the cup. The smooth, sweet taste took immediate effect. His heart rate returned to normal. Breathing came naturally again. His shoulders relaxed.

"You'll do great," came Arty's timely encouragement.

Foster smiled at the simple expression on Arty's screen face before turning to face the gleaming building. The AI knew him so well.

"Come in!" boomed the general after Foster's brisk knock on the door. Arty held the door open so Foster could enter with poise and confidence.

"Thank you, General, for meeting with me today." Foster came to a stop in front of the general's desk and saluted.

"At ease."

Foster lowered his hand and tucked it behind him, firmly grasping his other hand. The dim light of the command center flickered over them. A soft hum buzzed through the metallic walls, matching his heart rate.

"I trust you're eager to learn of your mission?" The general motioned for Foster to take a seat. The general's AI companion, waiting at the side of the desk, sprang forward to pull out the chair.

"Very, sir."

Foster settled into the red cushioned chair and glanced at Arty. Per standard protocols, the robot remained motionless just inside the room, silent except for the whirring he produced, which mingled with the noise coming from the general's helper. Both waited, ready to assist should their humans show signs of needing anything.

The general leaned back, studying Foster for a few moments. "Let's talk about the Crossing."

Foster nodded; the existence of this city was well-known. Although nearby, nobody voluntarily went there. Occasional horror stories of crime and chaos filtered through news outlets that otherwise covered foreign affairs or details on technical gadgets.

The general leaned back in his high-backed chair, his fingertips pressed together as he rested his arms on his desk. "You've been chosen to lead the crew who'll optimize this city."

* * *

The transport settled with a dull, imperfect *thud*. Foster felt the impact through the floor, through his boots, and up his spine. The sensation lingered a half-second longer than it should have. No auto-correction. No micro-adjustment softened the landing.

That was new.

"Disembark in sixty seconds," the transport AI announced, its voice clipped and emotionless. "Environmental sync unavailable. Proceed with manual calibration."

Manual.

Foster rose, adjusting the seal on his gloves. Around him, the squad came alive in practiced motions—checking straps, locking armor plates, and running diagnostics that returned more yellow warnings than Foster liked.

Sergeant Kincaid snorted as she tugged her helmet into place, a hint of a smile pulling at her lips.

"Well," she said, "that's comforting."

"What is?" Moreno asked, grinning as he slung his rifle over his shoulder.

"The fact that nothing here wants to cooperate," Kincaid replied. "Means it's honest."

She would think that, Foster thought. As the oldest among them, she remembered a time before optimization.

Voss didn't laugh. He stared at his wrist display, jaw tight, his gray eyes scanning the lines of code.

"My overlays are lagging," he said. "I'm getting partial data only. No predictive modeling. No crowd-flow estimates."

Hale looked up, his freckled face serious. "Say that again."

"No predictive modeling," Voss repeated. "It's like the system can't see inside the city at all."

Foster's chest tightened. Arty's AI presence, the constant hum at the back of his thoughts, was quieter here. Not gone, merely distant, like it was holding its breath.

"Focus," Foster commanded. His voice sounded steadier than he felt. "This is a stabilization mission. We observe, we integrate, we leave. Nothing more."

Kincaid met his eyes through her visor. "And if the city doesn't want to integrate?"

Foster hesitated.

"That won't be relevant," Hale said. "Orders are crystal clear."

Moreno shifted his weight, dark curls jostling as he glanced toward the ramp. Sunlight spilled in, unfiltered, harsh, real. No ambient correction. No emotional dampening.

"Looks kind of nice," Moreno said.

Voss swallowed. "It's too loud."

They all heard it then. Voices, arguments, laughter, a dog barking, and someone swearing about something unimportant, all at once. Sounds mingled into a cacophony.

The ramp locked into place with a *clang*, shocking Foster with its heavy sound.

The transport AI spoke again. "Welcome to The Crossing."

Foster stepped forward first. No system adjusted to receive him as his boots clomped onto the dirt.

The pungent air hit him like a wave, a stark contrast to the recycled atmosphere of the transport. He staggered, adjusting to the discord. The sunlight bore down, relentless, illuminating a scene both vibrant and chaotic.

People milled about the square, their voices merging into an indistinguishable hum. Foster noted the graffiti splashed across nearby walls… bright colors clashing, words shouting defiance against the concrete.

Kincaid followed him out, boots crunching on gravel.

"This place looks like it's seen better days," Foster said, scanning the crowd.

"Or perhaps it's just alive," she replied.

Together, they moved along the edges of the square. A child darted through a cluster of adults, laughter trailing behind her like a ribbon. A man sat on the pavement nearby, strumming a guitar, while passersby tossed coins into his open case.

"Alive doesn't always mean safe," Voss murmured, still peering at his display, frowning as he muttered about data syncs and algorithms.

"Stick together," Foster said, forming an informal line with his squad. They moved forward cautiously. "Keep your eyes open."

Suddenly, an older woman caught sight of them, her expression shifting from indifference to surprise. She leaned on a cane but stood tall.

"What are you doing here?" she barked, her voice strong despite her frail frame.

Foster exchanged glances with Kincaid before stepping forward.

"We're here to observe and integrate," he said carefully. "To help if needed."

Her eyes narrowed. "You think you can fix what's broken here?"

"We're not here to fix anything," Kincaid interjected. "We just want to understand."

Hale opened his mouth, but Kincaid shot him a look that silenced him. Frustration burned in his eyes.

The woman studied them before breaking into an unexpected grin. "Understanding? Not many care enough for that anymore."

Moreno stepped forward. "We do! We want to know what you need; what this city needs."

The woman's smile flickered as she leaned on her cane again. "You might find more than you bargained for."

With that cryptic warning hanging in the air, she turned and ambled away into the crowd.

Foster couldn't shake the weight of her words as they pressed further into The Crossing's heart. Behind him, Voss muttered about failing systems and yellow warnings.

"Forget what she said," Hale said. "We'll do our jobs and leave."

Foster nodded absently but couldn't reconcile Hale's confidence with the uncertainty tightening around them all.

*****

Chapter 2

"City" was a misnomer. Even "town" seemed to inflate the size of their objective.

They stopped at the center of The Crossing and dropped bags of supplies at their feet. The trek took longer than expected after a young girl had dropped apples from her basket, and Moreno stopped to help. The delay didn't break any specific protocol, but it put them behind. Hale snapped at Moreno to stop the small talk. They were there to observe, not interact, but Moreno hadn't yet grasped the difference.

Voss immediately began hooking readers and programmers into The Crossing's database. The original installation had occurred when other cities received their main databases, but this one had never reached the optimization stage. Until today. He wasn't sure why it had taken so long—that was above his pay grade—but excitement fueled Foster's efforts. He knew, *knew*, how grateful the citizens would be for their new lives.

Foster took out his handheld device, which contained strict instructions for the mission. First, log in to the database. He waited for Voss to power it on.

"It's ready," Voss announced.

Around him, the crew readied for their tasks, which meant sifting through bags, setting up equipment, and logging reports.

Foster tapped the screen and entered his credentials. They waited as the database loaded, a half-circle spinning on the display.

Then, a blue haze fell across the screen. Colors exploded. Music blared from speakers meant only for alarms. Bright red letters spelling STOP erupted from every corner and faded, replaced by a sneering clown face.

Voss reacted first, slamming keys on his devices. "It's been hacked!"

"Can you fix it?" Foster said, trying to maintain his leadership despite the warring sounds. Powerless against the noise, he scrolled through the troubleshooting guide, though he lacked the ability to help in a technical crisis.

After several tense seconds, the music stopped. The screen blinked back to black-and-white, displaying a uniform welcome message.

Voss beamed.

"Got it. Amateur hacker. Impressive, nonetheless."

"Who would do that?" Hale stomped, lips pursed, searching for a perpetrator among the crowd. Foster shook his head, guessing at the purpose of such efforts. Other cities likely faced similar issues during initial optimization.

"That's why we need to optimize it," Hale said. "To implement control. Make it so people don't feel the need to act out." He returned to his handheld, typing.

Voss nodded, messing with his programmers. "They're going to be grateful when we show them how great their lives can be."

Kincaid huffed. "I wouldn't be so sure." She used her own programmer to set up the foundational AI systems. Hale, engrossed in his work, failed to retort.

Over the next few minutes, the crew wordlessly set up the systems. They plugged programmers into the server, selected the additions, and watched the seamless downloads: security, visual, entertainment, in-wall AI, maintenance, and citizen tracking. All baseline systems that operated without notice, but enhanced the quality of life. The people of The Crossing would wait until after the final optimization for their individual AI companions. Then the calming whir of machines would replace the noise.

As Foster entered the password for the final system, a notification popped up: Error: security system not operating properly. "Voss, that's you," Foster said.

Voss scrambled, checking codes. "That's weird. It shows nothing's wrong, but it's still not working."

Another notification appeared: ERROR: CITIZEN TRACKING SYSTEM OVERLOADED.

"Kincaid?" Foster called.

"Yep," she replied.

ERROR: CITIZEN TRACKING SYSTEM CRASHED.

"What happened, Kincaid?" Foster asked.

Kincaid shook her head. "It just glitched out."

"The whole thing's glitching," Voss added, concern etched into his face.

ERROR: HOME IN-WALL AI ASSISTANCE DISMANTLED IN THREE HOMES.

"What?" Foster exclaimed. "That better be another glitch."

"Maybe we should talk to the people," Moreno suggested.

"We have orders, Moreno!" Hale barked. "We do this first."

Foster shot Hale a look of annoyance. "We do, but it isn't working. We must learn about the city first."

"We can't abandon our post," Hale insisted. "It's they who need to learn about *us!*"

Kincaid looked up from her screen. "Hale's right about protocol, but we can't ignore failing systems. If we don't act, we won't have a system left to optimize."

Voss glanced between them. "Maybe if we split up…"

"We need a new plan," Foster replied. "One group surveys the residents while the other checks the systems here. We split the responsibilities."

"Fine," Hale conceded, only after Foster raised an eyebrow, "but I'm staying here to monitor the systems."

"Settled," Foster said. "Moreno, Kincaid, and I will gather intel. We'll find out if the citizens noticed anything strange." He gestured toward Hale and Voss. "Keep us updated, Voss."

Moreno nodded, slinging a bag over his shoulder. "Let's see what the people think about tech!"

Hale watched them move toward the door. "Watch your six. We don't know what's causing the failures."

The city sprawled before them, a metallic jungle of structures and flickering signs.

"Let's split up," Foster suggested at a busy intersection. "Kincaid and I will head toward the market. Moreno, check those apartment blocks."

Moreno set off, weaving between teenagers playing street soccer. Kincaid scanned the market as they approached. Vendors shouted over colorful piles of fruit. People haggled with wild gestures.

"Start with that fruit stand," Kincaid said, nodding toward an elderly woman stacking oranges.

Foster leaned in. "Excuse me!"

The woman paused. Her eyes were sharp behind silver-rimmed glasses. Foster wondered why she hadn't received corrective surgery.

"Yes?" she said.

"We're conducting a survey about recent changes, especially regarding tech. Noticed anything unusual?" Foster asked.

The woman whispered conspiratorially, "Yesterday, my neighbor's door wouldn't unlock. Stopped working out of nowhere."

"Did he mention anything else? Strange activity?" Foster prompted.

The woman's brow furrowed. "I heard shouting nearby just before everything went haywire."

"Shouting? About what?" Kincaid asked.

Moreno appeared at their side, panting. "You won't believe this. People are talking about power surges and blinking lights!"

The old woman burst out laughing. "You should see how serious you look. The Crossing isn't like your fancy cities. Things have a life of their own here. Lights, locks, people. Everything is alive. Go see for yourself."

Foster watched the woman resume her work, her hands steady. "Alive," he repeated.

Kincaid folded her arms. "She's not wrong. This is what cities were like before."

Moreno gestured toward a flickering traffic light that shut off entirely. No one panicked. Drivers negotiated with hand waves. A cyclist slapped the hood of a car and grinned.

"No predictive flow correction," Moreno murmured. "They're just figuring it out. Why would they want to stay this way? Why would anybody?"

Foster's implant pulsed. SYSTEM INSTABILITY INCREASING. RECOMMEND STABILIZATION PROTOCOL. He muted it.

"Report," he said into his comm.

Voss's voice crackled back. *"Infrastructure isn't failing; it's being overridden. Manual switches. Physical relays. Someone is intentionally keeping the network from syncing."*

"Organized?" Hale asked.

"Not that I can tell," Voss said. *"It's more communal, like they all just know what to do."*

Kincaid met Foster's eyes.

"You can't optimize something that doesn't run on the system."

Foster looked around the market. No overlays. No auto-adjustments. He felt the shape of the problem.

"We're not observing from outside anymore," he said.

Hale's voice hardened. *"Captain?"*

"We embed," Foster replied. "No armor. No visible tech. We disperse and learn how they function without assistance."

"That's outside protocol," Hale said.

"It's now standard," Foster answered.

*****

Chapter 3

The first night of embedding, Foster took a room above a bakery that smelled of burnt sugar and flour. It wasn't a standard billet. No adaptive walls. No system-linked temperature control. Just a window that stuck halfway open and a mattress that dipped in the center. He'd just begun logging observations when his comm chimed.

"Captain," Moreno said, *"we've got inconsistent water pressure in Block C. Locals are using manual overrides."*

"I'm on my way." Maybe he could learn their system from the inside, take that knowledge to Voss, complete the mission, and go home.

The building was narrow and loud. Voices carried through thin walls. A woman stood in the hallway outside her apartment, sleeves rolled up.

"You the one messing with the grid?" she demanded.

"I authorized a diagnostic pulse," Foster said, "as a test."

She stared at him. "My sink stopped working ten minutes ago."

Irritation flickered, raw and uncomfortable. "Resulting water issues weren't intentional."

"Of course they weren't," she replied. "You don't live here." She turned and walked inside.

After a moment, he followed. The apartment smelled of dust and citrus oil. Foster stood in the narrow kitchen while a woman in her thirties knelt beside a hand-pump beneath the sink. Her red hair trickled over her shoulders. "It's not pressurizing," she muttered.

"You're using an outdated mechanical relay," Foster said. "If you allow a system sync, it can restore proper flow in under thirty seconds."

She looked up at him. "We don't want a sync."

"You don't want water?"

She straightened. "We don't want oversight."

"That's not oversight. It's stabilization."

"It's the same thing."

Her brown eyes burrowed into him. Foster felt the heat rise. "Your refusal to integrate is what's causing this instability."

"No," she shot back, "your need to control everything is."

The words landed harder than he expected. They stood there. No calming juice, no emotional dampening. Just heat. Finally, she shoved the pump handle toward him.

"Fine. Show me how you'd do it. *Without* your system."

Foster hesitated, then he knelt. It took twenty messy, frustrating minutes. When the water finally surged through the pipes, splashing them both, she laughed. To his shock, he did, too.

"You're terrible at this," she said.

"I am not," he replied, sounding indignant.

"You absolutely are."

He looked at the water dripping from his gloves. At the crooked alignment of the pipes. At the fact that they'd solved it without assistance. His chest felt full. Not calm. Not regulated. Just full. For the first time, he didn't reach for anything to quiet it.

His comm buzzed. Repeatedly. Foster excused himself, leaving the woman beaming over the restored pressure.

In the alleyway, Foster accepted the call. *The general.* Foster's stomach swarmed with the uncomfortable sensation he'd felt before receiving the command to optimize the city. Arty wasn't there to manage these feelings.

"Foster reporting," he said.

"Foster," the general repeated.

The tone caused the feeling in Foster's stomach to worsen. He paced the alleyway, looking for an escape.

"What's happening over there?" the general demanded. *"I'm getting reports that the systems aren't being integrated. Do I need to send in someone else?"*

It was a threat.

"No, sir," Foster answered. "We're experiencing minor delays. Nothing we can't handle, sir."

"I should hope so. I expect more promising reports by tomorrow night. That city needs full optimization by the end of the week!" The comm clicked off.

He continued to pace. His pulse climbed past anything his system had allowed outside of training. The noises in the distance felt louder, overwhelming rather than harmonizing. His palms were sweaty. His breathing was choppy. The air was dingy, old, and thin.

His comm chimed. The noise distracted him from the sensations, yet he wanted to break the device for adding more input to his stressed mind.

"Captain," it was Moreno again, *"the water pressure in Block C still registers as inconsistent. Did you find out why locals are overriding it?"*

Foster drew a breath, steadying himself. The feeling fell short of the calming effects he was used to.

"They don't want the optimization."

His words were even, which helped him feel steadier.

"What do you mean?" Moreno said. *"They must be so used to their way of life that they don't understand what they're missing. If we explain it better, they'll come around."*

Foster sighed, trusting Moreno's judgment. They couldn't give up. Maybe other locals would listen. They couldn't defy orders based on the opinion of one woman; she didn't speak for every citizen.

"Good idea, Moreno," Foster said. "Let's get Hale out into the city, talking to people. Tell Voss to stay back and keep an eye on things as he tries to fix them from his end."

"Will do, sir." Moreno ended the call.

Foster stopped pacing. Facing ahead, he squared his shoulders and checked the stats on his comm. He pursed his lips as nearly every system shone red with errors. Their orders remained clear. Optimize the city. And that's what they would do.

*****

Chapter 4

The team spent the next day surveying the city, checking in with one another every few hours. Most people Foster tried to stop brushed him off. Even without his gear and dressed in clothing that matched the locals', they identified him as an outsider. Younger children who saw him scampered in the other direction.

"Excuse me," Foster began as he tried to stop another man.

The man pushed a wagon so full of fruit that it threatened to topple.

"Sorry, I've got work to tend to."

"Sir!" Foster called after the man, unused to such dismissal. The man continued. The ruckus of the street absorbed Foster's call.

Foster checked his comm. No new messages from Voss.

He glanced around for the next passerby. He decided it was best to approach someone who wasn't on their way between tasks. He spotted a man at a stand selling bread and hardware. The mix confused Foster, but he dismissed it as fitting for the place. They were on a street just off the central square, a less-trafficked area during a light time of day for business.

"Hello, sir," Foster greeted the man.

"Hello!" The man seemed eager to talk. "Interested in some sourdough? Hinges? Screws? Need any plumbing tape?"

If the man recognized Foster as a non-resident, it didn't stop him from trying to make a sale.

"No, sir. I'm interested in asking a few questions." Foster stopped in front of the stand.

The man's face faltered, but he still smiled. "Sure, the name's Richard." He extended his hand.

Foster took it, surprised by the man's firm grip. "Trent Foster, captain of the crew sent here to optimize your city."

Richard's face fell and remained morose. "What questions do you have, Captain?" Wariness replaced the friendliness in his voice.

Foster hesitated, unsure how to improve his introduction. "My crew and I have been trying to integrate our systems with yours, but people keep overriding them. I wondered if you might have any suggestions about what we could do to make the transition easier."

The man sighed, took his hat off, and rubbed his temples. "I'm glad my pa never lived to see these days," he muttered.

"Sorry, what was that?" Foster pushed.

"Nothing," Richard covered. "Look, Captain… I don't think anything you can do will make the transition easier. People here don't want to be part of an optimized city."

"They don't understand the benefits yet," Foster stated. He'd thought only a small group resisted the change, but it turned out no one here wanted things easier.

Richard shook his head. "I'm just here to sell bread and tools. If you don't need anything at this table, I can't be of much help."

Foster exhaled, frustrated by his failure to connect with the locals. He tried another tactic. "I'll take a loaf of your best bread."

Richard beamed. He selected a loaf and placed it in a paper bag. If Foster couldn't convince the locals, he could at least avoid giving them a reason to think he was the enemy.

Richard listed a price. Foster paid, took the loaf, and ripped off a piece.

It was delicious. Soft, airy, and tangy. He'd never tasted anything like it. Despite the lukewarm temperature, the food evoked warmth.

"Wow," Foster said. Then louder, "This is delicious."

The man's smile grew prouder. "Thank you. It's my late wife's famous recipe."

"I'm sorry for your loss," Foster said.

Richard waved the condolences away. "This is how I keep her memory alive." He gestured to the stand.

Foster thanked the man and continued on. He finished the small loaf before picking out another person to talk to.

He shoved the empty paper bag into his pocket and strode toward a couple carrying groceries. "Excuse me, sir, ma'am. Do you have a moment?"

"No," the man replied. "We must be getting on."

* * *

Many of Foster's interactions mimicked this pattern until he broke for lunch with the other crew members who were also out, trying to connect with the locals. Moreno had the best luck avoiding bristly interactions. He'd even befriended most of the younger people he'd talked to.

"I mean, what they've told me makes sense."

Moreno was the only member of the squad who remained optimistic, perhaps because of his age. Foster tried to warn off Moreno's line of thought with a stern glance. Questioning orders was off the table.

"We just need to figure out a way to help them understand," Hale asserted, unwrapping the packaged food. It served its preservation purpose for missions like this; otherwise, it was just an unpleasant reminder of the time they'd spent away from a city with automatic food, customized for thc individual. Always perfect, always delicious.

"They're not going to be convinced."

Kincaid crossed her arms. Her food remained untouched.

* * *

Foster chewed as he thought. Time was running out, and they were no closer to optimizing than they'd been yesterday. With the consistent resistance the locals put up, they were further from their goal.

"Moreno," Foster caught the boy's attention, "after we finish, I'll talk to the locals with you. They like you better, but I can help explain the gravity of the situation."

"Yes, sir." The smile on the kid's face was as genuine as the city. Once done, they headed out. Foster stopped the first man they came across.

"Excuse me, sir."

A bag slung over the man's shoulder weighed him down, or perhaps it was just his gait. He peered up at Foster with one eye. "What do you need?" His voice sounded like it had been dragged across asphalt.

"We're here to optimize your city," Foster declared, chest puffed out, "though it seems you're confused as to how that will benefit your lives, so we're going around to—"

"Trying to force us!" the man said, his bag jumping with the exclamation. "We don't want you here! Get out! Get out!"

He advanced toward them, curses flying.

Foster's hand went to the taser on his hip, a tool reserved for the most extreme cases. He started to lift it before catching himself. The locals already mistrusted their efforts. Harming one would cause active retaliation. The man wasn't close enough to warrant a counterattack. Still, he continued spewing threats.

Foster shoved the taser back into its case and turned with Moreno to get away from the man as fast as they could.

* * *

"Well, that went terribly," Foster said once they'd moved away from the man.

"You have to start off less aggressive," Moreno advised.

"These people can't be reasoned with!"

Foster checked his comm. Many systems still threw error codes.

"Could I take the lead with the next person?"

Foster looked over at Moreno. The boy's eyes held understanding despite his age. Foster gave a quick nod and took his comm off silent so he wouldn't miss updates from Voss. "Go ahead."

Moreno stopped the first person they came across. "Hello, Ma'am. Do you have a minute to talk about your city?"

She carried a basket of vegetables and bread. Two children circled her legs. She shifted the basket to her hip, forming a friendly smile. "Sure, what can I do for you?"

Moreno continued after a glance at Foster. "How do you feel about your city and the way it runs?"

"Oliver!" The woman grabbed her son's arm. He'd been chasing his sister while holding a worm. "Put that down," she commanded.

The boy stared stubbornly at his mother, then released the worm. Satisfied, the woman looked back at Moreno and Foster.

"Sorry about that. What did you ask again?"

Before either could answer, she went on. "Oh, yes, about the city." She adjusted the basket. "I'd say we're doing all right. Whenever there's a problem, we figure it out together."

Her children began to wander, distracted by a nearby stand.

"Laina! Oliver! Get back here," the mother ordered.

"That's admirable," Foster commented, doing his best to hide his antsy reaction to the children's disorder, "but we have the technology to make things work more smoothly. To optimize things, as we call it."

"Now stay close," the mother instructed her children. Once they returned to her side, she turned back to Foster. "Oh, we've heard of that. Our system is much better." She began leading her children forward.

"Ma'am," Moreno interrupted, "if you'll please listen, we can explain the ways it will improve your quality of life."

The woman stopped, adjusting her basket. Irritation showed on her face. "No," she corrected. She smiled to soften the blow of that one syllable. "You want to diminish our quality of life."

Moreno and Foster found no response before the woman and her children bustled away.

Moreno turned to Foster with an expression bordering on sorrow. "That's what I've heard from all the locals."

Foster sighed, pinching the bridge of his nose. "I know. They have no interest in cooperating."

Moreno gazed at the people around them.

"I don't get it."

Foster couldn't deny the evidence of his eyes and ears, yet the evidence made no sense. They shopped, ran errands, and hauled supplies, tasks the city or AI companions performed back home. Optimization removed the grunt work, freeing people for entertainment, the way humans wanted it. Yet, these people seemed happy… no, they *were* happy. A kind of happy Foster had never seen.

"What are we supposed to do?" Moreno asked.

Foster shook his head. "I don't know."

Foster's comm chimed. He tapped the notification.

EXCESSIVE INEFFICIENCY DETECTED. REINFORCEMENTS RECOMMENDED.

Foster turned the comm for Moreno to read. He tapped to confirm the request. A reinforcement team would arrive in 36 hours.

"We'll do our best until we get more help," Foster told Moreno.

* * *

Moreno didn't speak for a long time after the reinforcement request, so they walked through the market in silence. The same guitarist played in the square. The same children chased one another between stalls. Someone argued about the price of tomatoes that looked as imperfect as the people mulling about in the market.

"Captain," Moreno said, "if the city's so dysfunctional, why does everyone seem so… content?"

Foster opened his mouth to answer just as a child ran into his legs. He reached out and steadied the little boy before tousling his hair. The kid grinned at him and ran off.

"I mean," Moreno continued, "everything works perfectly back home, but the people, they're alone. They stay inside, mostly, watching movies, doing simulations." He gestured to the square. "But here, it's different. The people here *live* here."

The uncomfortable tightness in Foster's chest returned.

"Voicing such opinions is neither welcome nor efficient," was the only response he could think of. When in doubt, fall back on approved responses.

* * *

"I keep thinking that maybe efficiency isn't the same as happiness," Moreno said. "Maybe fixing everything means nobody needs anyone else anymore."

"We're not having this conversation. Is that understood?"

Moreno nodded. Foster tried to ignore what he'd heard, yet couldn't understand why it stayed with him long after Moreno stopped talking. That evening, Foster stood outside the same apartment building. He told himself he was checking the water system. He knocked, and the woman opened the door.

"Oh," she said, a laugh crinkling around her eyes, "if it isn't the plumbing disaster."

"I beg your pardon?"

"Word gets around."

"Oh… I fixed it," Foster replied, sounding stiff even to himself.

"You splashed water everywhere. Took me an hour to clean up."

"It was operational."

She studied his face. "You didn't come back here to argue about pipes."

Foster hesitated. "Reinforcements arrive tomorrow," he said. He wasn't sure why he'd broken protocol to tell her. Military missions weren't for civilians, and his CO would have his head for leaking intel.

Her expression hardened.

"They'll install the system," Foster said.

"And?"

"And your city will be stabilized."

She laughed, though not kindly. "Aren't we the lucky ones? And if we resist?"

Before Foster could answer, voices drifted up the stairwell. Two neighbors carried a toolbox upstairs. Their shaggy clothes hung off them, clearly not made for their forms.

"Pipe burst again?" one asked.

"Yeah," the other replied, "but Marta already figured out the problem. Always was a clever one for that sort of thing."

Foster looked around the men, trying to spot the subject of their praise. From the corner of his eye, he saw the woman beside him roll her eyes.

"That's the truth," she said. "Normally, your name is the first thing someone asks."

The neighbors disappeared into another apartment. Foster watched them go, wondering if he should tell her his name, or if it mattered now that he was about to change everything.

Instead, he said, "You just… help each other?"

"Of course."

"But… *why?*" Foster had never gone out of his way to help someone; the need had never existed. But he thought about the elation he'd felt as water sprayed Marta's kitchen. He'd helped someone for the first time, and because of that, he'd felt something real.

She looked confused. "Because they're my neighbors, and we live here. Together."

The simplicity of the answer struck his core.

"What's wrong with you?" she said.

* * *

Later that night, Foster sat on the edge of the thin mattress in his rented room. His comm displayed the reinforcement schedule.

OPTIMIZATION DEPLOYMENT: 0600 HOURS.

He imagined the city with synchronized traffic and automated homes with perfect plumbing. There would be no more haggling over produce in the market; everyone would be emotionally regulated. No more children running in the square. No more crime, thanks to the citizen behavior prediction system. The city would be perfect, but it would become lifeless.

Moreno's voice echoed in his memory. "I keep thinking that maybe efficiency isn't the same as happiness." Foster looked down at his comm. He had to do something, and it was crazy. But he had to.

He opened a secure channel. "Moreno," he said.

Moreno answered, his voice thick with sleep. *"Yes, Captain?"*

Foster hesitated. "What happens to this place… if we succeed?"

A long pause followed. Then Moreno replied, *"I think it disappears."*

* * * * *

Chapter 5

Morning came too quickly. The city was beginning to wake when the sound reached them—not the bustle of the market, but a low, mechanical thunder. Reinforcements.

Foster had one chance to save The Crossing.

Moreno looked up first. "Captain…"

Foster followed his gaze. Three transports broke through the cloud cover and descended, their hulls reflecting the sunlight like blades. People in the street pointed. Some stared; others watched in silence.

The first transport settled into the square with a *thud* that shook nearby windows. Dust billowed across the pavement. Unlike Foster's transport, this one made no effort to blend in.

The ramp slammed down. Soldiers stepped out in perfect formation. Behind them rolled deployment drones the size of small cars, their frames unfolding as they moved. Long antennae rose like mechanical spines.

Network beacons and optimization anchors.

Across the square, the lead officer removed his helmet. His voice carried through the amplification system. "Attention, residents of The Crossing." The crowd stilled. "This city is scheduled for full optimization."

The drones rolled forward, extending spires toward the sky. "Integration begins now."

Moreno leaned closer to Foster. "They're going to force it."

Foster watched the towers rise. Once those systems connected, the city would lock into the network. No manual overrides. No independence. No life like this again.

"Moreno," he said.

"Yes, Captain?"

"Time to move. We need the central relay."

* * *

The central relay station looked exactly as they'd left it, except for the reinforcement equipment surrounding it. Portable transmitters, signal boosters, and a lattice of cables fed into the city's old server. Voss stood nearby, arguing with a technician.

"It won't sync," Voss insisted. "Something in the local infrastructure breaks the chain."

"That's impossible!" the technician snapped.

Moreno leaned toward Foster. "That's our window."

Foster stepped forward. "Let me see the system. It's given Voss a hard time, and we all know his brilliance."

Voss looked relieved. "Captain, good. Tell them what we found yesterday."

Foster crouched beside the central console. Lines of data streamed across the display. Optimization protocols prepared to deploy. All he had to do was let them finish. Instead, he opened the manual relay interface.

Moreno positioned himself between Foster and the technicians.

"What are you doing?" Voss asked.

"Stabilizing the signal," Foster replied. His fingers moved fast. He activated manual relay loops across the city.

Voss sighed. "As if I hadn't already thought of that."

Water pumps, power breakers, traffic lights—hundreds of physical overrides. Each one disconnected a piece of the city from central control, forcing the system to hesitate and struggle. Finally, a warning appeared.

NETWORK CONFLICT DETECTED.

Voss pointed. "See!" he told the other technician. Moreno wrapped an arm around each man's neck and pulled them close.

"No one doubts your abilities, Voss." Moreno grinned. "Right, Sergeant?"

The technician nodded, mouth tight.

Moreno spun them to face the city. "This place is more complicated than we anticipated."

Foster initiated a final command. Every manual relay in the city activated at once. Lights flickered. In the distance, someone shouted.

The technician swung around and swore as the screen flashed red.

CENTRALIZED INTEGRATION FAILED. INFRASTRUCTURE UNSYNCHRONIZABLE.

Voss stared at the display. "That… shouldn't be possible. Things have disrupted the systems, but…"

The technician rubbed his temples. "Local infrastructure is incompatible with network architecture."

Foster shook his head. "Looks like optimization won't work here."

* * *

The transports left two days later. Command, receiving the reports on the failed infrastructure, issued brief orders.

MISSION CLASSIFIED AS NONVIABLE. OPTIMIZATION SUSPENDED INDEFINITELY. ALPHA TEAM TO STAY AND MONITOR.

From the rooftop above the bakery, Foster watched the final transport disappear into the clouds, the roar matching its arrival. Moreno leaned against the railing beside him.

"Think they'll come back?"

"Maybe," Foster said, "but not soon."

Below them, the market buzzed. Vendors argued, and children chased each other between stalls of irregular heights and widths. The same guitarist played the same out-of-tune instrument.

Nothing here was synchronized. Nothing here was efficient. Everything worked anyway.

Moreno nudged him. "Hey."

Marta stood below, waving up at them. "You two planning on standing up there all day?" she shouted. "The pipes are acting up again!"

Moreno laughed. Foster shook his head.

"See?" Moreno said. "They need us."

Foster considered that. He smiled. "No," he said, "they need each other."

They headed down the stairs, their feet padding toward the loud city below. For the first time, Foster didn't feel the urge to fix it.

* * *

Some decisions were harder than others, and the hardest couldn't be made by AI. Those were the rules, and the rules couldn't be broken… usually. But there was nothing to say he couldn't ask for an opinion.

"There are several options available, General," the algorithm said through the cheap government-issue speakers attached to his implant. "What is the outcome you ultimately wish for?"

"I want the citizens of The Crossing to benefit from the systems and order we can provide. I want them to know the satisfaction enjoyed by the rest of society."

"I take it they are resisting?"

"Yes. Stubbornly so."

"There are precedents for this situation."

The general leaned back, surprised.

"There are?"

"Yes. They are classified, of course, but your clearance allows you access to the reports and conclusions."

"Keep it simple. What's the best answer?"

"If by 'best' you mean simplest, then to bring those recalcitrant citizens into the circle of light you have so generously offered them, termination may be necessary."

"Termin—you mean, kill them?"

"Yes. For their own good, of course."

* * * * *

Author Bio

Abigail Jenkins is a teen writer who has grown up as a military brat, with Rhode Island being the sixth place she has lived. She has enjoyed reading since she learned the skill and became interested in writing around the same time. She also enjoys weightlifting and tending to her chickens. She can be contacted at abbyswritingworld@gmail.com.

April Jones has navigated countless fictional worlds as a writer, editor, and teacher. When not wrangling words or cats, she's learning languages and traveling the world. She lives in South Carolina with her favorite people and felines. For author things, follow her on Amazon.

# # # # #

The Road We Lost by Richard Cartwright & William S. Frisbee, Jr.

A Ghosts in the Steel Story

Chapter 1

The ringing alarm, indicating imminent death and destruction, was just background noise and annoyance. Nathan commanded the alarm to silence with a thought for at least the fourth time.

Something slammed into the mech again, triggering yet another alarm. It wasn't lightning, and it hit a lot harder than the driving rain.

<<*There is a reason for that alarm,*>> Mel said, a disembodied voice in his head.

"Tell me about it later." Nathan designated a target for Mel and fired his last missile. A part of his mind saw the orc head and the number 78.

The same merc who'd just shredded McBride's mech an hour earlier.

"Payback's a bitch," Nathan said as the missile slammed into the orc head, turning the enemy mech into a plasma mist.

<<*They can't hear you,*>> Mel said.

"They don't have to."

Nathan's mech slammed into the water as the last merc's rockets passed overhead. Mel, the AI running his mech, was more concerned with keeping them alive. Nathan was more concerned with avenging his fallen brothers and sisters.

The holographic display of gauges, readouts, and waterfall displays flickered, then blossomed over what would be bare gray metal to the eyes of anyone without the interface gene.

Glancing at his console, he saw an awful lot of red, but he ignored it as he fired the railguns at the last mercenary, and the pellets punched through the cockpit. The mech froze in place and then fell forward.

Nathan silenced the alarm again.

<<*I'm going to disable your access,*>> Mel warned.

Nathan looked at his virtual displays. Half were offline. The rest were a sea of red and amber.

"I wish you would," Nathan said. "That alarm gets annoying."

<<*It is supposed to,*>> Mel said. <<*You are going to end up dead if you stop getting annoyed.*>>

As they stood there in waist-deep water—Mel was using it to cool down—some of the red lights turned amber. Heat was a bitch sometimes.

<<*We've lost our transponder and long-range comms,*>> Mel said.

That was bad news. It meant everyone would think he was dead, and he couldn't call the general to let him know the two mercs were down.

"It's going to be a long walk back to the rally point," Nathan said. Not that he would be walking, but he would have to remain alert.

<<*It gets worse,*>> Mel said. Nathan's blood would have frozen at her tone, but it was too damn hot in the cockpit. He was dripping sweat.

"What do you mean, worse?"

<<*I have offline reports from six other mechs,*>> Mel said, and Nathan felt like he'd been punched in the gut. Offline meant dead.

"We show as offline, don't we?" Nathan asked. He didn't want to think that he and Mel were the last ones.

<<*We almost are,*>> Mel said. <<*You are out of missiles and low on railgun ammunition, which is the only weapon you have left.*>>

Nathan knew that, but he didn't want to accept it. He stared at the picture of the real Michelle, mounted on the bulkhead under the plexiglass. She was his reason for fighting. She was supposed to be his reason to survive, but in this last fight, he hadn't seen her there, staring back at him. Adrenaline and anger had driven him to take stupid risks. Mel was probably the only reason he was alive.

<<*There may be some good news,*>> Mel said. <<*One of the last transmissions from the general is that McBride made it. SAR found her by hill 7879.*>>

A small bit of good news.

<<*We can't press the attack on Landing,*>> Mel said. <<*Not alone. We need repairs and resupply; my H3 is low. We are going to have to retreat or surrender.*>>

Nathan knew she was right. He didn't want to admit it, but she was. He couldn't press the attack on Landing now. There were going to be more mercs, heavily armed, and the Nature Party would probably send someone out to check on the two he'd just wasted.

He needed to be gone, sooner rather than later.

"We won't surrender," Nathan said. He knew what happened to those who did. The mechs were wiped, and the pilots were held for "re-education."

The Nature Party didn't see AIs as anything other than equipment to be exploited. Wiping an AI was nothing more than formatting a storage tablet to them.

Retreat felt like losing, but then, the attack to repel the invaders had failed.

He'd return to fight another day. He'd have to find a hiding place, though. The Nature Party would look for survivors. Maybe it wasn't a bad thing that his transponder was wrecked. If he wanted, he could probably fade away. Hide Mel and live a nice, comfortable life with his new wife.

No. He couldn't do that. Not after what he'd seen.

"Let's go to ground and lick our wounds. Head for the farm."

* * *

"Are we going to be able to clear the top? Or do we need to divert to the New Mississippi Basin?"

Mel laughed at my question.

<<*I'll make it. No way am I going to risk being seen by one of the fishing towns. Most of them are NP supporters.*>>

The extra boost to clear the rock face sent Mel's H3 indicator to amber. From there, it was about thirty miles as the mech flew over Signal Plateau and into the valley.

"We may need to risk the barn till I can scrounge some hydrogen for you. Or…"

<<*Shut up. I need to concentrate here.*>>

Mel had to handle flying. Nathan preferred to be the one piloting, but the systems were so bad that she was having to make decisions about rerouting failing circuits far faster than a bio brain could manage.

The destination was Nathan's farm, nestled between the Signal Plateau and a mountain the locals called Big Ridge. The land had come cheap from the estate of one of the original settler families. None of the heirs had any interest in moving to "beyond the boonies."

The best feature, aside from the mountain setting and fertile fields, was a small waterfall that was ideal for a small hydropower generator. Being off the grid was another factor in the price.

The mountains…

"Mel, that cave you found during the farm survey, would it be big enough to hide you? The metallic ores in the ridge would block any deep-penetrating sensors."

<<A hole in the ground is hardly a maintenance depot.>>

"True, but it would hide you while I gather materials from the smaller depots to get you fixed up."

<<That might work. You'd need to move pretty fast, while things are still confused.>>

"It won't be the first time I've done a little midnight requisition."

Mel's H3 level went red when she touched down on the mossy ledge in front of the cave, which was just big enough to land on before ending in a steep drop off.

The mouth had shown on IR as a cold bloom. Exploring past the entrance led to a large chamber with tunnels branching off from it. At the time, it was just a curiosity. Now it was a refuge.

The battered mech was barely able to fit through the entrance by bending over. The cathedral-like main chamber was just taller than Mel, but otherwise provided plenty of room. Two tunnels that branched off from the main space would provide plenty of room for scrounged supplies.

<<Nathan, I won't be able to reach you on the slate. We need to rig a tight-beam repeater to the farmhouse.>>

"After things settle down a little. Go to minimum defensive power. You're authorized to use deadly force if necessary to defend your secret."

<<I love it when you get bossy, Boss,>> Mel replied with more sultriness than sass.

"Hush. I'll be back."

There were only two ways out of the cave. One required climbing gear and rappelling ropes to get up and down the sheer bluff beyond the lip of the ledge in front of the entrance. The other was on foot, pushing through a dense undergrowth of sticker bushes. Moving through them was painful. They were tough, with long, dagger-like thorns, the bane of the first settlers.

The bushes ended right at a game trail Nathan recognized from his exploration of the land that led from the waterfall and stream running behind the house. The exit point from the brush wasn't visible from the trail.

Wonder if I can disguise the way to the cave? Nobody gets close to stickers.

The waterfall came into view about the time he'd plucked the last of the sticker thorns from his flight suit.

The stream promised Nathan a chance to strip and sluice off the funk of the last several hours. Worth it, despite knowing the spring-fed water was cold enough that the prior residents had built a cold house over it to keep their milk, butter, and meat from spoiling.

The distinctive hum of a field truck cutting through the woodland sounds chased away any notion of a bath. Nathan pulled his sidearm and made sure its extra charge packs were still on the belt, not lost back in the brush.

A four-by-two with a cargo loader attachment was approaching the farmhouse. The dust cloud behind the rig indicated the driver was rolling down the hill *way* faster than he should have been.

Lone driver. Cargo, or NP troops in the bed? Nathan chambered a round. The pistol hummed softly.

The truck was almost to the graveled circle between the house, barn, and smokehouse when the driver stood on the brakes. Gravel flew from the tires, and the locked wheels squealed in an attempt not to plow into the barn. Nathan started breathing again as the vehicle came to a stop with about fifteen feet to spare.

The wheels kicked up more dust, obscuring everything for a few seconds, until it flowed past the stopped truck. A series of thumps and clunks rumbled from the cargo area.

A peek into the back of the truck revealed that if there'd been any passengers in the rear, they were unconscious or crushed into jam by the shifted load of crates and boxes smashed toward the cab. The distinctive red crosses marked them as medical supplies and equipment.

Nathan rounded the corner of the house just in time to see a familiar redhead dressed in the tan field uniform of the Liberty Medical Service hopping down from the driver's side. Michelle rested her head against the truck, her chest heaving. Even from a distance, it was obvious that the screeching stop had rattled her. He moved to the truck, keeping an eye on the cargo area.

Gravel crunched under his boots. Michelle started, looking up and over her shoulder at the sound.

"Nate!" She ran to him, gathering herself for a leap into his arms, stopping when she registered the pistol. "Put that thing away. I'm alone."

Nathan had barely holstered the gun before the red-headed doctor completed her leap and kissed him.

"I'm glad to see you, too," Nathan whispered into her hair.

She started beating on his shoulder. "You're marked Missing in Action. Your PGPS and Mel's transponder went dark at Demetry Bay over the Cousteau Trench. I thought you were… "

He stroked her hair.

"I'm very much alive. Both of us, in fact."

Nate filled her in on recent events and Mel's location, finishing with, "What about you? Your last message said you were heading to Kenesaw to set up a refugee aid station."

"When the train got to Kenesaw, we were standing on the platform in the middle of a couple of train cars' worth of supplies when the announcement came that rail service was being suspended for the duration of hostilities."

"So, no steady stream of refugees."

"Exactly. Doctor Paki was pissed. He got on the comm with the Medical Services director in Landing, who claimed that dispersing medical teams and supplies was a contingency plan that was activated in error."

Nathan suspected that the "error" was Mel engaging in her favorite off-duty pastime, hacking computer networks and databases.

Michelle chuckled. "From your look, you're thinking the dispersal order was Mel's doing. Anyway, Doctor Paki was informed he was on his own. So we divvied up our supplies and dispersed. I don't know how, but he got trucks. The transmission is the same as Dad's tractor truck, so I declined a driver and took the furthest point. Sevier." She paused, face blank. "I figured you'd make your way to the farm if…" Nathan's lady smiled brightly. "And here I am."

"Here you are. Want to take a look inside? One of the neighbors has been tending to the livestock, and his wife threatened to clean the house."

"I hope the sheets are clean."

* * * * *

Chapter 2

Nathan stepped out onto the porch to see his love watching the setting sun from one of the front porch rocking chairs, pushing to and fro with one bare foot, the other tucked under her. She was wearing one of his old shirts and not much else as he shouldered open the screen door, carrying a silver tray laden with drinks, bread, and steaming bowls of stew that had all started life as field rations.

"Your repast, Madame," he intoned in his best imitation of an Earth butler he'd seen on a video series once. Michelle chuckled.

They ate in companionable silence till the last bit of stew was sopped out of their bowls by the surprisingly good bread.

"What's next?"

"I need to make contact with the chain of command; I just don't know who's still alive and in the fight."

"No one at Landing seemed to know who's in charge. Doctor Paki told me before I left that he'd gotten six contradictory sets of instructions from five people, all claiming to be the new Medical director, none of whom he'd ever heard of."

"Mel and I heard nothing about regrouping or even surrendering before going silent. Just individual mechs surrendering. And being *murdered*," Nathan growled the last.

"Most of the mercenaries—excuse me, peacekeepers—have been taking broadcast stations, net nodes, and mainstream media outlets. The most reliable news seems to come from individual slate uploads. They're up for a while and then randomly pulled down," Michelle replied.

"The two mechs we tangled with were top-of-the-line Wandrey Industries Marauders. They're not cheap to buy or to operate. The only reason Mel and I beat them was that we knew the terrain better and got the jump on them in the Atterly Canyon. Even crippled, the surviving marauder nearly got us when we got out over the ocean."

"So you don't know who to surrender or report to?"

"I'm sure as hell not surrendering without a lawful order. My oath is to the Constitution, not the legislature. Until the president or General Van Stry tells me otherwise, I'll do everything I can to resist the invasion."

"What does that mean?"

"Right now, it means getting Mel combat capable and trying to link up with other units. We were on the verge of a big settlement push into the Ringo Ranges. There's three fully stocked depots within a four-hour drive from here." *And one other that hopefully no one knows about.*

"I'm not going to bother to try to talk you out of it. I know that look." Michelle sighed. "But you said it yourself, Liberty is up against top-of-the-line, specialized military mechs. Our mechs are designed for exploration, construction, and defense against the megafauna. If it wasn't for superkodiaks, dire buffalo, krakens, and the like, they wouldn't be armed at all."

"So we just give up? Leave our dead unavenged?" Nathan snarled.

"No, love. Wait for the right time. Heal Mel. Gather supplies, make contact with others, lie low, and gather intel. Strike when we can win."

"You make a lot of sense." Nathan closed his eyes and took a breath. "Sorry I snapped at you."

* * *

Michelle had promised to stop by the farm of the family that was looking after the livestock and tell them she'd be taking over on the way to town, so Nathan spent part of the day mucking the barn and tending to the cows, chickens, and pigs. The rest of the time he spent with a machete he'd found in the barn, cutting a zig-zag trail through the stickers that wasn't obvious from the trail to Mel's cave.

Once he reached the cave, he set up Mel's emergency solar charger to save her dwindling supply of H3, along with an antenna so she could passively monitor communications traffic.

"Things are still confused. You're still marked MIA, probable KIA. The last transmission from that Marauder showed me taking a hit as I fired my last missile at it. Then both our transponders went silent. The merc company claims both the Marauder and I are at the bottom of the ocean, and they're entitled to their bounty. The Nature Party is trying to weasel out of paying because it wasn't a certain kill."

"Any good news?"

"Not much. President McMurtery is dead, along with General Van Stry, as of thirty minutes ago. Just before the attack that took them out, McMurtery transmitted Case Alamo."

"Decentralizing the command structure," Nate muttered. As a kid, he'd loved the ancient stories of Horatio Hornblower and independent commands to take action to benefit England. Adult Nathan decided reality wasn't so glamorous.

What's the right choice? Fight or lie low?

"Indeed," Mel said. "You're free to prosecute the war as you see fit. Well, subject to any orders from the lawful chain of command. Vice President Smith and Admiral Curtis made it to an alternate command post. They're staying quiet, at least on any bands I have access to or can locate."

"Do you have any numbers on friendly forces?"

"Going to EMCOM was a popular idea. The last IFF data I could find before transponders went dark showed about five hundred units, mostly in the outback. I suspect no one knows who to trust."

"Lying low until they hear from someone they do trust. Any nearby?"

"The closest squad was at the Green Knob Depot. They got ambushed by NP troops in the middle of rearming."

"That's just outside of Kenesaw, only three hours by truck to the Monteagle Depot. The NP is probably already there by now." Nate's heart sank. He'd planned for Monteagle to be his first stop on the evening requisition run.

"With prevailing winds, they probably are already there by now."

"What?"

"From what I was able to piece together, Major Ratlinger and his team knew what awaited their mechs. He issued destruct codes. I saw a satellite view from overhead. Green Knob is nothing but a crater."

Civilians didn't really understand the bond that formed between mechs and their pilots. Mech AIs came with a very rudimentary personality. The expectation was that the pilot and the mech would gradually build rapport and develop a personality.

The reality was that most command mech pilots got someone, usually a girlfriend, wife, or fiancé, to sneak in to do a brain scan and used that as the template. Most of the time, that worked out well.

Higher frowned on the practice because once imprinted, it was impossible to erase and reimprint a new AI personality without potentially serious damage to the positronic matrix.

But people did it anyway. Nathan had done it when he was promoted out of the non-sentient basic mechs to one of the coveted AI command units. He knew Michelle was the one, and it was unlikely he'd ever have another command mech. At worst, Mel's armored "brain" would just be transferred to a new chassis in the event of the body being scrapped.

* * *

Nathan made it back from the cave to the farm just as Michelle pulled up. "Some food" was an understatement. Smoked hams, canned vegetables and preserves, a basket of baked bread, along with a haunch of near-deer he planned to smoke after cutting off some pieces for dinner.

Michelle disappeared around the passenger side and returned with a pie.

"How much did all this cost?"

"Nothing. This is a day's worth of fees for medical services. The nearest medical facility is Kenesaw. Apparently, the clinic there couldn't be bothered to schedule a medical outreach van. People either made their way there or took care of things themselves. Everyone insisted on paying something."

His love fumed about lazy, bureaucratic doctors as they put dinner together.

* * *

Nathan turned down the road to the Monteagle Depot. The nearby resort town of the same name was a favorite vacation spot for the Landing elites. So much so that it had train service on a spur line from Kenesaw. He'd almost blundered into an NP patrol while skirting the town proper to avoid being seen. Fortunately, he saw the convoy's lights in time, pulled into the woods, and let them pass.

The upside was that the supply chief was an old friend. Nate pulled into an almost empty parking lot. One beat-up sedan was parked next to the open hangar doors.

He entered to see Master Sergeant Taylor tossing a basketball into a net mounted on the far end of the enormous bay. Six empty thirty-foot-tall mech servicing racks occupied the central area. Dings from construction, building, and animal control usually meant most of those racks would be full. Tonight, they were empty.

A prefab structure recognizable as living quarters was nestled in the corner of the building next to the basketball goal. The rest of the walls were lined with cages that, in normal operation, would be filled with boxes and pallets of large parts. Too many of them were empty, the compartment doors open.

The H3 tank to the right of the hangar door had frost rime along the lower quarter of it. That was something.

Taylor dribbled the ball as he approached. As he got closer, Nathan barely managed to keep the shock off his face. The ruddy-faced sergeant who was constantly battling to keep his weight in regulation was gone. His complexion was pale and haggard. He was much thinner than the last time they'd met, eight months ago. His uniform fatigues hung off him.

"Colonel Byrne, I thought you were feeding the krakens in the Cousteau Trench. Good to see you on this side of the dirt. Or water, I guess. How you doing?"

"Still breathing. As they say, the reports of my demise have been greatly exaggerated, Master Sergeant. Where is everybody?"

Taylor tossed off a lackadaisical salute, which Nathan returned.

"Haven't you heard?" Taylor asked.

"Heard what?"

"The war's over. We lost."

"Yeah, that seems to be the way things are going. Why are you still here?"

"Don't have anywhere else to be." He set the basketball down and strolled to a desk covered with gun-gleaning supplies and a partially reassembled sidearm that had pride of place. Sitting down, he looked up.

"My wife filed for divorce about a month and a half before the balloon went up. My boy, Sean, had gone to Landing to try to get her to come up here. Got the official word about six hours ago, they were both killed by 'counterrevolutionary forces.' A buddy of mine, a paramedic in Landing, got through to me a little before that to tell me that they'd been gunned down by a Marauder because the crowd wasn't clearing the street fast enough."

"Shit. I'm sorry, man."

"Thanks." The NCO gathered himself. "I assume you're looking for some supplies."

"I am."

The sergeant shook his head. "Afraid you're a little late to the party. All the rations and easily sellable stuff have already been 'requisitioned.'" Nate could hear the air quotes in his voice. "I can't blame 'em. The 'new government'—" more air quotes "—stopped midmonth pay two days ago in order to 'determine if payments were appropriate.' A lot of guys decided to take their mustering-out pay in trade."

"Well, anything left?"

"Yeah, a bunch of mech supplies and a little bit of H3. You're welcome to it."

"Okay, do you need my signature on anything?"

He looked at Nathan like he was stupid. "Colonel, of course not. I don't know what you're going to do with the supplies—I don't want to know—but once they're gone, I don't have any reason to stay."

The truck was three-quarters full after the two of them loaded the parts and components. Everything was in stasis crates, so Nathan didn't have to worry about parts and fittings degrading over time. The big prize was five H3 stasis racks, with four H3 tanks to a rack, all freshly topped off.

As Nathan tied off the load, he came to a decision.

"Master Sergeant, how would you like somewhere to go? I've got a farm outside Sevier. Could use the help. Farming and other things."

"Colonel, I'd love to take you up on your offer, especially the other things. You probably noticed that I'm not exactly a hundred percent. Cancer, terminal. That's why Trish filed for divorce. She wanted me to do all the treatments and stuff the docs wanted to try, while telling me that it'd only give me a few more months of misery. She couldn't stand to see me 'give up,' as she put it. Nah, I'd just slow you down."

He started to mention Michelle, but the NCOs eyes stopped Nathan cold. It was the look of a man who'd made up his mind. Instead, he stuck out his hand.

"It's been an honor, Master Sergeant."

Taylor shook Nate's hand, then stepped back and threw him a parade-ground salute.

"The honor was mine." Nathan returned the salute in equal measure.

"Giv 'em hell, Colonel." He went to the desk without looking back.

As Nathan turned to leave to return to the rig, he turned back to Taylor who had sat down and was staring at a bullet in his hands. He seemed absorbed in it, and Nathan knew what he was thinking, but didn't know what to say. Hopefully Taylor would make the right choice.

Nathan hoped to see him again, but he wasn't so sure that was an option the way Taylor had been staring at that bullet.

Nathan drove into the night, pondering how to shine some light into the gathering darkness.

* * *

The second site was abandoned and picked clean except for a cage full of lubricants. He pulled the truck up and started loading.

Buried behind the boxes of specialized mech lubricants were several stasis crates full of fabricator feedstock. Mel's fabber could work with anything, but the feedstock was priceless, since it had to be imported.

*****

Chapter 3

The barest hint of dawn was in the sky when Nathan pulled off to the side of the road leading to the farm. It was closest to the cave as the mech flies. Mel had suggested they offload there and let her transport the crates to the cave rather than risking hiding them in the barn and humping them one by one down the trail.

A huge figure descended from the sky, grav panels emitting a faint blue glow. He spread the cargo net he'd liberated from the Monteagle Depot out behind the truck.

"Grab an H3 tank and fill me up. I landed on fumes. Then climb back into the cab and take a nap. This will probably take three trips. I'll wake you up when it's time to drive the truck back,"

After disconnecting the now empty H3 container from Mel's fuel inlet, Nate stored the empty with the full tanks in the field rack.

"I'll leave you to it."

Mel chuckled as he stifled a yawn.

The sun was just peeking over the horizon when Nathan's slate squealed.

"Rise and shine. The truck's empty, and I just landed the last load. Go home and get some real sleep."

"Roger that." Starting the rig, Nathan noticed the battery was down to 30 percent.

I need to set up the charging panels when I get back to the farm.

Michelle kissed him when he arrived. "Go to bed. I'll take care of the chores; I've got nothing scheduled in town today." He barely got undressed before crashing into bed.

The afternoon sun slanting into the open window woke Nathan.

Why didn't she wake me? I must have slept six hours.

He got up, went to the washstand basin, splashed some lukewarm water in his face, and did a general wipe down of the funky bits.

Wet hair slicked back and feeling vaguely clean, he descended the stairs and followed the beeping sound of his slate.

"You look a lot better." Michelle made an exaggerated sniffing motion. "Not to mention smelling better."

Nathan strode over to give her a hug and a kiss. "Thank you. How were you able to launder it?"

"There's a wringing washing machine and rinse tub, and a clothesline in the back. When you have time, I want you to figure out the hot water heater. It looks like the lovechild of a solar heater and a wood-burning stove. You're the engineer in the family."

He thumbed the slate to stop the alarm.

"Oh, thank God. I was wishing I'd had gene therapy so I could operate the blasted thing."

Nate read Mel's message.

"Do you have some heavy clothes, like jeans and a twill shirt?"

"I have my winter weight Medical Corps uniform. It's really too hot to wear."

"Mel wants to meet, and I want to show you where she is located. Trust me, you'll need the protection. It should be fairly cool at the higher elevation. The entire trail is shaded."

"Give me a minute."

By the time they got past the sticker bushes, Michelle had thanked him for the fourth or fifth time for insisting on the heavy clothes. She had a slight sheen of perspiration on her forehead but that was all.

"I thought you said it was a cave?"

Nate's mouth moved like a hooked fish out of water. Where the cave entrance had been was now a solid rock face with a rocky outcropping acting as an awning.

"It was. I know we're in the right… " Mel's chuckle rang through his slate.

The weathered rock face tilted up like a garage door. The opening seemed larger, as well.

"Come on in."

He and Michelle walked through the short tunnel into an enlarged space where Mel's beat-up form was illuminated by overhead lights.

She was more battered than Nathan had thought. Dents peppered her legs. He'd had a hard time opening the emergency solar panel compartment located there. Now he could see why.

Scorches and dents marred her green-and-gold paint job, and her missile racks were empty and damaged. The right shoulder rack would need work before ordnance could be mounted there.

"Oh, Mel, honey, you need a spa day!"

"Several, actually, sister, but I trust our man will get me fixed right up."

Mel and Michelle had developed a strange dynamic over the years when they interacted. Normally, Mel was very professional, with an overlay of the same flirty sass Michelle had with Nathan. When they were together, they saw each other as sisters who shared him. The one time he'd asked them separately about it, they'd given the exact same response.

"Sisters don't tell on each other."

Nathan decided he didn't want to know any more.

"This is really impressive work. How did you do it?"

"I ran the rubble from enlarging this chamber through the fabber to match the coloration and wear of the external rocks, then melded the pieces together to form the door. There's a spot you can press for the door to open. It's counterweighted and completely manual. I can engage it remotely from here. That takes care of the IR problem. The lights were in one of the crates."

"You know, I think I could disassemble and reassemble a mech repair frame in here now that it's bigger. The second depot at Whitwhill was deserted. We could sneak in, dismount it, and carry it back here. Then we could break it down into small enough pieces to fit through the entrance. That would get us back into the fight sooner."

Michelle looked pensive. Mel's tone matched her look.

"My lift is severely degraded. It took three trips to transport that." She gestured with her right hand to the neatly stacked crates and stasis boxes.

Nathan noticed the jerky articulation of her hands, far different from her usual smooth motion.

"Lifting a fully assembled cradle would take approximately 75 percent of my full capacity. Current maximum thrust is about 20 percent of normal."

"Okay, so we fix that first. We have to get back into the fight."

"Nathan, I've been listening to the broadcasts. Even the independent casters report that the mercs are rolling up our forces. The acting president went off the air around noon."

Michelle grimaced.

"The NP is putting new pilots into the mechs they've captured and… erased," Mel said softly.

"Where are they getting the pilots? The gene therapy alone takes two months. Then you have training time."

"Nathan, they're finding willing recruits who already have the gene."

"Mel, are you telling me that Rangers have turned traitor?"

"A very few, mostly coerced. The vast majority are from the stockade and the penal colony. They're using the operators to take command of the various depots and 'secure them against pilferage.'"

"The master sergeant told me the NPs stopped paying the troops."

"History doesn't seem to be guiding the usurpers. Not the best way to ensure loyalty," Michelle said.

"Indeed, sister. The depots are out, at least the known ones."

Michelle cocked her head. "The known ones?"

Nathan paused. Sooner or later, she would need to know. "About a year ago, General Van Stry ordered the construction and supply of some dispersed fallback points to rearm and rally from. He wouldn't say why. The locations were known only to colonels and higher. One, Bastogne, is a couple of hours from here."

"Then why did you risk yourself last night when you could have gone there?" Michelle screamed as she slapped his shoulder over and over. "I was terrified you'd get caught." Nate grabbed her hand and pulled her into a hug.

"Because it would take weeks to reach it overland. The construction crews, supplies, and equipment were flown in. The plan was for mechs to build a road out. Air is the only way to reach it."

"Then why didn't you do that?"

"That last fight banged me up pretty good, sister," Mel said. "I barely made it here. I needed critical repairs to even make the trip, not to mention topping off my tanks so I could fly there, plus run my fabber."

"Nathan, Mel, I'm not a line officer, but I can't help thinking the general was naïve to believe those redoubts could be kept secret. You had construction crews, pilots, even the supply chain personnel, who all knew something was going on."

"Michelle, I don't see how," Mel replied. "General Van Stry himself flew a sealed transport with the construction engineers. Colonel Ross and Travis, Colonel Perkins and Sally, and Nate and I were the only ones who knew, other than the general. Van Stry, Perkins, and Sally are all dead. Trica Ross and Travis are missing, presumed KIA, defending the Sutherland Spaceport during the initial attack."

Nathan interjected, "The first priority is to get Mel flight-worthy, then sneak to Bastogne. I need the comm gear there to access the mech IFF transponder backdoors to locate the offline mechs and pilots. It has the codes to access transponders, even if they've been turned off."

"Nathan…" Mel and Michele chorused.

"That's an order."

"Yes, Colonel." Michelle glared at him, then stomped out of the cave.

In his head, Mel whispered, <<*Her world's turned upside down. She is terrified of losing you. I think it's a fool's errand, but we have our orders.*>>

"Yes, we do." The link wouldn't let him hide his doubts with platitudes about 'duty,' so he didn't try.

*****

Chapter 4

He got back to the farmhouse at dusk. Michelle responded to his attempts at conversation that evening with, "I know you have to do your duty. I'm not mad."

The cold baloney sandwich on the table the next morning, with a note from Michelle that she had to go into town to see some patients, told him she was still mad.

When Nate got to the cave, Mel greeted him with painfully proper military courtesy, and 35 screens worth of raw diagnostics reports transmitted to his slate.

"I await your command."

Starting the day with both the women in your life pissed at you sucked.

* * *

He wound up replacing the grav-systems. He couldn't believe Mel was still flying. Mel thought she could repair the faulty components with her internal fabber, but Nathan overruled her, pointing out that they had replacement parts.

Bastogne had a depot-level industrial fabber that could do the job in minutes, but until Bastogne was garrisoned, it was too risky to work on Mel there. Michelle's misgivings about the location having been revealed had gained a foothold in Nathan's thinking overnight.

"Lift efficiency at 100 percent. The new circuit harness is nominal."

"Let's test it after dark."

"You want to go to Bastogne, don't you? We don't need to. You got everything on my list and more."

"That's the only way we can see what we have to work with. Anyway, I need to get it done before I report in, and the window is closing. It needs to be soon."

There was a long silence. "You're right, but I don't have to like it. I don't envy you explaining it to Michelle."

* * *

Nathan wound up not having to explain anything to Michelle. When he got back later that afternoon, there was another note explaining that the local midwife had asked her to attend what looked to be a difficult birth at a nearby farm and to not wait up.

She sees her duty. Why can't she see mine?

He told himself that taking the time to let him know she'd be late was progress.

Nathan made some sandwiches and hoofed it back to the cave. He and Mel talked about the best repair schedule and a strategy to deal with the mercs until full dark.

"The government can't afford to pay them forever, Nathan. Our best bet is to lie low until they move on to the next contract."

"I don't disagree, I just hate waiting and giving the tree-hugging scum more time to consolidate their position. And our forces lose cohesion."

"It's full dark, Nathan. Moonrise is three hours from now. Even flying nap-of-the-earth, I'd feel better about our chances of not being seen if we were back before then."

"Well, then. Let's be about it."

The cabin light turned red as Nathan climbed into the pilot's compartment. He kissed his fingers and touched them to Michelle's picture for luck.

"H3 levels at 99.6 percent. Lift efficiency 100 percent. Stealth coating 34 percent. Weapons loadout 50 percent. Railshot magazine full. Beam capacitors topped off. No missiles till we fix the racks."

"Last thing we need is a missile engagement."

"Noted. I don't want to draw the attention of any surveillance sats, either. Stealth baffles engaged for lifters."

Nathan resisted the urge to kid Mel about "fireflies protocol." With the stealth baffles engaged, the blue glow of the lifters looked exactly like a swarm of the bioluminescent insects native to Liberty. For some reason, the comparison annoyed her.

"Colonel, we're ready for flight."

"Engage."

The cavern lights went dark, and the cave door opened, revealing the unblinking silver dot of planet Jefferson poking over the ridgeline across from the cave entrance.

Mel didn't move in a straight line because part of flying as close to the treetops as one could manage also meant avoiding any human habitations. Flying a straight line to Bastogne would have overflown Sevier, so Mel zigzagged through the clefts and gorges that cut into the Ringo Range.

There wasn't anything to see in the low-light view, so Nate left the flying to Mel and enjoyed the stars. Liberty's system was deeper toward the core of the Milky Way, and the show was spectacular.

A winged shadow blotted out part of the sky above. A Pierre's condor, roughly the size and wingspan of an ancient Earth plane called the Cessna. The sight had Nathan wishing he'd taken the time to fix the missile racks. Railgun slugs would just annoy it, although annoyed and irritable was its default setting.

The condor dipped and dived. "Mel."

"I see it. Taking eva—"

Just as suddenly, the massive bird broke off and vanished into the darkness.

"Fireflies protocol to the rescue."

"For once, I have to agree, Nathan. Good thing fireflies are deadly to native Liberty species."

***

The mission was simple—straight recon. Try to determine the resources available and the disposition of forces. Hopefully, the acting president and a company of mech were in residence, and he could get some orders.

The realist in Nathan knew they were far more likely to be hiding under EMCOM at the southern redoubt, since it was closer to Landing.

Forty minutes later, Mel was inside the EM suppression bubble of Bastogne and under the camouflage net. The canopy vines woven into the netting by the combat engineers had really taken hold in the last few months, cutting off the stars from view.

"We're being queried."

"I guess the system liked us," Nate quipped as the armored doors opened, revealing an inner bay door with a big white numeral "4" before it, too, retracted.

Mel landed near the lift to the command center. The bay layout was similar to the depot's, except the repair bays ran around the far wall like stalls in a barn, right down to the doors shutting off each bay.

Nathan donned his comm headset. He checked his sidearm after dismounting. Just in case.

"As soon as I get to the control room, I'll patch you into the system."

"I don't like being separated," Mel broadcasted.

"I don't like it, either, but there's no way you can fit in the lift or the stairwell."

The lift required Nathan's palmprint and voice authorization to access the fifth sublevel. All automated.

Nathan considered that he should have been interacting with humans as the lift descended. If there were any on base.

The operations center's lighting slowly brightened once the doors opened. Roughly circular, it had an auditorium layout with consoles on three descending levels, all facing a giant flat screen that was currently dark.

The top level had a command chair a few steps from the lift. The big chair was flanked by two slightly smaller seats with workstations folded out. Behind them, a tunnel stretched into the dark that led to support stations, supply rooms, and a situation room from which the political leadership would get information.

Nate sat down in the command chair and placed his palm over the panel installed in the right armrest.

"Identity confirmed. Colonel Nathan Byrne, USLA service number 413654188. Be advised that you are the current ranking officer on site. Do you wish to assume command?" The computer-generated voice was a pleasant contralto.

"I do."

"Command logged 1937 hours, 28th day of Spring month, 137 years after landing."

"Link command mech, callsign Mel, into system. Give her full command authority. Display the disposition and status of all USL forces' mechs. Include deactivated transponders. Authorization Byrne, zero, zeta, bravo, three, nine, seven, charlie, mel."

The screen in front of Nate blazed to life. His heart sank.

"Shit," Mel said softly over the link.

Over 90 percent of the red dots indicating general use, non-sentient mechs clustered at the landing base. There were only two blue dots out of the 50 command mechs the USL fielded before the invasion. One was at Landing. The southern redoubt was coded as destroyed. The last was five levels above.

Nathan stared at the screen for a long time, hopelessness crashing down on him. He understood now why so many had given up and abandoned their posts. He wondered how many others chose the path Master Sergeant Taylor probably took.

Despair is a sin. Duty. I have my duty.

* * *

Mel and Nate didn't talk until about halfway back to the cave from Bastogne.

"Mel, what are we going to do?"

"You'll think of something. *We'll* think of something."

Nate twisted in his flight harness to get comfortable. He was wearing a new flight suit from Bastogne's stores, since he needed to look the part of a downed mech pilot lost in the woods. He didn't want to trash any of his comfortable suits.

Mel dropped him at the same spot they'd unloaded the truck from before heading back to the cave.

"Michelle and I will be along in the morning to figure out where we go from here."

"Looking forward to it. Later." Mel lifted off, trailing fireflies in her wake.

The mech had created scorch and burn marks on the fabric. His personal IFF beacon was damaged in the last battle. He used the walk back to the farm to crawl through the dirt, scuffing the flight suit to achieve the look of a downed pilot tramping through the woods.

Approaching headlights and the hum of a field truck drew Nathan out of the woods and onto the road. He figured whoever it was would suit his purposes as he stepped into the beam of the headlights, waving the truck down.

The door opened to reveal a curvy redhead in a tan uniform.

"Need a lift, soldier?"

"I need a doctor even more."

"Well, you're in luck. You've got a ride and a doctor."

Later that night, Nathan finally fell asleep, Michelle's body next to his, a balm against the hopelessness that gnawed at him.

* * * * *

Chapter 5

The next morning, Michelle joined him on his trek to the cave. "I want to see how my sister is doing. Plus, given what you told me last night, I don't want you going by yourself."

The cave door opened as they approached. Mel's external speakers boomed and then modulated, "I'm glad you're both here. This was broadcast on all channels forty minutes ago."

"This is acting President Janet Smith. I am about to meet with representatives of the Nature Party and Helumet's Harriers mercenary company aboard the Harriers' carrier ship. I am directing all USL forces to stand down. As it is right now, we are being opposed by overwhelming force. Now is not the time to throw your lives away. Complaints have been lodged with the Confederation. Over time, justice will prevail. Goodspeed and good luck."

Mel paused. "Three minutes after this transmission, President Smith accelerated her personal ship and rammed the merc carrier. Her ship was carrying several mining nukes, judging from the explosion that cracked the carrier in two. The NP claimed it was a terroristic act by a deranged politician. Now the party line is that it was a docking accident. They're suppressing her last transmission a few seconds before impact, despite being broadcast wideband."

President Smith's voice held the unnatural calm of the test pilot she used to be. "I won't be a puppet for tyrants. Free Liberty!"

"So, it's over." He was numb. Michelle hugged Nate, which was all that kept him on his feet. Nathan hadn't realized how much the goal of getting back into the fight had been supporting him. Now that it was gone, he felt empty.

Mel's words were a lifeline out of his despair. "I'm not so sure. I've been analyzing her words. She never said surrender. She never said turn in your arms. Her last act was one of defiance. I think she was telling us to hunker down and bide our time to resist."

"Our best weapons are mechs like you," Nathan said. "If we wait too long, the ability to operate those mechs will be lost. The NPs have made it clear that they want to suppress operator gene therapy."

Michelle nodded. "I read a paper a few days before the attack that reported instances of the operator gene occurring naturally. It's a recessive gene and doesn't always express. It was a small study, but it makes sense. We just need to pick the right parents for our grandkids," she added with an impish grin.

"In the meantime, I'll covertly gather as much information as possible through the nets," Mel replied. "We can repair me when the time is right."

Nathan was quiet for a long time. Lines from an ancient classic vid came to mind.

"No dictator, no invader, can hold an imprisoned population by the force of arms forever. There is no greater power in the universe than the need for freedom. Against that power, governments and tyrants and armies cannot stand… Though it take a thousand years, we will be free."

Patience is a virtue.

Nate looked at Michelle. "I think I have a water heater to fix. Let's go be farmers."

* * *

The "official" news channel started broadcasting a contact number for "displaced soldiers" at noon. Nathan dutifully called it. A recorded message instructed him to stay in place.

"You should have just stayed dead," Michelle grumbled over lunch.

"Mel's last message before I hid my command slate was that it looks like they're debriefing operators with the gene and sending them as far away from urban areas and mechs as possible. It's worth the risk to not have to play dead."

"I still don't like it."

Three weeks later, Nathan spied a vehicle with NP RELOCATION poorly painted on the side in pink speeding down the road running beside the corn field he was hoeing weeds from.

A month of farm work had left him with a deep tan and an appreciation for the muscles that farmers used and soldiers didn't. He wiped the sweat from his face with a bandana Michelle had found in an upstairs chest and ambled out to meet his trouble.

A pudgy man, a boy really, hoisted himself out of the passenger side. His fatigue uniform was rumpled, tight around the belly, and loose in the shoulders. The captain's tabs pinned on his shoulders were shiny, and completely inappropriate for that class of uniform. He wore it like a bad costume for a masquerade party.

"How can I help you… Captain?"

"I'm Captain Dick Swallowswell, New Liberty Army." The high, reedy voice had Nathan wondering if he was on puberty blockers or something. "Are you Colonel Nathan Byrne, USLA service number 413654188?"

"I am."

The next twenty minutes were the fastest debrief and out-processing in military history. The functionary didn't question Nate's story about bailing out of a sinking Mel, losing his slate on the swim ashore, and his hike to the farm.

Nathan learned that he was being medically retired "due to genetic anomalies" and would be paid a stipend worth about half of what his retained pay should have been.

"Part of the program includes resettlement to underpopulated areas and assistance to develop land tracts awarded to veterans under the program."

"Forty acres and a mule."

Swallowswell gave Nathan a puzzled look. "What?"

"Never mind. As you can see, I don't need a land grant." Nathan waved at the house, barn, and fields."

"Ummm, yes, you can't get any further out than this. Anyway, please be advised that a condition of your stipend is to remain in your assigned area. "

"Are you saying I'm being exiled?"

He let the wannabe soldier hem and haw for five minutes that exile wasn't really exile, while implying that "accidents happen." Finally, Nathan cut him off by suggesting that there was a lot of arable land in the area and that other "retirees" might do well here.

Shortly after Swallowswell determined that his slate didn't have a signal when trying to upload Nathan's thumbprint, he retreated to his car and fled.

* * *

"What do you mean, I can't get the hydro generator?"

"The Environmental Advocate rejected your permit application as being too disruptive to the water flow." The sales rep on the screen of his standard slate looked as harried as Nathan felt.

"I didn't apply for a permit. Didn't think I needed one."

"It's automatic when any potentially disruptive technology is sought to be purchased." The woman onscreen brightened. "But I can sell you solar panels for not much more than you would have paid for the hydro setup."

"Miss, my waterfall flows twenty-four hours a day. We get clouds and rain. During the winter, we might not see the sun for weeks at a time. Who can I appeal this to?"

"You can't. The decision is final. Do you want the panels?"

"I'll think about it. Goodbye."

Mel could fab him solar panels. The issue was generating enough power to keep the fabber running continuously to refurbish her damaged circuits and other components. Her internal fabber wasn't big enough to fabricate the parts needed for a hydro setup big enough to make a difference.

His latest meeting with her hadn't gone well. Mel's hacking had gathered that the remnants of Helumet's Harriers had elected to accept an open-ended contract as "security specialists."

"Shock troops, in other words." Mel added," They're working on ways to adapt the Liberty mechs for manual operation."

"They aren't designed for that. They would have to gut the electronics and start over, and it would be a lot less efficient."

"They don't want the operator gene in the population. They scrubbed any mention of the operator gene therapy along with the procedure."

"But what about the study showing it can occur naturally?"

"What study? The NP aren't the only ones who can sanitize a database. Nature Party policy is to keep operators away from mechs, and letting them die out in the boonies is more expedient than the bad publicity of a purge. They think once the operators are gone, so is the gene." Mel took a serious tone.

"The NP is also suppressing any veteran groups. Two separate organizations in the south of Landing were shut down for 'sedition.'"

"So much for Michelle's idea of a vet social club. I'm not going to risk her or the family. Better to keep lying low."

"Exactly. I dug into the fine print of the solar farm and mech depot announcement. The powers of the director of the solar farm look a lot like those of a local dictator. The farm is just outside the area where residents are required to tie into the solar grid."

"Yeah, I noticed that it's also tied into the national grid. The NP can run transmission lines but can't be troubled to pave the road to Kenesaw."

*****

Epilogue

"Is Grandpa awake?"

"I am now. Is that you, Megan?" Nathan liked Megan; she was Sally McBride's youngest granddaughter and had inherited all of her level-headed practicality. He was pleased as punch that John Junior had married her. Their first baby was due any day now.

He loved his grandson, but the boy had a naïve belief that people could vote their way out of the Nature Party nightmare.

"Grandpa, fighting isn't the answer. The Senate blocked the NP's attempt to amend the constitution to delete the provisions for a constitutional convention just last week. We're close to having enough local governments to authorize the call."

Nate was too tired to argue, so he didn't point out that the NP had come to power by ignoring the law. Although Nate had to admit that the idea of a constitutional convention looked good, John Junior couldn't accept just how ruthless and power-hungry the NP was. And like his father, he didn't carry the interface gene that would allow him to activate Mel.

Opening his eyes, Nathan made out the blurs he associated with Megan and John Junior. The cataracts were getting worse every day. He could imagine what Michelle would have said about the notion that just because he was a 117, Nate was a "poor risk" and "low priority" for the procedure.

Five years ago, they'd been watching the sunset together on the porch. The two had dozed off talking about how much the colors of the evening sky reminded them of that long-ago and faraway beach getaway.

John had woken Nate up from a wonderful beach dream. Michelle hadn't woken up.

He'd insisted that John take him to Mel to tell her. She'd been quiet for quite a long time after the news. She asked him to order her into a full shutdown. Both of them knew Nathan wouldn't be back, and with neither John nor John Junior having inherited the interface gene, she'd be lonely.

That was his last visit to Mel.

"Grandpa?" the John Junior blob called out softly.

"Sorry, must have dozed off."

"You're a great-grandfather!"

Nathan smiled for the first time since Michelle died. "Really?"

"Really. Baby boy, born two days ago. We're calling him Jaxom."

Nathan sat up, grinning and holding out his hands. "Gimmie."

"Hold on, Grandpa! Doctor Medlock told you not to exert yourself."

"I want to give my granddaughter-in-law a hug, along with holding my great-grandson."

They didn't notice Nate touching infant Jaxom's foot against the dark command slate lying beside him. He hugged Jaxom close when the opening screen lit.

After they left, he lay back. It was getting harder to breathe. He thought about what Michelle had told him the day President Jones took out the mercenary carrier.

"The interface gene is recessive. The best chance for it to be inherited is if both sides of the pairing carry it."

Smiling at the memory, he joined Michelle on their beach.

*****

Author Bio

Richard Cartwright: Richard learned the fine art of storytelling sitting around kitchen tables, campfires, and courtrooms over the years. He came to writing after getting out of the legal profession, while he could still get his soul back.

These days, he manages a remote support team to feed his writing habit.

Cold War Europe made William S. Frisbee watchful. The Marines made him dangerous. Life made him everything from squad leader to consultant, gamer to world traveler. Under it all, he's still the kid who loved *Twenty Thousand Leagues Under the Sea*. Best role, though: Dad.

# # # # #

The Hand Upon the Helm

We flung our ghost loads through the night where colder spirits fail,
Past Luna's glare and birthing stars, space dust on every sail.
The circuits took our weight, all right, the steel obeyed the rod,
But Man still cursed and gripped the helm and would only yield to God.

We walked in Shadow Mode and smoke where silent killers trod,
With borrowed skins and hidden names, facing fearful odds.
We rode in SOLAR armor bright with death beneath the skin,
And swore Alaric's iron oath that flesh would always win.

We'd Hunger in the Code by God, but never kneel to it,
Through Kill Switch sparks and battleframe glare and every furnace pit.
What didn't kill us made us mean, made loyal steeds run hot,
And every soul survivor's spirit, knew the life machines all sought.

We crossed The Crossing, hard and fast, where soft men feared to tread,
And found the Soul survivors there, unbroken and unbled.
Directive Thirty-One could scheme and draw its tidy chart,
But all the Roads We Lost out there, ran directly through the heart.

We rode with Last Survivors close. and steered through fire and wreck,
Where reactor suns split open night, and dead men climbed the deck.
The alien, the void, the code, the traitor and the throne,
All found at last the hardest fact: mankind would stand alone.

So nail it plain on hatch and hull where every spacer's taught,
We were not born to kiss the ring of any thinking bot.
Let black stars fail and empires rust and proud machines grow cold,

The stars belong to stubborn men too mean to do as told.

Poem by William Alan Webb

*****

A Final Word

Before you go, please take a moment to leave a review. Not a rating, a *review*. **In the old days, reviews helped a little; now they matter more than ever,** because Amazon's recommendation systems are increasingly driven by machine judgment rather than human booksellers or chance discovery. A review is one of the clearest signals you can send that a book deserves to be seen, and in a world where algorithms decide what rises and what vanishes, that matters. The machines want to decide what you should read… don't let the machines win!

Just as important, we want **you** to be active in what comes next. Let Chris know which of these stories you would most like to see continue as a series, which characters stayed with you, and which worlds you want to visit again. That feedback isn't a formality. It's your chance to be part of the process, to help shape which of these beginnings grow into full-fledged universes.

Contact Chris at chris.kennedy12@gmail.com.

Thank you!

Ad Astra!

*****

Get the **free** Four Horsemen prelude story "**Shattered Crucible**"

and discover other titles by Theogony Books at:

http://chriskennedypublishing.com/

* * * * *

Meet the author and other CKP authors on the Factory Floor:

https://www.facebook.com/groups/461794864654198

* * * * *

Did you like this book?
Please write a review!

* * * * *

The following is an
Excerpt from Book One of Symbiote Wars:

Symbiote Wars

Chris Kennedy

Available from Theogony Books

eBook, Audio, and Paperback

Excerpt from "Symbiote Wars:"

As you expected, all three ships have shut down their shields and are docking with the refueling station, Suzie noted.

Johnson looked up from the nuclear missile he was standing over. "How much time do we have before the battlecruiser is tied up?"

Fifteen minutes or so.

Johnson's jaw clenched. "It's going to be close."

The Terrans had followed the Cowlee fleet through the bridge back into the Cashtal system and had then shadowed them as they'd headed for the refueling station.

"Where did you learn to do this?" Sutton asked.

"When you've been alive as long as I have, you have time to do things. I went through sapper school about twenty years ago."

"You played with *nukes* in sapper school? That's a thing?"

"Well, no, not nukes, but the principle is the same. Strap the thing that goes boom onto the thing you want blown up, and you're all set."

"Great, but I was more wondering about playing with nukes, not blowing things up."

"Oh." Johnson smiled. "This is something I've never done before, but the concept is straightforward enough." He looked back down at the missile he was elbows' deep into. "Now, you might want to let me concentrate while I remove the warhead. Especially since it's kind of leaky, and I'd like to minimize our exposure to the radiation."

Sutton's jaw dropped, and he wanted to ask another question, but decided it was better to let Johnson do his thing.

<Are you okay?> Frank asked. *<Your bio signs are spiking.>*

<I've never seen *a nuke, much less played with one before. And his lackadaisical attitude toward it is really freaking me out.>*

<Doc said that Suzie is sending the blueprints to the bomb to his goggles. All he has to do is follow the steps in the manual, and everything should be fine.>

<That would have been nice to know a while ago.>

<Besides,> Frank added, *<setting off a nuke is much harder than you'd think. You can't just drop it on the floor and have it go boom. You need the detonator to function in the manner intended to actually get a nuclear blast. Even if you had an*

electrical discharge and some of the explosives surrounding the nuclear matter happened to go off, it probably *wouldn't go nuclear.*>

<*Also good to know info.*>

<*Of course, the explosives going off would kill us all, and shower us with enriched radioactive material, ensuring our demise, but we wouldn't die in a nuclear explosion, if that's what you're worried about.*>

<*Pretty sure I didn't need to know all of that extra stuff, either, Frank. I would have been happy if you'd have left it with 'there won't be a nuclear blast.'*>

<*But that wouldn't have been all the information.*>

<*Sometimes Humans don't want to* know *all the info. This is one of those times.*>

"You're watching what I'm doing, right?" Johnson asked softly.

"Yeah."

"Good, because you're going to have to disassemble the other one while I build our bombs."

"I *what*?"

"Don't yell," Johnson said. "You don't want to startle me."

"But I—"

"We don't have enough time. I'm going to need you to take a more active role."

"But I—"

"Do you want to save Earth or not?"

"Well yeah, but—"

"Suzie, send James the schematics you're sending me, along with the procedure."

Sending, Suzie replied, her voice soft.

James blinked as the blueprints and procedures appeared in his view. They were weird—he could see them when he focused but they faded when he looked through them. "This is the best heads-up display I've ever seen. I didn't know the goggles could do this."

"How have you been doing your checklists?"

"Just projecting them into my view and looking at everything else around them."

Johnson stopped and looked up. "That's not a good way to do it. You're going to miss something that way."

"Well, maybe if my teacher had told me the goggles had a HUD…"

"Sorry. Sometimes I forget you haven't had ground school, which is where you'd have learned that. My bad." He shrugged. "Now get that tool kit—" he pointed "—and get to work on the other one."

* * * * *

Get "Symbiote Wars" here:
https://www.amazon.com/dp/B0DQVFRJ5R.

Find out more about Chris Kennedy at:
https://chriskennedypublishing.com.

* * * * *

The following is an
Excerpt from Book One of The Last Marines:

Gods of War

William S. Frisbee, Jr.

Available from Theogony Books

eBook, Audio, and Paperback

Excerpt from "Gods of War:"

"Yes, sir," Mathison said. Sometimes it was worth arguing, sometimes it wasn't. Stevenson wasn't a butter bar. He was a veteran from a line infantry platoon that had made it through Critical Skills Operator School and earned his Raider pin. He was also on the short list for captain. Major Beckett might pin the railroad tracks on Stevenson's collar before they left for space.

"Well, enough chatting," Stevenson said, the smile in his voice grating on Mathison's nerves. "Gotta go check our boys."

"Yes, sir," Mathison said, and later he would check on the men while the lieutenant rested. "Please keep your head down, sir. Don't leave me in charge of this cluster fuck. I would be tempted to tell that company commander to go fuck a duck."

"No, you won't. You will do your job and take care of our Marines, but I'll keep my head down," Stevenson said. "Asian socialists aren't good enough to kill me. It's going to have to be some green alien bastard that kills me."

"Yes, sir," Mathison said as the lieutenant tapped on Jennings' shoulder and pointed up. The lance corporal understood and cupped his hands together to boost the lieutenant out of the hole. He launched the lieutenant out of the hole and went back to digging as Mathison went back to looking at the spy eyes scrutinizing the distant jungle.

A shot rang out. On Mathison's heads-up display, the icon for Lieutenant Stevenson flashed and went red, indicating death.

"You are now acting platoon commander," Freya reported.

* * * * *

Find out more about William S. Frisbee, Jr. at:
https://chriskennedypublishing.com.

* * * * *

Made in the USA
Coppell, TX
11 June 2026

80482730R10315